PRECIPICE

Also by Robert Harris

PRECIPICE

A NOVEL

ROBERT HARRIS

HARPER

An Imprint of HarperCollins*Publishers*

PRECIPICE. Copyright © 2024 by Robert Harris. All rights reserved. Printed in the United States of America. No part of this book may be used or reproduced in any manner whatsoever without written permission except in the case of brief quotations embodied in critical articles and reviews. For information, address HarperCollins Publishers, 195 Broadway, New York, NY 10007.

HarperCollins books may be purchased for educational, business, or sales promotional use. For information, please email the Special Markets Department at SPsales@harpercollins.com.

Originally published in the United Kingdom in 2024 by Hutchinson Heinemann.

FIRST U.S. EDITION

Library of Congress Cataloging-in-Publication Data has been applied for.

ISBN 978-0-06-324805-2

24 25 26 27 28 LBC 5 4 3 2 1

To George Harris Parr –
welcome

AUTHOR'S NOTE

All the letters quoted in the text from the Prime Minister are – the reader may be astonished to learn – authentic, as are the telegrams, newspaper reports and official documents, along with the correspondence between Venetia Stanley and Edwin Montagu.

However, the letters from Venetia Stanley to the Prime Minister are entirely invented.

Paul Deemer is a fictional character.

PRECIPICE

PART ONE

PEACE

2 July–23 July 1914

CHAPTER ONE

L ATE ONE THURSDAY morning at the beginning of July 1914, a young woman with dark wet hair strode long-legged from the Serpentine in Hyde Park along Oxford Street towards Marylebone. In one hand she carried a cream linen sun hat, in the other a damp bathing costume and a pair of silk stockings rolled up inside a navy-blue towel.

Although she was evidently in a hurry, she did not break into a run – the pavements were too hot and crowded for that, and besides, being seen to exert herself was never her style. But she did walk quickly, tall and slim, her head erect, and in such a purposeful manner that most people instinctively cleared out of her way.

It was shortly after noon when she rounded the corner into the grand Georgian terrace where her parents had their London residence. On the opposite side of the street, the postman had made his midday delivery and was standing on the step, in front of the double-fronted, white-stuccoed mansion, checking his bag.

With luck, she was just in time.

She crossed the road, wished him good morning, slipped around him, beneath the portico, through the wide front door and into the stuffy midsummer gloom of the hall.

The mail still lay in its wire basket.

She managed to extract the familiar envelope moments before a manservant emerged from the depths of the house to fetch the post for her father. She hid the letter in her hat, handed over the rest, started up the stairs, and was halfway to the landing when her mother, Lady Sheffield, called from the morning room: 'How was your swim, darling?'

Without breaking step, she shouted back, 'Heavenly!'

She closed the door to her room, dropped her swimming things, tossed her hat onto the dressing table, lifted her dress over her head, and threw herself down on the bed.

Lying on her back, she held up the envelope between both hands.

Hon. Venetia Stanley, 18 Mansfield St., Portland Place, London, W.

She worked her finger beneath the flap, tore it open and pulled out a single sheet of thick notepaper, folded in half and dated that day.

2 July 14

I am in rather better spirits this morning – thanks mainly
to you. I hope I did not depress you unduly yesterday.
You were very dear and sympathetic, and helped me as
you always do. I am truly grateful in my heart of hearts.
I suppose at this moment you are plunging in the water
somewhere in the company of Lady Scott. I have a
rather drab day before me, including an interview with
the King at 4.30. Ottoline asked me to dine there tonight so it
is possible I may have a glimpse of you . . . Bless you darling.

It was unsigned. Recently, he had taken the precaution of not using her name or his own.

She read it again. He would expect an immediate reply, and would fret if he didn't get one, even though nothing of any significance had happened to her since she saw him yesterday. She carried the letter over to the dressing table, sat down, studied herself without interest in the mirror, and took out a sheet of paper. She unscrewed the top of her fountain pen, thought for a few moments, and then began to write rapidly.

I am just back from an invigorating swim in the Serpentine with Kathleen. Her energetic crawl put my languid breaststroke to shame. Remarkably, we managed to pass an entire hour without any mention of her late husband or even the South Pole – surely a record? The water was deliciously cool, if crowded. What a summer this is! – almost as hot as three years ago. I am so happy you are more cheerful. You will find a way through this Irish tangle, you always do. Dearest, I <u>can't</u> come to Ottoline's tonight as I've promised Edward & the Cossack I'll join their midnight river trip from Westminster to Kew. You know I'd much rather be with you. But I'll see you tomorrow. All my love.

Despite the speed of composition, her distinctive stylish calligraphy was clear as print. She too didn't sign her name. She blew on the glistening black ink, addressed the envelope – *Prime Minister, 10 Downing Street, London, S.W.* – added a penny stamp, and rang for Edith, her maid – German Swiss, reliably discreet – to take it to the post box. There were twelve deliveries a day in London in 1914. It would be in his hands by mid-afternoon.

★

His reply reached the house at eight o'clock as she was descending to the hall to greet Maurice Baring, her escort for the evening. She heard the flap of the letter box. Out of the corner of her eye she saw Edith go to the wire cage.

'Hello, dear Maurice.' She extended her hand. He was rich, forty, balding, a man of letters; indeed, a published poet (*Forget-me-Not and Lily of the Valley*, 1905 – now, alas, forgotten). He was wearing white tie and tails with a red carnation in his buttonhole. When he bent to kiss her fingers, his soft moustache brushed her wrist; she could smell his delicate lime pomade. Earlier, Lady Sheffield – baffled by her daughter's modern ways and increasingly concerned about her marriageability at the age of nearly twenty-seven – had asked if she was sure she would be 'safe' with him.

'Mama, I'd be safe with Maurice if I was stranded with him naked on a desert island for a year.'

'Venetia!'

'But it's true!'

Edith waited until her mistress was on the doorstep before slipping her the letter under cover of adjusting her dress. She opened it sitting next to Maurice in the back of his car. A short note, it was headed 4.15 p.m., which meant he must have scribbled it either before he left Downing Street to see the King, or while he was at the Palace waiting for his audience.

Don't if you can avoid it beloved go on this infernal river trip, but <u>do</u> come to Ottoline's. Couldn't you even manage dinner there? It would be so nice. But if that is impossible I look forward to seeing you there later on. <u>Do try</u>. Your own.

She frowned. *Infernal river trip* . . . He might be right. She had had her doubts about it, ever since she accepted the invitation, albeit for reasons different to his. The trouble with boat parties in her experience was that while one could get *on* them easily enough, it wasn't nearly so easy to get *off* them, and there were few things in life she detested more than feeling trapped.

Maurice must have registered the change in her expression. 'Trouble with an admirer?'

'I don't have admirers, Maurice, as you well know.'

'Oh, I wouldn't be so sure about *that* . . .'

She didn't much care for the tone of the remark, nor for the somewhat toothy leer which accompanied it. Dear God, had she been on the shelf so long even *Maurice* might be contemplating a pass?

She said, 'I suppose it's too late to chuck this whole boat trip business and go to Ottoline's instead?'

'What a peculiar thing to say! We haven't been invited to Otto-line's. And besides, the river will be fun. Everyone will be there.'

By everyone he meant 'the Coterie', as they called themselves, or 'the Corrupt Coterie' as the press preferred it – two dozen or so friends (the number fluctuated according to some mysterious collective judgement as to who was 'amusing' and who 'a bore') who went around together, sometimes to the Café Royal, occasionally to the music hall or a boxing match in the East End, most often to the Cave of the Golden Calf, a basement nightclub near Regent Street.

'Yes,' she said dubiously, 'I suppose everyone will be.' She stuffed the letter into her purse and snapped the clasp.

She was not one of the Coterie's leading spirits. She did not drink like Sir Denis Anson, the young baronet who could down two bottles of champagne before the evening even started, or take drugs like Lady Diana Manners ('the most beautiful woman in England'), who liked sniffing chloroform. She wasn't an intellectual like Raymond Asquith, whose father the Prime Minister had written the letter in her purse, or independently rich like Nancy Cunard, the shipping heiress, who was only eighteen. She went along with them to alleviate her boredom, to annoy her mother, and because nothing they got up to shocked her. And there was another characteristic that drew her to them: not cynicism exactly – although Raymond, the oldest and the wittiest, certainly was a cynic – but rather a curious sense of detachment from life. She felt as if nothing really mattered: not them, or the world, or even herself. They all felt rather like that.

It was in this familiar spirit of indifference that she surrendered herself to whatever the night might bring, borne along in silent luxury inside the cocoon of Maurice's Rolls-Royce Silver Ghost; first to a dinner for six at the Russian Embassy in Belgrave Square given by Constantine Benckendorff, 'the Cossack', the son of the ambassador, who had organised the river trip with Edward Horner, Raymond's brother-in-law; and then on afterwards in the Rolls again to the river, where the others were converging from their own separate dinner parties – sixteen guests in all, debouching from cars and taxis – Claud Russell and Duff Cooper, both diplomats at the Foreign Office, each clutching a brace of Bollinger rescued from Duff's mother's table, and Duff's sister Sybil Hart-Davis, and Iris Tree, a model and actress, who took her clothes off a lot, and Jasper Ridley who was a barrister and married to the Cossack's sister, and Raymond of course, and his wife Katharine, and Edward Horner her brother, another young lawyer . . .

They kissed and embraced and chattered on about what fun they were having – the young women in their different dresses as brightly coloured as birds of paradise, the men in their monochrome uniform of black tailcoats, white tie and top hats – pouring down the flights of stone steps from the Embankment to

Westminster Pier, watched by a curious crowd of onlookers leaning against the parapet. And Venetia went with them, gathering
her green silk gown in both hands so that the hem didn't brush
the ground.

The boat was more impressive than she had expected, a lengthy
Victorian pleasure steamer big enough for fifty passengers, named
King. A tall funnel rose between fore and aft decks strung with
coloured Chinese lanterns. Reflected orbs of lemon, lime and pink
shattered and re-formed on the black sheen of the oily water. It
was a hot night – bright, still, with a half-full moon. Through the
windows of the central cabin, she could see a buffet supper laid
out amid flickering candelabra and ice buckets stuffed with champagne. A quintet of musicians in the prow, hired from Thomas
Beecham's orchestra at Covent Garden, struck up 'By the Beautiful Sea', the hit of the summer, just as Big Ben, its round yellow
clock-face illuminated like a second moon, chimed eleven.

Denis was the first to board, running up the gangplank, swinging round one of the poles from which the lanterns were
suspended, and then climbing up onto the railing. He crouched
on the narrow handrail for a moment then slowly rose to his full
height, wobbling between the deck and the river, stretching out
his hands until he had gained his balance. The spectators on the
Embankment applauded. He turned precariously and began to
move towards the stern like a tightrope walker, cautiously putting
one foot in front of the other, toe to heel. When he reached the
end, he turned to face the pier. For a quarter of a minute, he stood
there, silhouetted against the river and the lights of the opposite
bank, swaying on the edge of disaster.

Diana said, 'Oh, Vinny, look at Denis – he can't be *that* drunk!'

'He's *very* drunk,' said Venetia, 'otherwise he wouldn't be
doing it.'

9

Suddenly he threw up his hands and fell backwards onto the deck and disappeared. They all laughed and cheered, apart from Venetia. What a pointless young bore he was, she thought. In that instant she made up her mind.

'Maurice, I'm awfully sorry, but I don't feel well. Would you forgive me if I slipped away?'

'Oh no, really? Must you? *Such* a shame . . .' He looked around. The others were queuing to board. She could tell he longed to join them, but was too much of a gentleman to desert her. 'I'll just tell everyone, then I'll take you home.'

'No, you stay. I don't want to spoil your evening. Could I ask your driver to take me back?'

'Of course – if you're sure?'

'Will you give my apologies to Conny and Edward? I'll call you tomorrow.'

She realised she was slightly drunk herself. She climbed the steps carefully without looking back, even when Raymond called her name and made it sound like a reprimand: 'Venetia!' She felt both guilty and exhilarated, as if she was leaving a bad play at the interval. Behind her the boat's steam whistle gave a brief warning toot. When she reached the Embankment and looked down at the river it had started to pull away from the pier. She put her bare elbows on the cool stone parapet and watched it for a while – the Chinese lanterns, the figures moving around on deck, the strains of the band, the laughter and singing carrying clearly on the summer air:

> By the sea, by the sea, by the beautiful sea,
> You and I, you and I, oh how happy we'll be . . .

She lingered until the boat disappeared under Westminster Bridge, then went in search of Maurice's Silver Ghost. Five minutes later she was gliding up Parliament Street, past the entrance to Downing Street. Along the dark side road, the red rear lights of a motor car glowed, and it occurred to her that he might just be returning from dinner. She thought of asking the chauffeur to pull over and set her down but banished the idea at once. She was tipsy. It might not be him. And even if it was, it would never do.

CHAPTER TWO

T HE NIGHT WAS brief, the air warm, the sky a fever of stars. When the sun rose over London at 4.45 the next morning, it was as if it had never been away.

On the third floor of that extravagant Victorian-Gothic fortress beside the Thames at Westminster known as New Scotland Yard, in the round turret at the south-western corner which housed the Metropolitan Police Night Duty Room, a young detective sergeant looked up from his newspaper and noticed the daylight seeping around the edges of the wooden shutters.

It had been a quiet shift. One by one, his more senior colleagues had pulled rank and gone home early, until only he was left holding the fort. The small office was stifling with the smell of stale pipe smoke and masculine sweat. He folded back the shutters, lifted the sash, and stood at the open window in his unbuttoned waistcoat and shirtsleeves, surveying the panoramic view – the shards of sunlight breaking on the tidal river; the crying seagulls swooping over the mudflats; the huge, silent building site on the opposite bank that would some day be the new headquarters of the London County Council; a solitary red omnibus crossing the bridge from Waterloo towards the Houses of Parliament; and finally, moored beneath him, on Westminster Pier, a pleasure steamer with a tall chimney, strung with extinguished lanterns.

It looked sad, grey, deflated.

Motionless along the pathway above the boat – sitting, standing, leaning against the stone balustrade – he could see more than a dozen elegant figures, men in white tie and tails and women in evening gowns, and what appeared to be a quartet of musicians holding their instrument cases, the whole group watched by a pair of uniformed police constables. Four cars, one a Rolls-Royce, were parked up on the Embankment, their drivers in a huddle, smoking.

He must have stared at this curious tableau for several minutes and still hadn't made much sense of it when behind him for the first time since midnight a telephone rang.

He stepped back from the window, grasped the candlestick stem with one hand, lifted the earpiece with the other, and spoke carefully into the microphone: 'Scotland Yard, night duty desk.'

'And who might I be talking to?' A man's voice, tinny down the crackling line. The trace of an Irish accent.

'Detective Sergeant Paul Deemer. Who is this?'

'All right, Detective Sergeant Paul Deemer, my name is Superintendent Patrick Quinn. You'll know who I am.'

'Yes, sir.' Suddenly, he was more alert. Quinn was head of the Special Branch, in charge, among other things, of armed protection for prominent dignitaries. Early in his career he had been Queen Victoria's bodyguard. 'Good morning, sir.'

'Is there an inspector available?'

'Not yet, sir. The first won't be in till six.'

Quinn made a rapid clicking noise with his tongue then said, 'Well, listen – there's been a fatal accident on a riverboat overnight. Two men missing, presumed drowned.'

'Yes, sir.'

'Among those on board were the son of the Prime Minister and the son of the Russian ambassador. I'm told the boat has now returned to Westminster Pier. She's called *King*.'

Deemer carried the telephone over to the window. The group had not moved. 'I believe I can see her from the office now, sir. Are they the two men who are missing?'

'No, no, they're both safe, thank God. But you can understand why I've been woken at home.' He didn't sound too happy about it. 'I need an officer to go down and take charge, check there's nothing suspicious about the circumstances, and then send them on their way before any reporters turn up. Can you do that for me, Detective Sergeant Paul Deemer?'

'Yes, sir.'

'Good man. Let me know how you get on. And be respectful, mind.'

Before he could answer, Quinn had hung up.

Deemer took his coat from the back of his chair and slipped it on, buttoned it, straightened his tie in the mirror over the fireplace, licked his fingers and smoothed his hair and moustache. Then he collected his bowler from the hat stand and set off, clattering rapidly down three flights of stairs. Technically, he wasn't supposed to leave the duty room unattended. But this was an order from a superintendent. Besides, he was keen and ambitious. In tragedy he sensed opportunity.

He crossed the courtyard and emerged onto the Embankment slightly out of breath, his heart beating fast. He paused at the gate so that he could look appropriately calm before crossing the wide empty street, past the chauffeurs, and down the steps leading to the water. He went first to the two constables and showed them his warrant card. They stared at him sceptically. It was no advantage in the police service, Deemer had discovered, to look younger than one's years. 'Well,' he said briskly, trying to convey an air of authority, 'this is a tragic business. Do you have the names of the missing men?'

The older of the two officers took out his notebook. 'Sir Denis Anson and a Mr William Mitchell.'

'How did it happen?'

'Anson jumped in.'

'Into the Thames?' It seemed absurd.

'The other victim, Mitchell, dived in to rescue him, then he got into difficulties as well. He was one of the musicians hired for the evening. A third gentleman, Mr Benck-en-dorff' – he pronounced the name as if it was slightly suspicious, and jerked his thumb towards a young man sitting on the steps, head bowed, a blanket across his broad shoulders – 'also went in to help, but he couldn't get to them before they both went under.'

Deemer was making notes. 'Where was this exactly?'

'Battersea Bridge. They were on the return trip.'

'When?'

'About three in the morning.'

'Have the bodies been recovered?'

'The river police at Chelsea are still searching.'

He looked up. 'So, there may be some hope?'

'No. The captain, William White, says there was an ebb tide, very strong. They searched for an hour, then gave up. I reckon we should let them all go home. No crime for you to cut your teeth on here, Sergeant.' The other constable smirked.

'You have statements from the witnesses on board?'

'More or less. Not everyone saw it – those who did all say the same thing.'

'I'll need your notes. Wait here.'

He went across to Benckendorff and squatted on his haunches in front of him. 'Are you all right, sir? I'm with the police. Should I send for an ambulance?'

The Russian raised his head. His face was pale and streaked with dark lines – oil, was it? He stank of foul water. 'No, I'm tired, that's all.'

'You did a very brave thing, sir.'

He shook his head. 'No, no, the musician was the brave one. I couldn't even get close to him. I never felt anything like that tide – as if some devil had caught my legs and was pulling me under . . .'

'You need to get out of those wet clothes and get home to bed. We won't keep you much longer. Which one is Mr Asquith?'

Benckendorff moved his head slightly and nodded towards a figure lying full length on the quayside, his legs crossed at the ankles, his arms folded on his chest, his top hat covering his face, apparently asleep.

Deemer went over to him. He coughed politely. 'Sir?'

A hand moved crablike across his chest and slowly removed his hat. He had fair hair, a thin face – sensitive, clean-shaven. His eyes were as blue as the sky. 'Yes?'

'I'm Detective Sergeant Deemer. I've been sent to make sure you're all right.'

'I'm perfectly "all right", Sergeant, thank you. I'm not really one of those you need to be concerned about.' He sat up and looked around. 'Well, I suppose we'd better get it over with.' He scrambled to his feet and brushed the dirt from his tailcoat. 'Someone needs to tell Sir Denis's mother. I should do it. Before that, I'd like to take my wife home.'

'I understand.'

By now, most of the survivors had started drifting over to see what was happening. A short, red-faced man, his coat draped over the thin shoulders of a woman leaning on his arm, said, 'Lady Diana's feeling faint. She needs to go to bed. I really must insist we be allowed to leave.'

Raymond murmured, 'Don't be an ass, Duff. There's a procedure to go through. Let the officer do his job.'

The woman said, 'Officer, I know it's simply awful about Denis and that poor violin-man, but we've all been here for *hours*.'

She had very wide blue eyes, oddly vacant – like a doll's. Deemer wondered if she'd taken something. There was a murmur of agreement from the other guests. He didn't care for their attitude, as if they were entitled to special treatment. If it had been up to him, he would have kept them for another hour or two. But his instructions from Quinn had been that they should all be sent away before the press arrived. So he said, 'Yes, you're free to leave,' before adding, as they turned to go, 'However, we may need to contact you to take statements later. I'll require the names and addresses of everyone on board.'

A young man spoke. 'I have the guest list if that's any help.'

'And you are, sir?'

'Edward Horner. I was the one who hired the boat with Count Benckendorff.'

He took a crumpled list from his inside pocket. Deemer scanned it quickly and handed it back, along with a pencil.

'If you could all please add your addresses beside your names before you go.'

They passed it around, scribbling on it without really looking, talking among themselves. How self-absorbed they were! He liked to think that if a friend of his had just died, and his body was not yet discovered, his first priority wouldn't be to go home. 'Excuse me!' He had to raise his voice and hold up his hand to attract their attention. 'One last question, while you're all still here. Sir Denis jumped into the river, is that correct? He couldn't have been pushed?'

'Good God!' exclaimed the red-faced man. 'What are you suggesting?'

'Well, it seems such a foolhardy thing to do. Was he drunk?'

'No,' said Raymond firmly. 'He was sober. It was an entirely deliberate decision on his part to enter the water.' (Was it Deemer's imagination, or did he exchange a flicker of a glance with Lady Diana?) 'He was a good swimmer. He left his watch and jacket on board before he dived in – you can ask the captain. That was the sort of fellow he was. Last year when we were in Italy he swam across the Grand Canal. Unfortunately,' he added with a shrug, 'London isn't Venice.'

'No, sir,' agreed Deemer politely, although he had never been to Venice, or even left England, 'I'm sure it's not.'

He watched them as they climbed the steps, helping Count Benckendorff to his feet and taking him with them. After they had said their farewells and their cars had pulled away, he sent the two constables off to write up their notes, and turned his attention to the four surviving musicians. They claimed they had all been too busy playing to give much attention to what was happening among the passengers. On the return trip, they had seen Anson dive overboard and had stopped playing and then one of the guests had called out, 'Denis, how are you?' and they heard him shout back, 'Quickly! Quickly!' That was when Mitchell stood up and started taking off his jacket. The guests all seemed paralysed.

The bandmaster said, 'I told him not to be a bloody fool but he took no notice. He went over the side and that was the last we saw of him. He had a little boy as well. Only a year old.'

'And Sir Denis Anson – he was sober, as far you could tell?'

For the first time the bandmaster seemed less confident. 'We know nothing about that, officer. We were just hired to provide the entertainment.'

Deemer took their names and addresses then went on board the boat.

Captain White was a retired Royal Navy man, nearly sixty. He showed him over the steamer, from the cabin to the stern deck where the awning was folded down and the musicians had been playing. He pointed to the railing.

'This is where the gentleman was fooling around. He got up three times, and each time I grabbed his foot and told him to get down. He must have got up again after my back was turned. By the time I stopped the engines he was about fifteen yards away, trying to swim back to the boat, but the current was too strong – when there's an ebb tide on that particular stretch you get a flush from the West London Railway Bridge that will suck anything under. That was when the musician went in, and not long after that, the Russian. He must be a damn strong swimmer – it was a miracle we managed to get a line to him.'

'Was Sir Denis drunk, in your opinion?'

The captain looked at the deck. 'That I wouldn't know.'

'Come now, Captain! No one sober would jump into the Thames at three in the morning! What had they all been drinking?'

'Champagne, mostly. They had supper in the cabin.'

'Show me.'

The captain led the way back along the boat. The dining table had been cleared, the cloth folded, bottles and plates packed away in boxes. Deemer looked around the cabin and frowned. 'You said they were drinking champagne.'

'That's right.'

'Where are the empty bottles?'

'Empty bottles?' The captain put on a show of mystification. He called out to the deck, 'Mr Lewis!'

The first mate appeared in the doorway. 'Yes, Captain?'

'What happened to all the bottles?'

Lewis hesitated. 'The gentlemen threw them over the side after the accident, sir.'

There was a pause. Deemer closed his notebook and put it away in his inside pocket. 'All right. What exactly happened here? Tell me now, man to man, or I'll take you both in.'

White and Lewis looked at one another. Eventually, White made a gesture, as if he was throwing in a bad hand of cards, and said, 'You tell him. You saw it. I didn't.'

'It was a bet,' said Lewis. 'Mr Asquith bet that pretty woman—'

'Lady Diana?'

'He bet her ten pounds she couldn't get Anson to swim to the riverbank. I didn't hear what she said to him, but he didn't take much convincing. He gave her his coat and his watch, then he just . . . dived in.'

Deemer turned to the captain. 'You have his belongings?'

White disappeared for a minute and returned with a tailcoat and a gold pocket watch. Deemer searched the jacket and took out a wallet and a set of keys. He opened the watch. An inscription was engraved inside the lid: 'To Denis on his 21st birthday, use your time wisely, love Mama.'

'What a waste of a life,' he said, handing it back. 'Of two lives.'

'You didn't hear it from us,' said the captain.

Deemer felt suddenly very tired. He left the cabin without

another word, walked across the gangplank, along the pier, and wearily climbed the flights of steps. It was after six, the day already warm, the early-morning traffic starting to run along the Embankment and across Westminster Bridge. In the duty room, he sat at his desk and studied the list of guests. Asquith, Manners, Baring, Cunard, Tree . . . It was like the society page in a newspaper. Two, he noticed, Russell and Cooper, had given their addresses as care of the Foreign Office. Raymond and Katharine Asquith listed theirs as 49 Bedford Square. Only one person hadn't provided any address at all. Venetia Stanley.

CHAPTER THREE

MAURICE HAD CALLED her with the news early in the morning. His nasal voice cut through her hangover: 'I'm afraid there's been the most dreadful accident . . .'

Her failure to feel much emotion had shocked her almost more than the tragedy itself. All the while she was listening to Maurice and saying the expected things – 'Oh no, poor Denis, it's too ghastly' – she was conscious of her detachment. What on earth was the matter with her? She was more affected by the story of the man who had thrown away his life trying to save someone he didn't even know. That struck her as extraordinary – heroic, mysterious. After a while, her questions about the musician began to irritate Maurice, who clearly hadn't bothered to find out much about him. 'Yes, yes, of course, I agree, something must be done to help his family – I'm sure the Ansons will make provision – but really, Venetia: *Denis*, with the whole of his life ahead of him . . .'

She said, 'It sounds an utterly crazy thing to have done, even by his standards. What on earth possessed him?'

'Well, between you and me . . .'

He pledged her to secrecy and told her about Raymond's bet

with Diana, and how they had all agreed to say nothing about it. 'You can imagine what it would do to Raymond's political prospects if *that* got into the press! As for Diana, you know how the papers love to portray her as some kind of narcissistic femme fatale—'

'I can't think where they get that idea.'

'Anyway, I'm so glad you were spared the whole thing.' He yawned. 'I'm turning in for a few hours. Can I take you to Eddy's tea dance later?'

'Sorry, Maurice, I have plans.'

'Plans! You always have plans!'

During the morning she took half a dozen more calls from members of the Coterie, each of whom told her in confidence about Raymond and Diana. Their accounts were the same, only the size of the wager varied: some said five pounds, some twenty.

That afternoon she put on the black and white striped satin dress she knew was his favourite, together with a straw boater encircled by a red ribbon, and just before half-past three slipped unnoticed out of the house and strolled in the warm sunshine around the corner towards Portland Place.

At the crossroads with New Cavendish Street, a newsboy was calling out the headline of the *Evening Standard* in a mournful Cockney plainsong – 'River tragedy, baronet's body still missing!' She watched him dealing briskly with his queue of customers, folding papers, taking coins, and for the first time felt a twist of real grief. This time yesterday, Denis had probably been playing cards at his club for stakes he couldn't afford on his allowance. Now he was making money for some ghastly press lord.

She moved further down the street and stationed herself on the kerb. She knew he would be punctual: he always was. A couple of minutes later, the big limousine, a Napier six-cylinder, came round the corner past All Souls church, its coachwork so brightly polished that as it drew to a halt, she could see the few high summer clouds reflected in the black mirror of its bonnet. The chauffeur, Horwood, sprang out and came round to open the door. As usual, he avoided catching her eye.

The commodious rear compartment had an interior of leather and walnut, like an old-fashioned carriage. Climbing in, she noticed the curtains had already been drawn across the thick sealed glass screen that separated the passengers from the driver's seat. The door closed. He leaned forward and pressed a button on a console. It lit a bulb on the dashboard instructing Horwood to drive. As the car moved off, she slid across the leather banquette and kissed him on the cheek.

The Prime Minister turned and smiled at her. 'Hello, my darling,' he said.

They took a drive together at least once a week, usually on a Friday afternoon for an hour and a half, either out into the country or just around London. They met often in between, of course, at lunches and dinners and country weekends, but always with other people around. The car was the one place where they could be sure of being alone.

Was she in love with him? She didn't know. She knew that she was fonder of him than any of the other men who had pursued her over the years – more than the sweet but ugly Edwin Montagu, Member of Parliament and Financial Secretary to the Treasury, who had proposed to her twice and even bought a house in Westminster where he hoped they might live together; more than 'Bongie' Bonham Carter, the Prime Minister's unmarried private secretary, who had kissed her and written her passionate letters;

more than Raymond, who had made it clear he wanted to have an affair with her; more than her handsome brother-in-law, Major Anthony Henley, who had indicated the same; and certainly more than Maurice Baring.

She liked him for his kindness, his cleverness, his fame and power, which he wore lightly. Her father had been a Liberal MP: she had grown up surrounded by talk of politics. Now she was probably the most well-informed woman in the country. And if she was honest, she also enjoyed the thrill of it – the secrecy, the illicitness, the *risk*.

As usual, he had brought some official papers to show her. They lay on the seat between them. Their clasped hands rested on the folder.

'I've been worried sick about you,' he said. 'When you didn't turn up at Ottoline's I assumed you must have gone on that wretched boat trip. Darling, I do wish you'd sent me a note to say you were safe.'

'I thought Raymond would have told you.'

'He did, but I'd have liked to have heard it from you.' He raised the back of her hand to his lips and kissed it. 'Poor Anson. He was ridiculous but I always rather liked him – all that animal energy and nowhere to direct it. It's terrible for his mother.'

'How is Raymond?'

'Shaken, though he tries not to show it. He's mostly concerned about the inquest now. His great fear is that Diana might be called as a witness. Apparently, the Duchess of Rutland is insisting on going to see the coroner to tell him her daughter's too fragile to give evidence.'

'Is that wise?'

'No. But it's important to keep her out of the witness box. Raymond too. God, what a mess!'

He turned away, brooding. His chin sank onto his chest. He knew about the bet, she realised – another problem for him to manage, on top of so many others. He had a fine profile – a noble head, like the bust of a Roman senator, with thick grey hair swept back off his forehead. It hung more than an inch over his collar. His wife was always telling him to get it cut, but Venetia thought it gave him a poetic look that suited him. Beneath the impassive mask of authority, he had a romantic, ardent nature. She looked beyond him through the big window, to the people walking along the street oblivious to who was driving past them: the Prime Minister hand in hand with a woman less than half his age. If only they knew – what a scandal there would be! She had a sudden mental image of Denis balanced on the side of the boat. Perhaps they were not so very different.

She wondered where they were going. He never told her in advance. He liked to surprise her.

'Let's talk about something else,' she said. 'Tell me what's going on.'

'Tell me about your life first.'

'But my life's so boring!'

'No, it isn't, not to me.'

The odd thing was, she knew he meant it. He was a sociable man – too sociable, his enemies said. In contrast to most of her father's political friends, he liked to draw people out, preferred listening to talking, preferred women to men. His charm was to treat the gravest matters of state as if they were nothing of any consequence, whereas the lightest of trivialities – dresses, card games, word puzzles, golf, poetry, popular novels – he discussed with the utmost seriousness. So, as the car sailed on around the edge of Regent's Park and headed north through Camden, she told him about her nephews and nieces, and what Iris and Nancy were doing, and what was new in Selfridge's, and what she might wear to the Islingtons' ball that evening, assuming it was still going ahead. This distracted him and seemed to cheer him up, until they reached Hampstead Heath, when he pressed another button on the console and the car came to a stop.

'Let's take a walk,' he said. 'There's something I want to show you.'

He opened the door himself – Horwood remained discreetly in his seat – and walked round the back of the car to let her out. It was a quiet, narrow street, shaded with plane trees, poplars, limes. A few people were out walking. None of them recognised him. He pointed with his cane. 'That was Keats's house.' He closed his eyes and recited:

> To sorrow I bade good morrow
> And thought to leave her far away behind
> But cheerly cheerly she loves me dearly
> She is so constant to me and so kind . . .

He opened his eyes again, swung round and pointed his stick at the house opposite. 'And that's where I lived with my first wife. I haven't been back for twenty years.' He offered her his arm. She took it and they crossed the road.

The house was set back from the street, half hidden by the fruit trees in the front garden – Georgian, whitewashed, with arched windows. Bees hummed in the orange blossom. The city might have been fifty miles away.

'What a pretty little place.'

'Isn't it? This is where I was happiest in my whole life – when the children were little, and my legal practice was just starting to thrive.' He shaded his eyes and squinted between the trees. 'There was a lawn at the back where I played cricket with the boys. We had no money. I was entirely obscure, just elected as an MP. But I knew somehow, with an absolute certainty, that a great future was about to open before me. Isn't that strange? Poor Helen never lived to see it. Mind you, she would have hated it. She loved her home and children. Politics appalled her.'

'She was different to Margot, then!'

'No man can ever have had two such dissimilar wives.'

'Shall we go in and ask if we might look round? I'm sure the owners wouldn't mind.'

He was still peering at the house. 'Raymond was only thirteen when she died. Beb was ten. Oc eight. Violet four. Cys was still a baby. Five children! It was a lot for me to cope with, and I was Home Secretary soon afterwards. Raymond was such a brilliant boy. A brilliant man too, of course . . . But I wonder if he would have turned out differently if—' He stopped himself and turned to look at her. 'No, I'd prefer not to go inside, if you don't mind, darling. I've taken us far enough down memory lane for one day. Shall we get some air on the Heath instead?'

They walked to the end of the road and followed a woodland path for a few minutes, past strolling families, and an ice-cream seller on a bicycle, until they came to one of Hampstead's ponds, where they sat on a bench looking across the water. Maintaining a careful distance, they played a game of his devising: which of them could name the most species of waterfowl. They took it in turns – moorhen, coot, mallard, swan, great crested grebe, black-headed gull . . . He won in the end when a mandarin duck suddenly surfaced a few yards away. 'They never last long,' he said wistfully. 'The ordinary ones attack them. Too exotic for this dull world . . . '

On the drive back, he was uncharacteristically quiet, staring out at the urban streets, cheerlessly bright and dusty in the midsummer heat. After a while, she let go of his hand and picked up the folder of documents. She glanced at him for permission. He nodded. 'Of course – that's why I brought it.'

The file was entirely devoted to Ireland. Census reports, maps of the north. Various counties, towns, even small villages, divided into a patchwork, some shaded red, some crimson, some pink. The darker the colour, the denser the Catholic population. The Catholics insisted on being ruled in future from Dublin; their Protestant neighbours refused to countenance leaving the United Kingdom. The Tories were pledged to support the Protestants, even if they took up arms against the government. She started to feel sick, reading in the moving car.

She looked up to find him watching her.

He said, 'It's the nearest thing I've ever seen to an insoluble problem – and by God, I've run up against a few these past six years.'

'Can't you postpone the decision?'

'We've put if off as long as we can. The Nationalists have made it clear that if we don't enact full Home Rule this session, they'll withdraw support, which means the end of our majority and a general election, which we'll probably lose. Either way, it's civil war.'

'Something will turn up. You're brilliant.' She tried to hand him the folder.

'Keep it. Give it back next time I see you. Perhaps *you* can see a solution.'

'That I doubt!' The idea that she could somehow solve the Irish Question lying on her bed in Mansfield Street was blatantly absurd, and he must have known it, but the gesture touched her. She reached over and stroked his hair. 'All will be well. I have faith in you.'

He put his arm around her. 'You realise I don't speak to anyone else like this? What would I do without you to confide in, my darling?'

They were passing down Primrose Hill. In the heavy traffic the car had slowed almost to a halt. She was conscious of people turning to stare at them.

'Wait,' she said.

She broke their embrace and slid along the banquette to pull down the blind on the nearside window. He did the same with the one next to him. She knelt on the seat and closed the final blind over the rear window. Once they were entirely secluded from public gaze, she returned to him.

They might have been in a pied-à-terre in Paris, or Venice. Only the sunshine filtering golden through the yellow silk softened the dark interior of their private world.

By ten past five – suitably recomposed – she was opening the door of her parents' house. A figure patrolled the hall. Edith, looking anxious.

'There's a gentleman waiting to see you, miss. I've put him in the morning room.'

'Who is it? Not Mr Baring, I hope?'

'No, miss.' She handed Venetia his card.

Detective Sergeant Paul Deemer
Metropolitan Police,
New Scotland Yard.

She turned it over to see if there was a message on the back. 'Good heavens! What on earth does he want?'

'He didn't say, miss.'

He was standing in front of the fireplace, a younger man than his rank suggested, about her own age, wearing an obviously cheap but well-pressed dark suit. She registered a few other details – highly polished black shoes, a bowler hat in his hand, a day's growth of beard across his chin, good-looking in a common sort of way.

'I'm Venetia Stanley. Can I help you?'

'Miss Stanley, good afternoon. I'm sorry to trouble you. I'm investigating last night's tragedy on the river.' He took out a note-book. 'I wondered if I might ask you a few questions.'

'Investigating?' She had a sudden sense of danger, and realised she was still holding the government file. She clutched it to her breast and folded her arms across it. 'What is there to investigate?'

'Nothing sinister, I assure you.' He opened the notebook. 'I'm gathering statements from the witnesses, but we don't seem to have yours. You left the pier this morning without providing your address.'

'That's because I wasn't at the pier this morning.'

'Why not?'

'I never got on the boat.'

He looked briefly puzzled, then his expression cleared. 'Ah! I see how the confusion has arisen! Mr Horner provided a list of the guests, but didn't say who actually boarded. That explains it. My apologies.' He cocked his head slightly and looked at her. 'Might I ask, Miss Stanley, *why* you didn't board?'

She was not normally flustered, but she felt her face flush. She hugged the file more tightly. 'It was late. I was tired. I decided to go home to bed.'

Why did she sound so guilty? It was ridiculous. But he didn't seem to notice.

'Quite understandable. And a wise decision, as it turned out. You spared yourself a very distressing scene.' To her relief, he finally put away his notebook. 'Well, I wish you a pleasant evening. I'll show myself out.'

He nodded as he passed her and went into the hall. She called after him, 'How did you find me if you didn't have my address?'

'Debrett's.'

He opened the front door and stepped outside. The moment it closed, she hurried back into the morning room and crossed to the window. He was standing on the opposite side of the street, looking at the house. He stood there for what seemed to her a curiously long time before he put on his bowler hat and moved away.

The Prime Minister wrote her a note as soon as he returned to Downing Street.

5.30 3 July 1914

I hear the Islington ball is put off on account of the river tragedy. I forgot to tell you that when I wrote to you asking you not to go & to come to O's instead, I had a kind of uneasy presentiment, and that after I got to bed, I dreamt that Edward's launch was wrecked. Isn't that rather strange?

We had a most heavenly talk, and there can never any more be any misunderstanding between us, my darling.

Dearest love.

CHAPTER FOUR

DEEMER WALKED TO the Underground station at Oxford Circus and descended into the sweltering catacomb of the Central Line. After eighteen hours on duty, trailing across London collecting witness statements, he was exhausted.

A hot gust stinking of oil and metal billowing from the tunnel mouth heralded the arrival of an eastbound train. He clung to a handle, swaying in silent unison with the other passengers eighty-five feet below the surface of the city, like weed on a seabed. Half an hour later, to his relief, he was back in the open air at Angel.

He lived alone in a little two-bedroomed terraced cottage in Islington with a tiny garden, front and rear, and a purple wisteria trained against the blackened brickwork beside the door. He had taken the lease on the expectation he would be marrying a girl he had been sweet on since school until he had realised he no longer loved her and had broken off the engagement. She had promptly married someone else, which made him wonder if he had made the right decision. He was lonely, yet he didn't altogether mind it.

There was something bracing about solitude. It gave one a sharper edge. His work absorbed him.

He picked up the bottle of milk from the doorstep, uncapped and sniffed it – it had curdled in the heat – then let himself in and went straight to the larder. There wasn't much – a piece of sweating cheddar, some biscuits, a bottle of warm beer. He took it out into the back garden and sat down on a wooden bench. He could hear children playing in the neighbouring park, chatter from the Albion pub across the road – reassuring sounds. A local cat, coal-black apart from a star of white fur on its breast, rubbed around his legs. He fetched the curdled milk, poured it into a saucer and watched her drink.

He thought idly about Venetia Stanley. She intrigued him. According to Debrett's, the mansion in Marylebone was merely the Stanleys' London address. Their main residence was listed as Alderley House in Cheshire, with another place at Penrhos in Wales. He wondered what an unmarried young woman of obvious intelligence could possibly do to occupy herself, drifting from one property to another according to the seasons, spending her time with the sorts of people who took night-time boat trips in the middle of the week and made fatal bets with one another. It seemed a pointless existence to him.

When he had finished eating and drinking, he carefully washed his plate, knife and glass and the cat's empty saucer, then went upstairs and undressed with similar deliberation, lining up his shoes and hanging up his one good suit. He drew the thin curtains and lay down on his bed in the summer evening light, closed his eyes and slept for twelve hours straight, until the following morning when he went back into Scotland Yard to work through the empty weekend, even though he wasn't supposed to be on duty.

*

Mitchell's body was pulled from the Thames near Wandsworth that Friday evening. Sir Denis Anson's remained submerged for nearly two more days, dragged around by the tide close to the footings of the West London Railway Bridge, before floating to the surface at dusk on Sunday.

The following afternoon, as soon as he had the pathologist's findings, Deemer wrote up his report. The cause of death in both cases was drowning. There were no injuries on either body, except for abrasions on Anson's face, which the police pathologist believed were posthumous and which he ascribed to contact with the riverbed. A joint inquest was scheduled for the Lambeth Coroner's Court in two days' time.

Deemer laboured hard to make his account as complete as possible, setting out all the circumstances of the tragedy, including the bet and the drinking. It ran to eight pages and concluded no crime had been committed. When it was finished, he took it upstairs to the Special Branch corridor. He had hoped to be able to present it to Quinn personally – to meet this mythical figure face to face – but his assistant informed him coldly that the superintendent was busy, and he was obliged to leave it in the outer office.

A few hours later on that Monday evening, just before midnight, the Prime Minister returned from dinner to Downing Street by taxi. As usual, he had taken the precaution of giving the driver, who had no idea who he was, precise directions – cabbies often tended to mistake Downing Street Whitehall, for Down Street Piccadilly, and several times after a journey spent lost in thought, he had looked up to find himself outside the Mayfair Underground station. He did not complain. He was proud to live in a country, possessed of an empire of some 440 million people, in which the head of the government passed unrecognised, and whose official residence was at the end of a side street hardly anyone could find.

He paid the fare and stood on the doorstep searching his pockets for his keys. After an evening of champagne and brandy he was a little unsteady on his feet, but his mind was clear enough. He opened the dark green door and locked it behind him then went upstairs. The house was silent, even though some seventeen servants slept on the premises – a butler, a housekeeper, a cook, three footmen, eight maids (three for housework, three for the kitchen, and one each for Margot and Violet), a governess, an odd-job man and a hall porter – this being the bare minimum Margot considered necessary to run a proper establishment. She used one of the three drawing rooms on the first floor as her bedroom, and it was there that he found her, sitting up in bed with a shawl over her nightdress, writing her diary. She laid it down as he came in to say good night.

'Darling Henry.'

'Darling.' He kissed her forehead.

'How was dinner?'

'Good.' He had been to Bedford Square to dine with Raymond and Katharine. Margot had cried off at the last minute, pleading a headache. She had turned fifty earlier in the year. Her migraines were constant.

'Is he prepared for the inquest?'

'I believe so. At least, he seems entirely unconcerned.'

'When is Raymond ever concerned about anything? If he'd shown more concern, this wretched business would never have happened. Do you know some of them actually went to the opera before poor Denis's body was even found?' *Flippant, callous, idle* and *blasphemous* were just a few of the adjectives she had hurled at the Coterie when she learned of the drownings, which had led in turn to a general rant about the degeneracy of the modern world – Cubists, Futurists, wishy-washy composers, Debussy, politicians who fomented civil war in Ireland, army officers mutinying, cynicism, sensationalist newspapers, Suffragettes slashing pictures . . .

'Well,' he said mildly, 'I have had a word with some useful people and we shall see how it all turns out.' He didn't want to say anything else in case he set her off again. 'Sleep well. I'll look in on you in the morning.'

He made his way through the darkened state rooms, to the large writing desk overlooking Horse Guards Parade where he liked to work late at night. It was six years since he and Margot had shared a bed. After the disaster of her last confinement – a baby boy, dead on his first day of life – the doctors had told her that another pregnancy would kill her. That had been the end of their conjugal relations. She kept a skull in her bedroom that had been found on her family's estate in Scotland, to remind her to live life to the full. He could never have made love under the empty eye-sockets of that skull.

He poured himself a glass of brandy, pulled a cord to turn on the shaded desk lamp, and sat down. Arranged around the blotter was a collection of several dozen little animals made of crystal, and miniature silver figures, which he had collected over the years and which he shifted into different groups according to his mood. He unlocked a dispatch box and took out the letter Venetia had sent him that morning.

It was wet over the weekend, so I had plenty of time to study your Irish papers, suitably hidden inside a copy of Tatler! – Papa asked several times if I could not find

something more elevating to read – & of course no
solution presents itself to my feeble brain that hasn't
occurred to your mighty one. Both sides must give up
some ground in the end.

The threat of civil war is so grave that I wonder if
there is not some means of <u>shaming</u> them into a
compromise. Would you not, in this situation, be justified
in turning to the King, & asking <u>him</u> to mediate? The
Unionists, of all people, can hardly object to a summons
from His Majesty, & the Nationalists will see how serious
you are. At the very least it will buy you more time.
Dearest darling, <u>do not despair</u>. Something will turn up, I
know it.

It wasn't a bad idea. He had been thinking along similar lines
himself. He opened the Irish folder and gloomily regarded the
counties of Fermanagh and Tyrone. After a while, in the hope of
a diversion, he pushed aside the maps and turned his attention to
his nightly folder of diplomatic dispatches. Afterwards he was to
remember that it wasn't even on top of the pile but buried halfway
down – a copy of a memorandum from the Foreign Secretary,
marked 'Secret' and dated that day.

July 6 1914

The German Ambassador spoke very warmly today of the
satisfaction and pleasure which had been given to the
Emperor and generally, by the visit of the British Admiral
to Kiel.

I said that I knew that it had given great satisfaction and
pleasure on our side.

The Prime Minister yawned and stretched out his legs. He took a sip of brandy before he resumed reading.

The Ambassador then went on to speak to me privately, he said, but very seriously, as to the anxiety and pessimism that he had found in Berlin. He explained that the murder of the Archduke Franz Ferdinand had excited very strong anti-Serbian feeling in Austria; and he knew for a fact, though he did not know details, that the Austrians intended to do something, and it was not impossible that they would take military action against Serbia.

He looked up. Ten days had passed since the heir to the Austrian-Hungarian throne and his wife had been shot to death by Serbian nationalists in Sarajevo and things had been very quiet – so quiet, he had put the matter entirely out of his mind. He felt as if he had suddenly struck a stone in the road. He put down his glass and resumed reading with quickened interest.

I said that surely they did not think of taking any territory?
The Ambassador replied that they did not wish to take territory because they would not know what to do with it. He thought their idea was that they must have some compensation in the sense of some humiliation for Serbia . . .
A second thing which caused anxiety and pessimism in Berlin was the apprehension in Germany about the attitude of Russia, especially in connection with the recent increase of Russian military strength . . . Russia now had a peace footing of one million men . . .
The Ambassador went so far as to say that there was some feeling in Germany that trouble was bound to come and

therefore it would be better not to restrain Austria and let the trouble come now, rather than later.

He finished the memorandum and stared out of the window at the lamps along Horse Guards Parade. His quality as Prime Minister – some said his genius, although he modestly thought that went a little too far – was his capacity to absorb a series of complex and unrelated problems, to discern various solutions and hold them in his head, and to have the patience to wait for the perfect moment to act – or not to act, which in his experience was often the better course, problems having a tendency, if left alone, to solve themselves. 'Wait and see' – that was the phrase for which he was most remembered and mocked, although it seemed to him eminently sensible. But what was he to make of this? It might be nothing. It could be Armageddon. There was certainly little he could do about it now. He wished Venetia was in London. It was a precious gift for him to have someone to confide in whose advice wasn't distorted by self-interest. But she was leaving town in the morning for a voyage to Scotland on the Admiralty yacht with Winston and Clemmie Churchill so there would be no afternoon drive with her on Friday. He hated it when he didn't see her.

He worked his way through the rest of the telegrams, finished his brandy and went into his bedroom. After he had washed and undressed and put on his nightshirt, he sat up in bed for a while reading a chapter of *Our Mutual Friend* before his eyes started to close and he fell asleep.

The following morning, Tuesday, Deemer was ordered to return to his normal duties. The assigning officer for the Metropolitan Police's Number 1 District seemed to derive considerable satisfaction in taking him down a peg or two after his job for Quinn and dispatched him to investigate a spate of burglaries in Pimlico. It was dull work, going from house to house to ask if anyone had seen anything suspicious – a uniformed constable could have done it equally well. Hours later, when he got back to Scotland Yard, he found a message that Quinn wished to see him, urgently. A few minutes after that, he was standing in front of the superintendent's desk. He was not invited to sit.

The head of Special Branch was a slight, gaunt figure, sixty or thereabouts, with hollow hairy cheeks, dark bushy eyebrows and a small silver goatee on a narrow angular chin. He might have been a distinguished retired amateur jockey from County Mayo. In his delicate hands he held Deemer's report and started making his odd clicking noise again.

'I had no idea you were doing all this. It's much more detail than anyone needs to know.' To Deemer's dismay, he was shaking his head. He looked agitated – irritated even. 'Your name is on the docket as the investigating officer, which means you're on the witness list for the coroner's court tomorrow. You must attend.'

'Yes, sir.'

'You must not, however, give evidence. If the coroner calls you, you're to say that you have nothing material to add to what has already been said. I don't want you to go perjuring yourself, so the wording is important. Have you got that, Sergeant?'

'Yes, sir.'

'It will only cause deep distress to the Anson family and further embarrassment to the witnesses if this story about a drunken wager becomes public.'

He picked up Deemer's report and dropped it in his wastepaper basket. 'Are we clear?'

'Yes, sir.'

'You may go.'

When Deemer was at the door, he called after him, 'Good work, by the way.'

Deemer passed a restless night and was up early the next morning. He shaved and dressed, taking even greater care than usual, and by eight he was in Lambeth.

The coroner's court and the mortuary were housed in two nondescript red-brick buildings next to one another. He showed his warrant card and went into the mortuary. The bodies had been transferred into coffins by the undertakers – Anson's casket polished mahogany with brass handles, Mitchell's plain pine. The lids were off. Both men looked shockingly young, innocent almost, in their suits and ties. They might have been brothers. Anson's face had scratches on the nose but was otherwise unmarked. Deemer stooped to examine the floral tributes heaped beneath his casket. On a huge bouquet of white roses, red carnations and lilies of the valley, a message read 'From the Prime Minister and Mrs Asquith'. Mitchell's coffin was unadorned.

He went back out into the cobbled courtyard. By now half a dozen photographers had taken up positions beside the entrance, and soon afterwards the witnesses and their supporting companions and the relatives of the dead began to arrive, all in black – black dresses, hats and gloves, even black parasols, the men in black suits and top hats. He recognised a few faces from the pier. Count Benckendorff striding on his own. Lady Diana Manners with an intimidating old lady he assumed must be the Duchess of Rutland. Raymond Asquith flanked by two lawyers in tailcoats, one of whom was the famous barrister and Unionist MP F. E. Smith. Sir Herbert Beerbohm Tree, the actor-manager, with his scandalous daughter Iris. The photographers' lights flashed continuously.

He waited until the last of them had walked past him before

following them inside. The court was no bigger than a schoolroom –
a bare wooden floor, whitewashed walls – stuffy on a July morning
even with the windows open. He managed to squeeze himself
into a corner at the back. Every square foot was occupied – officials,
jurors, witnesses, spectators, reporters, lawyers . . . Good God,
the lawyers! Lambeth Coroner's Court could never have seen such
a turnout. Two silks, neither worth less than ten thousand a year –
F. E. Smith representing the guests on the boat, Ernest Pollock,
another Unionist MP, appearing on behalf of the Anson family –
supported by junior counsel, both KCs jumping up and down to
pay tribute to the heroism of William Mitchell and to pledge financial support on behalf of their clients for his widow and her
eighteen-month-old son.

This set the tone for what followed, so that Deemer quickly had
the sensation he was watching not an inquiry but a play – one of
Beerbohm Tree's productions, perhaps – in which every character
had been given their lines and had learned their parts, not least
the coroner, who announced he saw no need to reveal the full list
of guests on board the boat, did not intend to comment on the
case, but would simply put the facts before the jury and ask them
to return a verdict.

Captain White was the first witness to be called and testified
that the party was definitely not drunk: 'merry, but sober'.

The Anson family's barrister rose.

Pollock: 'Sir Denis was merely in good spirits?'

White: 'Yes.'

Pollock: 'I am glad to hear you say that, because I should like
to hear you emphasise and say that there is absolutely no founda-
tion for saying that he had had too much to drink or anything of
that sort.'

White: 'I should say certainly not.'

Pollock: 'He was merry and full of life and only behaved as we would all like to see our sons behave?'

White: 'Yes, sir.'

The first mate backed up his captain: 'None of them was the worse for drink.' Count Benckendorff insisted that Anson was 'quite sober, skipping about and amusing people'. Mr Duff Cooper stated that 'Sir Denis drank a little champagne but was perfectly sober'. Mr Claud Russell said the same.

The coroner: 'Did you see him give his watch to anybody before he dived in?'

Russell: 'Yes, a second before he dived, he said, "Here take my watch", and handed it to someone.'

The coroner: 'Did you think there was any real danger?'

Russell hesitated. 'Yes.'

'Thank you,' said the coroner, quickly cutting off his own line of inquiry. 'You may stand down.' He looked around. 'Detective Sergeant Deemer?'

At the sound of his name, he felt his heartbeat accelerate. It seemed to take him an awfully long time to reach the witness stand, edging down the side of the courtroom and along the front, past the lawyers, stepping over Smith's outstretched legs. He was conscious of their scrutiny and sensed a slight tightening of the atmosphere, or perhaps it was just a projection of his own nerves.

'Sergeant Deemer, you attended the scene at Westminster Pier in the immediate aftermath of the tragedy and took charge of the police investigation. Do you have anything to add to what you have heard?'

Deemer glanced at the ranks of black-clad figures. Afterwards he wished he had found the courage to say yes, actually, he most certainly did, that this was all a fiction, that—

But instead, he found himself replying quietly, 'I have nothing material to add to what has already been said.'

'Thank you, Sergeant. You may stand down.'

As he returned to his place, he avoided the gaze of everyone in the courtroom. They were a blur to him. He felt humiliated, ashamed. Behind him, the coroner had begun his summing-up. He had not called Raymond Asquith to give evidence, nor Lady Diana Manners.

'Gentlemen of the jury, nothing has been kept back. All the facts have been placed before you. It is a short story, and a simple and a sad one. Sir Denis Anson appears to have been a young man of very high spirits and courage: plucky almost to recklessness. There is no evidence – and as far as I understand there is no suggestion – that Sir Denis was under the influence of drink . . .

'Unfortunately, the tragedy has involved the death of another brave man, whose wife is now a widow and whose child is father-less. This man paid a terrible price for his bravery. I am sure you all rejoice with me to hear what has been said in this court as to the assistance which will be given to his widow and child.'

The jury didn't even need to leave the courtroom to deliberate. After a whispered conference the foreman stood and in a confident voice returned their verdict: 'Accidental death by drowning in each case.' It was all over by eleven o'clock.

The coroner gavelled to signal the end of the hearing. The main body of spectators rose. Deemer pressed himself against the wall as the ladies passed by first – an expensive sickly odour of *eau de toilette*, a rustle of black silk, a flutter of fans, and a low murmur of relief that the business was done, that they could escape this stifling place with its talk of death and file out gratefully into the fresh air and the sunlight. Venetia Stanley, he noticed, was not among them.

*

First thing the next morning, when he arrived for his shift at Scotland Yard, he found a message in his pigeonhole summoning him to see Superintendent Quinn. He wasn't sure what to expect. He went upstairs at once.

The superintendent was signing letters. 'Sit down, Sergeant. I shan't keep you a moment.'

He had half a dozen newspapers spread out across the desk in front of him, arranged in a semi-circle, each folded to its report of the inquest. Deemer found himself trying to read the headlines upside down. Was he about to be commended or condemned? But when Quinn finally put down his pen and peered at him over a pair of half-moon spectacles, he made no reference to the case.

'What do you know about Special Branch, Sergeant?'

'Very little, sir.'

'Excellent – that's exactly as it should be. Well, let me tell you, we're a small division, one hundred and fourteen officers to be exact, including myself. Unlike the rest of the Metropolitan Police, we also operate outside London, across the entire country. We're responsible for checking suspects entering and leaving through the ports and railway stations, keeping track of aliens living here, protecting royalty and Cabinet ministers. We also have the task of arresting saboteurs, spies and any other such persons considered a threat to national security, at the direction of a certain department of the War Office that doesn't officially exist. It's a lot of work for a few score men. Are you married, Sergeant? Do you have children?'

'I'm unmarried, sir.'

'Good. That's an advantage. The days are long. The hours are irregular. Sometimes you'll be weeks away from home, doing work you mostly can't talk about. That puts a strain on a marriage. Parents still alive? Brothers and sisters?'

'My parents are both dead, sir.'

'Both? I'm sorry to hear that. When did that happen?'

'They were killed in a railway accident, sir, seven years ago. I have a younger brother. He's in the army.'

'What's his regiment?'

'Middlesex, Duke of Cambridge's Own.'

'Can you handle a firearm?'

'I've never tried.'

'Ah, well, it doesn't matter. We can soon remedy that. Now, do you have any questions?' Deemer had plenty, but before he could reply, Quinn said, 'Talk to my assistant.' And with that he concluded the interview.

CHAPTER FIVE

VENETIA WAS AT that moment aboard the First Lord of the Admiralty's official yacht, *Enchantress*, steaming north in calm seas and fair weather towards Scotland.

If she gave no thought to the inquest, either on the day of the verdict or on any of the days that followed, it was mainly because she had no time. Her cousin Clemmie Churchill, whose bridesmaid she had been, was six months pregnant, and it soon became apparent that the reason for her invitation was to assist the nanny with the children – Randolph, a demonic red-haired toddler, and Diana, whose fifth birthday party she was expected to help organise. When she wasn't running after Randolph to stop him climbing up on the railings, she had to try to keep them both occupied – reading them stories, teaching them to draw, devising games, playing hide-and-seek – while Clemmie lay in a darkened cabin with one of her nervous headaches and Winston worked on his papers and the speech he had to deliver in Scotland, emerging only at mealtimes to deliver monologues. So, this is what I have become, she thought, as she lay exhausted on her bed – the maiden aunt, the childless cousin, obliged to work my passage. It was not a vision of the future she relished. But if the alternative was to marry and have children of her own – was that not merely servitude of a different sort, a lifetime of obligation?

At Dundee on Thursday morning, she was cheered up to find a letter waiting for her from the Prime Minister (*My darling – you are dearer to me than I can tell you. Write – all love*) and at Queensferry on Friday there was another (*It is a lovely afternoon, and I wish more than I can tell you that I was on board the Enchantress . . .*). On Saturday night, on the return trip, when they anchored off the coast of Norfolk at Overstrand, there was a third, much longer, complaining about Lord Northcliffe, owner of *The Times* and the *Daily Mail*, who was supporting the Ulster Unionists (*I hate & distrust the fellow & all his works, but it doesn't do to say this to Winston . . . Have I worn out your patience beloved? You told me to tell you everything: there is one thing I can never tell you, but you know it.*)

When she looked up, Winston was watching her intently. Of course, she thought, he recognises the PM's handwriting. She coolly folded the letter and put it back in its envelope. He grinned at her and winked. 'I feel like a jealous lover,' he said, in his lisping voice. 'I wish he would write so ashiduoushly to *me*.'

H.M.Y. Enchantress,
Overstrand,
Sunday 12 July 1914
Thank you, darling, for your heavenly letter, which was here when we arrived. I feel guilty to be on holiday when you are so vexed with Ulster, tho' I can assure you the children are as demanding as the Unionists and Northcliffe rolled into one.

Pear Tree Cottage at Cromer wh. the Churchills are

renting for the summer is v sweet, & for Diana's birthday
we spent the night ashore. She is delightful & pretty, like
her mother, whereas Randolph is Winston in miniature (if
you can imagine anything so terrifying). This morning we
went to the beach & W. put on a curious baggy old red &
white bathing costume & built a vast network of
sandcastles & defensive walls, ostensibly for the children
but really for his own amusement. He took as much
pleasure in seeing these demolished by the incoming waves
as he did in building them & made a long speech about the
folly of human pretensions in defying Nature, etc. One
cannot help but love him. I made the mistake of asking
him to explain the difference between a Dreadnought & a
Super Dreadnought. You can test me when we go for our
drive on Tuesday.

I shall give this letter to Clemmie to post, as we are
leaving her and the children behind tonight so that
Winston can be back at Chatham in the morning.

Always yours.

She woke early the next morning and went up on deck. There
was a sea fog, chilly and saturating. The wooden lounging chairs
felt wet to the touch. She had to go back down to her cabin
and fetch a shawl. The mist didn't lift until they reached the
Thames Estuary. As the sky cleared, half a dozen aeroplanes
appeared, flying low overhead. The racket of their engines
brought Winston up from below to join her. He was wearing
a naval officer's cap and had a pair of binoculars hung around
his neck.

'Bristol Scouts,' he announced, studying the planes through his
binoculars, 'from the navy air station at Eastchurch.' He handed

her the field glasses. 'The wars of the future will be fought in the air, as well as on sea and land.'

They stood together, leaning on the railing, watching them climb and loop and dive.

'Is it not a most thrilling spectacle? Unfortunately, Clemmie won't let me fly any more. She made me promise her. Said it's too dangerous.'

'I'd love to fly.'

'Really?' He looked at her with interest. 'Would you like a flutter, Vinny?'

'Can you fix it?'

'Of course I can bloody fix it – I'm the First Lord of the Admiralty!'

Two hours later she was strapped into the passenger seat of a biplane behind a Royal Navy pilot, bouncing down the grass runway of Chatham Airfield in a borrowed leather jacket and a pair of goggles – *and oh! Darling it was so exhilarating! – you must promise me you won't be cross with Winston for letting me try it* – the bone-shaking speed along the ground and then the sudden hollowing in her stomach as the machine lurched into the air, the ecstasy of escaping the dull earth and seeing the familiar fall away then tilt on its axis and become entirely unfamiliar – summer-scorched fields dotted with tiny cattle, narrow brown lanes, church towers, miniature horses and carts, a limitless grey sea flecked by white waves and edged by a ten-mile line of surf breaking along the Essex coast – the rush of the wind in her face mingling with the racket of the engine and the scent of petrol, the danger of it, the possibility, the *freedom* . . .

She was returned firmly to earth that evening in Mansfield Street over dinner with her parents – formally dressed even though it was just the three of them, seated together at one end of the long table.

Having listened politely to her daughter's enthusiastic description of flying, Lady Sheffield waited until the meal was finished before announcing that they would all be going to the family estate in Wales at the end of the following week for their summer vacation, and that afterwards Venetia could expect to be away from London for a further three months: she was to accompany Lady Sheffield to India and then on to Australia, where Venetia's eldest brother Arthur had recently taken office as Governor of Victoria.

It was a moment before she felt able to reply. 'Where exactly are you hoping to find me a husband – in the Himalayas or the Outback?'

'We should be home in time for Christmas. Then we shall all go to Alderley.'

Her father was seated between them at the end of the table, smoking. He took his cigar out of his mouth just long enough to say, 'It will be an education for you.'

It was a plot, of course – she saw that at once – to separate her from her London circle: from the Coterie, obviously, but also, quite possibly, from the Prime Minister. His fondness for the company of attractive young women was well known, and they had certainly observed him with her often enough – the way he insisted on sitting next to her at table then patted the sofa for her to come and join him for an intimate talk afterwards. But she hadn't suspected until that moment that they might have realised things had gone much further.

She managed a brittle smile. 'I have no say in the matter, I assume?'

'The steamship tickets are booked.' Her mother smiled back at her across the table. 'Besides, what else do you have to do?'

She looked from one parent to the other. The Stanleys were
an intellectual family, not at all conventional; eccentric even.
Lyulph, her father, seventy-five and old enough to be her grandfather, had been a Liberal MP and a fellow of Balliol College,
Oxford, until his announcement that he did not believe in God
had obliged him to resign. He had inherited his title unexpectedly
on the death of his elder brother, Henry, who had converted to
Islam and had sat in the House of Lords as a Muslim peer. His
younger brother, Algernon, was a plump and worldly Catholic
bishop. Their nephew was the philosopher Bertrand Russell. And
Maisie, Lady Sheffield, who looked in the candlelight like an
eighteenth-century countess with her mass of white hair and her
dark eyes and brows, was clever enough to hold her own with
them all. But even in the Stanley household, unconventionality
had its limits, and a twenty-six-year-old daughter suspected of
having an affair with a sixty-one-year-old prime minister fell definitely beyond the boundary of what was acceptable. She knew
better than to argue.

'I have nothing else to do,' she said, 'as you well know.'

The next morning's post brought the inevitable letter from Downing Street, written the night before. Once again, she managed to
intercept the envelope before the servants got to it and took it
upstairs to read in the privacy of her bedroom.

I am extremely glad that I didn't know beforehand that you
were going to take to yourself wings & fly: even Winston
was shamefaced & apologetic when he mentioned your
exploit to me on the bench . . . I have had two interesting if
not very enlivening interviews. The first (which is most
secret) was with Lord Northcliffe – of all people . . . I long

to talk over this & other things with my most darling
counsellor. The choice is I think between tomorrow (Tues)
& Wed (when there is a singing party at our house in the
afternoon). Which wd. suit you best? We might take from 5
o'clock to 10 minutes to 7. Please let me know as soon as
you can . . . Write to me beloved. I love you.

She sat at her dressing table with her pen in her hand. For the
first time she was struck by the reality of what a long separation
would mean. She would not see him, or touch him, or feel his
touch. The flood of letters would dry to a trickle, arriving weeks
after they were written. Her daily window into his world – the
great world of politics and public events – would close. Her influence would end. And he would find a new confidante. Naturally
he would. She was the latest in a long line. She experienced a
sudden and unfamiliar stab of what she realised to her horror was
jealousy.

Really, it was intolerable.

A Stanley spirit of rebellion rose within her, and after a few
minutes, her pen began to move.

Darling, bad news I'm afraid. Mama is determined to spirit
me away to Penrhos for August, & after that on a long
voyage to India & Australia. Protest is quite hopeless. So,
let's do both! – can you pick me up from the usual place at
5 this afternoon? And then I'll come to the concert
tomorrow. We must make the most of our chances while
we can. I long to see you.

She took it to the post box herself.

*

Such was her determination to see him at every possible opportunity, and so insatiable was his need for her company despite the imminent Buckingham Palace conference on Ireland, that they contrived to meet six times over the next ten days: for a ninety-minute drive out to the Thames at Marlow that afternoon, when he showed her a telegram from the ambassador in Berlin describing the warlike feeling in Germany, and afterwards tore it up and scattered the pieces out of the car window; on Wednesday at the musical recital in 10 Downing Street (although, given the presence of both Margot and her mother in the audience, it was impossible to do more than exchange pleasantries); and on Friday for another two-hour car ride, this time out towards Goring-on-Thames, when he gave her the carbon copy of another telegram, this one from the British ambassador in Vienna, marked 'Confidential', warning that the Austrians were drawing up an indictment against the Serbian government 'for alleged complicity in the conspiracy that led to the assassination of the Archduke'.

She gave it back. 'Is that serious?'

'It might be. We must keep an eye on them.'

Once again, he screwed the telegram into a ball and threw it out of the window. It seemed to her a cavalier way to treat official documents, but she said nothing.

The following Monday, on the eve of the Irish talks, she called on him in Number 10 and they went out through the garden gate for an early-evening stroll in St James's Park. She couldn't resist slipping her arm through his. It was the end of yet another hot day in that improbably glorious summer. People were sitting in deckchairs, lying sprawled on the brown grass. Civil servants were going home for the evening. Some MPs were heading for their clubs. For once, he was recognised continually. He nodded politely to the men, raised his hat to the ladies.

A band started playing close to the lake. On impulse, she said, 'Why don't we have dinner together – just the two of us? We've never done that before. We could find somewhere quiet – it might be our last chance.'

'That would be wonderful.' He glanced around, hesitated. 'But I ought to prepare my thoughts for tomorrow.'

'Of course. I understand.' She disengaged her arm from his.

'Let's walk to the Mall,' he said miserably, 'and I'll find you a taxi.'

And she did understand. He had to be careful. But that didn't stop her feeling slightly crushed – either then, or the next morning, when she received his apologetic note.

I exercised real self-denial, darling, in regard to your suggestion that I should join you at dinner. I hate even the possibility of gossip about us.

Their fifth meeting was that afternoon when he picked her up from Portland Place. He had driven directly from the conference at Buckingham Palace, and she could tell at once, by the way he stayed hunched in his corner of the back seat, that it had not gone well. As they drove towards Regent's Park, he described the events of the day in a monotone. Himself and Lloyd George for the government, Bonar Law and Lansdowne for the Unionists, Redmond and Dillon for the Irish Nationalists, Craig and Carson for the Ulstermen – all around the table for hour after hour, once the King had made his appeal for agreement and left the room, those wretched maps spread out between them and no progress, no compromise, no surrender, just both sides sitting there refusing to make any concession, but not wishing to leave and take the blame for the failure of the talks.

'There was madness in the room. I tell you, having looked them in the eyes, I think they actually *want* a war. There's an instinct for destruction in these tribal conflicts beyond the reach of any rational argument.' He took her hand. 'And the worst thing is, you won't be here to help me face it.'

The idea came to her as she kissed his hand. 'If I can't be in London, why don't you come to me – at least for a day or two?'

'Come to Penrhos?' For the first time his expression brightened. 'That would be wonderful. Do you think your parents would invite me?'

'You'd have to be the one to suggest it. But they could hardly refuse.'

'Then I'll propose myself at the garden party on Thursday. I'm quite shameless when it comes to you.' Ireland seemed suddenly to have vanished from his mind. 'You are a wonder,' he said happily, 'you know that, don't you?'

The card had arrived a month ago, addressed to Lord and Lady Sheffield and the Hon. Venetia Stanley. It was meant to be the climax of the season.

Mrs Asquith

At Home

3 to 5 o'clock

Thursday July 23rd 1914

10 Downing Street London, S.W.

Margot made a point of always inviting Venetia to her social functions. Plainly she had decided the wisest course, as with all her husband's previous female friends – 'the harem', as she derisively called them – was to draw her in close, the better to keep an eye on her. Sometimes she even took Venetia aside and discussed 'Henry' confidentially, as if he were their shared project – his health, his drinking, the strain he was under, what they could do to ease his burden. At other times she froze her out completely. Then Venetia would turn occasionally and catch her staring at her across the room, those shrewd eyes narrowed, that bird-of-prey face rigid with distaste. She wondered which Margot she would encounter that afternoon.

As soon as she and her parents arrived in Downing Street, she saw that she need not have worried. Margot, never one to entertain by halves, had invited, as usual, seven hundred guests. The entrance hall, the state rooms and the terrace and garden beyond were crowded with MPs, Cabinet ministers, most of the diplomatic corps and half of fashionable society, red-faced and wilting in the heat.

In the crush it was scarcely surprising that she failed to recognise Detective Sergeant Deemer, whom she had only met briefly, and who was in any case trying to be as discreet as possible – standing in the lobby, part of a six-man team of Special Branch protection officers with orders to mingle among the guests. But he recognised her: one of the few people he did. On impulse, he followed her out through the French windows.

The Prime Minister and his wife were standing on the lawn at the foot of the steps, greeting each arrival. He kissed Venetia lightly on the cheek and Margot did the same. 'Dear Maisie,' he said to Lady Sheffield, 'just the person I wanted to see. I have to make a speech in Chester on Friday—'

Margot gave him a sharp look. 'You never told me that.'

Venetia didn't wait to hear the rest. 'Excuse me,' she said. 'There's Winston. I want to thank him again for my trip.'

'Don't go too far,' her mother called after her. 'We have to be at Euston by five.'

The First Lord of the Admiralty was in a group with his mother, Lady Jennie, and the German ambassador, Prince Lichnowsky, both of whom she knew. He introduced her to the others – a German count named Kessler and Comtesse Greffulhe, a French-woman, languidly cooling her powdered cheeks with a delicate Chinoiserie fan. They were discussing the Buckingham Palace conference, which had met again that morning and was due to hold its final session the next day.

'I hear it did not go well,' said Winston. 'What have you heard, Venetia?' He turned away from her to Lichnowsky. 'Miss Stanley,' he confided, in a stage whisper, 'knows *everything*.'

'Hardly!' She laughed.

'And if the conference fails,' asked the ambassador, 'what then?'

'Blood,' said Winston. 'Blood!'

She listened for a few minutes then moved away.

Deemer followed, no more than ten feet behind her. He felt conspicuous in his shabby dark suit which he was obliged to keep buttoned up despite the heat. He had only been an officer in the Special Branch for a fortnight. This was his first experience of protection duty, the first time he had gone out armed. He was sure the bulge of his Webley pistol in its shoulder holster must be obvious, at least to anyone who knew about such things. At one point, she turned round and looked directly at him, but didn't seem to see him. He thought she looked pale, unwell.

He was right. Despite the lightness of her lemon silk jacket and blouse she felt dizzy in the hot sunshine. She took a cup of tea from one of the servants and carried it to a patch of shade beneath a tree close to the garden wall. The Foreign Secretary,

Sir Edward Grey, was standing nearby in a huddle with the French and Russian ambassadors. His thin widower's face, melancholy at the happiest of times, but now accentuated by the dark glasses he wore to protect his deteriorating eyesight, looked positively sepulchral.

She realised she was in danger of fainting – and in Margot's house of all places.

She stooped and set her cup and saucer carefully on the grass then hitched up her skirt and sat down next to it. She took off her elaborate heavy hat, rested her back against the ivy on the brick wall and drank her tea. She closed her eyes. Conversations, indistinguishable from one another, brayed around her; people were having to talk ever more loudly to make themselves heard. When she opened them again the Prime Minister was standing over her, framed by the sun. She shaded her eyes against the glare to see him.

'No, don't get up,' he said. 'I only wish I could join you, but I must go and talk to all these ghastly people. It's been fixed – for the trivial price of making a speech to the Chester Red Cross Society, I can come for the weekend to Penrhos.'

'That's wonderful.'

'Isn't it?'

'I can hardly wait.'

'Till Saturday week, darling.'

'Till then.' He blew her the ghost of a kiss.

She watched him walk across the lawn towards the house – a politician's crab-wise progress, stopping to exchange a word or two here and there, remembering names, bestowing smiles – until he disappeared into the crowd.

Well, well, thought Deemer, who had been pretending to examine a nearby rose bush, even though it had shed its petals. He wasn't sure what he had witnessed exactly – he hadn't been able to hear a word of their exchanges – but it was definitely *something*.

In Belgrade, the ambassador of the Austro-Hungarian Empire was arriving at the Serbian Foreign Ministry to deliver his government's ultimatum.

PART TWO

WAR

24 July–4 August 1914

CHAPTER SIX

H IS MIND WAS so concentrated on Ireland, so haunted by visions of civil war and the imminent collapse of his government, that for once, the following morning, when he took the call from the Foreign Secretary, it took him a while to grasp the significance of what he was being told.

'We have the text of the Austrian demands,' said Grey. 'Their ambassador has just brought it over.'

'And what do you make of it?' He was looking at his watch, standing in his private secretaries' office. Margot was upstairs in bed with a migraine, brought on by the strain of her garden party. His car was waiting outside to take him to the Palace. Venetia was three hundred miles away. He felt harassed. If it had been anyone other than Grey, he would have refused to come to the telephone.

'I told him it was the most formidable document I'd ever seen addressed by one state to another.'

'Worse than we expected?'

'Infinitely worse.'

Now he absorbed the importance of the information. And in

the smoothly functioning filing system of his lawyer's brain, the European crisis moved up a drawer from low priority to high. 'You'd better bring it to Cabinet this afternoon. I must go now and deal with our own troublesome smaller neighbours.'

He handed the telephone back to his principal private secretary, Maurice Bonham Carter, donned his top hat, and together the two men went out into Downing Street. Horwood was standing by the Napier and opened the rear door. A solitary photographer took the Prime Minister's picture as he clambered into the empty compartment.

Venetia had arrived at Penrhos in darkness late the previous evening after a five-hour train journey and hadn't got to bed until long past midnight. She would have slept longer if it hadn't been for the piercing cries of a peacock just beneath her window.

She threw off her bedcovers and walked the considerable length of her room to draw back the curtains. After a summer in London, it was a shock not to hear the noise of traffic or see another human being. There was only the soft silence of north Wales, the wide empty flagstone terrace where the peacock was fluttering his fantail to a non-existent audience, the great expanse of the lawn, the encircling woods, and in the distance beyond the trees, glinting in the sunshine, the Irish Sea.

She quickly donned the bathing costume that had been laid out for her by Edith, slipped on a pair of canvas shoes and a warm robe, then went out into the corridor, past the suits of armour and the unsmiling ancestral portraits, and down the creaking wooden staircase. From the domestic offices came the sound of voices talking in Welsh and a smell of breakfast – of bacon frying and kippers grilling – that made her realise how hungry she was. But her ritual on her first day at Penrhos was always the same:

swim first, then eat. She called for Huck, her spaniel, let herself out through the French windows onto the terrace and set off over the dew-soaked grass towards the woods.

Penrhos House was huge – a sprawling grey-stoned, bay-windowed mansion dressed up to look like a castle, with towers and turrets and crenellated battlements, a walled garden, greenhouses, orchards, courtyards, barns, farms: six thousand acres in all. It was absurd really to have so much, that so many people should labour all year round to keep one family in luxury for a month or two. Her father had inherited it along with everything else when she was sixteen and she had accepted it without giving it too much thought.

Set into the garden wall, half-hidden by undergrowth, was a small Gothic door. In her teenage imagination, it had been a secret gate to an enchanted Arthurian world; sometimes, like this morning, it still was. She followed the narrow path through the silent woods. Sunlight filtered between the high branches and fell in translucent drapes of gauze amid the ferns and rhododendrons. Two minutes later, with Huck trotting ahead, she emerged from the trees onto a deserted curve of white sandy beach.

The flat line of the Anglesey coast formed the horizon less than a mile to her right; the port of Holyhead was the same distance to the left. And yet she might have been the only person on earth. She took off her dressing gown and waded into the sea.

It was too cold to swim for long. Afterwards, she went in search of the penguin she had bought from a pet shop in Liverpool a couple of years earlier with the vague intention of founding a colony. She had once kept a bear cub as well, in emulation of Lord Byron, until it got bigger and started chasing their house guests, at which point her father had given it away to a zoo. She found the penguin standing forlornly on a rock. But when she tried to approach it, the bird dived into the water and swam away.

On her way back to the house she stopped to pick some verbena. Later in the morning, after she had bathed and eaten breakfast, she sat on the terrace and wrote her daily letter to the Prime Minister.

> Here is some sweet-smelling green, my dearest, to remind
> you of what awaits you in Penrhos. I am remaking my
> soul, reading Pepys in the sunshine, & enjoying the quiet
> while I can. Tomorrow, Sylvia & Anthony & then Blanche
> & Eric all arrive with their children & the peace will be
> over. The last few months with you have been so heavenly.
> I fear I am rather dumb when it comes to telling you what I
> feel. But I wish so much that you were here with me, & I
> long for Saturday. All love –

★

He ploughed on through the day, like a ship in a heaving sea, with no higher purpose than to survive and get to the end of it.

First, he had had to deal with the King, who was in tears when he made his little speech at the break-up of the Buckingham Palace conference ('Farewell, I am sorry, and I thank you'); then it was back to Downing Street with Lloyd George to try to mollify the Irish Nationalists by promising to introduce the Home Rule Bill the following week; then, because he was also acting as Secretary of State for War to try to keep the army loyal, he had to endure a luncheon with various members of the military at the Marlborough Club; then back to Downing Street again for a Cabinet meeting – eighteen men, sitting around a long table on a hot afternoon, most of whom were determined to have their say on the Irish question, even though none had anything new to add. He bore it patiently, making a note of each contribution, with the result that it wasn't until after four that they finally got round to the Austrian ultimatum to Serbia. He kept his eye on the clock on the mantelpiece. He had to be in Parliament at five to give a statement on Ireland.

'Foreign Secretary?'

'Perhaps it might be helpful, Prime Minister, if I read out the text . . .'

Afterwards, in his imagination, whenever he relived the next ten minutes, it seemed to him that the air in the Cabinet room began to thin, the light fade, the sounds of the Friday-afternoon traffic through the open windows grow distant, as Grey's dry, precise voice intoned the demands of the Habsburg Empire: that the Serbs should censor all newspapers hostile to Vienna, dissolve all subversive organisations, sack all army officers and officials critical of the Emperor, allow His Imperial Majesty's security forces to operate inside Serbia to track down the terrorists who had assassinated the Archduke . . .

'Austria-Hungary,' concluded Grey, 'expects a reply by tomorrow, Saturday, at six p.m.'

He laid down his sheets of paper.

The Cabinet was for once stunned into silence as they struggled to clear their minds of the parishes of County Tyrone and adjust to this new threat.

The Prime Minister said, 'And what, in your judgement, will be the Serbian response?'

'They will probably do their best to comply with some of it. But they can't comply with it *all* – no state could.'

'And then?'

'In the worst case, Austria-Hungary will invade. Russia will come to the aid of her brother-Serbs. Germany will mobilise to meet the Russian threat. And once that happens, France will be bound by treaty to stand with Russia. In short – a general European war, such as we have not seen since Napoleon.'

Eventually, Lloyd George said, 'Just to be clear – if it comes to war, we are not legally obliged to stand with France?'

'Legally, no.'

Winston burst out, 'But France is our ally! If she goes to war, how can we, with any honour – whatever the legal position – remain neutral?'

That broke the silence. There was a sudden detonation of disagreement, hands flying up in horror, cries of 'No!' and 'Nonsense!'

The Prime Minister glanced around the table and noted down a few names. A large part of his job was arithmetic. He reckoned a good half were opposed to any British involvement, at any price. He decided to end this quickly.

'One thing we can all agree on is that a general European war would be a calamity. Our immediate policy is therefore equally obvious: to strain every sinew to prevent it.'

'On that point,' said Grey, 'I've asked the German ambassador to come and see me this evening to discuss the possibility of arranging a mediating group – ourselves, Germany, France and Italy – to put pressure on Austria and Serbia to avoid a conflict.'

'Good. Now I need to go and make my statement. In the meantime, I suggest we all take care not to say anything in public that might provoke a general panic. Let us show a united front.'

And with relief, he ended the meeting.

He desperately needed fresh air to clear his head. He decided to walk the half-mile to the Commons. Most of the Cabinet did the same, singly and in pairs, in front and behind, strung out along Whitehall. Winston fell in next to him.

'You know, this may not be entirely bad news.'

'How so?'

'It will divert attention from Ireland, and it will put the Tories on the spot. They can hardly push us to the edge of a civil war while the peace of Europe hangs in the balance.'

'I wouldn't put it past them.'

'The First and Second Fleets are still together at Portland after the summer review. I could announce we're keeping them intact, as a single fighting force – purely as a precautionary measure, of course. It might help deter the Germans from getting involved.'

He didn't like the sound of that, but he saw the logic, and it would certainly turn the screw on the Tories. 'Talk to Grey about it. But we must tread carefully. The stakes are very high.'

He put his head down to discourage further conversation, and after a few moments Winston lengthened his stride and caught up with Grey. He was twirling his cane. He looked almost jaunty. There is our War Party, the Prime Minister thought.

He entered the Commons to a half-hearted cheer from the Liberal MPs. The Cabinet trooped in and squeezed up beside him on the front bench. The grimness of their expressions was immediately noticed and seemed to spread a chill over the chamber. He glanced across at Bonar Law, whose treasonable behaviour over Ireland he regarded with contempt. The Tory leader looked unusually shifty. He guessed he must have heard about the ultimatum.

The Speaker said, 'Statement, the Prime Minister.'

He rose and briefly reported the failure of the conference and the government's intention of laying the Irish Home Rule Bill

before Parliament on Tuesday. Bonar Law stood and acknow-
ledged his statement without further comment. And that was it:
one of the great parliamentary anticlimaxes. It was all over in four
minutes.

He stayed in his seat while the chamber slowly emptied, watching the MPs as they left for the weekend. He had been prime
minister for six years. In the way of politics, he had been obliged
to disappoint more men than he had been able to promote, and
he noticed the way his own side looked at him – some fawning,
some envious, some hostile, not a true friend among them. He
felt a sudden stab of the melancholy that often stalked him when
he was tired. He forced himself to his feet and walked behind the
Speaker's chair to his office.

He sat at the long table, big enough for twenty men to gather
around, and reached for a sheet of notepaper. Oh, dearest, darling
Venetia, he thought – although he didn't dare put that down – how
I wish we had been taking our usual Friday-afternoon drive.

This is a black letter day in my Calendar – first & foremost
because the 'light has failed', which as you know means
that what I have come to rely upon most is removed far
away, and that I feel like a man who is being sucked away
from his lifebuoy.

He wrote on with great rapidity, imagining she was with him
in the room, describing the events of the day – the collapse of the
conference, the Austrian ultimatum.

We are within measurable, or imaginable, distance of a
real Armageddon, which would dwarf the Ulster &
Nationalist Volunteers to their true proportion. Happily

there seems no reason why we should be anything other than spectators. But it is a blood-curdling statement – is it not? Most beloved, I wish I could tell you what a stay you have been & are & will be to me. I wonder what sort of journey you had? & whether you found Huck & the Penguin? & what dress you are going to wear this evening? & – heaps of things. <u>Write fully.</u> Bless you my love.

He addressed the envelope and dropped it into the post box in the Central Lobby. Then, finding himself alone, and for want of anything better to do, he wandered down into the subterranean passages beneath the Palace of Westminster to the barbershop. At that hour on a Friday afternoon, he had the place to himself. He sat in the chair in front of the mirror, discouraged – by polite but monosyllabic responses – the barber's attempts at conversation, and submitted to the tedious business of having his hair cut. She would be pleased, he thought. Despite the latest crisis, he saw no reason why he would not be able to go to Penrhos in eight days' time.

He left Downing Street by car late the next morning, accompanied by Arthur – Oc – his third-eldest son. He was glad it was Oc. He was more soothing company than his intellectual brothers. He had left Oxford without a degree and had served in the Sudanese civil service. Now he was in business, something to do with trade with Argentina. Dear Oc: he could safely be relied upon not to want to talk about Serbia. They had lunch at Skindles in Maidenhead with the Home Secretary, Reggie McKenna, and his wife, Pamela, then the four of them played golf together at Huntercombe near Henley-on-Thames. The Prime Minister never talked politics on the links, striding along the springy Berkshire fairways with the wind in his face. He sank a couple of satisfyingly long putts, they beat the McKennas two and one, and afterwards he and Oc motored on to Margot's small country house at Sutton Courtney near Oxford for a long-planned family evening.

The Wharf, as it was called, was not at all grand. The front door opened onto the village street. But the Thames flowed past at the bottom of the garden, through a series of sluices and small lakes, which gave it charm. It had been renovated in the Arts and Crafts style, all bare brick, and hand-woven rugs on polished wooden floors. He had a small bedroom with a desk which he used as a study. Margot had her own quarters across a footbridge over the river in a converted barn. Raymond was already there, and Herbert – Beb – a lawyer who wanted to be a writer, and his elder daughter, Violet, who hurried downstairs to kiss him.

The evening was warm. The doors to the garden were propped open by flowerpots to let in a breeze. After a noisy dinner, over which he presided with his customary distant benignity, Raymond and Beb went off to play chess in the garden while he sat in the library, a glass of brandy beside him, for a game of bridge, partnering Violet against Margot and Oc. Stepmother and stepdaughter bickered as usual – first over some obscure bid, then over whether there was too little light or too much of a draught. Sometimes he thought it was worse than dealing with the Cabinet. Oc glanced at him across the table and gave him a wink.

It was just after ten when the telephone rang.

He finished the trick and waited while the maid answered the call and then came to fetch him. He took a sip of brandy and went out into the hall.

'Prime Minister?'

It was Bonham Carter, his private secretary.

'Yes, Bongie?' Whatever was the origin of this infantile

nickname he had no idea, but it amused him to use it. He much preferred the frivolities of the young to the formalities of the old. His children and their friends liked to call him Prime. He didn't object to that, either.

'Sorry to disturb you, sir. I'm in the office and I thought you'd want to know – a telegram has just come in from our embassy in Budapest.'

'Yes?'

'The Austrians have studied the Serbian reply to their ultimatum and announced that while it meets some of their demands, it doesn't go far enough.'

'Well, no surprise there. Don't work too late. Let me know if there are any further developments.'

He returned to the card table.

Margot said, 'What's going on?'

'Nothing that need interrupt our game. It's your deal, I think.'

An hour later, just before midnight, the telephone rang again. Wearily, he put down his cards and went back out to the hall.

'Sorry, Prime Minister.'

'Now what?'

'There are reports the Austrians have ordered their diplomatic staff to leave Belgrade and have started calling up army reservists. There's also a telegram from our ambassador in Serbia.'

'What does that say?'

'"Mobilisation ordered."'

After he had hung up, he stood for a short while staring at the wall. So, it was beginning! And yet it was unreal, as if a fire had broken out somewhere and wisps of smoke were beginning to curl beneath the door, but nobody moved because they couldn't believe it. A whole sequence of events – terrible events – briefly opened up before him with an awful clarity.

When he went back into the library, Raymond and Beb had come in from the garden with their cigars to find out what was happening. He looked at his sons, his darling boys, in their dinner jackets, three fit young men in their early thirties, men of military age, whom he had promised his first wife, as she lay dying, he would always look after.

Raymond said, 'Is everything all right, Prime?'

'Oh,' he muttered, 'just this wretched trouble in the Balkans.'

'There's always trouble in the Balkans,' said Margot briskly. 'It's nothing to do with us. Let's play a different game.'

The following morning, Sunday, was blessedly quiet. He played more golf before lunch. In the afternoon, Bongie Bonham Carter drew up outside the house in his bright new motor car, fresh from Downing Street, bearing a locked red dispatch box full of official papers. The Prime Minister took it with a sigh.

'You'll stay for dinner, I hope?'

'I'd love to, sir.'

At that moment, Violet came into the hall and insisted on taking Bongie for a walk. Bongie looked at him for permission. 'Yes, yes. Go ahead. I can deal with this alone.' He carried the box up to his room, set it on his desk, and watched them from the upstairs window, strolling arm in arm over the little bridge on the opposite side of the river – Bongie slim, serious, rendered older than his years by premature baldness; Violet swan-necked, statuesque, unexpectedly, in her late twenties, a beauty. Of all his children, she was the one to whom he was closest, had been so since her mother died. Now, looking at her, he wondered if she might not one day marry Bongie. He wasn't sure how he felt about the prospect. Margot, of course, would be delighted to finally get her out of the house.

He turned away, sat at his desk, unlocked his box and took out the papers.

Most were carbon copies of Foreign Office telegrams – 'flimsies' as they were known, on account of the onionskin paper on which they were typed. The carbon tended to blur the words in the bottom copies. Letters with enclosed loops – a, e, o, p, d – were often little better than black smudges. He had to hold the flimsies close to the desk lamp to read them. At the top of each was the time it was dispatched and the time it was decoded in London. The first had come in on Friday night, a long dispatch from the ambassador in St Petersburg: *Minister for Foreign Affairs expressed the hope that His Majesty's Government would proclaim their solidarity with France and Russia. He characterised Austria's behaviour as immoral and provocative. If war did break out, we would sooner or later be dragged into it, but if we did not make common cause with France and Russia from the outset, we would have rendered war more likely.*

There was another from the ambassador in Austria, received that morning: *War is thought to be imminent. Wildest enthusiasm prevails in Vienna. Russian Embassy is being guarded by troops to prevent hostile demonstrations.* The most recent pair were from Norway, where the Kaiser had been cruising the fjords on holiday: *German fleet, numbering twenty-eight large ships, received orders to concentrate during last night at predetermined point off the Norwegian coast.* And half an hour later: *Emperor William left Balestrand at 6 o'clock last night and is proceeding direct to Kiel.*

All across Europe, he thought – everyone moving into position, everything tending in the same direction, towards the precipice. The world had gone mad.

He reached into his inside pocket and extracted the letter he had received from Venetia just before he left Downing Street. He had re-read it several times already; he did so again. *The last few months with you have been so heavenly* . . . He tipped the verbena onto his desk, rubbed it between his thumb and forefinger, inhaled the sweet scent. He imagined the woods at Penrhos, pictured himself walking with her through the trees and along the seashore. He wanted to tell her everything, to show her the strain he was under, to elicit her sympathy. He sorted through the flimsies, selected the most interesting and picked up his pen.

My darling before I left London yesterday . . . and so on and so forth, one page after another, until he had told her everything. He hesitated. He had sent her a few pieces of correspondence before, but never anything that was technically secret. Still, why not?

Meanwhile, no one can say what is going to happen in the East of Europe. The enclosed telegram from our Ambassador at Petersburg wh. came on Friday night will interest you, because it shows the Russian view, & how even at this stage Russia is trying to drag us in . . .

A thin sheet of Foreign Office paper was a poor exchange for sweet verbena, but it was the only bouquet he had. What greater proof could he offer of his love, of his dependence upon her, of his absolute confidence in her loyalty and discretion? He folded the telegram into his letter and sealed the envelope.

CHAPTER SEVEN

T HE PRIME MINISTER'S letter was collected along with
the rest of the village's mail from the post box in Sutton
Courtney in the middle of the afternoon, taken by van
to the sorting office in Oxford, put on a train to London shortly
before 5.30 p.m., reached London an hour later, was sorted again
at the Mount Pleasant depot in Clerkenwell, and with ten minutes
to spare caught the Irish Mail train which left Euston every night
at 8.45 p.m. By 2.20 a.m., it was at Holyhead and a few hours later,
just before breakfast on Monday morning, the postman cycled
with it in his bag down the long drive to Penrhos House, where
Venetia was waiting in the hall to intercept it and spirit it away up
to her bedroom.

She sensed from the moment she opened the envelope and
unfolded the mysterious, almost tissue-like enclosure, that this
was something different to his normal letters.

Urgent.
Sir G. Buchanan to Sir Edward Grey.

Russian Minister for Foreign Affairs telephoned to me this morning –

She stopped reading after that first sentence.

Her first thought was that he had made a mistake and somehow mixed up his official papers with his private correspondence. But when she turned to his letter, she saw that he had indeed intended her to have it – *the enclosed telegram will interest you.* He had often shown her telegrams during their afternoon drives. He had never sent one through the post before.

Sitting on the edge of her bed in the silence of Penrhos, the dispatch in one hand, unconsciously twisting the beads of her necklace in the other, she read it right through to the end – thrilled at first by this glimpse into the secret world of high diplomacy, then riveted, and by the time she had finished slightly appalled, both by the content and by the sudden realisation that there was probably not another woman in the country who at that moment knew as much about the crisis as she did.

She sat for a few more minutes, absorbing the implications, until she was startled out of her reverie by the sound of the gong being struck downstairs, summoning the household to break-fast. Quickly she folded up the telegram and the letter, stuffed them back into the envelope, slipped it into the pocket of her skirt and went down to join the others.

Nobody looked up as she came in. They were all immersed in the morning papers – her father and mother, her three elder sisters and their husbands. Her nieces would be having their breakfast upstairs in the nursery and would not be produced until mid-morning. She went to the long sideboard which ran half the length of the dining room and contemplated the dozen silver dishes of devilled lobster and lamb chops, eggs and kidneys, potatoes and black pudding, tomatoes and mushrooms, sizzling from the heat of the tiny candles flickering beneath them.

For once, she had no appetite. She helped herself to some tea and a slice of toast from the rack and a footman immediately took both from her and stood waiting for her instruction. She looked around the table and pointed to an empty seat next to her mother. As she passed behind her, she glanced over her shoulder at the headlines in *The Times* – 'PEACE IN THE BALANCE', 'RELATIONS BROKEN OFF', 'WAR FEVER IN VIENNA'. It was the fourth that caught her eye: 'BRITISH NAVAL MEASURES'. He hadn't mentioned anything about that in his letter.

She said, as she sat down, to no one in particular, 'What are our naval measures?'

The eldest of her brothers-in-law, Bill Goodenough, a captain in the Royal Navy, said, without taking his eyes from his paper, 'Winston announced last night he's keeping the First and Second Fleets together at Portland.'

'Is that significant?'

'It makes it easier to mobilise. It doesn't mean we're going to get involved.'

'Why would we need to make it easier to mobilise if we're not going to get involved?'

'It's purely a precautionary measure. Nothing to worry about.' He continued reading.

The Stanleys were not a military family, so it was a slight source of bafflement to her parents that their three eldest daughters were all married to serving officers – Margaret, who was forty, to Bill; Sylvia to Anthony Henley, a major on the War Office staff; and Blanche to Eric Pearce-Serocold, commandant of the training school at Camberley. Venetia studied them across the table as she buttered her toast. They seemed entirely unconcerned by what was in the papers, lounging back in their chairs – hefty, fit, moustachioed fellows, looking forward to a day's leisure at the seaside.

She said, 'But might we not end up being dragged in, whether we want to be or not?'

Bill sighed and rustled his paper. 'How? By whom?'

'By the Russians, and the French.'

Her father said, 'I think you'll find that diplomacy doesn't quite work like that, my dear. It's governed by treaties, and we have no treaty obligations that would oblige us to go to war on behalf of either the Russians or the French.'

His tone was kindly but firm, indicating that the conversation was over, and after a few moments she rose from the table and announced she was going for a walk.

Sylvia called after her, 'Vinny, you won't forget, will you, that you promised to play with the children later?'

By the time she reached the bay the tide was out. Oystercatchers strutted across the newly uncovered sand. Curlews cried from the mudflats. Somewhere she had a photograph of herself and Winston digging for crabs on this same stretch of beach in the summer of 1910. It was only four years ago. Yet to her that morning it was already beginning to feel like a different world.

She took off her shoes, gathered her skirt in her hands and picked her way through the slippery rocks and shallow pools to the boathouse. An old skiff, rotted to its skeleton, lay beached on its side, chained to the wharf like some forgotten prisoner. She spread out her jacket on a shelf of rock, opened her satchel and took out her writing case. For several minutes she stared out to sea. The smell of salt and seaweed blown onshore by the breeze was thick enough to taste.

My darling, I've come down to the boathouse so that I
can answer your letter in peace & in a place where I can
think. No one disturbs me here – asks me to whom I'm
writing or demands that I look after the children or
make up a game of doubles at tennis. There's only the
sea & the rocks & the cries of the birds. The world
of diplomats & armies seems v. remote but you are
such a good correspondent I feel almost as if I were
beside you.

She noticed a clump of white heather growing in a cleft in the
rock. She broke off a stem and sniffed it.

Oh, beloved! You know how often I've told you, when
you were feeling 'down', that I wished I could change
places with you, & that I'd happily give up a whole
month of my dull existence for an hour of yours. Well,
today, I renounce my fantasy! This European crisis casts
Ireland into the shade. You say the only silver lining is
that it may at least take attention away from Ulster. Yes,
but at what a cost – like cutting off one's head to get rid
of a headache!
    Nobody here seems particularly worried & I had to bite
my tongue at breakfast, knowing as much as I do. But
please be wary of Winston, and the gleam that comes into
those blue eyes whenever the talk turns to war. What an
extra cruel twist of fate it is, that at this of all times I am so
far away from you. But I am holding you close in my
thoughts, and here – I am sending you some white heather,
fresh from the rocks, to remind you of me, and of this
place, and to bring you luck.

She wrote a couple more pages, filled with the sort of domestic trivia she knew he loved to hear, and when she had finished, she kissed the white heather, sealed it up with the letter and wrote his title and address on the envelope. They seemed much more incongruous here than in London.

It took her the best part of half an hour to make her way along the coastal path and over the railway bridge, past the little red-brick terraced houses to the post office in Holyhead. By eleven she was back at Penrhos and her nieces were running across the lawn to greet her.

His next letter arrived as usual in the first post the following morning. Once again it included, enfolded within its pages like pressed white petals, the torn-off fragments of diplomatic dispatches. They fluttered from the envelope onto the carpet as she pulled out the letter. The first part had been written at 11 a.m. and described the disaster in Ireland on Sunday night, when troops had shot into a Nationalist crowd in Dublin, killing three.

> We were placidly playing Bridge at the Wharf when a telephone message came in reporting the shocking news from Dublin. I at once came up with Bongie in his new motor, & we arrived here about 1 a.m., but there was nothing fresh.

The letter resumed at 4 p.m.

> I was calculating in bed last night that, roughly speaking, since the first week in December I must have written you not less than 170 letters. I have never in the same space of time written nearly so many to any human being, and

never come within 1000 miles of revealing so much that was my own secret property. Isn't it strange? How do you account for it?

I enclose 2 or 3 little extracts from the foreign telegrams, because they are not in the newspapers. We seem to be on the <u>very brink</u>.

We are now just about to have a Cabinet, & I must stop.

She retrieved the telegrams from the floor. One was from the embassy in Vienna (*Russian ambassador thinks that Austro-Hungarian government are determined on war, and that Russia cannot possibly remain indifferent*); another from the consulate in Odessa (*South-Western Railway here declared on war footing since midnight, all officials on leave recalled*); and the third from Oslo (*German men-of-war have all taken in considerable quantities of coal and are reported to be sailing at eight this morning . . . Four reported proceeding south, thirty miles south of Stavanger, possibly escort of Emperor . . .*).

She paced back and forth between the bed and the window. How frustrating to be stuck in Penrhos when so much was happening! If ever there was a time when he needed her presence, it was now. She tried to think of some excuse for returning to London. But her parents would be immediately suspicious and if she so much as hinted at the real reason they would be appalled. The notion that anyone might discover he was sending her secret telegrams was unthinkable. In fact, what was she supposed to do with them? It seemed wrong to destroy them – they were official documents: what if he needed them back? – yet risky to leave them lying around.

Concealed on the top shelf of her wardrobe behind her hat boxes was a Gladstone bag in which she kept all his letters, still in their original envelopes. She took it with her whenever she moved from house to house. She lifted it down and added the latest. There were so many now it was hard to fasten the clasp. As she stood on tiptoe and pushed it back into the furthest corner, it occurred to her that she ought to find a more secure hiding place, but just at that moment she couldn't think of anywhere better, and besides, the gong was sounding for yet another huge breakfast.

CHAPTER EIGHT

H E WAS RUNNING through the night – running, really *running*, breathless with panic – along dingy gaslit London streets of identical terraced houses, frantically searching for the only one which offered a chance of escape. Locked . . . locked . . . locked – door after door unyielding – until at last he plunged through one into a hall and a narrow winding staircase crowded with strangers he had to fight his way past along a passage to a dark bedroom with a bare wooden floor where there was a cheap cupboard which if he climbed inside would lead him back home to his mother and father—

For a fraction of a second he saw them in a garden, holding hands, and smiling at him, and then they vanished.

He cried out and opened his eyes.

His bedroom door was ajar. A figure was silhouetted in the light – his manservant, George Wicks, carrying the usual tray with a pot of tea, the newspapers and the morning post. He set it all down quietly on the bedside table, drew back the curtains, and stepped into the adjoining room to run the bath.

The Prime Minister lay staring at the ceiling waiting for his heart rate to subside. Variants of this nightmare had plagued him ever since he was twelve, when his father had died and he had been sent away from Yorkshire to live with strangers in Pimlico so that he could go to a good London day school. It was disturbing for a man of his age to revisit these childish feelings of panic at being lost and abandoned. It certainly didn't require the services of Professor Freud to tell him what it meant. He wondered if George had heard his cry.

His first impulse once he had recovered was to lean over to the nightstand and search through his letters in the hope of finding one from her. He performed this ritual every day. And yes, it was here, postmarked Holyhead, addressed in her distinctive hand.

He called out, 'Good morning, George!'

A distant voice answered, 'Good morning, sir.'

He propped himself up on his pillows and tore open the envelope. The white heather fell out onto the bedclothes. He raised it to his nose and inhaled the faint scent of the moss and woods of Penrhos. He read her letter through twice, the first time greedily, the second more slowly, savouring each word. He liked her description of a European war as a way out of the Irish mess – *like cutting off one's head to get rid of a headache* – and he smiled at her warning about Winston.

George reappeared. He was not quite thirty, had been his manservant in Number 10 for the past five years. If he had heard his cry, he would be too discreet to mention it.

'Your bath is drawn, sir, and I've laid out your clothes in the dressing room.'

'Thank you, George.'

The door closed.

When he was in London, he seldom bothered with breakfast:

Margot took hers in her bedroom and he had always had a horror of eating alone. He poured himself some tea, glanced through his other correspondence – nothing of much interest – and turned to page eight of *The Times*. 'BRITISH EFFORTS FOR PEACE', 'SIR EDWARD GREY'S PROPOSALS', 'NERVOUSNESS ON THE STOCK EXCHANGE'.

Yes, he thought, and there would be a lot more nervousness before the day was done. Things had looked almost hopeful the previous afternoon, when the German ambassador, Lichnowsky, had told Grey that Berlin would join his four-power conference. The news, announced by Grey at Cabinet, had cast Winston into a gloom: 'I suppose now we shall have a bloody peace!' But at midnight, just as the PM was leaving the Commons chamber after a noisy emergency debate about the shootings in Dublin, Grey had tapped his arm and showed him a telegram from the ambassador in Berlin. The Germans had changed their minds, or maybe Lichnowsky had misunderstood his instructions. At any rate, there would be no conference. The newspapers were out of date. The road was clear for war.

He went through into the bathroom, lifted his nightshirt over his head and lowered himself into his bath with a groan.

He spent the morning in the Cabinet Room, working at the long table. Whenever an official came in with papers for him to sign, he looked up expectantly. But there was no news from Berlin, Vienna, Paris or St Petersburg. Above the fireplace, the big clock ticked loudly – how many years had he spent listening to that? – while the trees beyond the high windows were dusty green and full of winking bursts of sunlight. The fine summer day seemed to mock him.

To be prime minister was to be a decision-making machine. He approved the withdrawal from Ireland of the Scottish Borderers, the regiment which had fired on the Dublin crowd. He appointed Sir John French as Inspector General of the Army. He insisted, despite the objections of the Chief Whip, that the Irish Home Rule Bill, postponed because of the Dublin shootings, be introduced on Thursday. And in the lulls between his decisions, he continued his morning missive to Venetia – *at this moment things don't look well, & Winston's spirits are probably rising* – stopping whenever Bongie or his other private secretary, Eric Drummond, appeared, when he would discreetly cover the letter with his official papers.

In the afternoon, following a dull lunch organised by Margot with guests he didn't particularly want to see, he walked down to the Houses of Parliament, posted his letter to Venetia, and then strolled into the chamber to answer questions on the reform of the judiciary, income tax, the House of Lords, and the fees levied on bishops when they were consecrated. It was absurd and yet at the same time reassuring to go through these motions as if everything was normal. Finally, Bonar Law asked him if he had any fresh information on the European crisis and he replied truthfully that he did not. And that, it turned out, was the end of normality.

He was just passing behind the Speaker's chair, heading towards his Commons office, when a bulky figure stepped out from the crowd of MPs, so abruptly they collided with one another.

'Sorry, Prime Minster. So sorry! Excuse me! I needed to catch you before you left the chamber—'

'Good heavens, Montagu!' As usual, he found himself laughing. Montagu had once been his parliamentary private secretary – clumsy, devoted, lugubriously funny. Over the years he had become part of his official family. The fact that he – a Jew! – had twice proposed marriage to Venetia only added to his slightly comical absurdity. Their private nickname for him was the Assyrian. 'What on earth is so urgent?'

'Lord Rothschild wants to see you right away.'

'About what?'

'I think he should tell you himself.'

He had given Montagu a promotion earlier in the year. He was now Financial Secretary to the Treasury.

'All right, I suppose so – if you think it's so important. Where is he?'

'He's anxious no one should see him, so I took the liberty of showing him straight to your room.'

Mystified, he followed Montagu along the corridor.

The old man, stout, massively grey-whiskered, had chosen to remain standing in the centre of the large room, his beautifully brushed black silk top hat resting on the table beside him. The most powerful banker in London, an ally once, now supported the Unionists and was hardly a friend of the Liberal government. There was no small talk, not even a handshake.

'Thank you for seeing me, Prime Minister. I shan't keep you a minute. What I have to say is strictly confidential, but I feel it's my patriotic duty to warn you that I've just received an order from our Paris house to sell a vast quantity of consols held by the French government and savings banks.'

'How vast?'

'Enough to collapse the market.'

The Prime Minister rocked back slightly. Consols were the bonds that funded Britain's sovereign debt – seven hundred million pounds' worth of it. 'Well, at this particular juncture, given everything else that's happening, that would certainly be' – he groped for the least alarming adjective he could think of – 'unhelpful.

Thank you for warning me. Is there any chance that you might be able to dissuade them?'

'I've managed to delay them for twenty-four hours by telling them it's technically impossible – there aren't sufficient buyers. But they need the money to fight the war they're certain is coming, and therefore I'm afraid that sooner or later . . . The atmosphere in Paris is . . .' His voice trailed off. Usually cool and detached, he seemed to be in the grip of strong emotions. It was a few moments before he could continue. 'I never thought I'd live to see it, but I really believe this could be the end of European civilisation.'

The Prime Minister's equable temperament recoiled from such hyperbole. 'Come now, Lord Rothschild, we're not at that point yet! I assure you we're doing everything we can to keep out of it.'

'Nobody will be able to keep out of it! Not if it collapses the world financial system! Trade will come to a stop. There will be revolutions all over Europe. As a short-term measure I suggest you should consider closing the exchanges before the start of business tomorrow morning.'

There was a brief tap on the door and Bongie entered. The Prime Minister was still staring at Rothschild in amazement. He said, without turning round, 'Yes, what is it?'

'Austria has just declared war on Serbia.'

As soon as Rothschild and Montagu had gone and he was alone, he went into the large water closet next to his room, ran the taps and splashed his face. Drying himself on the small towel, he studied his reflection in the mirror above the basin.

In his experience, two qualities were required above all to be a successful prime minister. First, the efficient dispatch of business. And second, optimism. Optimism! There was simply no point in giving way to despair. It sapped one's energy, confused one's thinking, spread like a contagion among one's colleagues and sub-ordinates, solved nothing, made matters worse. He knew that some people interpreted his equanimity as complacency. It didn't bother him. He was prime minister, and they were not.

So when, a few minutes later, Major Hankey, secretary of the Committee of Imperial Defence, was brought in by Bongie, and placed in front of him on the table the large red and blue leather-bound volume known as the War Book, he opened it sceptically. On the title page it said: 'Co-ordination of Departmental Action on the Occurrence of Strained Relations and on the Outbreak of War'. Hankey, a spare, neat figure, who reminded him of his old school gym instructor, had spent years of his life devising this bureaucratic masterpiece.

'Remind me how it works.'

'The Foreign Secretary formally warns the Cabinet that he can "foresee the danger of this country being involved in war in the near future" and that sets the machine in motion. Eleven government departments will then send out the warning telegram across the Empire – ports, railways, post offices, army headquarters, police stations, town halls and so forth – initiating the precautionary phase. The recipients have already been issued with instructions, so they know what to do when they receive the warning telegram.'

'And what does this telegram say?'

Hankey showed him.

IN THE CIRCUMSTANCE THAT GREAT BRITAIN IS AT WAR WITH_____, ACT UPON INSTRUCTIONS.

'We will simply insert the word "Germany".'

'How many telegrams will be sent?'

'I don't have the precise figure. Several thousands.'

The Prime Minister pushed the book back across the table. 'No, it's too soon.'

'It's purely a defensive measure, Prime Minister. It merely readies the machine in case the situation suddenly deteriorates.'

'It may seem defensive to you, Major, but news of it will leak and to the rest of the world it will be seen as belligerent. Public opinion isn't yet prepared for war.'

No sooner had Hankey gone than Winston burst into the room and began striding up and down, lapels gripped between fingers and thumbs, as if he were lecturing on a public platform. The Prime Minister remained seated at the table and watched him calmly.

'There will be a general European war, Prime Minister – now that Austria has announced her intention to invade, nothing is more certain. And I say to you, with all the power at my command, that it would be a disaster of the absolute first magnitude – it would strike at the very existence of the British Empire! – if the bulk of our naval forces were to remain bottled up in Portland Harbour and were later obliged to run the gauntlet of a Channel infested with German submarines. We could lose this war before it even starts.'

'What is your proposal?'

'That under cover of darkness, without lights and at high speed, we move the combined fleets – an eighteen-mile convoy of dreadnoughts, destroyers and cruisers – to battle stations in the North Sea.'

'This would be done when?'

'If we issue the orders today, they could be ready to embark at nightfall tomorrow.'

The Prime Minister calculated the risks. It was really a step further than he wished to take. Constitutionally, he ought to consult the Cabinet. But they would be split, it would cost a day, and as ever Winston's advocacy was compelling.

He didn't say yes or no but reluctantly gave an upward tilt of his chin and grunted.

Amid these swirling storms and currents, his one fixed point, his guiding star, remained Venetia, and the prospect of seeing her on Saturday. He slipped out to the Central Lobby and sent her a telegram – *SITUATION DIFFICULT BUT STILL HOPE COME PENRHOS END OF WEEK* – and when he returned to his room he wrote her a second letter, describing the events of the afternoon, including the visit of Lord Rothschild, eventually finishing it just before six. *There – I must stop now, having given you more than enough to read at one stretch. Bless you – own beloved.*

After he had posted it, he strolled out through St Stephen's entrance and walked back alone around Parliament Square, through the early summer evening to Downing Street. He had left it to his daughter Violet to rustle up a few old friends for dinner followed by bridge, a diversion to take his mind off Serbia and Ireland. But when he stepped into the upstairs drawing toom, she told him that Margot had taken over the arrangements and had invited Winston – of all people! – and the Russian ambassador, Count Benckendorff, and his wife.

He groaned. 'Oh Lord!'

'I'm sorry, Papa. I did tell her you would probably have had enough politics for one day. But you know how much she does like to be in the swim of things.'

'I do indeed.'

In the early days of his premiership, Margot had gone around calling herself 'the Prime Ministeress'. He had been obliged to warn her that this was not a wise idea, that it was causing envy among his colleagues: 'I place the very highest value on your advice, my dearest, but it's best expressed to me in private. People *do* dislike the idea of *petticoat government*.' She had dropped the title but continued to write to ministers behind his back and even occasionally to summon them to private meetings. Her judgements were often shrewd, but her instincts were conservative, and she especially disliked the radicals like Lloyd George. Sometimes it was like living with a particularly garrulous leader writer from the *Morning Post*. Still, he thought, as he dressed for dinner, it did at least mean that he could sit quietly with his own thoughts and leave most of the talking to her.

There were eight around the table. On his left, he had Violet, on his right, Sophie Benckendorff, the mother of the hero of the boat disaster, still beautiful in her fifties. Margot, at the opposite end of the room, had placed herself between Winston and the monocled Count Benckendorff. He watched her turning from one to the other, talking more than she was listening: quite an achievement when Winston was in the room. The two central seats facing one another were occupied by a pair of elegant, slightly effete bachelors – Eddie Marsh, Winston's private secretary, and Harold 'Bluey' Baker, a junior minister.

The countess chatted to Eddie, Violet concentrated on Bluey, and for a few precious minutes he was left undisturbed. He still felt vaguely unsettled by that morning's dream. It lingered in his head like the mild after-throb of a nettle sting, or an electric shock. He sipped his champagne and glanced around the candlelit room, at the dark wooden panelling and the soft-glowing portraits of his predecessors. He wondered what his parents would have made of the scene. Not much, probably – dour northern Nonconformists that they were – although they would surely have been proud of him. But then again – perhaps not? They might have thought he had 'got a bit above himself'. Sometimes he couldn't quite believe it either. The King had once been heard describing him as 'not a gentleman'. He tilted his champagne glass to the candlelight and studied the streams of golden bubbles. He knew one of his nicknames among the Tories was 'Perrier Jouet'. Quite amusing, really. Could it be true that this sophisticated society which had enabled him to rise from a Yorkshire mill town to be head of His Majesty's Government was threatened by some fanatical assassin in the Balkans? Rothschild had said the crisis could be the end of Western civilisation. But that couldn't be right, could it? Old Rothschild of all people!

He drained his glass, and a footman refilled it.

After dinner the women withdrew and Benckendorff went off briefly to telephone the Russian Embassy to discover if there was any news. He returned to say – 'this is in confidence' – that thirty-one divisions were now mobilising on the southern front. 'There is only one chance left of averting war, Prime Minister. That is if the British government declares immediately it will support us and France. Then I believe the Germans and Austrians might yet take fright and draw back from the brink.'

'Is that so? Germany of course says the opposite: that if we stay neutral, you and France won't dare to fight without us.' He stubbed out his cigar. 'Let's play cards.'

Two tables had been set up in the drawing room. He partnered Sophie Benckendorff against Winston and Violet. Margot and the ambassador played Eddie and Bluey. Footmen served port and brandy. Normally, he could lose himself in the precision of the game, in the vivid emerald green of the table and the colours of the cards, the balance between luck and skill, the mild flirtation with one's partner, the competitive desire to win – the entire world blessedly reduced for a couple of hours to a single square yard of baize. But that evening he couldn't quite surrender himself to it and was relieved when at eleven o'clock Winston, after playing in his usual crazy fashion, announced that he needed to get back to the Admiralty, at which the Benckendorffs also declared they ought to leave.

He walked them down to their car. The ambassador took his hand in both of his, and said, with deep emotion, 'Tomorrow may be decisive. Please think about what I said.'

The Prime Minister waved them off. He watched the Rolls-Royce turn into Whitehall. It was a starlit evening – quiet, warm: body temperature, so that there seemed no friction between his skin and the London air. He stood on the doorstep, smoking his cigar. On the opposite side of Downing Street, chandeliers burned in the windows of the Foreign Office. He crossed the road and walked through the big iron gates into the courtyard and turned right up the flight of stone steps. He nodded to the night porter and ascended the stairs to the Foreign Secretary's room. He went straight in.

Grey was slumped on the brown leather sofa, his feet on the low table; in the armchair next to him was Haldane, the Lord Chancellor. Strata of cigar smoke hung suspended over the vast office. On the table beside Grey's feet was a decanter of brandy, half-empty.

'Ah,' said the Prime Minister, 'I thought I might find you here. Do you mind if I join you?'

Grey patted the seat next to him and reached for the decanter.

They were his oldest friends in politics, a relationship going back thirty years, to a time in the mid-1880s when they had just been a trio of ambitious young Liberal MPs of like-minded moderate views. He was not as close to the patrician Grey, with his love of fly-fishing and birdwatching, as he was to the intellectual Haldane. When Raymond and Beb were boys, Haldane used to come over to Hampstead to play cricket in the garden.

Yet there was no such a thing in politics as true friendship. There could never be absolute trust, not when one was Prime Minister. Even with these two, as midnight passed and they tried to find some way out of the quagmire, he was careful not to give away all that was in his mind. Only with Venetia was he completely unguarded. Haldane knew more about Germany than any other man in the government. He spoke the language, had lived there as a young man studying German philosophy, had tried, in his last job as Secretary of State for War, to bring about closer relations with Berlin – he had even publicly described the University of Göttingen as his 'spiritual home'. All to no avail. He now had the bitterness of a spurned lover. He rated the chances of peace at nil.

'They could have stopped the Austrians if they'd wanted to. The fact they chose to stand aside tells us everything we need to know.'

'What will they do next?'

'I assume they'll follow the plan Field Marshal Schlieffen drew up years ago: first attack the French in the west, and try to finish them off quickly, before moving their main force east to deal with the Russians. To do that according to their timetable necessitates going through Belgium, and if the Belgians appeal for our support, how can we stand aside?'

'We can't,' said Grey. 'It's unthinkable. And we've also given private undertakings to the French that if it ever came to it, we'd do all in our power to help them.'

'Private undertakings,' said the Prime Minister, 'but not an actual treaty. That's what Lloyd George and the others will say. I'd estimate three-quarters of the parliamentary party will oppose our getting involved.'

'But we do have a treaty with Belgium,' said Grey, 'guaranteeing her neutrality. Suppose we break our word, and the French are defeated. If we allow Germany to dominate Europe, we'll no longer be seen as a great power. Our strategic position will be jeopardised, our moral authority to govern the Empire gravely weakened. And on a purely personal level – I regret adding to your problems, Herbert, but I must speak frankly – if we don't fulfil our undertakings to the French, I shall feel honour-bound to resign.'

They sat in silence. How rare to hear his Christian name in the mouth of a male friend – it was a sign of crisis in itself. He could feel his optimism drifting away, breaking and dispersing like the cigar smoke above them. At least the politics were becoming clearer. If Grey resigned, he would have to go too: privately he had no doubt about that. The government would collapse. The Tories would come in. And there would still be a war. It was a matter now of political survival – and that at least was a fight he understood.

He reached into his inside pocket and pulled out the list of names he had made at Cabinet the previous Friday. He had counted ten – Lloyd George, Morley, Beauchamp, Simon, Harcourt, Pease, Samuel, McKinnon Wood, Runciman and Burns – who were opposed to British intervention. Some he could probably win over once they realised the gravity of the situation. But some would resign whatever happened. It was the very devil of a mess.

He said to Grey, 'You must formally warn the Cabinet tomorrow that you can foresee us being drawn into a war in the near future. It doesn't mean we're committing ourselves. It's merely a statement of fact, to which even our most peace-loving colleagues can't object. But it will open the War Book, the telegrams can go out, and we can move to the preparatory phase.'

'And then?'

'And then we must pray for a miracle.'

It was one o'clock when he finally left Grey's room and walked back across Downing Street. He locked the door of Number 10 behind him and made his way through the slumbering house to his bedroom. He couldn't face saying good night to Margot, even though he could see a crack of light beneath her door. After he had undressed and brushed his teeth he climbed into bed. Often before he went to sleep he liked to scribble a pencilled note to Venetia describing the events of the evening. Tonight, he was too tired, even though he had so much to confide in her. He put her sprig of lucky white heather under his pillow, reached over, turned off the lamp and, as he had done since he was a boy, pulled the blankets up to his chin. He hoped he would wake to discover a letter from her; he hoped he would not dream.

CHAPTER NINE

THE NEXT MORNING, Wednesday 29 July, Paul Deemer rose early, walked around the corner to the local shop and bought *The Times* and the *Daily Telegraph*. It was a rare day when he had no work to go to, but this was such a day. He was halfway through his annual week's leave.

Back in his house, sitting at his kitchen table, a cup of tea beside him, the little black cat rubbing against his legs, he read the news.

WAR DECLARED BY AUSTRIA
GRAVE CRISIS ON THE STOCK EXCHANGE
THE FATE OF EUROPE IN THE BALANCE

Normally, he didn't much bother with the papers. But his leave had given him plenty of spare time – more time than he knew what to do with – and the result was that all week he had been following the international news, finding each day's developments more ominous than the last's. Turning the pages, his mind went back to the politicians and diplomats he had seen at the Downing

Street garden party – the Prime Minister, the Foreign Secretary, the German and Russian ambassadors. They had all seemed so languidly confident, such masters of the world. But now in the press they appeared to him as helpless, diminished, almost puny figures, when set against the tidal wave of the crisis. He wondered if he shouldn't go in to Scotland Yard, leave or no leave: at least he would have someone to talk to. But then he thought, no, that was stupid, his colleagues would laugh at him. His philosophy was to worry about only those things over which he had some control. He therefore resolved to stick to his original plan and spend the day in his garden. He folded the papers and changed into his work clothes.

The north London soil was poor exhausted stuff, scarcely better than black dirt, but soon after he had moved in, he had dug in horse manure and gradually over the summer, despite the fact it had barely rained in London throughout the whole of July, he had brought the flower beds back to life. By late morning, the wisteria was pruned, the geraniums cut back, and the delphiniums and foxgloves deadheaded. The simple tasks absorbed him. They satisfied his instinct for order. But mostly they took his mind away from what was in the papers, and more especially what it all might mean for his brother in the army.

Three miles to the south, in central London, St James's Park was quieter than it had been all summer, the ducks on the lake unfed, the deckchairs mostly empty despite the sunshine. Instead, crowds had begun to congregate outside the Houses of Parliament and the Foreign Office, in front of the Admiralty and along Downing Street, as if proximity to the buildings in which the grave decisions of life and death were being made might somehow give them a sense of what was happening. When ministers arrived for their emergency Cabinet meeting at eleven o'clock, they had to thread their way through a silent, motionless throng.

At two o'clock that afternoon, from all the main government departments, dozens of clerks carrying manilla files disgorged onto the streets and began making their way on foot towards the three nearest main post offices – on Whitehall, in Parliament Street, and on the Strand. They commandeered all the telegraph operators, posted CLOSED signs at the counter windows, turned away the queuing customers, and began the process of sending out the thousands of warning telegrams as specified in the War Book.

Such was the meticulous planning of Major Hankey and his staff that the task was completed in thirty minutes.

Deemer – his back aching after bending over all day, his shirt glued to his skin with sweat – was just filling the watering can with the last dregs from the rainwater butt and contemplating a trip across the road to the Albion for a pint and some company more rewarding than the cat when he heard the flap of the letter box. It was shortly before 6 p.m.

He walked through the kitchen, and down the narrow hall to the front door. On the doormat lay a pair of telegrams. He frowned at them. One buff-coloured envelope would have been ominous enough; two for some reason made him think immediately of his brother. He carried them into the kitchen and wiped the soil off his hands before he opened the first.

It was an impersonal instruction from the Assistant Commissioner of Scotland Yard informing the recipient that in view of the international situation all police leave was cancelled, and officers were required to present themselves for duty the following morning.

The second was from Commander, Special Branch, instructing him to report to Captain Holt-Wilson, 3rd Floor, Watergate House, 13 York Buildings, Strand, at 09.00 the next morning.

The cancellation of all leave could only mean that things were even worse than the newspapers were reporting. The name Holt-Wilson and the address meant nothing to him. Presumably this was the 'certain department of the War Office that doesn't officially exist' which Quinn had mentioned when he had recruited him to Special Branch. He sensed he was about to become a small component in some vast and well-prepared machine that was even now being set in motion. He also concluded that if he was to see his brother before God-knew-what descended upon them, this might be his last chance.

He abandoned his watering, changed his shirt, put on his jacket, locked up the house and went out into the street. From the Albion came the sound of a piano, but he turned his back on it and walked quickly in the opposite direction. Fifteen minutes later, he was on a northbound Underground train to Mill Hill.

He was six years older than his brother, and this gap in age had defined their relationship, especially after their parents had been killed. It was Paul who had used nearly all their small inheritance to pay for the fourteen-year-old Fred to board at a decent school; Paul who had tracked him down when he ran away, taken digs where they could live together, and arranged an apprenticeship with a local garage; and Paul – when that had gone wrong, and Fred had started hanging around with a rough crowd and getting into trouble with the police – who, in despair, had suggested he should try the army, which was being expanded by the new Secretary of State for War, Haldane: not so much *suggested*, in truth, as marched him to the recruiting office in Hounslow and stood over him to make sure he signed. And it had proved a success, or so it seemed: at any rate, Fred was still in the army five years later.

The train was filled with off-duty soldiers – noisy, larking around, jostling one another, stealing one another's caps and skimming them across the carriage. They tumbled out onto the platform at Mill Hill station, and he followed them, across the road and up the slope towards a sprawling complex of modern red-brick barracks that looked like a factory with warehouses. The closer they came to it, the more well-behaved they became. Next to the iron gates was a sign, *Middlesex Regiment (Duke of Cambridge's Own)*. After they had gone through, the sentry stopped him.

'No visitors allowed.'

'I've never had a problem before. When did this start?'

'About an hour ago.'

Deemer showed his warrant card. 'I need to see Private Fred Deemer.'

'Police? In trouble, is he?'

'I'm his brother.'

'Well, I suppose . . . Seeing as you're the law . . .'

He stepped back into his box, checked a printed list, and directed him to one of the accommodation blocks in the grid of streets on the far side of the parade ground.

Everywhere – activity.

At the entrance to the dormitory, he hailed a soldier going in and asked him if he knew Fred Deemer.

'I'll see if he's inside. Who's asking?'

'His brother.'

While he waited, he took in the scene. Soldiers in uniform drilling in the centre of the vast open space, soldiers in singlets running at the double around the perimeter. Lorries being loaded and unloaded – heavy ribbed wooden crates of what he guessed must be ammunition. In the distance somewhere, the crackle of rapid rifle fire on a shooting range. When he had persuaded Fred to sign up, the country had been at peace so long, it had never seriously occurred to him that his brother might one day have to fight. He had seen the army as a way of keeping him out of harm's way.

'Hello, Paulie!'

He swung round to confront a young man in khaki uniform and flat cap, smoking a cigarette. If he'd passed him in the street, he would never have recognised him. He could have been one of the soldiers fooling around on the train.

'Hello, Fred.' He stuck out his hand. 'It's been a while.'

Fred transferred his cigarette to his mouth and shook Paul's hand firmly. He looked him straight in the eye. 'Not since Christmas, I reckon.'

'It can't be!'

'It is, you know.' His voice hadn't changed, nor the look in those pale blue eyes, always faintly mocking, as if he was enjoying a private joke at his elder brother's expense. But the rest of him – the thick moustache, the broad shoulders, the strength of his callused grip . . . 'So – what? – you were in the area, were you?'

'No, I came specially. I wanted to see you. You've read the papers? God knows what's going to happen.'

'You don't have to worry about me. Not any more. We're well trained. If it comes to a fight, we're ready.'

He took a furtive drag on his cigarette. He was hiding it in his palm, holding it between his thumb and two fingers. No doubt he wasn't supposed to be smoking on the parade ground. Deemer found this characteristic bit of minor rule-breaking oddly reassuring.

Fred said, 'You still with that girl of yours?'

'Not any more.'

'Came to her senses, did she?'

'Something like that. And you? Are you—'

'Nah, not me! Not yet. Not likely!'

There was a brief silence. Fred glanced around. 'Listen, Paulie, it's good of you to come – I appreciate it, really – but they've cancelled all leave and we've an inspection any minute.'

'You need to get back?'

'D'you mind?'

'Of course not.' He was ashamed to realise he felt relieved. 'Let's try to keep in touch a bit better.' He took out his notebook, scribbled his address, tore out the page and handed it to Fred.

'You've got a new place?'

'Yes. A house, actually. Small, but still . . .'

'Still – a house – nice.'

He folded the paper up very small, unbuttoned his breast pocket and tucked it away.

'Write to me,' said Deemer, 'if you're sent away. Let me know how you're getting on, where I can get in touch.'

'I'll do that.' Fred licked his fingers and nipped the end of the cigarette to extinguish it then put it in his other breast pocket. 'Cheerio, then.'

'Look after yourself, Fred.'

'And you.'

He turned and walked back into the barracks – a jaunty figure, as Deemer afterwards always pictured him, shoulders swinging, passing out of the evening sunshine into the dim light of the dormitory.

In the garden of Penrhos House, in the lengthening shade of the great beech tree – planted, it was said, in the reign of Charles II, and only recently starting to rot – a game of croquet was just coming to an end. Venetia, in an ankle-length white cotton skirt, stood with her legs apart and swung the mallet. Her blue ball hit Anthony Henley's red with a satisfying crack and sent it flying a good twenty yards – 'Oh, I say, Vinny,' he complained, 'there's no need to be quite so brutal!' – then she positioned it in front of the hoop, knocked it through cleanly and struck the peg.

'Good shot,' said Eric, her partner. 'Well done.'

'Let's play one more,' said Anthony. 'Give us a chance to level the score.' He and Blanche were three–two down. He hated losing, especially to Venetia.

'The best of five,' said Venetia. 'That was the agreement.'

She shouldered her mallet and walked towards the terrace, where the rest of the family were sitting. The other players followed. It was that peaceful interlude between afternoon and evening. The children had been put to bed by their nannies. The tea things were being cleared by a maid. From the kitchen, the smell of dinner wafted on the warm breeze over the lawn. That was the way at Penrhos: meal followed meal followed meal in a never-ending round. As she neared the house, the butler, Jones, emerged out of the French windows from the drawing room carrying a silver salver which he presented to her father. Lord Sheffield inspected it over the top of his spectacles and called out, 'Telegrams!'

She came up the steps quickly. 'Is there one for me?'

'Not today,' he said, handing round the envelopes. 'Anthony – there's one for you; one for Eric and one for Bill.'

'Good heavens!' Her mother laughed as they tore them open. She always laughed when she was anxious. 'How funny! It's like a game of consequences.'

The officers showed their telegrams to one another – all leave cancelled, report to base immediately – while their wives murmured variously that it was 'too awful', 'such a bore', 'how ridiculous', as if the main issue was the interruption of their holiday.

Eric, the oldest and most senior in rank, said, 'Well, speaking for myself, I'm relieved. I think it's about time the country took a stand. There's nothing like a war for making men see the true value of things.'

'Hear, hear,' said Bill.

Lady Sheffield said, 'But you'll be able to stay for dinner, surely? A few hours won't make any difference.'

'War!' said Venetia's father abruptly. 'How utterly ridiculous!' She glanced at him. He was sitting low in his deckchair, shaking his head. 'You were right, Venetia. We *are* being dragged in.'

She hadn't expected a letter the next morning. She presumed he would be too busy to write. But it arrived punctually as usual. Edith brought it up to her. She could hear her brothers-in-law downstairs preparing to leave.

'Thank you, Edith. Tell the others I'll be down in a moment.'

She waited until the door was closed before she opened the letter. He had written the main part at lunchtime:

I was more touched than I can say by the little piece of white heather & what you wrote about it . . . Like you I count the hours till Saturday . . . We have just had a long Cabinet . . . The main conclusion to which we came was to issue this afternoon what is called in official language the 'warning telegram . . .' I am just off to the War Office to see that the 'warning' is in full force . . .

The second part was shorter:

6 p.m. I have just finished an Army Council – concerned
entirely with arrangements during the 'precautionary
period'. Rather interesting because it enables one to realise
what are the first steps in an actual war. You will think of
me tomorrow darling won't you? and I shall have your
white heather very near my heart. Post just going – tho' I
have still lots to say to you. All my love always.

She slipped it into her skirt pocket. *The first steps in an actual
war* . . . That sounded chilling. And yet clearly, he was still intent
on coming to Penrhos for the weekend. How could that be
possible?

She went downstairs. In the hall, the valets were carrying their
masters' luggage out to the car.

'Where is everyone?'

'In the drawing room, miss.'

The mood over dinner had been surprisingly cheerful, excited
even, as though the officers were about to embark on a thrilling
adventure. But now that they had changed into their uniforms,
the prospect of war suddenly felt more real and the atmosphere
in the room was subdued. Venetia went from one to another kissing them goodbye – Eric first, whom she liked the most, then Bill,
who had been so sure the crisis would come to nothing, and finally
Anthony, who put his hands on her waist as he kissed her and
whispered in her ear, 'What if I'm killed and we've never made
love?'

She stepped back and glanced across the room at Sylvia, but
she was looking in the other direction and didn't seem to have
noticed.

'Don't be so melodramatic, Tony. You'll probably be back in a week. Those are only the warning telegrams.'

'How do you know about the warning telegrams?'

He was on the staff at the War Office. She had got him the job as a favour when the PM took over as Minister of War. Now she wished she hadn't.

'I must have read it in the papers.'

'But it isn't in the papers.' He gave her an unpleasant grin. 'It's secret.' He seemed pleased to have caught her out. 'But of course, *he* tells you everything. Everyone knows that.'

'I don't know what you're talking about.'

'He's over sixty. What on earth do you see in him – apart from the obvious?'

'You should go and say goodbye to your wife.'

She walked away. Her hands were shaking. It took an effort to control herself, to force a false smile and somehow to get through the next few minutes, carefully avoiding eye contact with him as she moved with the others out of the drawing room into the hall, standing on the doorstep with her sisters and parents, waving the three men off as the car pulled away and travelled slowly down the long drive that curved through the deer park, before turning right onto the road towards Holyhead, and vanishing out of sight.

Deemer had allowed himself plenty of time to find Watergate House. It turned out to be a modern office block, solidly built of bright red brick and pale grey masonry, tucked away at the end of a narrow street that ran down from the Strand to Victoria Embankment Gardens and ended in a cul-de-sac.

He loitered against the garden railings opposite for ten minutes, pretending to read a newspaper, studying the people as they arrived for work. Ordinary office types mostly – he imagined them to be insurance brokers, perhaps, or accountants – but he did also note a couple of older men carrying briefcases, walking with the straight backs and brisk strides of retired soldiers.

At five to nine exactly he dropped his paper into a wastebin, strolled across the road to Watergate House and went inside. A cold, impersonal lobby of marble and steel led to a staircase. The first and second floors appeared normal enough. Through the half-open doors, he could hear telephones and typewriters, people talking in the corridors. The third floor was silent. He stood listening for a few moments then cautiously tried the nearest door. Locked. A spyhole. No nameplate. He walked the length of the deserted landing, trying all the doors, and when he reached the end and turned, he found a woman had emerged and was watching him.

'Good morning.' He moved towards her. 'I'm here to see Captain Holt-Wilson.'

She was late middle-aged, tall and broad, formidable in a brown woollen suit. As he drew closer, she put her hands on her hips to block his path.

'And who are you?'

'Detective Sergeant Deemer.'

'Do you have some identification?'

He gave her his warrant card. She held it up to the light and turned it around, examining it suspiciously, as if it were a counterfeit banknote, before handing it back.

'You'd better come in.'

She ushered him into a small office, closing the door after her.

'Wait here.'

She went into the next room, closing that door as well, a careful procedure that reminded Deemer of a prison. She would have made a good wardress, he thought. He had met a few of those in his time.

'The captain will see you now.'

Holt-Wilson stood as he came in. He was fortyish, wiry, bald, with protruding ears, a huge sharp nose and a toothbrush moustache. His whole face seemed to come to a point in that vast proboscis, jutting out like the prow of a ship. He wore a regimental tie of dark blue and crimson. He leaned across his desk and shook his hand.

'So, you're Deemer?' Even his well-educated drawl was nasal.

'Yes, sir.'

'Sit, please.'

Deemer took a seat. He briefly registered the desk loaded with files, the bare walls, the big iron safe in the corner.

'You're young. How old are you?'

'Twenty-nine.'

'Know why you're here?'

'No, sir.'

'You've been following the news, I take it?'

'Yes, sir.'

'Then you'll know the reason. We're a small outfit; too small frankly for the task we've been set, so we're having to expand fast – literally overnight, in fact. I asked Superintendent Quinn to recommend a couple of men of junior rank who might be suitable for the work, and one of them was you. Are you willing to take things further?'

'Yes, sir.'

'Good. However, before I fill you in, I'll need you to sign this.' He slid across the desk a sheet of paper and a pen. 'It's an annexe to the Official Secrets Act in which you undertake not to disclose any aspect of your work, and state that you understand that you may be prosecuted if you do.'

Deemer signed without reading it and passed it back. Holt-Wilson gave a brief, welcome-to-the club sort of smile.

'We're part of the War Office, but you'll retain your position as an officer of the Metropolitan Police. Our immediate task is to arrest German spies – as a police officer, you have the power of arrest, which I and most of my colleagues do not possess. We already have a list of about two dozen enemy agents we need to take into custody as soon as war is declared.' He paused. 'I'm not going too quickly for you?'

'No, sir.'

'Sorry to throw you in at the deep end, but we haven't much time and the threat is extremely urgent. This is the man we'd like you to concentrate on over the next couple of days.' He held up a blurred photograph. 'Karl Gustav Ernst. Forty-three years old. Ugly swine. Owns a barber's shop in Caledonian Road, close to Pentonville Prison – he even cuts the hair of the prison governor and chaplain, can you believe? He lives above the premises, acts as postman for the Germans' spy network, and as a recruiter. We've been following his activities for several years.'

'What do you want me to do?'

'For now, just keep an eye on him. Above all make sure he's still living at the same location. Watch his visitors if you have the chance. But be discreet. We don't want him to panic and disappear or warn the others. Is that clear? His address is on the back.' He handed over the photograph and took out his pocket watch. 'I can just about spare five minutes to show you around. Any questions?'

'Yes, sir, if I may. Who exactly is it I'm working for?'

'Technically, the department is called MO5(g), but no one will ever ask you, so you don't need to bother about it. All correspondence is addressed care of Kelly's Letter Bureau, Shaftesbury Avenue. You've already met our caretaker, Mrs Summer. She's our guard dog.'

He opened the connecting door to a larger room lined with filing cabinets. In the centre several desks had been pushed together around which sat four well-dressed young women with typewriters.

'This is Miss Westmacott, Miss Newport, Miss Holmes and Miss Bowie. They're responsible for the Registry, which is the heart of our operation. Ladies, this is Detective Sergeant Deemer, who's joining us today.'

They looked up at him and smiled and he nodded back politely. They were pretty. He wouldn't have minded exchanging a few words, but Holt-Wilson was already opening the next door.

'And this is the duty room. Here is where you'll be based. I'll arrange a key. You enter from the landing.' A big space with fine views across the public gardens to the river; glass doors opening onto a wrought-iron balcony and railings. More desks, more faces, more names to remember – all male this time. 'Captain Booth, Captain Brodie, Captain Fetherston.' They barely glanced in his direction. 'The two men over there' – he gestured with his head to a pair of old sweats – 'are Sergeant Regan and Sergeant Fitzgerald, both retired from Scotland Yard. And those are the offices of the senior commanders.' He pointed to four doors in turn. 'Colonel Haldane, Major Drake, Superintendent Melville, and our commanding officer, Major Kell. I'd introduce you to him, but I believe he is on the telephone to the Home Secretary even as we speak.'

He turned back to Deemer. 'Well, that's the tour. You'll soon get the hang of it. We aren't very many to protect the country from the German menace, but we do have one supreme advantage.'

'What's that, sir?'

Holt-Wilson seemed surprised he should even ask. 'We're British, of course.'

CHAPTER TEN

DESPITE EVERYTHING, THE Prime Minister still clung to his hopes of seeing Venetia at the weekend. He sat at the Cabinet table that morning, her white heather tucked inside his shirt, surrounded by maps and statistical tables, composing the speech he would have to give in the Commons later in the day proposing the introduction of Irish Home Rule. It was grinding, uninspiring work – nothing new to say, so much else to worry about, absurdly small in the scale of things – and from time to time he paused to refresh his mind by re-reading her latest letter.

Penrhos House
Weds. 29 July 14
Darling, by the time you receive this, it will be exactly a week since we were last together at that wretchedly crowded garden party, when we barely had a chance to talk. Who could possibly have predicted how much the world would change in so short a time? It makes one realise how vital it is to live for the moment, & to snatch

such pleasures as one can, for none of us knows the future!

I wish I could <u>do</u> something. You can have no idea of how frustrating it is to be a woman at a time like this, to sit & watch men running the world, saying stupid things & making a mess of it all. I'm sure we could take on the job & do it better.

I don't have to tell you – do I, dearest Prime? – that I shall be really disappointed not to see you on Saturday & that the prospect of a whole weekend together has been like a distant oasis in this desert heat? (My poor Penguin has been suffering equally badly & we have been sitting on his rock together today & comforting one another.) But <u>please</u> don't dream of coming so far when you have so much to do . . .

But he *did* dream of going, so much so that when Bongie came in and reminded him that they really ought to cancel his visit to Chester the next day to address the Red Cross – the journey alone would take four hours by train, during which time he would be out of touch with events in London – the Prime Minister said irritably, 'I don't see why I should alter my plans just yet.' Conscious that he sounded like a spoilt child, he added, 'The Red Cross do important work. It would be wrong to disappoint them.'

And there was in fact an unexpected easing of the pressure that morning. At eleven o'clock Bonar Law left a telephone message asking for a private meeting at his home in Kensington to discuss 'an important matter'. He even sent his car to fetch him, which struck the Prime Minister as a cheek: presumably the rogue didn't want to be seen entering Number 10 by the crowds now almost permanently hanging around in Downing Street. He ought to refuse and get on with his speech. But curiosity overcame his caution and he decided to go, stepping out into the sunshine, ignoring the stares of the public and climbing into the back of Bonar Law's motor – if indeed it was Bonar Law's motor. It crossed his mind that it might be a plot by the Ulster Volunteers to kidnap him. That would be amusing.

Fifteen minutes later, he arrived at a detached suburban villa in a leafy square just south of Kensington High Street to find the Tory leader with Carson, who proposed, as a 'patriotic duty', that the debate on Irish Home Rule should be postponed for the duration of the crisis. He listened for ten minutes, tried to conceal his relief, and rose from his chair with dignity.

'Thank you for the offer. I shall consult with my colleagues and give you an answer within the hour.'

Back in the Cabinet Room, he piled up all the wretched maps of Ulster and the statistical reports and his draft speech and deposited them on Bongie's desk. 'I feel like Cicero, who freed a slave when he came with a message that the speech he had to give that day was cancelled.'

'You're freeing me, Prime Minister?'

'Oh no, my dear boy! You're not free!' He was in a great good humour. He could imagine himself walking along the beach with Venetia. 'Leave it twenty minutes, then telephone Bonar Law and say we accept.'

He summoned Lloyd George and Grey to tell them what he'd done and afterwards invited Grey to stay for lunch. Margot had already asked Waldorf Astor, Ettie Desborough and the Gladstones. The mood was light-hearted. They kept off politics. After ninety minutes, Grey announced he ought to return to the Foreign Office, at which point the lunch party broke up. Twenty minutes after that, he was back, slightly breathless, bearing the latest telegram from the British Embassy in Berlin. The German Chancellor, Bethmann Hollweg, had made an offer: if Britain would agree to keep out of the war, Germany would undertake not to annex Belgium, Holland, or any of France's territory, apart from her colonies.

The Prime Minister said, 'This is very crude stuff.'

'Crude?' The normally desiccated diplomat was biting his lip in anger. 'What sort of country do they think we are? They're asking us in effect to act as their accomplices.'

'How should we reply?'

'We must reject it immediately. The longer we leave it, the likelier they are to interpret our silence as carte blanche to invade.' He gestured to the Cabinet table. 'May I?'

'Of course.'

Grey pulled out a seat and lowered himself onto it, flicking the tails of his coat to either side, like a concert pianist about to perform. The Prime Minister watched him as he started writing. He shared the Foreign Secretary's distaste, but he distrusted any action taken in a burst of emotion. He liked to revisit every angle of a problem before making an irrevocable decision – a final mental check, a lawyer's habit – and now he asked himself: what if their line of reasoning was entirely wrong? France had been smashed on the battlefield by Germany in 1870, and the world had gone on turning, and it had not involved the loss of a single British soldier. What did it matter if the Germans went through Belgium, so long as they withdrew afterwards? The thought hit him like an attack of vertigo. But when he tried to imagine how he might pick his way back from the cliff edge, the path had vanished.

'Prime Minister?'

He realised Grey was showing him his draft telegram to the British ambassador in Berlin.

You must inform German Chancellor that his proposal that we should bind ourselves to neutrality on such terms cannot for a moment be entertained. For us to make this bargain with Germany at the expense of France would be a disgrace from which the good name of this country would never recover.

An image of Venetia came into his mind, standing on the beach in a white dress and a straw hat, framed by the sea, stretching out her arms to him but receding into the distance.

'Very good.' He handed back the draft. 'Send it.'

The Caledonian Road ran north to south close to where Deemer lived – a commercial thoroughfare, wide and grey and filthy like the Thames, embanked along this particular stretch by small shops with flats above them.

Karl Ernst's barbershop was in a mean terrace in the shadow of a railway bridge, hemmed in by a greengrocer on one side and an ironmonger on the other. Its red-and-white-striped barber's pole was cracked, its window painted bottle-green, making it impossible to see inside, its door – unlike most of its neighbours' and despite the heat – kept firmly closed. Deemer walked past it twice without encountering a customer. He didn't think he could risk a third attempt.

A few doors down on the opposite side of the street was an Italian café. He bought a newspaper, went inside and took up a position at a table in the window. A net curtain strung across the lower half of the glass shielded him from the passers-by. He heard a lot of foreign voices – Polish, Russian, German, Yiddish, French. Whenever a train passed over the nearby bridge, his spoon rattled in its saucer.

He lingered as long as he could, ordering food he didn't want, picking at a congealing dish of macaroni cheese and fending off the waiter who kept trying to clear his plate, all the while maintaining his watch on the barber's shop. He counted half a dozen men going in and out and made a note of the times and a brief description of the visitors in the margins of his newspaper. Three he reckoned were probably normal customers, but the other three seemed to stay too briefly, and their hair, as far as he could tell, was the same length when they emerged as when they entered. He assumed Ernst must be inside, but he couldn't be certain. What if he had an accomplice?

It was after four o'clock by the time he finally paid his bill, stuffed his newspaper into his pocket and went out into the street. In little more than half an hour it would be closing time, and yet still he hadn't set eyes on Ernst. He would have to take a risk. He crossed the road and walked cautiously towards the barbershop. The OPEN sign was still hanging on the door. He took a brief glance left and right then turned the handle. As he stepped inside, a bell tinkled.

The shop was empty. He took it in briefly – a revolving leather chair with a footrest, a mirror in a heavy frame, shelves full of bottles, a basin in the corner with a mound of hair swept up beneath it, a single bright electric light in a pink glass globe, a smell of sweet pomade – and then the curtains at the back parted and a man emerged wearing a white jacket. They looked at one another.

Ernst said, 'I was just about to shut.'

It was him, no question – the accent, the broad face, the thinning blonde hair, a nose that looked as if it had been broken and badly reset.

'Your sign says open.'

Why did he say that? He had got what he came for. He should have just left.

The German shrugged. 'Well, then . . . It is early.' He inspected Deemer more closely. 'But your hair is cut quite recent, is it not?'

'I just wanted a shave. But if you're closed, it doesn't matter. I was only passing.'

'It's not a problem.' He went to the door and changed the sign to CLOSED. 'Give me your coat.'

The comical aspect of the situation did not escape Deemer. Neither of them wished to arouse suspicion, so now they each found themselves doing something they didn't want to do, Deemer shrugging off his coat and giving it to Ernst, hoping he would not notice the scribbles on his newspaper, Ernst turning the chair outwards so he could sit, tucking a towel around his collar and swinging him back to face the mirror. The German disappeared through the curtains to fill the basin with boiling water – was it Deemer's imagination, or did he hear him whispering to someone? – then he returned and started lathering the soap.

Ernst said, 'You are from this district?'

'More or less, just a few minutes' walk.'

Ernst pressed a lever and the chair tilted back sharply until Deemer found he was almost horizontal. The German loomed over him with a cut-throat razor. His warm breath exuded an unpleasant, spicy smell.

'And what is your business, may I ask?'

'Oh, this and that. I have various irons in the fire.'

'"Irons in the fire". This is a good expression. Very English. Be still, please.'

Deemer did not enjoy the vulnerability of being shaved at the best of times. To find himself nearly flat on his back with a German spy scraping a blade up his throat was peculiarly unpleasant. He gripped the sides of the chair. Mercifully, Ernst seemed to have lost interest in their conversation, and the shave continued in silence. Ten minutes later, having paid him a shilling and promised to return, Deemer was back on the street, thankful for the every-day traffic and the heat, running his hand over the unfamiliar smoothness of his chin.

The next morning – Friday – Venetia received the usual dispatch from Downing Street. It was shorter than normal, written at the end of the previous afternoon, and briefly recounted what had happened during the day, including his secret visit to Bonar Law and the menacing terms of the German offer. She could tell the strain he was under.

> I think the prospect very black today. We are going to have another Cabinet at 11 tomorrow morning. It will depend a good deal on the state of things then whether I can fulfil my Chester engagement (about wh., except as a means to an end, I am not very keen). But unless Fate is very unkind I shall all the same hope to come to you on Saturday, and see you – perhaps in your new striped dress, not the 'yellow peril' – You say you wd. be 'really disappointed' if I didn't come. I wish I cd. tell you how I should feel! All my dearest love beloved.

She folded the letter and stared blankly out of the window. She supposed she should be flattered that he was pondering what colour dress she might wear – but at such a time? She certainly hadn't given the matter a moment's thought. In any case, the whole trip must surely now be a fantasy. It worried her that he could not see it.

The Cabinet met at eleven and it was quickly clear that travelling up to Chester to give a speech that evening was indeed out of the question. He pressed the button under the table that rang in the private secretaries' office and summoned Bongie to tell him to cancel it, and to bring him a copy of *Bradshaw's Railway Guide*. As the argument about Belgian neutrality and Britain's moral obligations to France raged around him, he looked up the Saturday trains to Holyhead. There was one at noon that would get him to Penrhos in time for dinner. He was aware of Lloyd George looking at him quizzically across the table. He closed the *Bradshaw* and handed it back to Bongie then returned his full attention to the debate.

The split remained the same, roughly half opposed to British intervention and half who regarded it as inevitable, with Winston as ever the most bellicose. He steered it to a conclusion, satisfactory from his point of view, of agreeing to do nothing except reject France's request for a public guarantee of support if she was attacked by Germany. That at least postponed any resignations.

Afterwards, he left by the garden gate and walked with Winston across Horse Guards Parade for lunch at Admiralty House with Lord Kitchener of Khartoum, the Consul General of Egypt, who had come home to be invested with an earldom and had stayed on for a month's leave. He found the Field Marshal's mood, as he had expected, belligerent, which was presumably why Winston had arranged the lunch – 'If we don't back France when she's in real danger, we'll never be regarded as a great power again' – but also fatalistic – 'The Germans will walk through the French army like partridges.' At six-feet-two, Kitchener towered over Winston. Decades in India, Africa and the Middle East had burned his face to a complexion resembling red marble. His vast moustaches were dark, his eyes an unnaturally bright blue and, due to an old injury, fixed and staring slightly, like a hypnotist's. He was resolutely unmarried. No wonder the public was so obsessed by him, thought the Prime Minister. An idea began to form in his mind.

'When are you returning to Egypt?'

'On Monday.'

'Can you postpone it?'

'Impossible, I'm afraid.'

If it had been anyone else, he would have ordered him to stay. Instead, he said mildly, 'Perhaps you could let my office know your movements over the next few days, in case we need to contact you.'

He walked thoughtfully back across the gravel of the parade ground to Number 10, to discover a message from the King asking to see him straight away. He didn't really have the time to spare, but he could hardly refuse. He took Bongie with him. Horwood drove them slowly through the crowds gathered in Downing Street and outside Buckingham Palace. They parked in the courtyard. He left his private secretary downstairs while he went up to the royal sitting room. George V was a gruff, unsubtle, non-intellectual type, who had never had an original thought in his life. The Prime Minister always liked to say that whenever he wanted to know what the ordinary man on the Tube was thinking, he would go and talk to the King.

'Good of you to come, Prime Minister. I've just received a rather worrying personal telegram from the Kaiser. What do you make of this?'

It was in English – 'My dear Georgie . . . Yours, Willie' –
complaining about their mutual cousin the Tsar – 'Nicky' –
duplicitously mobilising his forces even while 'the talking' was still
going on. The German Emperor's tone was sulky, bombastic,
peevish – he would not put up with it, two could play at that game,
now there would be fighting and the world would see it was not
his fault . . . *Georgie, Willie, Nicky* – the Prime Minister had a vision
of three boys in stiff court dress playing soldiers in some enormous palace nursery.

'That is indeed ominous,' he agreed.

'Such an odd fellow, the Kaiser. My father couldn't stand him.
Obviously, it's private, but I thought you ought to see it. If you
want me to reply, perhaps you could prepare a draft.'

'I'm most grateful, sir. With your permission, I shall inform the
Foreign Secretary.'

He sneaked a look at his watch. By now it was almost four. He
was due in Parliament within the hour to make a statement on
the latest situation. He asked to be excused, bowed his way out
of the room and hurried along the red carpet, down the wide
ceremonial staircase, past the huge oil paintings of various plump
and bewigged Hanoverian Georges – all Germans, of course – and
into his car. Five minutes later, he was entering the precincts of
the Palace of Westminster.

He had barely settled into his Commons room when William
Tyrrell, Grey's private secretary, arrived with a statement from the
German Chancellor that had been delivered to the Foreign Office
fifteen minutes earlier by Baron Schubert from the German
Embassy. The Baron had insisted on standing and reading it out,
mopping away his sweat: Russia had mobilised her army and fleet;
therefore, Germany was declaring martial law; and unless Russia's

mobilisation was halted within the next twelve hours, Germany would mobilise in turn.

The Prime Minister absorbed the blow without emotion. 'That's that, then.'

'It would appear so.'

At five, he entered the Commons chamber and stood at the dispatch box. The murmur of voices around him died to a hush. 'We have just heard – not from St Petersburg, but from Germany – that Russia has proclaimed a general mobilisation of her army and fleet.' A swell of noise rose and then dropped away as soon as he raised his hand to quell it. 'In the circumstances, I should prefer not to answer any questions till Monday next.'

He walked behind the Speaker's chair, conscious of the chatter that immediately broke out in his wake. They would be meeting on Monday? But Monday was the August bank holiday!

At half-past five, he scribbled a note to Venetia.

Things look almost as bad as can be, & I fear much about tomorrow. I will wire in the morning. If I come, it will be by the train wh. gets to Holyhead 6.45 p.m. If I can't, do telegraph & write to me most beloved, and give me your love, & tell me your plans. I must see you. All my dearest love.

He dropped it into the post box on his way back to Number 10, where Lloyd George, Montagu and the directors of the Bank of England were waiting for him. Hitherto Olympian in their contempt for politicians, the directors now had the strained expressions of lost and frightened schoolboys. Confidence in the City had evaporated. There were queues outside the Bank. They had been forced to suspend the exchange of gold for paper currency for the first time since the Napoleonic Wars. They had already doubled interest rates from four per cent to eight. Now they proposed to raise them again the next day, to ten. The entire financial system was on the edge of collapse.

The Prime Minister, a former Chancellor of the Exchequer, tried to exude a calmness he did not feel.

'Things will settle down once the situation is clearer. The economy was sound last week, and it will be sound next. You have taken the right measures, gentlemen. We shall weather this storm.'

After they had gone, he went upstairs with Montagu, dropped into the nearest armchair, and asked him to pour them both a brandy. It wouldn't be much of an economy, he thought, if it had no one left to trade with.

There was no formal dinner that night. Margot had arranged instead a buffet in the dining room. People wandered in and out and helped themselves and sat in small groups, talking quietly. Winston came, and Grey. Bongie and Drummond brought in telegrams. Afterwards, he could not remember exactly who was there. He drank several more glasses of brandy. He was glad of Montagu's company. Such a loyal friend. And Venetia liked him. He must put him in the Cabinet soon, something junior.

'I'm hoping,' he said, 'to visit Venetia tomorrow.'

'I didn't know she was in London.'

'She isn't. She's still in Penrhos.' He saw Montagu's surprise. 'There's a very good train,' he muttered. 'I could be back by Sunday evening.'

He felt he had said too much and dropped the subject.

At midnight, Montagu left to walk home. Most of the others had drifted away. Margot had gone to bed. But he still felt fully awake, his nerves fired up, as if he had come straight off the platform after delivering a big speech. At half-past twelve, Tyrrell crossed the road from the Foreign Office. A telegram from the Kaiser had just arrived. Bongie and Drummond joined them, and the four men read it together: a more formal version of his telegram to the King – personal, hurt – blaming everything on the Tsar's decision to mobilise.

It was a strange feeling, to stand in that otherwise deserted room, to have the words of the German Emperor in their hands, and to imagine him sleepless in Berlin.

The Prime Minister said, 'What does he hope to achieve by this?'

Tyrrell said, 'He's trying to pin all the blame for the war on the Russians.'

'Is it just that? Or has he got cold feet at the last minute and wants to find a way out?' He saw the scepticism on their faces. 'If the Russians could be persuaded even now to halt their mobilisation, the Germans might follow suit. We ought to do something. It's worth a try. Bongie – order a taxi.'

'To go where, sir?'

'Buckingham Palace. Eric, ring the King's private secretary and tell him I'm coming over. Let's draft an appeal from the King to the Tsar, cousin to cousin.'

At one o'clock in the morning, the Prime Minister, with a quarter of a bottle of brandy inside him, climbed slightly unsteadily into the back of a taxi and was driven by an amazed cabbie to Buckingham Palace. After he had dropped him, the cabbie refused to take his fare, and called after him, 'God bless you, sir!'

Up the staircase for a second time, past Georges I, II, III and IV, and into the sitting room, where presently George V appeared, wearing a pair of slippers, a brown dressing gown over his nightshirt, his eyes full of sleep, his thinning hair sticking out at the back in tufts.

'Thank you for receiving me, Your Majesty. We would like you to send an immediate personal telegram to the Tsar. May I read it to you?'

'If you must.'

'It begins: "My Government has received the following statement from the German Government" – and here we will put in the Kaiser's message, and then you might say: "I cannot help thinking that some misunderstanding has produced this deadlock . . ."' He read it through to the final sentence. '"I feel confident that you are as anxious as I am that all that is possible should be done to secure the peace of the world."'

'Is that it?' The King sounded dubious. Having gone through it again, the Prime Minister didn't blame him. It was a feeble message – a pebble of platitudes flung at an advancing tidal wave of a million men under arms.

'That's it, sir.'

'Very well. Give me a pen.'

He carefully wrote 'My dear Nicky' at the top, added 'Yours Georgie' at the bottom, and returned it to the Prime Minister.

'Now if you don't mind, I'm going back to bed.'

*

I got home again about 2 a.m. and tossed about for a little on my couch – (as the novelists say) – but really I didn't sleep badly, and in that betwixt & between of sleeping & waking, thank God the vision of you kept floating about me and brought me rest & peace.

CHAPTER ELEVEN

THE PRIME MINISTER'S letter, written the previous day, informing Venetia that he might yet arrive on the 6.45 p.m. train, provoked expressions of disbelief in Penrhos that Saturday morning when she mentioned it at the breakfast table.

'Is he reading the newspapers?' Her father held up *The Times* and showed her the headlines.

EUROPE IN ARMS

GENERAL RUSSIAN MOBILISATION

MARTIAL LAW IN GERMANY

FRONTIER INCIDENTS

'Will Margot be with him,' asked her mother suspiciously, 'or is he planning to come alone?'

'*If* he comes, I should imagine he'll just bring a private secretary. Bongie, probably. Anyway, he won't come. It's only a daydream, something to take his mind off the crisis.'

Lord Sheffield said, 'But how can he possibly even think about removing himself from London at such a time?'

'I should have thought that was obvious,' said Sylvia. She looked across the table at Venetia. 'You know he can't go a day without seeing you, darling. It's already been more than a week.'

'Venetia,' said Lord Sheffield, 'is this true?'

'Of course it's not true! Sylvia's just trying to cause mischief.' She glared at her sister. 'You should worry about your own life, *darling*, before you start concerning yourself with mine.'

She saw Sylvia flinch.

'Venetia!' exclaimed her mother.

'I have a headache,' she announced. She stood and dropped her napkin onto her plate. 'I'm going to my room.'

His telegram arrived later in the morning.

REGRET INTERNATIONAL SITUATION REQUIRES MY PRES-
ENCE LONDON. MANY APOLOGIES. WILL WIRE YOUR MOTHER.
LETTER FOLLOWS.

It was a relief, especially after the scene at the breakfast table. But now that he'd done the proper thing, she was surprised by how disappointed she felt.

Penrhos House
Holyhead
Sat 1 Aug. 1914
Darling, I've just received your wire. It really is a bitter
blow. I already hate this beastly war & it hasn't even started
yet! Perhaps, if you can keep us out of it, you'll be able to
come to Penrhos next weekend instead, & if you <u>can't</u> keep
us out of it, at least it should mean this wretched trip to
India and Australia will be off, & I can come up to
London & see you there.

She wrote a few more inconsequential sentences and found herself becoming maudlin. She decided to walk down to the sea to blow away her mood. But she had barely emerged from the woods and was still only at the edge of the beach when she saw something rolling in the shallow surf – black-backed, white-bellied. She prayed it was a dead fish that had been washed ashore, even though she knew, with growing certainty as she drew closer, that it was her penguin.

She waded into the sea up to her knees, heedless of her shoes and skirt, seized it by one of its tiny wings and dragged it up onto the sand. It was pathetically light, and when she knelt and cradled it like a baby in her lap, its head lolled and its small dark eye was dull and opaque in the sun. Everyone had told her this would happen, but for two years she had proved them wrong, until this wretched summer with its endless unnatural heat. Why did everything she touch go wrong? Why was she so hopeless? She started to weep. She cried for the bird and she cried for herself, because it seemed to her that she and it were not so different. Neither of them had had the life that their natures demanded.

This bout of self-pity, entirely uncharacteristic, lasted for all of five minutes, then stopped as abruptly as it had begun.

It was absurd.

She carried the corpse across the beach and laid it on a rock close to the woods. Then she walked back to the house to find a spade.

Dearest, I'm sorry to add to your sorrows, but poor
Penguin has passed away. He was only a bird but I know
you were fond of him too. I suppose it must have been the
heat. I gathered all the children together & we processed
down to the sea & gave him – or was he a her? I never

knew – a solemn funeral as befitted his dignity. I dug a
grave quite easily in the sandy soil within sight of the sea &
piled up rocks to make a cairn to stop Huck or the foxes
digging him up. We can visit his tomb when next
you come.

   I hope that will be soon, but only when things are
clearer & you can be spared from London, otherwise there
will be Talk. Sylvia (of all people!) made a cheap remark at
breakfast, so we must be careful. I love you & miss you
more than I can say.

She walked into Holyhead to post her letter. On the outskirts
of the town, she heard music in the distance, but it wasn't until
she was crossing the railway bridge and saw the hordes of day-
trippers streaming out of the station that she remembered it was
a bank holiday weekend. The Holyhead Brass Band was playing
beneath the clock tower. People were queuing at the stalls to buy
cockles and hot sausages; a penetrating smell of vinegar and fried
onions pervaded the centre of the port. Strung across the street,
lines of Union Jack pennants flapped in the warm sea breeze.

   She climbed the hill to the post office and bought stamps,
although the woman behind the counter didn't think there would
be a delivery the next day because of the bank holiday. She posted
the letter anyway and lingered afterwards at the top of the steps,
looking across at the big Dublin ferry in the harbour, the pleasure
boats moving around it, the train steaming into the station with
passengers hanging out of the windows. She wished she was in
one of the crowded carriages. It was an eccentricity of hers, much
mocked by her family, always to travel third class rather than first
whenever she was alone. She loved the smells and sights of
common life compared to the one she led – the unaffected voices,

the cigarette smoke, the frank looks, the casual swearing, the bodies pressed against hers, the energy of it.

The Cabinet meeting the Prime Minister chaired that morning was the most fractious he could remember. Several times it degenerated into a shouting match that wouldn't have disgraced an East End pub, with Winston, whose declamations took up half the time, demanding the immediate authority to mobilise the Fleet and the majority resisting. The pacifists most violently opposed to him were led by John Burns, the President of the Board of Trade, a teetotal working-class socialist from Battersea, who took the line of the *Manchester Guardian* and wanted a public declaration that in no circumstances would Britain go to war. Grey, once again biting his lip, pale with anger, announced that if that was to be their decision, he would resign. At noon, the Prime Minister, glancing wistfully over his shoulder at the clock and thinking of the train now pulling out of Euston, suggested they adjourn till the following day.

In the afternoon came a frustrating hiatus. He knew that dramatic events must be occurring in Europe, but he found it impossible to discover any definite information. Telegrams from the embassies, carried by commercial operators, went to the general post offices, and then had to be picked up by government messengers, taken to the relevant ministries and decoded. It wasn't until eight o'clock in the evening that he discovered the French had mobilised, and it was nearly midnight, and he was having a nightcap with Grey and Haldane in the drawing room of Number 10, when he received a one-sentence wire from the British ambassador in St Petersburg: *German Ambassador handed to Russian Minister for Foreign Affairs formal declaration of war this evening at 7 o'clock.*

ROBERT HARRIS

'Click, click, click,' said the Prime Minister, passing the telegram
to Grey, 'just like a machine. There's something quite mesmerising
about the way these alliances are playing out.'

'Unfortunately, the system is so intricate that once it starts it's
almost impossible to stop. Now it's accelerating the very catastrophe it was designed to prevent.'

The following morning, there was no letter from Venetia. He
lay in bed, staring at the ceiling, listening to the Sunday-morning
bells in the Abbey and St Margaret's. This, he knew, would be the
decisive day. It was quite possible – likely even – that unless he
played his hand cleverly, by the evening he would be on his way
to Buckingham Palace to tender his resignation. Sometimes in the
past, when he was exhausted and things were going badly, he had
thought he wouldn't mind giving it all up. But now it came to it,
he realised he would mind it, very much.

After he had dressed, he looked in on Margot. She was wearing
a dark grey outfit, ready for church. 'I'm going to St Paul's,' she
announced, 'and I'm taking Frau and Rolf with me.' Frau was
their old German governess, still employed by the family, now
married to Rolf Meyer, a fellow German. Margot looked at him
defiantly. 'You don't mind, do you?'

'No, my dear.' He kissed her on her cheek. 'It's the sort of
bravery that made me want to marry you in the first place.'

The German ambassador called in to see him, to plead with
him in fact – 'as a man, as a friend' – to keep Britain out of the
war, and at the end of the interview he burst into tears, much to
the Prime Minister's embarrassment. After that, he sat and worked
at the Cabinet table until just before eleven, when he heard the
ministers starting to gather in the corridor outside. Bongie
appeared from the private secretaries' room. 'They're here, Prime
Minister. Shall I show them in?'

'Leave it for a couple of minutes.'

He went over to the window and looked down into the garden.

Anthony – 'Puffin' – his eleven-year-old son, was playing with Megan, the Lloyd Georges' girl, who lived next door. They saw him watching and waved, and he waved back. Damn the Cabinet, he thought. Let them wait. Let them realise I can make them wait as long as I like: that their positions entirely depend on me. His leadership style was emollient, but there were times when one needed to crack the whip. After five minutes, he opened the door and briskly invited them in. When they were settled in their places, he asked the Foreign Secretary to update them.

Grey said, 'I'm afraid that since we last met, the position has deteriorated exactly as we feared. France has mobilised. Germany has declared war on Russia. This morning we have reports that Russian formations have already crossed the border into Germany and that fighting is in progress. Eight German army corps are poised on the frontier with France and there are said to have been several incursions and clashes.

'I understand the desire of colleagues that we should stand aloof from all this, but whether we eventually decide to fight or not, there is now an imminent threat to France's Channel ports, which is obviously a threat to us as well. I would therefore like the authority of the Cabinet to assure the French government that we will not allow the German fleet to make the Channel the base of hostile operations.'

'And how are we to stop them?' asked Burns.

Winston said, 'By threatening to sink the buggers if they show their faces.'

'Then we might just as well declare war now!'

The familiar argument flared up again. The Prime Minister let it run. He counted Morley, Simon, Harcourt and Lloyd George on Burns's side – the latter was the most significant: what was he playing at? – with himself and Grey and Winston on the other, and Crewe, McKenna and Samuel in the middle. Haldane was a mystery. The rest would form themselves into a pack – 'the beagles', he called them – and follow the majority.

Shortly after one o'clock, Drummond came in with a telegram for Grey, who brought it up close to his weak eyes to read it and waited for a lull in the discussion before intervening. 'With permission, Prime Minister, I've just received a message from our ambassador in Brussels. It appears that early this morning German troops invaded Luxemburg.'

In the silence that followed, the Prime Minister finally saw his moment. 'That at least has the benefit of clarifying matters. As a government, we have a responsibility above all to safeguard British national security.' He turned to Grey. 'Foreign Secretary, in the light of this development, I believe you should tell the French we will protect the Channel from German domination, for our sake as well as theirs.'

Burns said, 'With respect, Prime Minister, I do not believe that that is the mood of the Cabinet.'

'And with respect to you, Mr Burns, it is my constitutional responsibility to sum up our deliberations and advise the King of our decision.'

'We should vote on it.'

'There are never votes in Cabinet. That is the convention.'

'Then I am afraid I must tender my resignation.'

'Well, I'm sorry to hear it.' He looked around the table, daring anyone to challenge him. Lloyd George opened his mouth as if to speak, then closed it. 'The kaleidoscope is turning rapidly. Let us hold off talk of resignations for the time being. I suggest we meet again at six-thirty, when we may have more information.'

He went upstairs to his desk to work, spreading out his files amid the miniature silver shepherdesses and the little crystal animals. There was a big crowd in the street outside. He could hear them cheering each time they recognised a minister leaving.

In mid-afternoon, Drummond brought him the latest telegram from the British Embassy in Paris: *German situation. Movements of large bodies of troops continue. All telegraphic, telephonic and railway communications between neighbouring countries cut excepting those to Austria . . .*

From Cologne it was reported that almost a hundred German troop trains had been counted leaving the central railway station since six o'clock that morning. Destination: the Belgian border.

And from Brussels, most ominously of all: the Germans had just issued an ultimatum to the Belgian government demanding free passage for their army through Belgian territory, with a deadline of twelve hours for a positive reply.

At six o'clock, despite constant interruptions, he started his daily letter to Venetia.

> Germany is now in active war with both Russia & France, and the Germans have violated the neutrality of Luxemburg: we are waiting to know whether they are going to do the same with Belgium . . .
> Happily, I am quite clear in my own mind as to what is right & wrong. I put it down for you in a few sentences.

Explaining a complex problem to her required him to see it more clearly himself. That was one of the joys of talking things through with her, either when they were alone together or on paper. So it was now: half a dozen principles, numbered one to six, that suddenly seemed to light a route through the fog.

Just as he was finishing, Bongie came in and tapped his watch. The second Cabinet meeting of the day was due to start in ten minutes. He quickly added a final paragraph:

That is all I can say for the moment. If only you were here, my beloved! How I miss you – in this most critical of crises. Think of me & love me & <u>write</u>. Every day I bless & love you more.

In the Cabinet Room, the ministers had already seated themselves by the time he made his way to his place. It was the first Cabinet meeting ever held on a Sunday evening. There was a golden summer light in the windows he had never seen before.

'Before we proceed, I wonder if it might be helpful if I set out six basic statements of fact which I believe we can all agree on, that should guide our policy . . .'

He read them out, pausing after each sentence, giving an opportunity for objections: (1) that Britain was under no obligation to help France or Russia; (2) that there was no question of sending troops to France at that moment; (3) that France was an intimate friend and ally; (4) that it was against British interests for France to be wiped out as a great power; (5) that Germany couldn't be allowed to use the Channel as a hostile base; and (6) that Britain had obligations to Belgium to prevent her being overrun by Germany.

Nobody spoke, not even after the last statement. One could

argue the toss for ever about who or what was responsible for the crisis – Serbia, Austria, Russia, Germany, France, capitalism, imperialism, nationalism – but on that Sunday evening only one belligerent had already invaded one neutral country and was about to invade another. He could sense the altered mood in the room, as palpable as a change in air pressure. The stubborn Mr Burns repeated his determination to resign, but the others were muted, stunned. By eight o'clock, with only five dissenting voices, he had secured an agreement that Grey should warn the Germans the next day that any serious violation of Belgium's neutrality would compel His Majesty's Government to take appropriate action.

He closed the meeting at eight o'clock with a quiet sense of accomplishment. He had kept his government together. But politics is merely a process of replacing one problem with another. Now there was just the little matter of the impending war.

He dined with Reggie and Pamela McKenna at their house in Smith Square. The Home Secretary and his wife were old friends; it was exactly what he needed after such an arduous day. He took Edwin Montagu with him, and Violet, and Cyril – Cys – the youngest of his sons by his first wife, and Elizabeth, his seventeen-year-old daughter by Margot, who was known as the Bud.

The big sash windows were raised to their furthest extent to let in the slight evening breeze. They dined on lamb cutlets followed by ices and afterwards played bridge. Word of the Cabinet's stiffening resolve was already in the first editions of some of the morning papers, and as the night went on, the noise of the large crowds wandering the streets towards Buckingham Palace became ever louder – a distant and slightly unnerving roar, interspersed occasionally with the singing of 'God Save the King'.

'The government seems to be very popular,' said Montagu, looking up from his cards. 'You'd think we'd already won.'

'I don't much care for it,' said the Prime Minister. 'It reminds me of Walpole's remark before the war with Spain: "Today they are ringing the bells; soon they will be wringing their hands."'

The commotion was still audible at one in the morning, when he left with the others to walk back to Number 10.

It was unnaturally light, the gas lamps burning around Parliament Square, a three-quarters moon overhead. Not long after they started making their way up Whitehall, somebody stepped right in front of him, stared into his face, called out, 'Bloody hell, it *is* him!' and he found himself surrounded by several dozen members of the public, some fairly drunk. The small crowd was friendly enough, shouting out compliments and chanting 'For He's a Jolly Good Fellow', much to the amusement of his children. But he had never courted popular fame, unlike Winston and Lloyd George, and the experience was disconcerting. At the corner of Downing Street, at Violet's suggestion, he stopped briefly and reluctantly removed his top hat. He doffed it this way and that, then clamped it firmly back on his head and fled towards the safety of his front door.

Venetia did not swim for long next morning – even in August the temperature of the Irish Sea rarely got out of the fifties, and if she stayed in for more than ten minutes, she knew she would have a chill in her bones it would take her hours to dispel. She waded ashore, wrapped herself in her towel, checked the beach was deserted, and wriggled out of her swimming costume and into her dress. For once she didn't bother to hurry back. There would be no delivery of letters to intercept.

She let down her hair, shook it loose and walked along the wet sand. At the top of the low headland was a ruined, roofless grey stone structure, its origins lost beyond living memory, romantically known as King Arthur's Seat. Here last summer in a sudden squall she had sat sheltered from the wind with the Prime Minister's arm around her. And here, the summer before that, Edwin Montagu had proposed to her – unexpectedly, touchingly, hopelessly. She had tried to refuse him as gently as she could.

'I'm afraid that can never be.'

'Is it because I'm Jewish?'

'No, of course not. I'm not like that.'

'Because you ought to know, in case you change your mind – which I hope one day you will – that under the terms of my father's will, if I marry outside the faith, I'll be disinherited.'

'So, what are you saying? That if we did marry, we'd be poor?'

'Yes. Unless you converted.'

She'd started laughing; she couldn't help herself – 'Well, there's certainly no point in marrying a *poor* Jew!' – until she saw his expression, then she'd quickly taken his hand. 'I'm sorry. I didn't mean to be an ass. Really, I am very fond of you. But as a friend, not in the other way.'

'You think I'm ugly?'

'Dear Edwin, *everyone* thinks you're ugly!'

'My God, I am, aren't I? Really ugly!' And then it had been his turn to laugh, throwing back his head, showing his terrible teeth and the underside of his bristly black moustache. She joined in, and when they had both stopped, he said seriously, 'But I do love you, Venetia. I've never loved anyone so much, and I never shall.'

'Why?' She was genuinely puzzled.

'I think,' he began, and hesitated. 'You won't be offended?'

'No. Go on.'

'I think it's because you have a man's mind in a woman's body.'

'Now that's a rather feminine observation if I may say so. Perhaps it's you who has a woman's mind in a man's body?'

'It's true, I do! I'm neurotic and I detest male company and all masculine pursuits. I much prefer choosing fabrics. You see – we are made for one another.'

She could never marry Montagu, but after that she liked him more. She wasn't offended by what he said because she recognised the truth in it.

She took a longer route back to the house than usual, climbing over the padlocked gate that marked the edge of the family's estate and following the coastal track rather than going through the woods. The tide was receding, exposing black rocks and shallow pools. Oystercatchers stabbed at the muddy sandbanks. She walked past an empty farmhouse with whitewashed walls and turned onto the main road that ran along the western boundary of the house, and she had almost reached the big iron gate when the postman emerged from the grounds on his bicycle and began pedalling away towards Holyhead.

As she hurried through the park, she told herself he needn't necessarily have been delivering letters, it could have been a telegram. But when she reached the house and went straight into the dining room, she found the family still sitting around the remains of breakfast, obviously waiting for her, and the Prime Minister's letters – two of them – laid beside her plate.

She was conscious of everyone looking at her – wet hair trailing down her back, dishevelled, still holding her towel and swimming costume.

Her mother said, 'You're late.'

'Sorry.'

'Well,' said Sylvia, nodding towards the letters, 'aren't you going to open them?'

'I shall, of course, when I'm ready.'

Her instinct was to seize them and run to her room, but then she thought, *How pathetic! How cowardly!* and instead she forced herself to pin up her hair, to collect some cold eggs and bacon, to sit at her place and begin chewing mechanically. She looked around. Lord Sheffield was watching her over the top of his newspaper.

She said, 'What's the news, Father?'

'How should I know? You're the one who gets it straight from the horse's mouth. Why don't *you* tell *us*?'

'Very well. I'll see what he has to say.'

The letters were postmarked Saturday and Sunday evenings. She slit open Saturday's with her butter knife and skimmed it quickly.

Sylvia said, 'Don't keep us in suspense. Read it out!'

'Yes, I will. Just give me a moment.'

Disclosing the first paragraph would have sunk her – *your counsel & your understanding & your sympathy and your love . . . My darling, without you, I tremble to think what wd. have happened to me . . .* – but the rest was factual and she read it aloud casually, as if it were the most natural thing in the world to be sharing the Prime Minister's first-hand account of his visit to the King at one-thirty in the morning (*one of my strangest experiences, & as you know I have had a good lot*), followed by the details of a Cabinet meeting: *If it comes to war I feel sure (this is entirely between you & me) that we shall have <u>some</u> split in the Cabinet. Of course, if Grey went I should go, & the whole thing would break up.*

Her audience was riveted. When she finished, there was an impressed silence.

'Good heavens, Venetia,' said Lady Sheffield, 'he really does confide in you.'

'It's far more political than I'd expected,' said her father. He nodded towards the other letter. 'Do you think we might hear what happened yesterday?' His tone had become almost deferential. 'Only if you think he wouldn't mind, of course.'

'I'm sure if he were here, he wouldn't object.'

Her hands shook as she opened the second letter. He had put two stamps on it, she noticed, which no doubt explained why it had been delivered despite the holiday.

'Start from the beginning,' commanded Sylvia. 'Give us the whole thing.'

'If you insist. "After all there was not as I thought & hoped a Sunday delivery: so I got no letter from you this morning, which is the saddest blank in my day."' She held it out for inspection. 'That's exactly how it begins, you see?'

Blanche said, 'How sweet.'

It was lucky for her that he had been too busy to include his usual declarations of love. She read out his account of the visit from the German ambassador (*He was very agitated poor man & wept*) and the morning Cabinet meeting (*It will be a shocking thing if at such a moment we break up*) and finally his six guiding principles. Her gaze skittered over the next few lines – *beloved . . . miss you . . . love you . . .* – and she swerved to a halt.

'And that is how it ends,' she said, folding it and putting it back into its envelope, 'on a cliff-hanger, like all the best dramatic novels. And now, if your curiosity is satisfied, I'd like to go and change out of my wet clothes.'

In her room, she wrote to him at once.

Darling, don't be alarmed, but I wasn't expecting your two lovely weekend letters & they were waylaid by the family this morning while I was down by the sea & I found myself either risking a 'scene' or sharing at least a part of the contents. I chose the latter, & all was well, they were most impressed, but it's a reminder that we must take care – the simple precaution of never using our names is not enough . . .

*

The Prime Minister had been trying all morning to get hold of Lord Kitchener. Just before he went into yet another Cabinet meeting, he told his private office to track him down. But the Field Marshal was nowhere to be found in London. At Broome Park, his country estate near Canterbury, his butler, after some persuasion, finally revealed that his lordship had just departed for Dover and was intending to catch the one o'clock Channel steamer to Calais.

Bongie came into the Cabinet room and whispered in the Prime Minister's ear: 'He's on his way back to Egypt.'

'Well, tell him I need to see him urgently.'

An hour later, Bongie returned to report that they had wired the Dover harbourmaster and the steamship company, that the ferry was being held in port, that he had managed to speak to one of Kitchener's aides on the telephone, but that the Field Marshal was insisting on staying on board and continuing his journey.

'Then tell them to remind him that I am Secretary of State for War, and he is a serving officer, and I am ordering him to return!'

It struck him as odd – he might have used a stronger word – that on the eve of the greatest war in history, the most famous officer in the British Army should prefer to slip away to Egypt. But he had no time to brood on it for the next twenty-four hours, as he had so much else to worry him: mobilising the army and navy, dealing with four resignations from the Cabinet – Burns, Morley, Simon, Beauchamp – responding to the Belgian government's rejection of the German ultimatum and the appeal from the

Belgian King Albert to George V for support. At two-thirty, he had to set off for the emergency session of the House of Commons, sitting in the back of the Napier, trapped behind the big glass windows and gawped at like an animal in a zoo, inching his way through the cheering crowds, and arriving to find the chamber so packed that chairs had been set up along the central aisle. And then Gray's statement on the crisis, which lasted more than an hour, about which he had been anxious, Gray being a dull and often confusing speaker, but which proved to be a triumph, so much so that the Liberal MPs – three-quarters of whom had been peace-at-any-price men a few days previously – were suddenly cheering the government on to declare war against Germany at once.

He looked around at the contorted, transformed faces and the blizzard of waving order papers, and he experienced a curious sense of detachment, of floating away and regarding the scene from somewhere up near the galleries, as if the world had become an alien place, full of raging passions and absolute certainties, that were entirely uncongenial to his nature.

With all the telegrams, interviews, meetings, orders, decisions, letters to be read and written, it was not until the following afternoon that he finally had his meeting with Kitchener in the formal state drawing room of Number 10.

'It was good of you to come back to London.'

'Under the circumstances, I did not feel I had been left with any choice.'

'I expect you can guess why I wanted to see you so urgently.'

'Not really.'

The Field Marshal's face, half-hidden by those monstrous moustaches, was immobile, his blue eyes fixed like gemstones. Really, he was impossible! It was like trying to hold a conversation with an Easter Island statue. The Prime Minister almost abandoned his plan. But he pressed on.

'Well, we have this morning notified the German government that unless they undertake by midnight to withdraw their forces from Belgium and France, we shall consider ourselves at war with them.'

'I see.'

'For the past four months, I've been acting as Secretary of State for War, but obviously that can't continue in the present circumstances. Therefore, I would like to submit your name to His Majesty as my replacement.'

He studied the Field Marshal and waited for a reaction.

Eventually, Kitchener said, 'I think that would be a bad idea.'

'Why?'

'Because I am not a politician.'

'Precisely, and I have no wish for you to become one. That is your great strength. You would exercise unparalleled authority over the army because you're not political, and the country and the Opposition would be reassured by your presence in the counsels of government.'

'I would still prefer to return to Egypt.'

'And you shall – I give you my word – as soon as the war is over. We will keep the consulship open for you.'

'But that may not be for a very long time.'

'Not as long as all that, surely? I keep hearing Christmas mentioned as a time when the war is likely to end.'

'That is nonsense.'

'Really? How long do you envisage it lasting?'

Kitchener raised his hand and let it fall. 'Who can say? I certainly think it's likely to go on until nineteen-seventeen.'

'*Nineteen-seventeen?*' The Prime Minister drew back slightly. 'That seems very pessimistic!'

'To defeat the Germans, we will need to raise an army of at least two million men. To recruit, arm and train such a number will take three years. Hence, the earliest the war can possibly be won in my opinion is nineteen-seventeen.'

'My military advisers say it will be much shorter than that.'

'Then with respect, Prime Minister, you need new advisers.' He was silent for a while. 'You understand, Prime Minister, that the casualties will be enormous?'

'Yes, I know. We shall have to brace ourselves for a hard time.'

'The best precedent for what we face is the American Civil War, which killed more than six hundred thousand soldiers. But that was a war confined to one country – mostly to one part of one country – which is trivial compared to the scale of a general European land war. Also, that was fifty years ago. The effectiveness of artillery and small arms has greatly advanced since then. If this conflict lasts until nineteen-seventeen, the deaths will be in the millions.'

The Prime Minister tried to imagine what millions meant – the misery of each loss magnified four times, ten times, fifty times by parents, grandparents, brothers, sisters, aunts, uncles, friends, children . . . But how could one's mind possibly begin to encompass so much grief? It was unfathomable, unthinkable. He understood now why Kitchener had been so keen to remove himself to Egypt.

He said, 'All the more reason, then, for you to stay here and do your duty.'

Another silence. 'I should like to think it over.'

He will do it, thought the Prime Minister. He has no choice.

'I can give you until tomorrow morning. By then the war will have started.'

The pressures on him were such that he didn't get round to reading Venetia's letter until nearly six that evening. Her opening paragraph transfixed him. He tried to remember what he had told her, but so much had happened, the events were a blur in his mind. She assured him that 'all was well'. Even so!

I am rather alarmed at the family curiosity as to the contents of my letters, & I am sure you were judicious in what you read to them (& didn't read): I suppose (and hope) that it was an exceptional case, due to the lateness of the Bank Holiday post. You feared, did you? that I should forget the extra stamp! You don't quite know me – even now . . . Winston, who has got on all his war-paint, is longing for a sea-fight in the early hours of tomorrow morning. The whole thing fills me with sadness. We are on the eve of horrible things.

★

The British ultimatum to Germany was set to expire at midnight Central European Time: 11 p.m. in Britain. All over the country, people sat up as if it was New Year's Eve to see out the peace and see in the war. Some went out into the street to stand with their neighbours. In London, Trafalgar Square and the Mall all the way down to Buckingham Palace were once again crowded with revellers, waving Union Jacks and the French tricolour.

In Penrhos, all was silence. Venetia sat with her family in the drawing room. They had dressed formally for dinner as usual, even though there were no guests. Her father had his fob watch open and was counting off the minutes. Her sisters sat slightly apart and together on the long sofa, holding hands. She couldn't keep still. As the hour approached, she went over to the French windows and stared across the terrace to the distant trees, motionless in the calm evening, their outlines silvered in the moonlight, and thought of him – where he was, what he might be doing – and wished she was with him.

'One minute to go,' said her father.

In Downing Street, perhaps half the Cabinet had assembled – Grey, Lloyd George and McKenna among them; ministers and officials constantly coming in and out – most of the ministers smoking, either cigars or cigarettes, drinks in their hands, brandy and soda, whisky and soda, sprawled in the hard leather chairs or standing at the fireplace – the windows open to let out the fumes – listening to the bursts of noise from the crowds that drifted occasionally over St James's Park like the sounds of a distant battle. Margot, the only woman, was sitting in the corner with a cigarette, holding forth to the Leader of the House of Lords, Viscount Crewe. The Prime Minister was standing at the window, thinking of Venetia and how soon he might be able to see her. It was a kind of delicious ache in the pit of his stomach, a hunger that he cultivated but could never satisfy, that seemed to get a little more acute with each day they were apart. He would need her more than ever. He barely noticed when Big Ben began to chime eleven, the doors flew open and Winston strode in smoking a huge cigar and beaming with happiness.

On the Caledonian Road, Deemer was sitting in the front seat of Holt-Wilson's little car, next to the captain, who was studying his watch, with Sergeant Regan and Sergeant Fitzgerald crammed in behind them. The lights in the flat above the barbershop had gone out half an hour earlier. A nearby church clock began to chime the hour.

'That's it,' said Holt-Wilson, snapping shut his watch. 'Let's go.'

Deemer closed the car door quietly. He opened the lid of the boot and heaved out the metal battering ram, hoisted it onto his shoulder, then led the way across the street. Uniformed police were deploying from a van parked outside the Italian café. The four officers of MO5(g) reached the barbershop. Three halted. Regan walked on and turned right into the little alley that ran between the row of shops and the railway embankment. As soon as he was out of sight, Fitzgerald drew his pistol.

Deemer looked at Holt-Wilson, who had also drawn a gun. The captain nodded. Deemer swung the battering ram, the flimsy door frame splintered, the lock gave way, he pushed open the door and they stepped into the shop, Deemer in the lead – past the barber's chairs, through the curtains. It was too dark to make out much. He dropped the battering ram and groped around on the wall for a switch just as a light came on upstairs which lit the way to the upper floor. He took the stairs fast, Fitzgerald and Holt-Wilson behind him, and there on the landing was Ernst, in a dirty white singlet and drawers. He started to shout something in German, then saw the guns and quickly raised his hands. In less than a minute, Fitzgerald had him cuffed, and was steering him downstairs.

'Well done, Deemer,' said Holt-Wilson, clapping him on the shoulder. 'That's how you take a German spy.'

Deemer's heart was pumping wildly. He was aware of a dog barking somewhere, and suddenly the sound of a police whistle from the alley at the back. He exchanged a mystified glance with Holt-Wilson and stepped through the open door into a bedroom – Ernst's, by the look of it: the blankets were thrown off the bed and a pile of clothes, including his white jacket, was on the chair. He crossed the landing and went into the second bedroom. Empty, but the bed had been slept in – he felt it: the sheet was still slightly warm – and on the nightstand a candle flickered in the draught from the wide-open rear window.

PART THREE

INVESTIGATION
5 August–6 September 1914

CHAPTER TWELVE

NOBODY OBSERVING DEEMER over the next two weeks would have guessed his profession. In his bowler hat and cheap dark suit, he would leave his house at seven o'clock each morning, often not returning until nearly midnight. He would walk to the Angel Tube station. At the kiosk beside the entrance, he would buy a copy of *The Times*, and as the train jumped and jolted, he would read the war news, carefully avoiding eye contact with his fellow passengers. After changing lines at Euston, he would alight at Charing Cross and join the hundreds of other office workers swarming up to the surface. Ten minutes after that, he would be on the third floor of Watergate House, unlocking the door to the duty room of MO5(g), the border crossing from normality into his secret world.

In this foreign land, for all his efforts, he remained a stranger. Men like Booth, Brodie and Fetherston were not his type, nor he theirs: officers seconded from county regiments, whose braying conversation when not discussing work centred around hunting, skiing, polo or tennis, and who took great delight in using the private nicknames they had invented for everyone in the office:

Captain Drake of the Staffordshires, the head of counter-espionage, was 'Duckie'; Holt-Wilson, the son of a clergyman, was 'Holy Willy'; Deemer had become 'the Dreamer'. The well-spoken young ladies in the Registry were polite to him, but their sole qualification for the job was that their parents were known socially to the department chief, Major Kell, and Deemer felt slightly awkward in their presence. The old salts from Scotland Yard kept their distance.

And then there was the nature of the work itself. In the first few days of the war, MO5(g) had arrested twenty-two suspected German spies. But Deemer was considered too junior to take part in their interrogations. Instead, he was assigned to follow up the dozens of reports from members of the public forwarded to the department by Scotland Yard – of German waiters in Maidstone suspected of plotting acts of sabotage against the railway line in Kent, or anglers on the Channel coast accused of signalling to U-boats. One army officer denounced the Lord Chancellor, Lord Haldane, for allegedly keeping a wireless set hidden behind a cupboard in his bedroom. The First Sea Lord, Prince Louis of Battenberg, had been born in Austria, and that was enough to make him a suspect. A German woman, Frau Anne Meyer, employed by the Prime Minister, was said to be still living under his roof in Downing Street and stealing documents. These were the imaginings not of cranks, but of solid, sensible members of the middle class, who expected to have their fantasies taken seriously. It did not make Deemer think more fondly of his fellow citizens as he trudged from one informer to another, filling his notebook with nonsense. Overnight, the entire country seemed to have become paranoid. 'Spy mania', they called it.

In between chasing down these dead-end leads, he spent his spare time in the Registry, working through the card index of

actual spies, familiarising himself with the German espionage network, searching for some clue that might identify the man who
had escaped from the bedroom above Ernst's barbershop. Could
he have been Hauptmann Kurt von Weller, a former Prussian
officer, arrested a few days later? Or Harold Dutton, an army clerk
who had copied information on the Portsmouth defences? Or even
Marie Kroener, widow of the German agent Wilhelm Kroener?
Or was it someone too cunning to have found their way onto the
Registry's card-index system? Whoever he or she was, they had
been agile enough to elude Sergeant Regan in the darkness and
escape via the alley and across the railway embankment into the
night.

When he had exhausted the spy index, he moved on to the
growing index of thousands of German and Austrian nationals,
whose cards were marked by a system of double initials to denote
their trustworthiness, from AA ('Absolutely Anglicised': undoubt-
edly friendly), through AB ('Anglo-Boche': probably friendly) and
BA ('Boche-Anglo': probably hostile) to BB ('Bad Boche': undoubt-
edly hostile). Bad Boche! The schoolboy language made him
wince.

It was in this section of the Registry on the morning of Monday
17 August, thirteen days after the declaration of war, that Holt-
Wilson came up behind him, his great beak of a nose red and
dripping from a summer cold.

'Ah, Deemer! Good morning. Thought I'd find you here.' He
blew his nose on an enormous white handkerchief. 'The chief's
got something he wants you to look into.'

'Good morning, sir.' He felt a flicker of hope. 'What's that?'

'Some interesting stuff's been handed in by members of the
public. Come along. He'll fill you in himself.'

Swallowing his disappointment, he followed Holy Willy

through the duty room to Kell's office. He had received a few curt words of welcome from the chief at the beginning, but this was the first time he had crossed his threshold. There was an army camp bed in the corner, with blankets neatly folded – Kell often worked through the night – and French windows with a balcony looking out to the Thames. The major was seated behind his desk. He was about forty years old. In his tweed suit, with his round spectacles and his hair combed back off his wide forehead, he looked more like a young headmaster than a soldier. The captains privately called him 'Kelly', although never when he was within earshot. He had a reputation for cleverness – he was said to speak six languages – and strict discipline.

'Take a seat. Settling in all right?'

'Yes, sir, thank you. I think so.'

'Well, here's a job for you. Quite a puzzle. Take a look at that.'

He lifted the lid of a small cardboard box and pushed it across his desk. Inside were various pieces of what looked at first glance to be wastepaper, typed on tissue-thin paper, dirty and weather-blown. They were separated into three groups, each with a strip of paper clipped to it, marked respectively 'SJP', 'M' and 'G'.

Deemer glanced at him.

'Those are classified Foreign Office telegrams dispatched just before the outbreak of war, recently discovered in three separate locations: in St James's Park, near the river at Marlow, and in a field just outside Goring-on-Thames.'

'Discovered by members of the public?'

'Indeed, all quite independent of one another. They've been handed in to local police stations at various times over the past ten days, who then forwarded them to Scotland Yard. Now we've been asked to look at them. Obviously, one's immediate anxiety is that there's a German agent inside the Foreign Office. But that doesn't seem to make any sense. An agent would surely guard such material very carefully, not scatter it around the south of England like confetti.'

Holt-Wilson said, 'It's like a mystery out of Sherlock Holmes.'

'What's most troubling is that high-grade messages like these would have been encrypted. Two are actually telegrams from the ambassadors in Berlin and Vienna, so the encoded texts would almost certainly have been intercepted by the Germans and Austrians, which means that if the enemy ever got hold of the decrypts, they could match the two and break our ciphers.'

'A real mystery,' repeated Holt-Wilson. He blew his nose and inspected his handkerchief. 'Whoever's responsible should be prosecuted.'

'Our first task,' said Kell, 'is to get some kind of explanation from the Foreign Office. I've alerted William Tyrrell, Sir Edward Grey's private secretary, and told him what's happened, and that I'll be sending the telegrams straight over. I want you to show them to him personally and ask him what he makes of them. We need to make sure they don't try to sweep this under the carpet just because it's embarrassing, but co-operate with us in carrying out a full inquiry.' He replaced the lid on the box and looked at Deemer. 'Well, what are you waiting for? That's the job.'

Deemer walked along the Embankment towards the Foreign Office, carrying the cardboard box. He wondered what exactly was in the telegrams. Kell hadn't invited him to read them, but he hadn't forbidden it either. He got as far Whitehall Gardens before his curiosity finally overcame him.

There was a row of park benches. He chose an empty one at the end and cautiously opened the box. Thanks to the fine summer weather, the telegrams were still entirely legible – if there had been a heavy shower, he guessed they might have disintegrated. The one found near Goring was from the ambassador in Vienna: two pages, both intact, warning that the Austrians were preparing an ultimatum to Serbia. A quarter of the telegram discovered in Marlow was missing; the rest showed that it was from Berlin, describing the increasing hostility to Serbia in the German press. The most recent had been retrieved in St James's Park the weekend before last: from the embassy in Paris, reporting that the Spanish government had assured the French, in confidence, that they would be friendly in the war and France could safely withdraw its troops stationed along the border.

He put the telegrams back in the box. He might only be a glorified errand boy, but at least the errand was important.

At the grand entrance to the Foreign Office, he told the caretaker that he had been sent by the War Office and that he had an appointment to see Mr William Tyrrell. The information was relayed to a uniformed messenger, and very soon afterwards a clerk appeared, who conducted him up an immense staircase, showed him into a room the size of a tennis court and asked him to wait. He sat on the edge of a studded red leather sofa with the box and his hat beside him and looked around. Everything was gargantuan – the acreage of carpet, the high ceiling, the huge windows, the monumental oil paintings of ambassadors and soldiers of the British Empire in gilt frames a foot thick; even the tick of the clock seemed to echo off the walls. When eventually the door opened, he half-expected a giant, but the only thing large about Tyrrell was his head, which was disconcertingly out of proportion to his slender body.

The diplomat's reaction to the telegrams was to purse his lips. 'And these were found in fields and a park?'

'Yes, sir. They are authentic, I take it?'

He nodded. 'They're carbon copies – what we call flimsies.'

Deemer took out his notebook. 'May I ask how many people will have seen them?'

'Very few. Telegrams at this level are sent round to ministers in a locked box.'

'How many ministers?'

'Five.'

'And who are they?'

Tyrrell looked at the notebook. He hesitated. 'I'm not sure I can disclose that.'

'Why not?'

'It's confidential.'

'Like the telegrams?'

He smiled faintly. '*Touché*! Well, purely for your information the five ministers who automatically receive telegrams from the major embassies are the Foreign Secretary, the Prime Minister, the First Lord of the Admiralty, the Secretary of State for War and the Colonial Secretary.'

Deemer wrote them down. 'I'm afraid they'll all need to be interviewed.'

Tyrrell stared at him for a few seconds, then laughed. 'Well, that is most certainly *not* going to happen! Do you think men like Winston Churchill and Lord Kitchener are going to interrupt their vital war work to talk to *you*?' He put the lid on the box of telegrams and tucked it under his arm. 'Leave it with me. I'll speak to the Foreign Secretary.'

Deemer eyed the box. 'Shouldn't our department hold on to the telegrams for now – as evidence? Major Kell is keen to get to the bottom of it.'

'I'm afraid that's out of the question. Thank Major Kell for returning them and tell him we'll handle the investigation from now on. I presume you can see yourself out.'

Two minutes later, Deemer was standing in the courtyard, looking up at the monumental building with a kind of wonder. These people! They were the same type he had observed at the inquest into the riverboat tragedy. They seemed to believe themselves above the rules that applied to ordinary citizens. Anything that might embarrass them was made to disappear.

And there matters might have rested, at least as far as Deemer was concerned, were it not for the fact that soon after he had returned to Watergate House and hung his bowler on the hatstand in the duty room, Mrs Summer, the caretaker, came over to his desk with an envelope and a message clipped to it from Holt-Wilson, who had gone to the Travellers Club for lunch with Kell: *Sgt Deemer – here's another one! This was handed in to Roehampton police station on Saturday. It should be included with the other documents for further investigation. E. H-W.*

'Thank you, Mrs Summer. I'll deal with it.'

He waited until she had gone before he opened the envelope. Inside was a single sheet of the now-familiar thin paper – this one from the British ambassador to Germany, typed and dated 4 August, the day war broke out.

My interview with the Chancellor was very painful. He said that he could not but consider it an intolerable thing that because they were taking the only course open to them to save the Empire from disaster, England should fall upon them just for the sake of the neutrality of Belgium. He looked upon England as entirely responsible for what might now happen. I asked him whether he could not understand that we were bound in honour to do our best to preserve a neutrality which we had guaranteed. He said, 'But at what price!'

The flimsy was barely crumpled. He doubted it could have lain out overnight – there was no moisture damage from the dew. It must have been picked up very quickly. Since its discovery, only forty-eight hours had elapsed. The trail might still be warm. He glanced around. Nobody seemed to be paying him any attention. He returned the telegram to the envelope, tucked it into his jacket, collected his bowler and walked back out into the summer's day.

To reach Roehampton in the suburbs of south-west London required a bus journey and then a train to Barnes station. He arrived just after two and strolled down a country lane towards the centre of the village. It felt good to be out of town for the first time in many weeks – families picnicking beneath the trees, the women in their elegant light dresses and sun hats, the men in blazers, the fresh air full of birdsong. For a quarter of an hour it was possible to forget entirely the country was at war.

At the police station, he showed his warrant to the duty sergeant, and asked him to check for an entry in the log book made on Saturday, when a government document had been handed in. The sergeant remembered it very well. He had been on duty himself that day. Late morning, as he recalled – he leafed through the ledger – yes: here it was. 11.45 a.m. Brought in by an elderly gentleman, a Mr Albert Hardy of Medfield Street, a bit of an old busybody, always dropping by to complain about something or other – litter, stray dogs, lewd behaviour on the Heath. The sergeant hadn't paid the discovery much attention, but the inspector had been excited.

'Medfield Street,' said Deemer. 'Is that easy to find?'

'Yes, just go out of here, carry on for about half a mile and turn left off Roehampton Lane – it's a nice spot overlooking Putney Heath. Important, is it?' The sergeant folded his arms and leaned forwards on the counter, hoping for some information in return.

'I can't tell you that, I'm sorry.'

As he left, he heard the sergeant muttering something about 'bloody Scotland Yard'.

Medfield Street was indeed a pleasant place to live, a row of neat red-brick three-storey villas, built in a rustic style, facing south across the open heath, where the grasses were tall and golden as a field of hay ripe for cutting. Mr Hardy's door was sturdy plain oak, iron-studded, with an iron knocker. As soon as Deemer rapped on it, a dog started barking inside, and then its owner appeared holding a small terrier by its collar.

'Mr Albert Hardy?'

'Yes.'

'I'm Detective Sergeant Deemer of the Metropolitan Police. I'm sorry to disturb you . . .'

But Mr Hardy was only too delighted to be disturbed. He plainly had nothing to do all day except observe the passing scene in his little patch of Arcadia. He insisted on taking Deemer into the parlour and making him a cup of tea. He had lived in the house with his wife for thirty years, but she had passed away and he was on his own. The room was full of books about mathematics – he had taught the subject until he retired – and he started to talk about his career, until Deemer politely brought the conversation back to his discovery.

'Ah, yes, the telegram.'

He had been walking his dog on Saturday morning and had just emerged from the woodland onto Roehampton Lane when he saw 'a very smart motor, with a chauffeur, and a man and a woman in the back', coming towards him, and through the open window 'came a little ball of paper, deliberately thrown' – an act of littering unforgivable in Mr Hardy's opinion, but all too common on that particular stretch of main road. He had waved his walking stick at the car as it passed, and had retrieved the litter, as he always did, to place it later in the appropriate receptacle. Intrigued by the thinness of the paper, he had opened it up and seen to his astonishment the words 'confidential', 'Berlin' and 'Chancellor'.

Deemer was writing it all down with increasing excitement. This had been worth the trip – an eyewitness who had seen the culprit! He had not expected that. 'Can you describe the passengers in the car?'

'I'm afraid not, it went by too quickly.'

'Young? Old?'

'I had the impression the man was older than the woman, but I can't be sure.'

'Was it heading towards London or away from it?'

'Away – driving out into the country.'

'What sort of car, can you remember?'

'I don't know anything about cars. It was large, rather grand.'

'Well, that's useful in itself.' My God, thought Deemer, a big car with a chauffeur – it might well have been one of the five ministers. He was suddenly in a hurry to get back to the office. 'You've really been most helpful.' He put away his notebook and finished his tea. The old man's loneliness was starting to depress him. He wondered if this would be him in thirty years. 'I'd better be going.'

'I could take you to the spot where it happened, if you like.'

'Thank you, but I don't think that's necessary.'

He was halfway to the door when Mr Hardy suddenly said, 'I do remember the car's registration number if that's of any use.'

Deemer stopped and turned. 'It is indeed.' He took out his notebook again.

Mr Hardy recited it very slowly: 'A3141.'

'How on earth did you remember that?'

'Very easily. They are the first four integers of pi.'

Oh, but he loved the routine of police work! The unheroic solitary nature of it, walking from place to place, interviewing, checking, thinking, methodically filling his notebook, acquiring the skeleton of facts that gradually solved the mystery of a case. By the middle of the afternoon, he was back in the centre of town, in Spring Gardens, close to Trafalgar Square, climbing the steps into the grandiose headquarters of the London County Council.

A3141 was a London numberplate – the A prefix denoted that. The details of every number issued since 1903, including the make and model of the vehicle and the name and address of the owner, were kept at County Hall. The police were entitled to consult the register; Deemer had done it often, and his face was well known. He waited on the familiar hard leather bench in the corridor, looking at a mural depicting scenes from London's history, and afterwards he would long remember the expression of the clerk when he came back with the information he had requested.

'Are you pulling my leg, Sergeant?'

'No. What do you mean?'

By way of reply, the clerk handed him a slip of pale blue paper. The car was a forty-five horsepower, six-cylinder Type 23 Napier, registered to the Right Honourable Herbert Henry Asquith, 10 Downing Street, Whitehall SW.

The moment he returned to Watergate House, he asked to see Kell. As he made his report, the chief sat back in his chair, listening, saying nothing, with his fingertips pressed together. His spectacles reflected the light from the window and made it hard to read his reaction. The silence after Deemer had finished lasted for at least a minute.

Eventually he said, 'In the five years since I established this department, I've heard some extraordinary tales, but this beats everything. The Prime Minister of the United Kingdom motoring around the country, throwing decrypted telegrams out of his car window? And with a *woman* sitting next to him? Who the devil was she?'

'I suppose it could have been Mrs Asquith.'

'That's hardly reassuring. She's one of the greatest gossips in London! Besides, I thought your witness said she was a younger woman? I'm not sure she fits that description. What an utterly intolerable mess!'

His thin lips compressed so tightly they disappeared. His face became rigid. He brought his hands down onto the desk with a thump and jumped to his feet, then threw open the French windows and stepped onto the balcony, leaving Deemer to stare at his back. He had entered expecting some words of praise for solving the case so quickly, but now he saw that he had been naïve. He had landed Kell with a political nightmare.

After a few minutes, the major returned to the office, closed the windows and sat down at his desk. He was entirely composed.

'We can't just leave it here, much as I'd like to. How big a security risk is he? In particular: who was the woman in the car? That's what troubles me the most. What if it was this German governess, Frau Meyer, who's apparently still living in Number Ten? I expect it wasn't – but how do we know? We need to establish the identity of the passenger before we go any further. Do you think you can do that, discreetly?'

'I'll try, sir.' He couldn't begin to imagine how he might go about it. 'What should we do with the Roehampton telegram?'

'I don't think we should tell the Foreign Office about it, not yet – if we do, it will only disappear with the others. I'll keep it in my safe. In fact, don't mention a word of this to anyone, not even Captain Holt-Wilson.' He swivelled in his chair towards the window. Once again, the light on his glasses rendered his expression opaque. 'We should keep this whole affair just between the two of us for now.'

CHAPTER THIRTEEN

THE FOLLOWING MORNING, the Prime Minister was working in the Cabinet Room when Bongie entered with a red dispatch box that had just been sent over from the Foreign Office. It was small, only a foot long and six inches wide, with *GRV* embossed in gold on the top and a brass handle at one end. It was locked: one of the type to which only the most senior ministers had a key.

His private secretary said hopefully, 'Would you like me to deal with it, sir?' He hated it whenever he suspected that secrets were being kept from him.

'No, you'd better leave it with me.' He signed a couple of orders, closed the file and handed it over his shoulder to Bongie. 'This needs to go across to the War Office right away.'

The decisions he was required to take each day had grown massively in scale and significance. For example, he had been obliged to ask Parliament for a Vote of Credit of £100 million to recruit an army half a million strong, to be ready by the spring. He had authorised the dispatch of the British Expeditionary Force of some ninety thousand soldiers to France, most of whom had already crossed the Channel in conditions of absolute secrecy. And he had been called upon to decide where they should be deployed, arbitrating between the General Staff, who wanted them detrained around Maubeuge on the Franco-Belgian border, and Kitchener, who thought that such an exposed position put them at imminent risk of being overrun and instead favoured Amiens, due north of Paris. In the end he had come down on the side of the General Staff, but the decision still nagged at him – the thought of all those young men so close to the oncoming German steamroller. His anxiety stemmed from being asked to make rulings on matters he knew little about. And yet he had never been more popular! When, on the first Sunday of the war, he had gone alone to evensong in Westminster Abbey to soothe his nerves by listening to the hymns, he had been recognised on leaving and once again escorted home by a large and enthusiastic crowd of sightseers. *Loafers*, he thought as he hurried down the street.

Once the door had closed behind Bongie, he searched in his trouser pocket for his bunch of keys and opened the dispatch box.

For circulation Tuesday 18 Aug. 1914
From: Foreign Secretary
To: Prime Minister
First Lord of the Admiralty
Secretary of State for War
Secretary of State for the Colonies

The enclosed diplomatic telegrams have recently been discovered by members of the public in St James's Park, and in the countryside near Marlow and Goring-on-Thames. As we five are the only ministers who receive copies of these telegrams, I fear one of us must be held responsible for a grievous breach of confidentiality. It is not merely the disclosure of the contents that is potentially harmful; much more serious is the risk that the security of the Foreign Office cipher may have been compromised.

I cannot stress too highly the importance of safeguarding secret material, especially in wartime when we must be on our guard against the activities of enemy agents. I would be grateful if each of you could respond to this memorandum and state frankly whether you can shed any light on the matter.

(Signed)

E. Grey

He poked at the crumpled papers with his forefinger. He picked up a couple with disdain. What a ridiculous fuss about nothing. It was not as if the telegrams were any longer sensitive. Did Grey really imagine that German agents were wandering the country lanes, on the off-chance they might find stray government documents?

He had long ago developed the vital political defence mechanism of not remembering those things which it was more convenient to forget. Now he told himself that none of this had anything to do with him. There could certainly be no proof that he was responsible. True, he had shown a telegram to Venetia on Saturday when they were driving down to Surrey and had then disposed it out of the window, but that wasn't in the box. Next to his name on the list of recipients he wrote 'Not guilty, H.H.A.'. He replaced Grey's memorandum in the dispatch box, locked it, took it through to Bongie's office and told him to send it on to the next addressee, Winston at the Admiralty.

He went back to the Cabinet Room and started his daily letter to Venetia. He must tell her all about it. He was sure she would find it amusing.

Venetia was still in bed on Wednesday morning when Edith brought up his letter, slotted into the toast rack on her breakfast tray.

It was the first time all summer that she had taken breakfast in her room. Normally, she was up and about much earlier. But her ten days away from Penrhos, which had included three separate house parties in three different parts of the country, had left her for once exhausted. After a first weekend in London, and a brief but joyful reunion with the Prime Minister, she had gone to Mells in Somerset, the country home of the Horners, to stay for a week with Edward, Raymond, Katharine and various other members of the Coterie. She had not enjoyed it as much as she had expected. How trivial they and their brittle cynicism now seemed in this transformed world! Edward was determined to enlist, for which Raymond mocked him: he had done a much more amusing thing and put his name down for something called the London Volunteer Defence Force, on the grounds that it was full of his friends, it didn't actually exist, and no member of it could possibly be killed before Goodwood 1915 at the earliest.

Afterwards, she had gone back to London and had driven with the Prime Minister down to the Jekylls' house party at Munstead, near Godalming, where they had been able to get away for a couple of long walks together, arm in arm through the Surrey pinewoods. She had left the following afternoon and travelled by car to Stanway House in Gloucestershire for another party, given by Lord and Lady Wemyss, whose daughter, Cynthia, was married to Beb Asquith. And finally, back to Anglesey. How many miles was that? It had to be a thousand. And how many meals, and games of charades and bridge and tennis, how many late nights, and how much talk about the war? It was a relief to be back in the silence of Penrhos.

She waited until Edith had gone before she opened the envelope.

My darling – of course there was no letter from you this morning: how could there be when you were in the motor all day? (Beb reported having seen you at Stanway). All the same its absence left a blank feeling, and I look forward eagerly to tomorrow.

Do you remember remonstrating with me for throwing out of the window that little rolled up ball of 'flimsy' as we drove thro' Roehampton lane on Sat? The only people – except E Grey – who get these secret flimsies are myself, Winston, Kitchener and Harcourt. It appears that the police have discovered fragments of them in St James' Park, in Oxfordshire near Goring, & one or two other places in the country. These they have laboriously collected and the pieces came round in a box this morning with a severe admonition from E Grey as to the dangers to wh. the Foreign Office cypher was exposed from such loose handling of secret matters! My conscience was quite clear as to St Jas's Park & Goring: so I simply wrote 'not guilty' – nor was our little ball among the pièces de conviction: but what damning evidence you might have given!

Her first reaction was a smile of amused relief. That could have been embarrassing. But then she read the paragraph again and her smile faded. Surely the involvement of the police was ominous. Obviously there had been some kind of official inquiry. Perhaps it was still going on. And what did he mean, his 'conscience was quite clear'? Who else did he imagine could have been the culprit? She had noticed this about him before. Sometimes he seemed to live in a fantasy world.

She climbed out of bed and went to the wardrobe, stood on tiptoe and reached behind the hat boxes for the Gladstone bag, now so heaped with letters it threatened to overflow: she had to lift it down carefully by both handles. She set it on the carpet and knelt beside it, searching through it until she found the telegram he had sent her from the ambassador to Russia. She sat back on her heels and gave a sigh of relief. At least it was still there. For the first time it struck her that having it in her possession was a criminal offence. What would happen if one of the servants found it and reported it to the police? She wasn't frightened she might be sent to prison – people like her were never sent to prison – but the scandal could be appalling for them both.

She folded up the flimsy and put it into her purse, then hoisted the bag back up onto the wardrobe shelf and rang the bell for her maid.

'I've had enough breakfast, thank you, Edith. Could you take it away, please, and lay out my pale blue dress? And could you see if the car is free for an hour this morning? I need to go into Holyhead.'

There was a hardware store in the middle of the town from which she bought a plain wooden box with a lock and two keys and half a dozen tins of paint and some paintbrushes. She had the chauffeur carry it all into the nursery and for the rest of the day, to the grateful relief of their mothers, she played a game with the children of decorating it. That morning, for the first time, the papers had reported that the British Expeditionary Force was moving into position. Eric was with it. Anthony, too, on the staff of the Commander-in-Chief, Sir John French. Bill's squadron was in action in the North Sea. It gave her sisters some respite not to have to worry about the children as well. By the end of the afternoon, the box was finished, a garishly coloured riot of flowers, animals, birds and butterflies.

'And now,' said Venetia, 'we must leave it to dry.'

Rosalind, Sylvia's eldest girl, who was seven, said, 'What are you going to do with it, Aunt Vinny?' Her face was covered in paint.

'I'm going to take it up to my room and keep my toys in it, of course.'

'Grown-ups don't have toys!'

'Most grown-ups don't, but I do.'

In Downing Street, the Prime Minister was in the Cabinet Room with Lord Kitchener, bent over a large-scale map of northern France and Belgium which the Field Marshal had brought over from the War Office. The Prime Minister had always enjoyed reading maps. They reminded him of Baedeker guides and family holidays abroad when he had always insisted on leading the way to the best galleries and the most interesting churches.

Kitchener said, 'The German thrust is developing exactly as I predicted. They're coming through Belgium in huge numbers, and plainly intend to break through into France over the frontier here' – he tapped the map – 'between Maubeuge and Lille, exactly where the BEF is concentrating.'

The Prime Minister found Kitchener's certainty unnerving. He did not debate, he issued edicts. Already, the War Office staff were complaining about him. One said that meetings with him were 'like hell with the lid off'. Still, he was determined to maintain his optimism. 'The French disagree, of course. They believe the main attack will be further south. Somewhere here.' He indicated vaguely.

'The intelligence reports tell us otherwise. Perhaps as many as three-quarters of a million men are pouring across the country. My fear is that they'll be upon us before we are even properly deployed.'

'Well, the French say the Belgians are putting up a strong resistance that is slowing the German advance.' *The French disagree . . . the French say* . . . He was conscious of parroting back what he had been told by the General Staff. 'And then there are the two great forts at Liège and Namur which stand in their way. Surely they will hold out for weeks?'

'They might. They might not.' Kitchener gave a mournful smile. 'We shall just have to *wait and see.*'

Deemer in the meantime had not been idle. He had, with Kell's permission, invented as a cover story for his investigation what he grandly called 'A Review of the Transport Security of Senior Ministers in Wartime', and had made a request, via Special Branch, to interview the Prime Minister's driver. He had reckoned it a long shot, but the private office at Number 10 had replied promptly the following day: the PM's chauffeur, Mr Horwood, would be available for interview on Thursday 20 August at 2 p.m.

'For God's sake, be careful,' warned Kell as he left Watergate House. 'Remember, it is the Prime Minister we're dealing with.'

He arrived with five minutes to spare. The Napier was one of three large cars drawn up outside Number 10. He didn't stop to inspect it but mastered his nerves, marched straight up to the big green front door, grasped the large brass knocker and brought it down hard. The door was opened at once by an elderly caretaker, who nodded when he said he had come to interview Mr Horwood, didn't ask to see any identification but took him straight across the large lobby and along a corridor towards the rear of the building, where he pointed him to a staircase that led into the depths.

The basement passage was crowded with uniformed servants. Luncheon was just being cleared. He was startled by the number of maids and footmen carrying dishes, by the noise and the heat and the low ceilings and the warren of tiny, dingy rooms. He found his way to the kitchen and asked a cook with a sweating red face, holding a tray of pastries, where he might find Horwood. She gestured irritably with her chin to a man in a dark suit sitting at the table, calmly reading a newspaper amid the chaos.

'Mr Horwood? I'm Detective Sergeant Deemer.' He showed his warrant card. 'Is there somewhere quiet we can talk?'

'I suppose so. If we must.'

The chauffeur reluctantly folded his paper and led him into the butler's pantry. The tiny space was almost entirely taken up by a rolltop desk piled with bills skewered on metal spikes, and two chairs. He closed the door.

'I hope this won't last long. I have to take the Prime Minister out at two-thirty.'

'I just have a few questions.'

'You'd best make a start then, hadn't you?'

Deemer always tried hard not to take an instant dislike to anyone – he considered it unprofessional – but it was difficult not to with Horwood. He was a ferrety middle-aged man with a centre-parting and a toothbrush moustache, and like many servants, in Deemer's experience, he assumed a manner appropriate to the rank of his employer. His answers were offhand: he had been driving the Prime Minister for seven years; no, they had rarely travelled with a detective, except at the height of the Suffragette nonsense a year or so ago ('But surely,' he said suspiciously, 'if you're with Special Branch, you should know that?'); most of the PM's journeys were around London, or to his country home near Abingdon, or to a golf course.

'Does he ever go for drives out into the countryside, purely for pleasure?'

'How do you mean?'

'Marlow, Henley, Goring – places like that?'

'Yes, but I don't see that's any of your business.'

'Does he take official papers with him, to work on in the car?'

'You'll need to ask him that question. I just sit at the front and drive. What exactly is the point of all this?'

Horwood's tone was increasingly hostile. Deemer decided he had gone as far as he could. He put away his notebook and asked if he might take a quick look at the car.

Once they were outside in Downing Street, the chauffeur became more friendly. His pride in the Napier was almost paternal, and she was indeed a beauty – even Deemer, who didn't drive and had no interest in cars, could see that – a gleaming anthracite-black body, set off by a silvery metal radiator grille and trim. Horwood lifted the bonnet and showed him the engine. She was fast, he said: a similar model had set a new British record at the Brooklands racetrack, maintaining an average speed of sixty-six miles per hour over twenty-four hours.

'Does the Prime Minister ever drive it himself?'

'Good Lord, no!' Horwood laughed at the very idea. 'You'd have to clear the streets!'

The spacious interior was cushioned, the roof high enough for a man to wear his top hat, the passengers separated from the driver by a thick glass screen with curtains – there was no rear-view mirror, Deemer noticed – so that instructions had to be passed from the Prime Minister to Horwood by means of a console that activated lights on the dashboard. There were blinds on all the windows. Not so much a car, he thought, as a private saloon on wheels.

'Does the Prime Minister usually take someone with him when he goes on a drive?'

Deemer noticed how Horwood's smile shrivelled instantly. 'I'm his chauffeur, Sergeant,' he said stiffly, 'and proud to be so. Whoever he takes along as a passenger has nothing to do with me. I wouldn't tell you their names even if I knew. And now, if you'll excuse me, I have to start the engine. The Prime Minister will be out in a minute.'

Deemer walked to the end of Downing Street. He paused at the corner with Whitehall and glanced back. Horwood was bent over the starting handle. The chauffeur had not just been defensive, he thought, he had been embarrassed. There was something about those drives that had made him uncomfortable. He heard the engine ignite, stutter into life and begin noisily ticking over. He wondered where the Prime Minister was going.

On impulse, he turned and stepped into the wide road and hailed a taxi coming up the slope from the direction of the Houses of Parliament. The driver lowered his window.

'Afternoon, sir. Where do you want to go?'

'I'm not sure yet. Do you mind waiting?'

'No, sir. It's your money.' The driver started the meter.

Deemer climbed into the back of the cab. A few minutes later came the sound of a powerful engine and the Napier passed directly in front of them. He had a clear view of the Prime Minister in the back seat, his chin in his hand, gazing out of the window, seemingly lost in thought. Horwood waited for a bus to pass, then pulled out and swung left towards Trafalgar Square.

'Would you mind following that car?'

The taxi driver eyed him in the mirror – eyebrows raised, mouth turned down, bemused – then let out the handbrake. They tucked in behind the Napier. In Trafalgar Square it sailed in a wide arc around Nelson's Column, then headed up Regent Street. Five minutes later, it drew to a halt in Oxford Street outside a shop with an imposing sign in black and gold: 'J. & E. Bumpus Ltd., Booksellers to H.M. The King'.

'Pull over here,' said Deemer.

They passed the Napier and parked a little further up the street. Through the rear window, he saw Horwood opening the car door and the Prime Minister clambering out and crossing the pavement, where he stood wearing his top hat, his hands clasped behind his back, inspecting the books on display in the windows. Presently, he went inside. Deemer paid the taxi fare and walked towards the Napier. He pulled his bowler down and kept his face averted in case Horwood, who was sitting in the front seat, recognised him, but the chauffeur had brought his newspaper and didn't look up.

Bumpus was a big bookshop – a sign by the till boasted it was the largest in London – its stock arranged over five storeys, with second-hand volumes in the basement, rare and collectible on the ground and first floors, and general books above. It was too warm a day for book-buying and the shop was mostly empty, dust drifting in the shafts of sunlight, a drowsy aroma of old paper. The Prime Minister was standing in front of one of the high stacks on the ground floor, reaching up to replace one volume and taking down another. Deemer pulled out the nearest book and pretended an interest in eighteenth-century French literature, occasionally looking up from the pages to watch the Prime Minister. For the leader of a country embroiled in a vast war, he appeared remarkably unhurried. Deemer wondered if he was waiting to meet someone, but it seemed not: he was simply absorbed in his reading.

After about a quarter of an hour, he moved away, carrying a small volume, but instead of taking it to the counter, he went upstairs with it. Deemer waited for a few minutes before following him up the wooden staircase, and found him settled in an armchair, with a book in his lap and two more on a small table beside him. His head kept nodding forwards. He dozed for a while, came awake with a start, raised his head and looked around, as if he was worried someone might have seen him. He hauled himself upright, picked up the other two books and walked past Deemer, who descended a few steps and watched him from the turn of the stairs as he carried his small pile to the till. He had a brief conversation with the young sales assistant, opening one of the books and pointing out a page. After a further exchange, he wrote something in a ledger, produced his wallet, counted out a sizeable amount of paper money and left the shop. The assistant put the books under the counter. Through the glass door, Deemer watched the Prime Minister climb into the back of the Napier and the car pull away.

He went over to the assistant and showed his warrant card. 'The gentleman who just left, do you have any idea who he is?'

'No, I don't know his name.' He was a young man, nervous to find himself in the presence of the police, anxious to be helpful.

'Does he come in often?'

'Quite often. He's very knowledgeable. A true bibliophile. Has he done something wrong? He seems so respectable!'

'May I ask what he bought?'

The assistant bent down and produced four books, and set them in a row on the counter, spines out, all finely bound in red Morocco.

'Sheridan's *The Critic*, published 1775; and a three-volume edition of *Oliver Twist*, 1838. Both first editions.'

'They look expensive.'

'They are.' The young man suddenly turned pale. 'Oh dear, is he a criminal? Has he paid with forged notes?'

'No, nothing like that. Why didn't he take them with him?'

'We offer a delivery service. They're a birthday present. He asked us to dispatch them on his behalf.'

'Who are they going to?'

The assistant hesitated.

'I can speak to your manager if you prefer.'

'He's not here at the moment.'

'Well then . . .' Deemer smiled.

The bookseller opened a ledger and turned it round so that he could read the entry, written in the Prime Minister's own hand: 'The Honourable Venetia Stanley, Penrhos House, Holyhead, Anglesey'.

When he returned to Downing Street, the Prime Minister wrote to Venetia. His mind was full of images of her opening his present. He longed to be able to watch her.

One ought not to complain, in times like these, that life is
imperfectly arranged. Sometimes, at odd moments, I dream
dreams & draw pictures, & fancy imaginary conditions,
which, if they cd. only be realised, would make everything
so much easier, remove grim barriers of time and space,

annihilate distance . . . I wish with all my heart – every day,
all day, & most of the night – that Penrhos was 200 miles
nearer London . . . I wd. give more than I can put down on
paper to be able to – some sentences are best left unfinished.

★

Deemer met Kell that evening, at the chief's request, not at Watergate House but at Kell's club in Pall Mall. They sank into a pair of
deep chintz armchairs in a corner by the window. Kell lit his pipe,
ordered a whisky and soda, and asked Deemer what he wanted.
Deemer asked for the same. He waited until the waiter was out
of earshot before he opened his notebook and relayed the gist of
his interview in Downing Street.

'Horwood essentially confirmed that he's driven the Prime Minister out to all these places where the telegrams were discovered,
and when I asked whether anyone ever accompanied him, he
became noticeably shifty and refused to answer. I had the definite
impression he knew more than he was letting on. So I decided to
follow him.'

'You followed Horwood?'

'No, I followed the Prime Minister.'

Kell removed his pipe. His mouth hung open. 'You tailed the
Prime Minister? Where to?'

Deemer described his visit to the bookshop.

Kell said, 'And you think the Prime Minister's companion on
these drives – to whom he showed the telegrams – could be Venetia Stanley?'

'I think it's highly probable. She fits the description of a possibly
younger woman seen in the back of the car in Roehampton on
Saturday. And there's something else.'

'Go on.'

'As it happens, I interviewed her earlier in the summer in connection with the riverboat drownings – you remember the Prime Minister's son and daughter-in-law were on board?'

'She's part of *that* set? What do they call themselves? "The Coterie"?'

'Yes. In fairness to her, she didn't board the boat in the end – she changed her mind for some reason. But I saw her again a couple of weeks later when I was on protection duty at the big garden party in Downing Street. She was talking to the Prime Minister, and I sensed there was some kind of relationship between them.' He shrugged. 'Well, there must be, if he's taking an hour off in the afternoon to buy her an expensive birthday present.'

They were silent while the waiter brought them their drinks. After he had gone, Kell said, 'I must say, this whole business is really starting to stink to high heaven. What do we know about this woman? Is she married? How old is she?'

'I'm fairly sure she isn't married, sir. I think she still lives with her parents. I'd say she's mid to late twenties. Her father's Lord Sheffield. They have a big house near Portland Place, a family seat in Cheshire, and this other estate in Wales.'

'She's in her twenties, the Prime Minister's in his sixties – good God, she's young enough to be his daughter!' He sat back in his chair and sucked noisily on his pipe. For a few moments his face almost disappeared in a cloud of smoke. 'He really must be mad. Apart from every other consideration, he's leaving himself wide open to blackmail. Of course, as you probably know, there's been gossip about him for years – his drinking, his liking for the company of young women.'

'I didn't know that, sir.'

'Oh, yes. These things never get into the press, but they don't go unnoticed. He's only managed to stay in power thanks to the Irish and the socialists. He's devilishly clever at political juggling. A month ago, it looked as though he and the government were finished. The only thing that saved him was the war.'

He took a sip of whisky. Deemer did the same. During the lull in the conversation, he glanced around the room. Gentlemen in their armchairs reading the evening papers. A couple of officers in uniform talking at the bar.

Kell said, 'I heard back from Tyrrell this afternoon. The Foreign Office have concluded their investigation. All five ministers have denied responsibility, and as far as the FO are concerned, that's it. Case closed. Can't be taken any further. But frankly, Deemer, I'm not inclined to leave it there. What's the point of a security service if it doesn't investigate what could be the biggest breach of security in the country? At the very least, we need to discover more about Miss Stanley. For all we know, she could be a German sympathiser. But it needs to be kept very quiet. What do you say to going up to Holyhead for a few days and seeing what you can find out?'

'I think it's certainly worth a try, sir. I could just about make the evening train. I'd be there first thing in the morning.'

'You're keen! I like that.' Kell consulted his watch. 'No, it's too late now. Go up in the morning. You'd better not come back to the office. I'll tell Captain Holt-Wilson you're doing a job for me.' He took out his wallet and extracted three five-pound notes. 'This should cover your expenses.' He held out the money, but when Deemer reached for it, he briefly pulled it away. 'I'll want receipts, mark you.'

'Of course, sir.'

He disliked it when people did that. It reminded him of the way adults made fun of children.

He folded the money carefully and inserted it into his notebook.

When he arrived home that evening, he found a letter from his brother. It was written on a small official form. There was no date and no address.

Hello, old man, just a line to say I've made it to France. I can't tell you where, but I guess you'll read about it soon enough. The lads and me are all in good spirits, so not to worry, and I'll see you soon. Look after yourself. Yours ever, Fred. PS Here's something to help you remember my ugly mug.

Enclosed was a sepia-tinted studio photograph of Fred in uniform standing against a painted wall hanging of Doric pillars entwined with ivy, his hand resting on the back of a plain wooden chair.

He studied it for a while. Fred looked stiff and awkward in front of the camera, not really like himself at all. He propped the picture on the mantelpiece and went out through the kitchen into the garden. The summer was coming to an end. The sun had already gone down behind the houses backing on to his. Beyond the serrated line of roofs, the sky glowed crimson and purple, as if the city was on fire. He watered his flowers and tried to imagine Fred bedding down for the night in France. Would he be under canvas, or billeted in some farmhouse, or in the corner of a field? He couldn't imagine it – his little brother about to fight the Germans – the whole thing was unreal.

He poured some milk into a saucer for the cat and went over the road to the pub. Customers were already being turned out onto the pavement, and he realised he had forgotten that the Defence of the Realm Act now required all pubs to close at nine-thirty. There was nothing for it but to go to bed. But his worries about Fred, and the prospect of his mission to Holyhead, and his memory of the Prime Minister and Venetia Stanley together in the garden of Number 10 chased one another around in his mind, and it was several hours before he fell asleep.

CHAPTER FOURTEEN

Penrhos House,
Holyhead
Fri. 21 Aug. 1914
My darling, your letter has just arrived. Isn't it awful that
we won't be together on my birthday? Your presence is the
only gift I want. I treasure your beautiful words about
removing the grim barriers of time & space, & annihilating
distance. Do you know Shakespeare's 44th Sonnet?

> If the dull substance of my flesh were thought,
> Injurious distance should not stop my way;
> For then despite of space I would be brought,
> From limits far remote where thou dost stay.
> No matter then although my foot did stand
> Upon the farthest earth removed from thee;
> For nimble thought can jump both sea and land
> As soon as think the place where he would be.
> But ah! thought kills me that I am not thought,
> To leap large lengths of miles when thou art gone,

But that so much of earth and water wrought
I must attend time's leisure with my moan,
Receiving nought by elements so slow
But heavy tears, badges of either's woe.

That sums up how I feel, my dearest, & better of course
than I could ever hope to do.

The only direct train to Holyhead on Friday morning left Euston
station at eight-thirty, and to judge by the crowd at the platform
entrance, half London was determined to be on it. As soon as the
barriers opened, Deemer joined the charge, running along the
side of the carriages until he reached an empty third-class compartment. He stowed his case in the luggage rack and took a
corner seat beside the window moments before three generations
of a noisy Irish family piled in after him, occupying all the remain-
ing places, the adults balancing toddlers and a baby on their laps.
From their conversation he gathered they were on their way to
catch the Dublin ferry, which meant they would be with him for
the entire six-hour journey.

The train pulled out on time, moving slowly past the smoke-
blackened houses and factories of north London. It was hard for
him even to open his copy of *The Times*, let alone concentrate on
it, amid all the chatter and the jolting of the train, but what he
could make out was not reassuring. A map of Belgium showed
the front marked by a thick dotted line, and although there was a
lot of praise for the gallant resistance of the Belgian Army, it was
clear that they were retreating. The Germans had occupied Brussels, and only the forts at Liège and Namur stood between them
and north-east France.

He gave up trying to read. He offered his paper to the Irish grandfather and for the next couple of hours stared out of the window at the towns and villages and the ugly sprawl of the industrial West Midlands. He knew he ought to have a plan ready to put into action when he got to Holyhead, some cover story to explain his interest in Venetia Stanley, but he found it hard to think of one. By the time they reached Crewe at eleven-thirty, he wished he had never started.

But gradually his mood began to lift. The train pushed on into Wales, the views turned from dreary fields to distant mountains and lush green hills, and by early afternoon the track was running alongside the seashore, close enough to see the waves breaking, past empty dunes and crowded beaches, piers and bathing machines and beach huts, and little brightly coloured pedal boats. They stopped at Rhyl and Colwyn Bay; people poured off the train. How many years was it since he had seen the sea – a real blue sea, dazzling in the sunshine? He could hardly remember it.

They crossed the long bridge over the Menai Strait into Anglesey and not long after that the causeway that linked Wales to Holy Island. He saw great flocks of birds on the mudflats, and thick woodland. Five minutes later, they pulled into Holyhead. He helped the family lift down their luggage and carried one of their suitcases along the teeming platform towards the ferry terminal. He shook hands with them all, including the children, wished them bon voyage, then made his way out of the station and into a little town square beside a clock tower – a dusty London policeman, incongruous in his dark suit and bowler hat, accompanied by the cries of seagulls and a fresh sea breeze that seemed to carry with it the promise of adventure.

The town rose steeply up the hillside, looking out north-eastwards towards the railway station and the harbour. A huge modern hotel stood midway between the two, but he guessed it would be filled with travellers on their way to or from Dublin. He needed a different sort of place.

He walked around for half an hour, noting a civic building named Stanley House, a pub called the Stanley Arms, a Stanley Street, the Stanley Sailors' Hospital, a row of Stanley almshouses. Only God was more all-present than Venetia Stanley's family, in the multitude of chapels and churches jammed into the slopes, their crowded graveyards filled with memorials to men lost at sea. The houses were mostly whitewashed, the streets cobbled. In the northern part of the town, he found a road of detached villas, built in the 1880s, most of them guesthouses, all advertising vacancies. He chose one at random, named Bay View. It had a small garden at the front enclosed by a brick wall, a porch with a wrought-iron balcony above it, and lace curtains at all the windows. Mr Griffiths, the portly landlord, declared he would be happy to offer him bed, breakfast and an evening meal for fifteen shillings a day, breakfast at seven-thirty, supper at six-thirty. He paid thirty shillings in advance and carried his suitcase upstairs.

His room was at the top of the house, tucked under the eaves, with a window that did indeed offer a view of the bay, although the glass was streaked with salt and the panorama was accordingly misty. He laid his suitcase on the single bed, opened it, and changed into an old pair of trousers, an ancient tweed jacket with patched elbows, and a flat cap. He knotted a large red handkerchief around his neck, tucked it into his collar, and inspected the results in the mirror on the dressing table. He would pass, he thought – just about – as a schoolteacher or a solicitor's clerk, up from London for a few days' holiday.

He walked back into the centre of town to a bicycle shop, handed over a £5 deposit, and hired a bicycle for five shillings a day; the owner insisted he take a padlock and chain to prevent it being stolen. In the marine chandler's next door, amid the coils of rope and brass winches and cleats, he found a small telescope and a knapsack, and from the bookshop a pocket guide to birds and a local map. For each purchase he asked for a receipt: he was already running through Kell's money at an alarming rate. He wheeled the bicycle up the hill, rounded a corner, and saw a queue of young men outside a doorway. When he came closer, he saw that an insurance office had been converted into an army recruiting centre. A corporal stood on the pavement and called after him as he went past, 'What about you, mate? Are you going to fight for King and Country?'

He put his head down and walked on, ignoring the jeers behind him.

In his room, he spread out the map of Holy Island on the dressing table. Penrhos House was only about a mile and a half east of the town, but it might as well have been on the moon as far as his chances of getting inside it were concerned. He lay on his bed and considered the problem.

At half-past six, he went down to supper in the small dining room. The other guests were already seated: two couples, one young – honeymooners, holding hands across the table – and another in their fifties, who said they came every year on a walking holiday. After an initial polite 'Good evening' and a brief exchange of explanations of why they were there – Deemer said he had come for the birdwatching and hoped none of the others was an ornithologist – general conversation ceased, and the couples talked quietly to one another. He read his guide to birdwatching without much interest: sparrows and blackbirds were all he had ever noticed. Dinner was grapefruit segments followed by mutton stew and steamed ginger pudding, cooked by Mrs Griffiths and served by her husband. At the end, when a maid came in to clear the dishes, he took the opportunity to escape.

It was a warm evening, glassy-aired, the sun still up, the road quiet. He walked into the centre of town. The first pub he came to was small, smoke-filled, noisy. When he entered, he could hear voices talking in English, but he was conscious of people turning to stare at him, and by the time he reached the bar, the customers had all switched to speaking Welsh. He bought half a pint of local beer, drank it standing alone and ignored and left at once.

The next pub was larger and less crowded. This time he bought a pint and sat at a small table close to the bar. He took out his bird guide and pretended to read it, all the while looking around and trying to catch someone's eye. Eventually, an elderly man in a fisherman's smock, drinking on his own, started to take an interest in him. He bent his head to look at the book, and Deemer held up the cover for him to inspect.

'Ah,' he said, 'so you're here for the birds?'

'I'm only a beginner. I'm trying to work out the best place to go.'

'Well, if it's seabirds you're after, you've come to the right spot.'

'Will you join me?' Deemer pulled out the chair next to him. 'Can I buy you a drink?'

Five minutes later, he had managed to steer the conversation round to Penrhos.

'Now that's the best place on the island,' said the fisherman. 'You've got your oystercatchers and your curlews. But you should also be able to see cormorants, grey plovers, egrets. Brent geese, if you're lucky.'

'Is it easy to get to the sea?'

'Just go out to the causeway. There's a little road runs along the shore.'

'What about the woodland?'

'Now that's private, belongs to the big house. There are tracks up from the beach you can follow, but mind you don't get caught. That's Lord Sheffield's place, and they like their privacy. They have all sorts of grand folk staying.'

'What kind of grand folk?'

The old man dropped his voice and leaned in close. 'The Prime Minister, for one. They say he goes to stay quite regular.'

'Now then, Dafydd,' said a younger man at the bar, 'what're you gossiping about?'

'I'm just telling my friend here how the Prime Minister goes to stay at Penrhos House.'

'You don't want to go talking to strangers about that kind of thing. Don't you know there's a war on? He could be a German spy.'

At the word spy, several heads turned.

'I'm not a *German* spy,' said Deemer. 'I'm an *English* spy.'

The young man cocked his head and stared at him. 'That's even worse,' he said.

Deemer joined in the general laughter and offered to buy him a drink as well. After that, the rest of the evening passed off merrily. He put his book in his pocket and was careful to keep off the subject of Penrhos House and the Stanleys. They talked about the town and fishing and the war, and the number of young men who had already volunteered to fight.

'I think they must be bloody mad, the lot of them,' said the young man, whose name was Gethin, and who worked for the ferry company. 'They've no idea what they're letting themselves in for.'

That provoked a general argument about the war. Dafydd was keen on teaching the Kaiser a lesson ('he's an arrogant bugger'), but Gethin declared himself a socialist and said that wars only occurred because of imperialism, which was a product of capitalism. 'Or is it the other way round?' He seemed genuinely puzzled; he was quite drunk.

At nine-thirty, the landlord threw them out.

They shook hands in the street, clapped one another on the shoulder, and went their different ways, the two Welshmen down towards the harbour and Deemer up through the town. Unlike his new friends, he was sober. There was no moon, the gas lights were sparse, the streets silent apart from the occasional dog barking in the distance. Twice he thought he heard footsteps behind him, but when he turned it was too dark to make anything out. Still, he had the uneasy, prickling sensation of being watched, and it was a relief when he recognised the street of Victorian villas. There was a light on downstairs in the Bay View guest house. He had to knock and wait for Mrs Griffiths to let him in. She was a narrow, pinched-faced woman – unlike her husband, who was as round as a barrel – and she made it clear by her crimped lips and a slight toss of her head that she didn't think much of guests who came back late and smelling of beer.

He wished her good night and quietly mounted the stairs to his room, where – tired from his journey, and filled with strong Welsh beer and fresh sea air – he lay stretched out fully clothed on his bed and for once fell immediately asleep.

CHAPTER FIFTEEN

HE LEFT BAY View shortly after breakfast on Saturday morning, wheeling his bicycle along the side passage from the back garden where Mr Griffiths had allowed him to keep it overnight and out onto the road. It was a long time since he had ridden a bike. He swung his leg over the crossbar, took a deep breath and pushed himself off. The front wheel wobbled beneath his hands and didn't stabilise till he picked up speed, after which he descended alarmingly quickly through the town, his fingers clenched tightly on the brakes, his feet skittering over the cobbles at the corners to slow himself down until he reached the level ground in front of the railway station.

He rode past a row of tiny whitewashed terraced cottages, along what rather prematurely styled itself the London Road, and out into the open country. The land was flat and scrubby, the sea close but invisible somewhere to his left. A strong breeze blew against his face and made the going hard. After about five minutes, woodland began to rise on either side, and not long after that he noticed a pair of large brick gateposts surmounted by stone griffins, well set back and so hidden by the hedgerow he almost missed them. He braked hard and skidded to a halt in the gravel.

He glanced up and down the London Road. The only traffic was a horse and cart. He lifted his front wheel, planted it firmly in the centre of the drive and set off.

He couldn't see the house at first, but then the drive began to rise slightly and curve, and it came into view dramatically about a quarter of a mile across the park – a grand stately home, a palace almost, with a turreted central section and wings on either side. He dismounted and took his telescope from his knapsack. A red Post Office van was parked in front of the door. As he watched, it started to move. He quickly put away his telescope, remounted and pedalled back to the gates, and was safely off the Stanleys' property by the time it reached the road and turned towards the town.

The parcels were carried by a footman into the drawing room, where Venetia was seated on the long sofa, surrounded by her sisters, parents and nieces. It had been an annual family tradition at Penrhos ever since she was sixteen: to watch her open her presents.

Margaret had given her a dressing-table set decorated with mother-of-pearl, Sylvia a pink silk camisole from Somatoff's in Oxford Street, and Blanche – dear Blanche! – had knitted her a scarf. The little girls had drawn her pictures and picked her bunches of flowers. Her parents produced a set of luggage, monogrammed B.V.S. for her full name, Beatrice Venetia Stanley, doubtless bought in anticipation of her now-cancelled expedition to India and Australia; and a very welcome cheque. After they had all been opened and cooed over, she moved on to the morning's post: a pair of evening gloves from Winston and Clemmie, a book of love poetry inscribed by Maurice Baring (from him but not by him, she was relieved to see), and a hideous and doubtless expensive glass ornament from Edwin Montagu.

She read the Prime Minister's letter before she turned to his present.

It will be 27 years tomorrow since you opened your eyes on this sinful world, and it is not yet quite 3 since I made my great discovery of the <u>real</u> you. I sometimes wonder, looking back, whether you would rather that I had <u>not</u> made it, and that things had continued between us as they were in the early days . . .

She skimmed through the rest of the letter and put it back in its envelope. The family watched her but said nothing. Since their scene over the breakfast table, they had managed to stifle their curiosity, but even so Sylvia couldn't resist asking, 'I wonder what he's sent you.'

She knew from her quick reading of his letter that the contents were eminently respectable (*I hope, darling, you will like them: no books since the world began, or at any rate since people took to printing, ever took with them a deeper & truer message of love*).

'Let's see, shall we?'

She tore away the thick brown wrapping paper, and although the volumes were hardly romantic, they touched her. Despite all his cares and responsibilities, he had taken the trouble to go out and choose them himself. Dear, darling Prime!

Sylvia said, '*Oliver Twist*? Isn't that rather like a school prize?'

Lady Sheffield said, 'Well, I think it's very thoughtful of him.' She went over to the French windows and scanned the sky. 'You know, the sun is definitely breaking through. We'll be able to have our picnic after all.'

There was always a picnic on Venetia's birthday at Penrhos, weather permitting. That was another part of the family tradition.

Deemer had cycled along the edge of the estate to the start of the causeway that linked Holy Island with Anglesey – the 'Stanley Embankment', according to his map. What a bleak landscape it was, he thought, like the first day of Creation – a great, grey, formless expanse of mud and water, stretching as far as the eye could see, covered in flocks of seabirds searching for food across the newly uncovered shore.

He rode slowly along the coastal track, between low dry-stone walls and yellow gorse, for about half a mile until his way was blocked by a padlocked gate with a sign: 'THE STANLEY ESTATE. PRIVATE. KEEP OUT.' He dismounted, lifted his bicycle over the wall and jumped down after it. He dragged a couple of dead branches over it until it was fairly well hidden, then began to make his way into the woods.

He could not see the big house at first, but he soon began to sense its presence. There was a bench beside a path, and a stone obelisk with an inscription that had been weathered away by the years. A little bridge crossed one of the streams. He followed the path from the bridge and glimpsed through the undergrowth a high stone wall covered in ivy with a small Gothic oak door set into it. The wall extended a good fifty yards in either direction, each side ending in a crenellated round tower, like a fortress in a storybook. He turned the iron ring on the door, expecting it would be locked, but it opened easily. He stood, listening. All he could hear were the hollow cries of the wood pigeons and the rat-a-tat of a pair of woodpeckers drilling in the distance. He stepped into the doorway. The wall was four feet thick. On the other side were more trees. He walked on, the woodland thinned, and there was the house again, a few hundred yards away, across a sweep of lawn dotted with ancient beeches and cedars. Not a soul to be seen. He took out his telescope and scanned slowly from left to right – three storeys, immense windows, towering chimneys, a wide terrace set with deckchairs and tables, steps down to the lawn. No sign of movement except for a peacock strutting across the lawn.

He lowered the telescope. Now he had come this far, he wondered what else he should do. What could he report to Kell, except that Miss Stanley lived in the most extraordinarily grand style? Caution told him he ought to leave before he was discovered. But he was reluctant to go. It seemed such a waste of all his efforts. He sat down with his back against a tree, drew up his knees and tried to think.

By now it was late morning. The breeze had dropped; the sun was high and hot. He took off his cap and wiped his face. Insects buzzed around him. He felt ants biting his ankles. He stood again to brush them away and noticed movement on the terrace. Through the telescope he saw a procession of uniformed servants emerging from the house, crossing the terrace and coming down the steps onto the lawn straight towards him – half a dozen, more like a dozen, carrying wicker hampers, blankets, folding chairs and tables. He withdrew into the trees and waited for them to file past. One of the men was complaining – he couldn't hear the words, but he could tell by his tone he was grumbling – and a woman told him that if he didn't like it, he should go and join the army, to which the man replied that he would be doing exactly that on Monday. They disappeared in the direction of the sea.

He trained his telescope back on the house. It was another

half-hour before the Stanley family came out, dressed as if for the races. He counted five ladies in long dresses and elaborate wide-brimmed hats and carrying parasols, one older man in a grey frock coat and top hat, two little girls, and two nannies in dark uniforms, one with a pram and the other a pushchair, and a dog trotting in front of them. He didn't like the look of the dog and retreated further into the trees, but not so far that he didn't recognise Venetia Stanley as she went by, holding hands with one of the girls. After they had gone, he looked back at the house. It must be almost empty. Did he dare risk pushing his luck and going inside? He might find something. But if he was caught and his identity discovered, it would be the end of him. He decided against it.

He left it a couple of minutes before he walked back to the Gothic door, along the path, over the stream and down to the edge of the treeline. For the last few yards, he dropped to his knees and crawled on his stomach through the undergrowth to a spot where he could survey the beach through his spyglass. An elaborate picnic had been set up – trestle tables pushed together and covered with a long white linen tablecloth set with napkins, silver cutlery and crystal glasses; the Stanley family seated in eight chairs around it, Venetia at the head; servants hovering, pouring drinks and serving food; the tableau framed by the distant glittering sea. So much for the war! he thought. He watched for a while, then wriggled backwards and retraced his steps through the woods, pulled away the branches, mounted his bike and began pedalling back towards the main road, listening to the cries of the curlews, feeling dwarfed and suddenly lonely in that desolate primordial landscape.

The Prime Minister left Downing Street late in the afternoon, to drive the sixty miles to Lympne Castle in Kent, for a family gathering of his in-laws, the Tennants. Violet and Oc went with him, as well as the inevitable Bongie; Margot was in Scotland, staying with her sister.

He was unusually quiet, sitting in his usual place in the right-hand corner of the back seat, his elbow pressed against the window, his chin resting on the heel of his hand, staring blankly at the London streets. Kitchener had just told him the British Army was likely to be in action against the Germans before the end of the day. He had almost decided not to leave. But what was the point of waiting around in London for news? What could he do? He was both powerful and powerless, responsible for what was happening but ignorant of what was taking place – the very devil of a position in which to find oneself.

Gradually the others became aware of his silence.

'You know what would cheer you up, Prime?' said Oc. 'A round of golf. Signal Horwood to stop the car.'

They drew to a halt somewhere in the suburbs of south London, Oc got out and spoke to Horwood, and a couple of hours later, when they were almost at the coast, the car diverted to the course at Littlestone.

The Prime Minister played badly, but what did it matter? The sky over Romney Marsh was vast, the course dramatically flat and bounded by the sea. For a blessed hour he forgot about the war. They managed to play seven holes before the light faded, the sun sinking behind a mass of purple cloud, radiating broad golden shafts across the marshland in a way that reminded him of twilight in a cathedral. Not for the first time, he thanked God for his uncomplicated third son, for whom no problem was so great that it couldn't temporarily be eased by a spot of physical exercise or a game of cards.

As they walked back to the car, he asked Oc what he was planning to do.

'I've applied to join the navy.'

'Have you really? I never had you down as a sailor.'

'Oh, I shan't go to sea. Winston's cooking up a scheme to have a naval division that will fight on land.'

He had to laugh. 'Winston with his own private army! What can possibly go wrong?'

Lympne Castle was medieval, six hundred years old. At dinner, he sat happily between his two pretty nieces, Dinah and Kakoo, both unmarried in their twenties, and talked across the table to Margot's brother, Frank, the castle's owner. Their father had been the richest man in Scotland. When he died, he had left a fortune of more than £3 million, but while the two older brothers had inherited an income of £40,000 a year, the girls had got nothing. Now Frank announced he was planning to sell the castle or let the government have it and turn it into a hospital for wounded soldiers. That reminded him of the war, and he asked Bongie to telephone London to see if there was any news, but he returned to say there was nothing.

The following morning, as he was lying in bed, Bongie brought in the Sunday post: a brief letter from Venetia, thanking him for her presents – *you are a darling, I shall treasure them* – and another from Kitchener to say that the Fourth Division was just crossing to France and Sir John French was satisfied with his position. He didn't report any fighting.

As it happened, at that moment, through his bedroom window, he could see a squadron of eight battleships and two cruisers moving slowly up the Channel like great grey phantoms. They must be carrying the new division – twenty thousand men – just embarked from Southampton and now steaming towards the front. The sight stirred him. He had already written to Venetia twice on Saturday. Now he took up his pen again:

Your darling little letter came just as I awoke: it was most considerate of you to write so early. I wrote to Kitchener that I wished to be kept informed well in advance of any movements to the front, and you may like to see his answer.

He described the scene from his window, sealed the two letters in the envelope and took it downstairs for Bongie to post. He wanted to share everything with her.

He stayed at the castle all day, strolling through the grounds, playing golf and bridge. It wasn't until after dinner that he left with Oc and Bongie. By then a thick sea fog had rolled across Romney Marsh.

The Napier crawled along the narrow lanes. Its headlights bounced off a sickly yellowish wall. He tried to make a joke of it – 'The fog of war!' – but it was unnerving. He cursed himself for not setting off earlier. Twice they were flagged down by Kent police on the lookout for spies and saboteurs, and he had to sit and listen as Horwood explained that he was taking the Prime Minister back to London. Torches shone in his face as he was examined. He stared stonily ahead. The fog didn't lift until Maidstone, and it was half-past one by the time they reached Number 10, where Margot was waiting up for them. He was in no mood to listen to her stories of hunting in Scotland and went straight up to bed.

He was woken just after seven, in the middle of a dream, by George, holding out his dressing gown and telling him that Lord Kitchener was downstairs, asking to see him urgently. He slipped on the dressing gown, and a pair of slippers, and tied the cord as he hurried across the landing.

He found the Field Marshal in the Cabinet Room, wearing a business suit and a bowler hat, which he removed as soon as the Prime Minister walked in. In the same hand he held a slip of paper which he passed over without uttering a word. It was a decrypted telegram, handwritten by the cipher clerk, with SECRET stamped in red in the top right corner.

From Sir John French
To Lord Kitchener
August 24th

My troops have been engaged all day with the enemy on a line roughly east and west through Mons. The attack was renewed after dark but we held our ground tenaciously. I have just received a message from General commanding 5th French Army that his troops have been driven back, that NAMUR has fallen, and that he is taking up a line from MAUBEUGE to ROCROY. I have therefore ordered a retirement to the line VALENCIENNES to LONGUEVILLE-MAUBEUGE which is being carried out now. It will prove a difficult operation if the enemy remain in contact. I think that immediate attention should be directed to defence HAVRE. Will keep you fully informed.

He sat down heavily. 'Namur has fallen?'
Kitchener said, 'So much for holding out for weeks or months.'
He read the telegram again. 'And now French is worrying about defending Le Havre?' He could not believe it. 'That's a hundred and fifty miles to his rear!'
'He fears the Germans are planning to sweep around his left flank and take Dunkirk and Calais. He'll have to look sharp to avoid the entire army being trapped. I did warn this would happen.'

Kitchener turned on his heel. For a moment, the Prime Minister thought he was about to walk out. Instead, he marched to the end of the room and gazed out of the window. The Prime Minister suddenly wished he was properly dressed. He pulled his dressing gown around himself more tightly. By the time Kitchener returned, his granite mask was back in place. 'Evacuation from France would be a serious reverse, no question of it. But one must expect these shocks in war. By the spring we'll have raised a whole new army of six or seven hundred thousand.'

By the spring!

The Prime Minister said, 'I suppose the question is: can the French hold out till then?'

The Field Marshal shrugged. 'Well, if they can't . . .'

He left the sentence hanging.

CHAPTER SIXTEEN

DEEMER WAS READING that morning's *Times* over breakfast. The tone of the articles was still relentlessly optimistic (*Namur is perfectly capable of taking care of itself for the next three months*), but the map told a different story. The black lines showing the German advance appeared ever more ominous. A month ago, he would have taken what the government said on trust, but now he suspected that the situation was more perilous than the public was being told.

He glanced around his fellow diners – the older couple, dressed for a day's walking; the smiling honeymooners; and a new guest, a blonde man in his forties sitting at a table in the corner, who had arrived on Sunday afternoon and kept himself to himself. He put his paper aside and finished his bacon and eggs.

He had, at last, a plan. It was not exactly foolproof – it was, to be frank, a long shot – but it was something.

It had come out of a conversation he'd had with his new best friends, Dafydd and Gethin, over warm beer in the pub on Saturday night, when he had described his visit to watch the seabirds on the bay and the talk had turned quite naturally to the Stanleys of Penrhos House. He casually mentioned that he had seen their elaborate picnic in the distance.

'This war will be the end of them and their way of life,' said Gethin, 'you mark my words.' The prospect clearly gave him considerable satisfaction.

'So how do you come up with that then, Karl Marx?' demanded Dafydd.

'You can laugh all you like, but I'm telling you, this is the inevitable crisis of capitalism. The whole system that supports them and their class is going to break down.'

Dafydd snorted into his pint.

'No, no, listen to what I'm saying. The system depends on the exploitation of cheap labour, and from now on that's not going to be possible. Men can earn more going off to fight than they can in their regular jobs, and when they come back, they're not going to put up with the Stanleys and their slave wages.'

'It'll never happen!'

'Look around you, man! It's happening already! I hear they've lost half their servants, and the war's only been going three weeks. There were three of their gardeners joined up just on Friday. Then there's taxation. Someone's got to pay for this bloody war, and who's got all the money? What do you say, Paul?'

'Oh, I don't know about all that, I'll leave the politics to you.'

But in his mind, he had already seen an opportunity.

He drained his tea and left the dining room to fetch his bicycle. Twenty minutes later, he was cycling through the gates of the Stanley estate, along the snaking drive, all the way up to the great house. He dismounted at the front porch and wheeled his bicycle past one of the turrets, along the front of the mansion to the end of the north-west wing. In the courtyard, a chauffeur was cleaning one of the family's cars and directed him to the walled garden where he might find the head gardener, whose name, he said, was Mr Geddings.

He followed a path past a series of large greenhouses, under a rose arch that must have been a good twenty yards long, strewn with dead petals in need of sweeping up, to a wrought-iron gate set into a high red-brick wall. The huge garden beyond it stopped him in his tracks – a world within a world: gravelled walkways between immense flower beds, a fountain with a fish-pond in the centre, the walls lined with espaliered fruit trees – sheltered, warm, fragrant, silent apart from the drone of bees.

An elderly man was on his knees, weeding one of the beds.

'Mr Geddings?' The man looked round. Deemer took off his cap and held it respectfully between his hands. 'I've come to offer my services.'

Geddings looked up at him. 'You're quick off the mark! The advertisement's not even in the paper yet.'

'I heard in town you were in need of men.'

'Well, that's true enough. I'm practically running the place on my own. Let me have a look at you.' He held out his hand. 'Give me a pull, would you? I'm too old for this lark.'

Amid much groaning and cracking of joints, Geddings heaved himself to his feet. He stayed bent over, his hands on his knees, and craned his head to inspect Deemer. 'You're English?'

'From London.'

'London!' The Welshman pronounced it as if it was Sodom or Gomorrah.

'We do have gardens in London, Mr Geddings – though nothing to compare with this.'

'Steady on, boyo – don't overdo it!' But he looked pleased at the compliment.

Deemer explained his situation, as he had carefully rehearsed it: that he had come to Holyhead for a few days' holiday, that the trading company where he was employed as a clerk had lost most of its business because of the war, that he had been laid off, and that he was not looking for a permanent position, just a few weeks' work to set him back on his feet.

Geddings shook his head. 'I'm sorry, young man. I'd like to help you out, but I need fellows with experience.'

'I have experience.'

'You're a gardener?'

'I've worked as a gardener.'

'Have you now?' The old man straightened painfully, keeping one hand pressed in the small of his back. He pointed with his trowel to a mass of pink blooms. 'Tell me, then: what are they?'

'They're petunias.'

'And those?'

'Dahlias.'

'And those?'

'Geraniums.'

Geddings grunted and rubbed his chin. 'All right, it proves you know a weed from a flower, which is more than most. I'll give you a try. Threepence an hour. But just for a couple of days, mind – I'm not making any promises.'

Threepence an hour! No wonder all his under-gardeners were joining up.

'Is there somewhere I can sleep? I can't afford to live in town on threepence an hour.'

'Oh, I see, so I'm to be a hotel keeper as well now, am I?' and Deemer briefly feared the offer was about to be withdrawn, but then the old man winced and rubbed his back and looked with hatred at the flower bed. 'Young Owen Parry had a mattress above the stables. It isn't much, but I suppose you can have that. When can you start?'

'This afternoon if you like. I just need to get my things.'

'All right. This afternoon.' They shook hands. 'What's your name, by the way?'

'Merryweather,' said Deemer. 'Paul Merryweather.'

Bay View was silent, the guests all gone for the day, the scullery maid cleaning the stairs. He collected his suitcase from his room, settled his bill, and cycled into town. He sent a telegram to Kell, addressed to The Manager, Kelly's Letter Bureau, Shaftesbury Avenue, London: *HAVE SECURED EMPLOYMENT WITH THE FAMILY. WILL REPORT SOONEST. SEND FUTURE CORRESPONDENCE C/O HOLYHEAD POST OFFICE.*

By two o'clock he was back at Penrhos House and Mr Geddings was showing him his accommodation – a hayloft above an empty stable, with a mattress and a roll of dirty bedding, a plain wooden table and chair, and an enamel chamber pot and basin. Thin grey light filtered through a tiny window.

Even Geddings seemed embarrassed. 'I warned you it wasn't much.'

'It'll do me fine.'

'At least the nights are still warm. You can get water from the pump in the courtyard. The kitchen will give you something to eat at six.'

He took him into the walled garden, handed him a trowel and told him to start weeding.

Deemer worked hard all afternoon, stabbing into the hard, dry earth, dragging out the roots, filling four wheelbarrow loads with bindweed and ground elder and pushing them out of the far end of the walled garden to the compost heap. He didn't dare slacken.

By the end, his back ached, his hands were scratched and sore. But it was worth it when, at six o'clock, Geddings came up behind him, inspected his efforts and grunted his approval.

'That'll do well enough. You'd best knock off for the day.' He called over a couple of under-gardeners and introduced them: Coslett, who looked too young to join the army, and Elijah, who looked too old. 'Show him the way to the kitchen.'

They led him out of the walled garden, into the courtyard, down a flight of steps and along a wide subterranean passage that ran the length of the house. In the kitchen, two rows of uni-formed maids and footmen were making noisy conversation over their evening meal, facing one another across a long butcher's table. A scullery girl gave him a plate of fish and boiled potatoes and a piece of fruit cake. He looked for a place to sit, but Elijah said, 'We're not allowed to eat here, man, we're outdoor staff,' and took him back down the passage and up above ground to a bothy at the edge of the garden.

The bothy was a brick-built outhouse, a combination of store-room and shelter, lined with shelves holding small tools, canes, netting, oil cans, glue pots, bits of machinery and the like. There was a seed company's calendar for 1912 on the wall, a rickety table and a few old chairs with wicker seats, a Primus stove emitting a sweet stink of paraffin, and a cupboard with tins of tea and sugar and a bottle of milk. Coslett lit the Primus and set a kettle to boil.

Deemer hadn't had any food since breakfast. He ate quickly and in silence while the other two talked in Welsh – talked about him, judging by their occasional sidelong glances. Coslett left the table to make a pot of tea. When they'd finished their meal, Elijah lit his pipe and said, 'New man gets to take the plates back.' He car-ried the dirty dishes to the kitchen and by the time he returned, the Welshmen had gone.

He went out of the bothy. The grounds were deserted. He guessed the gardeners must have gone home and the Stanleys would be getting ready for dinner. He went up to the hayloft and retrieved his telescope.

For the next hour he explored the property – the Victorian greenhouses full of heavily scented lilies, and orchids that smelled more delicately of cinnamon and vanilla, the walled vegetable garden, the rose garden, the herb garden, the maze, the elaborate sundial, the grass tennis court, the summer house, the pagoda, the gravelled paths between the box hedges with elegant wrought-iron benches spaced along them. Eventually, he worked his way round to the woodland closest to the sea where he had hidden on Saturday. He could hear the waves breaking on the shore behind him as he scanned the house through his telescope.

By now, it was almost eight, the sun had gone, the sky was overcast, and some of the lights upstairs had been switched on. Figures were moving back and forth in one of the bedrooms, but he was too far away to make out who they were. He decided to venture onto the croquet lawn. He crossed it quickly in the gathering twilight, hoping he would not be seen. Standing beneath a great decaying beech tree, he trained his telescope on the window. A moment later – silent, remote, unearthly, like an apparition in a ghost story – Venetia Stanley materialised in his eyepiece. She was in a pink chemise, bare-armed, half-undressed. She stood, motionless, staring across the garden, seemingly straight at him. He quickly lowered the telescope. He felt embarrassed, guilty, a voyeur. Cautiously, he raised the telescope again. She was still there. Suddenly another figure – slim, blonde: her maid, he guessed – appeared beside her, holding a dress in her outstretched hands. The maid ducked down out of view, Venetia moved a pace to one side, and moments later the maid resurfaced, tugging up the dress and helping Venetia guide her arms into it. She fussed around behind her, stepped forwards and drew the curtains, and the vision disappeared.

He closed his telescope.

When Venetia returned from her swim the following morning, Edith was waiting for her with the Prime Minister's letter, written the previous day.

Early this morning I was aroused by Kitchener bringing French's telegram, which I enclose. Very bad news.

She put aside the letter and read the Commander-in-Chief's telegram. She thought of the people she knew, her friends, her brothers-in-law, caught up in this cauldron, and bit her knuckle. She was aware of Edith in the corner of the room, gathering up her clothes from the night before. 'Edith, dearest, would you mind just leaving me alone for a moment? You can finish all that later.'

After her maid had gone, she went over and sat at her dressing table to read the rest of his letter.

I wish we had something like a code that we cd. use by the telegraph. This morning for instance I longed to let you know before anyone else what had happened & was happening. Do you think it is impossible to invent something of the kind? You might think of it, & even elaborate it, in the intervals of prawn-hunting. There are many occasions on which it might save us both anxiety, and convey our real thoughts & wishes.

Darling I love you: how much I cannot put into words, but <u>some day</u> you will know.

She picked up the telegram again. He had been sending her more and more documents lately: a handwritten letter from the Queen last Thursday, another yesterday from Lord Kitchener about troop deployments. But this was easily the most extraordinary. The telegram was stamped SECRET, it contained the exact details of the defensive position to which the army was retreating, and he had sent it through the ordinary post! What was she supposed to make of it? She could hardly offer him advice on military tactics.

And although he insisted his spirits were good – *Kitchener is not at all downcast: nor am I* – she could sense the strain he was under. Sharing it with her every day was his way of relieving the pressure. And, in a peculiar way, without flattering herself – which was not in her nature – she knew that the most important practical contribution she could make to the war effort at that moment was to shore up his confidence. She must encourage him, support him, love him more than ever before.

She took up her pen. *My darling . . .*

But it was not so amusing any more, she had to admit, having access to all this life-and-death information, especially living under the same roof as her anxious sisters. How much should she tell them? Nothing, she decided. Once she had finished her letter, she would go into Holyhead to post it, and send him a wire asking him to let her know if he should hear any details of casualties, especially if they included Anthony or Eric. She wondered what else he would send her, what more risks he would run, and how long she would have to keep up a pretence of ignorance before this ghastly war was over.

CHAPTER SEVENTEEN

I T TOOK DEEMER two days of careful observation to find a
way of getting inside the house.

From the moment he arrived, he had been trapped in the
Sisyphean labour of weeding. No sooner had he finished clearing
one massive flower bed than Geddings set him to work on the
next. Kneeling with his trowel, he cast wistful glances up at the
roofs and chimneys of the mansion, just visible above the parapet.
The walled garden had become his prison; the only chances he
had to escape it were in the middle of the mornings and the afternoons, when the gardeners were allowed to go to the bothy and
have a fifteen-minute tea break, or when he wheeled his barrow
to the compost heap: then it was possible for him to wander off
briefly, round to the edge of the lawn to catch glimpses of the
family and their guests on the terrace, or to observe them playing
tennis and croquet.

It was on the Wednesday afternoon, about five o'clock, as he
was pushing his empty barrow back towards the walled garden
from the compost heap, that he passed one of the three immense
Victorian glasshouses and saw Geddings with a pair of secateurs

cutting the stem of a lily. He stopped to look. The head gardener noticed him, tapped on the window and beckoned him inside.

'Do me a favour, will you, boyo – take these round to the house-keeper? Her ladyship likes to have fresh lilies for the dinner table every night. Go to the front door and ask for Mrs Protheroe.'

He carefully laid out six dozen sprays of white, pink and yellow blooms in his wheelbarrow and set off around the side of the house. At the front door, he reached out his hand to ring the bell, then checked himself and turned the handle instead. The hall was deserted. He filled his arms with lilies and stepped over the threshold.

It was a grand space, the walls covered almost entirely with oil paintings, a suit of armour at the foot of a wide staircase, a Gothic side table next to a dinner gong, a flagstone floor with rugs, a high and elaborately plastered ceiling. The doors were all closed. A nearby grandfather clock ticked loudly. He could hear voices somewhere, a woman's laughter, dance music playing on a phono-graph. He moved into the wide passage leading towards the back of the house.

He had gone about a dozen paces when around the corner came a blonde woman carrying a dress over her arm – the maid in the window the other night. She walked straight past him. He called after her, 'Excuse me, miss.' She stopped and turned. 'Could you help me? I'm looking for the housekeeper.'

'She's in the dining room.'

'I'm afraid I don't know where that is.'

'Ah, you're new. I'll show you.'

A foreign accent – German, was it? Good God! They walked together, side by side.

He tried to make conversation. 'I only started on Monday. My name's Paul Merryweather.'

She opened the door and called inside. 'Mrs Protheroe? One of the gardeners is here with the flowers.' *Viz de flowers* . . . She stood aside to let him enter. 'Beautiful flowers.' She smiled at him.

'Thank you. May I ask your name, miss?'

She gave him a cool look. 'Edith,' she said eventually. 'Edith Winter.'

The next afternoon, he made sure he was passing the greenhouse at the same time, and Geddings duly asked him to take the lilies to the mansion. But even though he lingered in the hall until one of the footmen challenged him, he did not glimpse Miss Winter. By Friday, when he presented himself at the greenhouse once again, it had become an unspoken part of his duties: in the under-staffed garden he was now the man who delivered the flowers to the big house. But for the second day in succession, he failed to encounter her.

Saturday afternoons he had off. He collected his pay from Geddings at one o'clock – twelve shillings, counted out into his palm one by one – and after he had hidden it in his quarters with the rest of his money, he cycled into Holyhead. It was the first time he had been able to get away during normal hours since he started work. At the post office he sent a wire to Kell: *REQUEST URGENT INFORMATION MISS EDITH WINTER, APPROX THIRTY, POSSIBLE GERMAN NATIONAL.* It felt like the first proper piece of detective work he had accomplished.

He wheeled his bicycle through the crowded streets, enjoying the sunshine and the breeze. He had just bought himself an ice cream when he saw a large car pull up opposite the Hippodrome Picture Palace, and Venetia Stanley get out, accompanied by Edith Winter. They crossed the road and went straight inside. He finished his ice cream, chained his bicycle to a lamp post and followed them.

They had already bought their tickets by the time he reached the kiosk and paid his fourpence. The small auditorium was almost full. He could see the two women six rows in front. They had taken off their hats. He found a seat at the back, the lights dimmed, the pianist abruptly ended his selection from Gilbert and Sullivan and struck a dramatic chord. The newsreel began – a caption, 'Fierce fighting in France', flickering film of troopships leaving Southampton, soldiers marching jerkily along a straight road lined with poplars, machine-gunners firing amid clouds of smoke, and then Lord Kitchener in a bowler hat climbing out of a cab and paying his fare, with another caption – 'Kitchener's recruits reach 200,000' – which drew a cheer. At the end came a shot of the Prime Minister sitting at a desk, turning his head slightly back and forth, looking grim. 'Mr Asquith tells Parliament: "We do not repent our decision."'

The main feature was an American thriller entitled *My Official Wife*, supposedly set in snowy St Petersburg but obviously filmed in California, about a man taking a glamorous woman over the Russian border, whom he allowed for no very plausible reason to pose as his wife, and who then turned out to be a terrorist determined to assassinate the Tsar, the whole nonsense climaxing with a model boat being torpedoed in a tank of water. It lasted about an hour before mercifully the lights came up, the pianist started hammering out the National Anthem and the audience stood.

He doubted Venetia would have recognised him from their interview at the beginning of July, but he left quickly in any case, squeezing past his neighbours as the last notes of 'God Save the King' were dying away. Outside, he waited in a shop doorway across the street. A couple of minutes later, the women emerged. Venetia climbed into her car. Edith gave her a wave and then set off down the hill.

He unlocked his bicycle and followed her on foot, wheeling it. He allowed himself to imagine she was on her way to meet a fellow agent, or that she might be planning to hide a package somewhere. But she descended quickly through the town without glancing in any of the shop windows, reached sea level, ignored the entrance to the station and crossed the railway bridge. He kept a hundred yards behind her.

Rather than taking the main road back to the house, she headed towards the sea and joined a track that swept around the curve of a bay. The wind was stronger here, flicking foam from the tops of the waves, wrapping her dress tightly around her slight figure. She had to keep one hand pressed on the crown of her hat to stop it being carried away. Gradually his fantasy of uncovering a German spy ring single-handed began to fade. He decided that tailing her any longer was pointless. He mounted his bicycle and pedalled after her.

'Miss Winter!'

She glanced over her shoulder. He braked and climbed off the bicycle.

'I'm sorry to interrupt you. We met the other day.' She looked at him blankly. 'The man with the lilies?'

'Ah yes, of course! The new gardener.'

'I'm sorry – I just saw you there. May I walk with you? Or would you prefer to be alone?'

'As you wish.'

She resumed walking and he fell in beside her, pushing his bicycle. He tried to think of something to say. 'I went into town to see a film.'

'Yes, I saw it too. What did you think of it?'

'I thought it was entertaining.'

'Really? I thought it was the most awful rubbish.'

He felt crushed. 'I suppose it was. Do you see many films?'

'In London, yes. Not here.'

'So, you don't live all year at Penrhos?'

'No!' She sounded amused at the suggestion.

'You travel with the family?'

'Yes.'

'As a lady's maid?'

'Yes.'

'How much longer will you be staying?'

'So many questions! Are you a policeman as well as a gardener?' He felt his face redden but she didn't seem to notice. She said, 'The house will be closed for the winter at the beginning of October. Then we return either to London or Cheshire.' She was plainly bored with him already. She stopped and stared at the horizon. 'You go on ahead, Mr Merryweather. I think I shall go down to the sea.'

'Of course. Goodbye.'

He rode on. When he reached the far side of the bay, he paused and looked back. She had taken off her shoes and was walking across the sand – a small, purposeful figure, bent into the wind.

Early the next day, he cycled back to Holyhead.

It was a Sunday morning. The town was quiet, apart from the church bells. The only businesses open were a newsagent and the telegraph counter at the post office, where a telegram was waiting for him from Kell: *SUBJECT SWISS NATIONAL BORN ZURICH 1884 RESIDENT BRITAIN 1906. AWAITING YOUR REPORT.*

So, she was a citizen of a neutral country. That didn't mean she wasn't a German sympathiser. And Kell was clearly becoming impatient, even though the Stanleys wouldn't be leaving Penrhos for another month. He didn't think he could bear to stay that long.

Outside the newsagent's a queue had formed. People were muttering and shaking their heads. Something must have happened. He joined the back of the line. When he reached the counter, he saw that *The Times*, which never published on a Sunday, had produced a special edition. Instead of the usual advertisements, it had put news on its front page.

FIERCEST FIGHT IN HISTORY

HEAVY LOSSES OF BRITISH TROOPS

THE GERMAN ONSLAUGHT

He bought the last copy in the shop and read it standing in the street.

Since Monday morning last the German advance has been one of almost incredible rapidity . . .

In scattered units with the enemy ever on its heels the Fourth Division, all that was left of 20,000 fine troops, streamed south . . .

I have seen the broken bits of many regiments . . .

We have to face the fact that the British Expeditionary Force has suffered terrible losses and requires immediate and immense reinforcement . . .

He stood rigid with shock, oblivious to the anxious conversations going on around him. He tried to think. Might Fred's regiment be part of the Fourth Division? He had no idea. All that he had of his brother was a scribbled note, an awkward photograph, and a memory of him walking back into the barracks on a summer's evening.

★

The first the Prime Minister knew of the *Times* special edition was when a manservant brought it into his bedroom in Lympne Castle, where he had once again gone for the weekend. His first reaction was astonishment, and then – as he imagined the reaction spreading across thousands of breakfast tables at that moment – dismay. He bathed and dressed quickly and went downstairs to find Margot and Edwin Montagu sharing a copy over the breakfast table.

'Henry,' said Margot, in a worryingly calm voice, 'this is terrible.'

'Yes! Terrible, terrible . . . Secret military information plastered all over the first page for everyone to see! Think of the distress it will cause to the men's families.'

Montagu said, 'Is it accurate?'

'Broadly accurate, yes – which makes it even more unforgivable.'

'Something broadly accurate in *The Times*,' murmured Montagu. 'That's worth a special edition in itself.'

But for once the Prime Minister was in no mood for his drollery.

'How on earth did it pass the censors? Try to get hold of F. E. Smith, will you? Ask him what the devil's going on.'

He went out to walk around the castle grounds. He found the view from the terrace, with its endlessly shifting play of light and shade across the marshland leading to the English Channel, always calming. People had been looking out at the same vista for a thousand years; they would be doing the same a thousand years from now, when this day, and he and his problems, would be long forgotten. By the time he went back inside, he had regained his composure. Montagu had spoken to F. E. Smith, the Unionist MP who had appeared for Raymond at the riverboat inquest, and who was head of the government press bureau. Smith had not only confirmed that he had authorised publication, but boasted in his bombastic way that he had added a sentence or two of his own, to encourage recruitment.

The Prime Minister said, 'What on earth possessed us to appoint him?'

'He's Winston's best friend. And of course, he's a friend of Northcliffe's.'

'Northcliffe!' That bullying, arrogant, vulgar menace: he hated even hearing the man's name.

In the afternoon, Horwood drove him and Margot over to a big army camp near Folkestone to visit the wounded recently evacuated from France. She was good at this sort of thing – better than he was – sitting on the edges of the beds, talking to the men naturally as if they were ghillies on her family's Scottish estate. He was tongue-tied. Their ordinariness, their humility, their bravery moved him. They were the reason he had entered politics, why he had fought to introduce a universal old-age pension so that they would not be destitute at the end. They had suffered minor wounds mostly – the more serious cases were still in France, being treated in the field hospitals. A colonel in the 5th Lancers who had been shot in the calf told him he had seen Anthony Henley two days previously alive and well. The place stank of disinfectant. At the end of the visit, he slipped away to the adjutant's office to wire Sylvia in Penrhos with the good news.

That evening, he left the castle in darkness after dinner to drive back to London with Montagu. Just outside Maidstone their headlights picked out a broken-down car with a family of four standing helplessly by the roadside. Suddenly he pushed a button and signalled Horwood to stop. He climbed out himself and walked back to ask if they needed help. The children were crying. It was clear that they did. Horwood fetched a rope, and the Napier towed them to the next village. The parents thought they ought to stay with the car, so the Prime Minister offered to drive the children back to their home. The boy was about twelve, the girl eight – a bright little thing, she reminded him of Violet at that age. She sat on his lap and prattled away in a cockney accent about the family holiday in Margate. It turned out they lived above a grocery shop in Lewisham, where their aunt was waiting for them. After he had seen them safely inside, he got back into the car.

Montagu said, 'Those parents had no idea of your identity, did they?'

'I hope not.'

'You know, we ought to give this to the press. It would make an excellent little story.'

'What an abominable idea! Why? All so that Northcliffe can put it in the *Daily Mail* and sell a few more copies? I can't think of anything worse.'

The Prime Minister closed his eyes. The rest of the journey passed in silence. By midnight, they were back in Downing Street.

Monday was a bad day.

It began with a telegram from Sir John French, brought over by Kitchener, describing his army as 'shattered' and requesting permission to withdraw it from the front line completely and retire to La Rochelle.

'But that's way further back than Le Havre,' protested the Prime Minister. 'That's on the Atlantic coast – the opposite side of the country!'

'He's lost his nerve,' said Kitchener, 'or his senses, or possibly both.'

'We can't simply cut and run. It would be the most blackguardly betrayal of France. I shall have to ask the Cabinet to overrule him.'

When he read out the telegram at that morning's meeting, the reaction among ministers whose nerves were already on edge after Sunday's *Times* was explosive – outrage, consternation, belligerence, panic. He let them vent their emotions for an hour and then summed up that the Secretary of State for War should instruct the Commander-in-Chief that his proposal was unthinkable, that it would seem to the world that Britain was deserting France, that he must stand his ground.

After that, he found it hard to concentrate, waiting all day for French's reply, describing to Venetia what had happened (*all this is most secret*), scanning the eight hundred names on the casualty lists for the sons of his friends. He picked at his lunch and dinner, played a lacklustre game of bridge with the President of the Board of Education, and tried to make polite conversation. Just before midnight, Bongie came in to tell him that Kitchener's office had called – French's reply had finally arrived, and he was bringing it over.

The Prime Minister put down his cards. 'Find Winston, the Home Secretary and the Chancellor and tell them to meet me in the Cabinet Room.'

He finished his brandy. He was sober enough to know he had drunk a good deal. He took the stairs slowly, pausing at the turn to collect himself. For a moment, gripping the handrail, he pictured the soldiers he had met in the hospital, the thousands of lives now hanging in the balance. But he couldn't allow himself to dwell on all that. He must shut down his imagination. The business had begun, men were going to die, and it had to be seen through to the end. He continued his descent.

Winston was the first to arrive, cheerful as ever. Now here was a man made for war, thought the Prime Minister. Here was a man who clearly relished every minute of it, even the disasters.

McKenna came in next, and then Kitchener, who had been at a formal dinner in the City and was wearing white tie and tails. He had the telegram in his hand and was clearly irritated to find other ministers present.

'May we start?'

'We should wait for the Chancellor.'

'Must we? We don't have much time.'

'Why? What does Sir John say?'

Kitchener read it aloud. '"I do not see why I should again run the risk of absolute disaster in order a second time to save the French."' He skimmed the telegram across the table towards the Prime Minister. 'He's refusing to obey.'

Winston said, 'If he was a German general, the Kaiser would have him shot.'

The Prime Minister read the telegram for himself. The tone was insufferable, hysterical. 'I agree with Winston. Unfortunately, I'm not the Kaiser.'

'If not shot, then sacked.'

'I fear that sacking the Commander-in-Chief at this moment would only compound the public impression of chaos.' He turned to Kitchener. 'I think you need to go over to France and stiffen his backbone.'

'Willingly.'

'How soon can you leave?'

'Let me go home and change. I'll be ready in an hour.'

Winston said, 'I can arrange for a fast cruiser to take you across from Dover tonight.'

The Prime Minister pushed the bell to summon Bongie. 'See if you can arrange for a special train to take Lord Kitchener to Dover.'

'When, sir?'

'Now. Tonight. And it's secret. Don't tell them the name of the passenger.'

Lloyd George arrived, his mane of thick grey hair dishevelled, as if he had just got out of bed. He and Kitchener exchanged curt nods. The Prime Minister was discovering that his Secretary of State for War hated discussing military matters with any politician, but especially Lloyd George, who had opposed every imperial war Kitchener had ever fought in. Over the next ten minutes they settled a few more details. Kitchener would go first to Paris to reassure his French counterpart that the British would stay in the front line, then track down Sir John and tell him to pull himself together.

'I shall put on my field marshal's uniform before we meet – just to remind him I outrank him.'

'Bloody generals,' said Lloyd George after he'd gone. 'If they fought the Germans half as well as they fight each other, we'd win this war tomorrow.'

CHAPTER EIGHTEEN

O N TUESDAY, THE first of September, as if obeying some ancient almanac known only to himself, Geddings announced that this was the day when Deemer should move from the walled garden to the front of the house to begin preparing it for the autumn, trimming the hedges and the ivy, mowing the lawns and replenishing the gravel.

It was the perfect spot for surveillance. At seven o'clock, the newspapers were delivered. At eight o'clock, the postman cycled down the drive with the morning's mail. Various tradesmen came and went. Just before noon, the family's large limousine was driven round to the front porch, followed by a smaller car that drew up behind it. Maids and footmen carried out the familiar minimum requirements for a Stanley picnic – wicker baskets, folding tables and chairs, boxes of cutlery, napery and glassware – and loaded them into the boot of the limousine. The family emerged soon afterwards, led by the gaunt and elderly Lord Sheffield, Venetia carrying one of the little girls. Deemer kept his head down and raked the drive. The servants climbed into the smaller car – Edith, he noticed, was not among them – and the expedition drove away.

That afternoon when he brought in the flowers, the hall was deserted. He decided to go in search of Miss Winter, wandering in and out of the empty rooms, carrying the lilies as a shield in case he was challenged. In the drawing room, through the French windows, he saw her sitting on the terrace, sewing the hem of a dress. He opened the door quietly and came up behind her. She jumped a little at the sound of his footsteps and put her hand to her heart.

'You startled me!'

'I'm sorry. The house seems to be deserted.'

'The family have gone on an outing to Prestatyn, so there will be no dinner tonight. I fear there is no one to appreciate your beautiful lilies.'

'When will they be back?'

'Tomorrow.'

'That's a pity. They won't be so fresh tomorrow.' He had a thought. 'Would *you* like them – or some of them? For Miss Venetia?'

She gave him a wry look, then shrugged. 'Why not?' She bit off the thread, put the needle in her sewing box and gathered the dress. 'Do you mind carrying them upstairs for me?'

She led him back through the drawing room, across the hall and up the staircase, past the family portraits and along the wide passage on the first floor. 'This is Miss Venetia's room.' She opened the door to an enormous bedroom and laid the dress on the bed. 'Wait a moment.'

She went out into the corridor and left him alone. He could hear her rummaging in a cupboard. He looked around at the splendid bed, the dressing and writing tables with their array of silver-framed photographs, the sofa and chairs, the huge wardrobe, the Persian carpet. He considered quickly searching the drawers, but his arms were full of flowers, and besides she was back in less than a minute, holding a large cut-glass vase. She carried it into the bathroom, filled it with water, and placed it on the writing table. She took the lilies from him a stem at a time until the vase was full, then stepped back and considered her arrangement. She made an adjustment, then nodded.

'Thank you. They are lovely.'

'Worthy of the room.'

'If you think this is impressive, you should see her room in Alderley.' Her diction was perfect; only the accent betrayed her.

'Your English is excellent, if I may say so.'

She smiled at him. 'I notice you have not accused me of being a German.'

'Are you?'

'Of course not. The circles they move in – I would not be here.' She glanced at the door. Her tone became abruptly brisker. 'And now you must go. I'll take the rest of the flowers down to Mrs Protheroe. You really ought not to be inside the house.'

The following morning, he made sure to start work early. At eight o'clock as usual, the postman cycled up to the porch and went inside with a bundle of letters, re-emerged, nodded to Deemer and pedalled away. Deemer watched until he was out of sight before he slipped into the hall. The mail was on the side table next to the dinner gong. No one was around. He sorted through it quickly. A dozen letters to Lord and Lady Sheffield, three to the Hon. Mrs Anthony Henley, a couple to the Hon. Mrs Pearce-Serocold, five to Venetia. He recognised the handwriting on one of them: her name and address written in the same distinctive style he had seen in the ledger at the bookshop. He tucked the letter carefully into his inside pocket.

He left it until after the other gardeners had finished their morning tea and had gone back to work before he went into the bothy. He re-lit the Primus stove and waited for the kettle to boil, then held the envelope to the steam. The stationery was thick, of good quality, but after a minute the seal of the flap began to loosen. He took a pot of glue from the shelf, checked the courtyard was empty, and walked quickly across to the hayloft.

Inside the envelope were two sheets of 10 Downing Street notepaper, each folded in half to make four sides. He extracted them carefully and held them between the tips of his fingers. Eight full pages of cramped text. *My darling*, the letter began. He stood with his back to the window. The light was poor, some of the words were indecipherable. He could only read it slowly. When he had finished, he hunted in his suitcase for his notebook and scribbled down a few of the more startling sentences: *French has greatly underestimated his total losses, more likely to be 10,000 than 5,000 . . . In his telegrams (Secret) he speaks of his force as 'shattered' . . . We decided the only thing to be done was for Kitchener to go there without delay . . . Hardly a dozen human beings realise that he is not at the War Office today . . . You had better keep it quiet for the time. I have just come back from seeing the King who knew nothing until he heard from me this morning . . . I don't think you know at all how much I love you . . .*

He didn't dare copy more. He folded the letter and gently inserted it back into envelope, and was in the delicate process of applying glue to the seal with the end of his little finger when he heard Geddings call his name from the stable below. 'Are you up there?'

'Yes, yes, I'm coming down now.'

He pressed the flap closed, slipped the letter inside his jacket and descended the ladder. Geddings was waiting at the bottom, arms akimbo, foot tapping in irritation.

'Sleeping on the job?'

'Just felt a bit faint, Mr Geddings. Only for a few minutes. Better now.'

The old man conveyed a lot of scepticism in his grunt. 'Don't make me come looking for you again. You can save your faints for your own time.'

He trotted round to the front of the house and let himself into the hall, where he saw to his relief that the morning mail was still on the table. The envelope was slightly smudged by his dirty hands, a little crumpled from the steam, but nothing hopefully that might not have happened in transit from London. He slipped it into the pile.

A few minutes later, the two cars swept up the drive. From his position halfway up his stepladder, trimming the ivy beside the porch, he had a good view of Venetia Stanley as she climbed out of the limousine. She was handsome rather than beautiful – lithe, vivacious, her face flushed from a day on the beach. He could see why the Prime Minister might be in love with her. But to share so many state secrets with a young woman less than half his age, to send them through the ordinary post, and to show her decrypted telegrams – that was beyond love, surely? That was a kind of madness.

She went inside. He waited for a reaction, a shout of anger or dismay. He half-expected her to re-emerge, looking to see who had tampered with her letter. But the forecourt gradually emptied of servants, the cars drove away, and soon from the hall resonated the sound of the gong summoning the family to lunch.

For the rest of the week, he maintained his surveillance and brooded on what he should do. He observed the postman coming to the house two or sometimes three times a day and speculated on how many more letters he was bringing from the Prime Minister. He took flowers to the house every afternoon and twice saw mail lying on the hall table, but servants were around and he didn't dare risk searching through it to check the handwriting.

He lay on his mattress in the evenings, studying his notes – *10,000 casualties, a shattered army* – thought about Fred and wished he could see what other military secrets she might be receiving. What did she do with the letters after she had read them? Destroy them or keep them? Show them to the rest of the family, or to friends? Leave them lying around where anyone might see them? Did Edith read them – a foreign national? The potential for a breach of a security was vast. The wisest course would be to obtain a warrant, bring in the police and search the place. But that was a decision for Kell, not him, and it was impossible to slip into Holyhead during the working week and make contact now that Geddings was keeping a closer eye on him.

On Friday, he lost his vantage place at the front of the house and was put back weeding in the walled garden. He took the lilies in as usual for the dinner table and returned to work just after five, pulling out tendrils of sticky goose grass, which raised irritating red welts on his forearms and the backs of his hands that spread to his neck when he touched it. He was wiping the sweat off his face with his sleeve when he glanced up and saw Edith at the gate, peering around, looking for something. She spotted him and came over. He stood and took off his cap.

She said, 'I was hoping to catch you in the house. Miss Venetia was delighted with the lilies and told me to ask if you could bring some regularly for her room.'

'Of course.'

'You can leave them with Mrs Protheroe.'

'Yes, I will. Would you like to take some now?'

'No, we are going to London tomorrow for a week. But when we return.'

He thought she had been avoiding him since their encounter at the beginning of the week. Now, though, she seemed to want to linger. She asked him the names of some of the flowers. He was conscious of his blotchy skin, his hair plastered down, damp with perspiration. Nevertheless, he said, 'I'm sure you know the grounds better than I do, but it would be a pleasure to walk around with you and point out the flowers some time – if you have a free hour.'

She nodded judiciously, as if weighing up a business proposition. 'I should like that,' she said finally. 'Thank you.'

After he received his wages on Saturday, he cycled into Holyhead. There were noticeably fewer holidaymakers, a chill edge to the wind, a hint of rain; an end-of-summer feeling. At the post office, no letter or telegram awaited him. He asked the postmistress to check again, but the answer was the same. After two weeks of living alone undercover, he felt as if he had been forgotten and abandoned.

He sat on a bench overlooking the harbour and read *The Times*. For the first time it carried a list of casualties – 'The Roll of Honour', they called it – officers killed, wounded and missing. The names of the dead took up almost a column of small type. There was a list of other ranks being treated at Woolwich Hospital but not of privates, corporals and sergeants killed, presumably because there were too many to print. Fred's name was not among the wounded. He didn't know whether to feel glad or sorry. The map of the front line now showed the Germans within twenty miles of Paris.

He cycled back to Penrhos along the coastal track. Clouds were massing on the horizon. The sea was gunmetal grey. He needed either to make some progress, he decided, or to leave. He leaned his bike against the wall in the courtyard and walked all the way round the house. There was no sign of Edith or Venetia. He assumed they must have caught the train to London. He lay down on his mattress until six, when the servants would be having their evening meal, then made his way to the front door. The hall was empty. He went quickly up the stairs, along the passage to Venetia's room, and stepped inside. He sat in an armchair and took some deep breaths, told himself to calm down, take his time.

He looked around and wondered where to start. He settled on the writing desk as the most obvious place. There were several dozen letters in the drawers but none from the Prime Minister. He moved on to the dressing table. Jewellery, make-up, perfume, nail scissors, tweezers, hair grips and the like – nothing more. He flicked through the books on the bedside cabinets, looked under the bed, lifted the mattress. In the wardrobe was a painted wooden chest. It was locked. He took down the hat boxes and checked inside, then returned his attention to the chest and carried it into the centre of the room. It felt very light. He went back to the desk, the table and the cabinets and looked in each for a key. He found several, but none fitted. Finally, he took the tweezers and a hair grip, and set about trying to pick the lock.

Beyond the high window, darkness gathered. It started to rain. Kneeling on the carpet, he felt for the lock pins. There were only three. It was a fiddly task to raise them one by one with the grip and keep them raised with the tweezers. He heard footsteps in the corridor and froze. But whoever it was walked straight past. After about half an hour, he had the pins in position and turned the tweezers clockwise. The lock opened. He wiped his hands and lifted the lid.

★

What had he expected? A dozen letters? Two dozen? Instead, he reckoned there were more than a hundred, loosely stacked. He hesitated before he touched them. He didn't want to disturb the order. He inspected the dates on the first half-dozen. They seemed to have been deposited in the box as they had arrived, with the most recent on top, but it was too dark to read them properly, and he didn't dare turn on the lights. He went into the bathroom, fetched the largest towel and shifted a couple of chairs to make a tent over one of the bedside lamps. He knelt beneath it, with the chest beside him, and reached for the first letter. It was two days old. It began *My darling*, and ended *My own love, how I long for you*. In between it described Kitchener's return from France, the tension between the British and the French high commands, and the progress of recruitment: *30,000 men a day . . . we have got now nearly 300,000 . . .*

It was similar to the letter he had read earlier in the week – there was sensitive intelligence in almost every paragraph. He sat back on his heels, his mind struggling to encompass the scale of it. How should he proceed? After a few minutes' thought, he decided to concentrate only on those letters she had saved since the start of the international crisis – the Prime Minister seemed to write to her at least once a day: that would suggest about forty in all – and to make a list of breaches of the 1911 Official Secrets Act, a law which after all the Prime Minister had himself brought in. He supposed he would have to copy out at least some of the more compromising personal declarations as well, if only for their blackmail potential, although he felt grubby merely reading them.

He only had his notebook and a pencil. From Venetia's writing desk he helped himself to a handful of paper, one of her pens and a bottle of ink. He set to work.

In the early hours, as he was getting to the end, he heard people coming upstairs and along the passage, murmured voices, the creak of floorboards, the closing of doors. The ribbon of light from the passage that had been shining beneath Venetia's bedroom door all evening disappeared.

He spent another hour trying to eliminate every trace of his presence, putting everything back in its proper place. The hardest task was relocking the painted chest. His fingers were sweaty and clumsy with frustration. Finally, fearful that if he went on much longer he would damage the lock, he gave up, and put it back in the wardrobe. He would just have to hope she wouldn't notice or would conclude she hadn't locked it in the first place.

He waited until four o'clock on Sunday morning, when he was reasonably sure everyone would be sound asleep, then quietly left the room, his notes in one hand, his shoes in the other, and descended to the hall. The huge key of the front door was in its lock. He turned it slowly, drew back the bolts as silently as he could, and let himself out into the soft, wet darkness.

After a restless few hours' sleep, he packed his suitcase. He wrote a note to Geddings and left it on the table in the bothy, thanking him for giving him the opportunity to work in such a beautiful garden, apologising for his abrupt departure, which he blamed on a family emergency, and hoping to be back in touch. Then he cycled away down the empty drive.

In Holyhead, he sent a telegram to Kell, informing him that he would be back in town by eight o'clock, and requesting a meeting as soon as possible. By noon, he was on the train to London.

As soon as he turned into his street that evening, he noticed a car up ahead in the twilight, parked outside his house. A man was in the driver's seat. When he drew closer, he saw that it was Kell. The major lowered his window.

'Sorry to call round unannounced on a Sunday night, but your telegram made it sound rather urgent.'

'It's perfectly all right, sir. Would you like to come in?'

He unlocked his front door and pushed it open, sweeping aside the small pile of letters that had accumulated since his departure. He switched on the light. The house was dingy after standing empty for more than two weeks. It had a vaguely unpleasant smell, as if something had gone off in the larder. He felt embarrassed at its meanness.

'I'm afraid it's rather stuffy, sir. We could walk over the road to the pub if you'd prefer.'

'Better not,' said Kell. 'In a public house you never know who's listening. Why don't you close the shutters?'

'Of course.'

By the time he had finished, Kell had already helped himself to a seat in one of the two battered old leather armchairs. He drew his fingertips through the dust on the armrest and examined them carefully.

'Can I offer you a drink, sir?'

'No, thank you. I've come straight from the office and I'm just on my way home.' He took out a pipe full of half-burned tobacco and struck a match on the sole of his shoe. 'So – tell me what exactly you've been up to.'

Deemer sat opposite with his suitcase on his knees. He took out his notes and explained how he had assumed a false identity as a gardener, and how he had gained access to the Prime Minister's letters to Venetia Stanley.

Kell's eyes widened slightly. 'You broke into her room?'

'I didn't break in, sir. I let myself in. Shouldn't I have done?'

'Well, it's a bit late to worry about it now! No, no, you did well. We have to allow ourselves some licence. And what does it amount to, this correspondence?'

'He writes to her every day, and in almost every letter he tells her secrets – Cabinet discussions, military movements, diplomatic developments, future plans. And occasionally he sends her documents.'

'What sort of documents?'

'Well, for example, I found a copy of a telegram from the ambassador to Russia – exactly of the kind he showed her in the car in August. She has a letter from Lord Kitchener describing the deployment of troops to France, which I copied out.' He handed it to Kell. 'She has a handwritten letter from the Queen—'

'Good God!' This seemed to shock him more than anything.

'And most sensitive of all, a decrypted secret telegram from Sir John French, which gives the exact position to which he proposes to withdraw the Expeditionary Force. The Prime Minister sent it to her on the day he received it.'

He passed his copy of the text to Kell, who read it slowly, then looked up in disbelief. 'But this would have been operationally sensitive – if the Germans had seen this . . .'

'It certainly gave me quite a shock, sir.' He didn't add the reason: that his brother was one of the soldiers whose safety might have been put in jeopardy.

'But there's no evidence Miss Stanley has shown these to anyone?'

'No, she keeps them in a locked box.'

'The letters are – what? – intimate in tone, one would imagine?'

'Very intimate, yes.'

'What sort of things does he say?'

Deemer flicked through his notes. '"Darling I love you: how

much I cannot put into words . . . My own love, how I long for you . . . I would give more than I can put down on paper to be able to – some sentences are best left unfinished . . ." And this passage struck me as significant: "I wish we had something like a code that we could use by the telegraph. This morning for instance I longed to let you know before anyone else what had happened and was happening. Do you think it is impossible to invent something of the kind?"'

Kell gaped at him. 'He's acting as if he were a spy inside his own government! What about this maid of hers – this Swiss German?'

'She's a Swiss citizen,' corrected Deemer, 'who speaks German. I formed the impression she was reliable. Obviously, I couldn't say for certain.'

Kell sighed and sank into his chair. He tilted his head back and stared at a damp patch in the ceiling which Deemer hadn't noticed before. He said, 'If the culprit was an ordinary person – say, a Foreign Office clerk – we'd arrest them tomorrow, and they'd be prosecuted under the Official Secrets Act and almost certainly go to prison for a very long time. But – the Prime Minister? It's unthinkable!'

'Could you speak to someone in confidence, sir – Sir Edward Grey, perhaps – and ask them to have a word with him? Warn him it has to stop?'

Kell gave a gasping laugh. 'Well, that would be a tricky conversation, wouldn't it? To reveal that we had broken into the bedroom of the Prime Minister's mistress and read his love letters! I doubt I'd still be in my job by the following morning. And what proof do we have of it, apart from your notes?' He sucked at his pipe, but it had gone out. He didn't bother to re-light it. After a while, he said, 'I don't think there's any alternative but to carry on watching and waiting. Do you think it's worth your going back to Penrhos?'

'I don't see there's much more to be gained by further surveillance, sir. In any case, the house is due to be closed at the end of the month.'

Kell thought it over. 'If it's evidence we want, there's only one possible course of action.'

'Sir?'

'We shall have to intercept Miss Stanley's mail.'

'Can we do that, legally?'

'Technically not without a warrant from the Home Secretary, but in wartime we can do pretty much what we please. And if anyone starts asking questions, I can always justify an operation on the grounds of this Swiss German maid of hers – say we had a plausible suspicion of espionage: we should intercept her letters as well. It's certainly better, though, if we keep it "off the books". You can join our team at the sorting office in Mount Pleasant – they'll show you the best techniques: photographs are what we really need – but you'll have to operate separately from them, without telling them what you're doing, and report only to me. Are you comfortable with that?'

'I think so, sir.' He wasn't very comfortable, in truth, but he didn't feel able to refuse. And besides, he had sunk his teeth so deep into the case now, he couldn't bring himself simply to walk away from it. 'Yes, I can do that.'

'It'll be tedious work, I'm afraid, but I don't think we have any alternative.' Kell stood. 'You'd better start tomorrow. I'll warn them you're coming. Continue to stay away from the office. We can meet at my club whenever you have anything to report. I know I can rely on your discretion.' He patted him on the shoulder. 'You have the makings of a first-rate intelligence officer.'

After Deemer had shown him out, he stooped to pick up his small pile of mail. There was a letter from his brother, dated the previous week.

Hello, old man. Well, it's been a pretty hard show, I can tell you that! I've had a few close shaves, & we've lost a lot of good fellows. But not to worry. It's starting to get cold. Could you send me a few things? Socks, gloves, long johns, muffler, maybe a half-bottle of brandy if you can manage it, & cigarettes? I'll pay you back when I see you. Take care of yourself & send me a letter about how you're getting on. Ever yours, Fred. PS It won't be over by Christmas!

The words were reassuring but the writing was not. It looked as if it had been written by a very old man.

PART FOUR

INTERCEPTION

24 September–21 October 1914

CHAPTER NINETEEN

NEARLY THREE WEEKS later, as September drew to an end, the Prime Minister at last achieved one of his war aims, thanks to a plan of campaign both cunning and circuitous, and entirely of his own devising.

First, he had suggested to the Lord Mayors of London, Edinburgh, Cardiff and Dublin that he should deliver a recruiting speech in each of the four capital cities of the United Kingdom. Then he had so managed to arrange his schedule that his visit to Dublin would occur on Friday 25 September. Finally, he had written to Lady Sheffield proposing himself as a guest on the night before he sailed from Holyhead and the night after his return. She had responded at once: 'That would be wonderful for us, especially as it will be the last weekend before the house is closed for the winter. I shall write to Margot at once & invite her & the girls as well.'

He would have preferred to have gone alone, but he bowed with good grace to the inescapable demands of propriety, and on Thursday morning, 24 September, the prime ministerial party set out from Euston station in a reserved first-class compartment:

Margot, Violet, Elizabeth, Bongie and – because the trip involved Ireland, with its ever-present threat of violence – a protection officer from Special Branch.

The one great drawback to his scheme was that it required him to deliver an hour-long speech, and to an Irish audience, which was always a delicate business. For most of the journey, while the others chattered on around him, he was obliged to sit in his seat by the window, making desultory notes. His mind kept sliding off such lofty matters as the formation of an Irish army corps and on to the more congenial prospect of seeing Venetia, and how he might engineer some time alone with her.

They pulled into Holyhead just before half-past five. Lady Sheffield had sent two cars to meet them, and a few minutes later they were turning through the high gates towards the Arthurian towers and battlements of Penrhos House – a romantic vision that had sustained him for the best part of two months. But of course, fantasy dissolved upon first contact with reality: when had that ever not been the case? They climbed out of the car to be informed by the butler that tea was being served in the drawing room, and instead of leading Venetia out onto the terrace and into the woods, as he had been hoping all day, he found that she was almost lost in a crowd, surrounded by Lord and Lady Sheffield, Blanche, Sylvia and Margaret and their daughters, Reggie and Pamela McKenna and their two small boys, Edwin Montagu – she hadn't told him *he* was invited – and the usual Stanley private army of maids and footmen and nannies. Once Margot, Violet, Elizabeth and Bongie had poured into the room behind him and headed for their hosts, she disappeared entirely.

Such was his childish sense of disappointment he considered asking the butler if he could be shown straight to his room, but then Lady Sheffield saw him standing alone in the doorway and came over to greet him and lead him into the throng, and after that it was all handshakes and kisses and the admiring of sullen infants, and trying to balance his tea and plate of cucumber sandwiches in one hand, until at last Venetia was in front of him, wearing the striped green dress she knew was his favourite. 'Hello, Prime.' She leaned in to peck him on the cheek and whispered, 'Don't worry, it won't always be like this.'

But it always *was* like that, at least for the next day and a half. Although his room was handsome, it was situated at the very end of the guest wing, as far from Venetia's as it was possible for Lady Sheffield to contrive (he suspected she had done it deliberately), and in the adjoining room where a male visitor's valet would normally have slept, his Special Branch detective was installed to watch over him: there would be no nocturnal corridor-creeping this weekend. At dinner, he was placed between Lady Sheffield and Pamela McKenna, and managed only a brief conversation with Venetia afterwards, sitting on a sofa, the back of his hand brushing lightly against her leg.

The next day after breakfast, the entire party – Venetia, Lord and Lady Sheffield, Margot and the girls, Bongie, Montagu and the detective – was driven to the docks at Holyhead and boarded the steamer to Dublin. The ferry departed at noon – shadowed, at Winston's insistence, by a destroyer stationed a few hundred yards to starboard in case of an attack by German submarines. It was, the Prime Minister had to admit, an awful lot of inconvenience for a great many people, just so that he could see Venetia. He wanted to deliver a memorable speech, not least because she would be in the audience. But although he spent almost the entire four-hour voyage below decks in his cabin, working with Bongie, he somehow lacked inspiration. He was still working on his text that evening in Dublin, when he left the Viceregal Lodge in Phoenix Park accompanied by the Viceroy, Lord Aberdeen, in his ceremonial Rolls-Royce.

The Mansion House in Dawson Street was ringed by five hundred Irish soldiers. The audience crammed into the round auditorium was at least as large. He sat on the platform with Aberdeen, a fossil-like aristocrat whose grandfather had been prime minister at the time of the Crimean War, and the Nationalist leader John Redmond. Below him he could see Venetia in the front row, and when he rose to speak, he pulled out all the stops.

'I come here not as a partisan, not even as a politician, but I come here as for the time being the head of the King's Government, *(cheers)* to summon Ireland, a loyal and patriotic Ireland, to take her place in the defence of our common cause.' *(Cheers.)*

His reception throughout was enthusiastic. He spoke for forty-five minutes, sat down to an ovation, then had to go and repeat the performance to an overflow meeting in another part of the building. It was late by the time he got back to the Viceregal Lodge, tired but triumphant. Venetia took his hands in hers and told him he was wonderful. He replied, smiling, 'Yours is the only applause I wanted.' At dinner he was seated next to Lady Aberdeen, who lobbied him tirelessly for her husband's reappointment as viceroy now his term was coming to an end. As soon as he could, he excused himself and went to bed.

The Times the next morning described him as speaking 'in a low voice, which can hardly have been audible at the other end of the great chamber. He seemed to be a little tired.'

He crumpled the paper between his hands. Damn Northcliffe, he thought.

On the voyage back to Holyhead, he sat moodily on deck with his arms folded and a blanket over his legs and watched Venetia as she strolled around, first with Bongie then with Montagu. Both were bachelors, both were young enough to be his sons, and both, he knew, would marry her like a shot if she gave them any encouragement. He felt a great sense of hopelessness.

They returned to Penrhos in the middle of the afternoon. He told his detective to leave him alone, went out onto the terrace and stared unseeing at the view, leaning on his cane, still wearing his top hat and frock coat. He felt a touch on his arm and turned. It was Venetia, with a couple of dogs at her heels.

'I think we've earned an hour to ourselves,' she said, 'don't you?'

She had observed how out of sorts he had been ever since he arrived. She was sorry for him, but really – what could she do? There were so many emotional cross-currents swirling beneath the roof, it was dizzying. Violet was jealous every time she saw her talking to Bongie, as was Montagu – not that she felt the slightest romantic inclinations towards either of them. Margot gave her the evil eye whenever she caught her so much as looking at her husband. Her parents and her sisters watched her constantly. This was her first opportunity, now that the other women were all changing in their rooms, to have him to herself.

'I'd like that very much,' he said.

They strolled across the lawn towards the trees, the dogs running ahead of them, and talked about his speech in Dublin and the awful grasping pushiness of the Aberdeens.

'Who do you think I should replace them with? You don't have to tell me now. Think about it and write to me next week.'

It amused her the way he liked to flourish his powers of patronage in front of her, sharing his secrets, performing his speeches – he was like the peacock beneath her window, she thought, showing off his plumage. As soon as they were out of sight of the house, she took his arm.

'Where shall we go?' he asked. 'What about that place where we took shelter from the storm last year?'

'King Arthur's Seat? That's awfully hard and cold, don't you think? I've found us a much better place.'

She led him out of the gate and deep into the woods. They turned off the path and onto a barely discernible trail that must have been made by animals. The branches hung low. He had to take off his hat. She went first and held his hand to guide him. He was laughing at the absurdity of it, taking swipes at the vegetation with his cane, pretending to protest, but when they emerged into the clearing, he stood stock still and exclaimed, 'Oh, this is wonderful!'

It was a gentle slope running down towards the sea, covered in high grass – a hollow cleft in the land, entirely secluded.

'I discovered it in the summer,' she said, 'and I thought to myself: this is where I shall bring the Prime if he manages to make it. Listen.' She held up a forefinger. The only sounds were the cooing of wood pigeons, the rustle of the dogs foraging in the undergrowth, and somewhere close by a trickling brook. 'No cars,' she said. 'No Horwood sitting six feet away behind a pane of glass.' She turned to face him and put on a good-humoured frown. 'You're somewhat overdressed for the occasion if you don't mind my saying so. May I?' She unbuttoned his coat and helped him to slip it off his shoulders. Together, they spread it out on the soft ground.

The Prime Minister was in unusually high spirits that evening. Everyone remarked upon it. Montagu, sitting next to Venetia at dinner, nodded towards the other end of the candlelit table, where he was holding forth to Sylvia. 'The sea air seems to have done him good. It's either that, or seeing you.' He gave her a meaningful look.

'Well, if it's seeing me, I'm glad. What's wrong with my taking his mind off things, and making him happy? He needs *someone.*'

They both glanced at Margot. She was dressed flamboyantly in black, with an array of jet-black feathers at her thin bosom, and a couple more in her jewelled headdress. She was talking loudly about Kitchener. People stopped to listen as her piercing, huntswoman's voice cut across the table. 'As I said to Henry, he may not be a great man, but he's certainly a great poster.' Everyone heard her. Most laughed. The Prime Minister grimaced. Conversation resumed.

Montagu muttered, 'She said exactly the same thing over dinner in Dublin last night.'

'A good line is always worth repeating.'

'That's the trouble. It will be repeated. These things get around.'

At the end of dinner, the women retired to the drawing room, leaving the men to their port and cigars. Venetia, standing talking to Violet, was conscious of Margot perched on the edge of the sofa in her black plumage, her glittering eyes watching her keenly.

'Don't turn round,' she whispered, 'but your stepmother is staring at me as if she'd like to murder me.'

'Well, I'd often like to murder *her*, so I suppose that's only fair.'

They laughed. Once, they had been best friends. Nowadays they were not so close. Venetia wondered how much she had guessed.

Margot, provoked by their laughter, rose, and headed directly towards them.

Venetia said, 'Oh Lord, she's coming over. Excuse me, will you, darling? I simply can't face it.' She stepped out onto the terrace.

It was a clear, slightly chilly night on the cusp of autumn, with a brilliant moon and stars that were invisible in the artificial brightness of London. She went down the steps into the garden and walked round to the rose garden, where there was a favourite wooden bench that gave her the widest view of the heavens. From the fading blooms came a vague sweet scent, like a memory of summer.

She sat and thought about what Montagu had said about her and the Prime Minister. Was it really that obvious? She supposed it must be. But half the people around that table were probably having affairs. Even her mother was said to be enjoying a discreet *amitié amoureuse* with the Earl of Carlisle, not that Venetia would ever have dreamed of bringing it up. Frottage was the commonest form of pleasure. Even full intercourse was considered permissible, just as long as the man was careful not to get his lover pregnant – 'leaving the church before the sermon' was the favoured euphemism. Naturally, accidents happened. Several of her friends were known to be the product of their mothers' infidelities – Diana Manners, for example – but even then, nobody really cared, so long as the husband was willing to bring up the child as his own. Becoming pregnant when one was unmarried was a different matter – *that* would make one a social outcast. She had been careful not to go that far.

A dot of red light glowed briefly in the darkness. She caught the whiff of a cigar. A moment later the Prime Minister appeared before her.

'I thought I might find you here. How are you, my darling?'

He sat down and rested his arm along the back of the bench behind her. He took another pull on his cigar. She could feel the heavy rhythm of his breathing. After a while, he clasped her bare shoulder gently with his free hand and drew her towards him. She nestled her cheek against his chest, glad of his warmth. He always seemed to exude more heat than most people. They sat in contented silence as he smoked and stared at the stars. He said, 'At this moment, we might be the only two people on the planet.'

She heard a rustling noise and pulled away slightly.

She whispered, 'I think someone may be watching us.'

'Let them watch. What is there to see? Two dear friends sitting together looking at the night sky.' He pointed with his cigar. 'The North Star is always the brightest. That is what you are to me, my dearest. The fixed star that guides my life.'

She leaned over and kissed him. He threw away his cigar. It arced across the gravel path and landed in a cascade of bright orange sparks.

It was only the next afternoon, after he had left to go back to London on the Sunday train, that she returned to the bench and discovered behind one of the hedges a single black feather.

CHAPTER TWENTY

ROM THE MOMENT he had set foot in it three weeks earlier, Deemer had taken an intense dislike to the Mount Pleasant sorting office. It was only a twenty-minute walk from his house in north London, but even though he must have passed it dozens of times, he had somehow never registered it: a huge, anonymous, two-storey Victorian depot on King's Cross Road, occupying the site, and some of the buildings, of an eighteenth-century prison. Through it streamed all the millions of letters and parcels that flowed into and out of the capital every day.

On Kell's orders, he had been allotted a small room to himself, with a tiny, barred prison window set up high in a chute-like opening in the thick outside wall. He could just about see a patch of sky. This former cell lay at the end of the restricted corridor assigned to the mail interception division of MO5(g). He had the only key. Entry was forbidden to the other interceptors. They did not mingle with him. He barely knew their names. There was an ancient cast-iron safe, a chair, and a table with a camera apparatus fixed above it which he had learned to use in a day. In one corner was a stove with a hot plate where he kept a kettle simmering on a low heat for steaming open the letters. A sharp knife, a thin piece of split bamboo (should he need to roll the letters into a cylinder and extract them without breaking a seal) and a pot of glue were his only other tools. In an alcove which had once housed a lavatory, a thick black curtain concealed a photographic darkroom with a sink. The whole place stank of acetic acid and ammonium sulphate, which irritated his eyes and gave him an almost permanent headache.

He arrived punctually that Monday morning at half-past ten to begin his nine-hour shift. He took off his coat and put on a postal clerk's brown linen jacket, slipped on a pair of cellulite cuffs, stoked the stove, set the kettle to boil and made himself a pot of tea.

The letters came in three waves – usually around eleven in the morning, four in the afternoon and seven in the evening. The Prime Minister's letters mostly arrived from the Westminster sorting office in the afternoon or evening, Venetia's from the main post office in Anglesey in the morning. The secret intelligence he had so far passed on had ranged from logistics (*Kitchener told us that we have by now sent out to French 213,000 men & 57,000 horses*) to strategy (*Kitchener down in the dumps, thinks the forces are too close – suffering in fact from lockjaw, and is rather doubtful whether Joffre has enough men to outflank the German right*). The work was at once fascinating and dull, long periods of tedium punctuated by bouts of anxious, concentrated activity. He had at least been able to take the last three days off – Kell had passed on word from Special Branch about the weekend in Penrhos – but the Prime Minister had reportedly returned to Downing Street on Sunday evening and the correspondence was almost certain to resume later in the day. Deemer picked up his newspaper and settled down to wait.

The first delivery was brought to him half an hour later: two letters addressed to Venetia in Penrhos – neither from the Prime Minister, so he left them untouched – and one for Edith Winter with a Zurich postmark. He steamed it open and photographed it, more for something to do than because he expected it to be interesting. It was signed 'Aloisia' and was in German: he would pass it along to be translated. He resealed the envelope and took all three letters to the collection room at the end of the corridor, from which they would be returned immediately to the immense sorting hall in the building opposite. It was a matter of professional pride that every letter should go off whenever possible for delivery by the correct post.

The afternoon wave contained three more letters for Venetia, including a thick envelope in the Prime Minister's hand, posted in Westminster half an hour earlier. He steamed it open, quickly photographed each of the many pages without having the time to read them properly, glued the envelope and sent the letters on their way.

He turned on the red light in the darkroom and set to work. In the tray of developer, the familiar Gothic script of the 10 Downing Street letterhead materialised clearly in the top right-hand corner, along with the text beneath, written that morning:

My darling – I feel as if I have had a most heavenly dream, too beautiful & rare to correspond to anything on this gross & disappointing earth. But Heaven be praised it was not a dream, but the realest of realities.

He carried on developing. And then this, which made him whistle under his breath:

These figures may interest you (of course secret)
Western Theatre
Allies 70 divisions
Germans 66 divisions
Eastern Theatre
Russians 75 to 80 divisions
Germans 42
Austrians – almost negligible
P.S. I have not said a tenth of what I feel. <u>Do write</u>.

On the next sheet, the heading of the notepaper changed to 24 Queen Anne's Gate.

Do you notice my change of address? I will explain it directly . . . I was alone after the Cabinet in Downing St & gladly came back with the Assyrian & Eric Drummond to the silken tent for luncheon . . .

Deemer had begun his own card index system to make sense of the correspondence, in which he recorded nicknames, proper names and their private slang. 'The Assyrian' he had worked out was Edwin Montagu, Financial Secretary to the Treasury. The 'silken tent' was his house in Queen Anne's Gate. Eric Drummond was one of the Prime Minister's private secretaries.

Drummond has now gone back (in the absence of Bongie) to deal with No. 10 & the Assyrian to one of his numerous committees . . . Do you think Cardiff is at all possible? As you know it would make all the difference. I am alone in the tent, looking out over St James's Park, & thinking &

remembering & longing & hoping: and all thoughts &
memories & longings & hopes centre around & in <u>one</u>
<u>person</u>, & if only I could take the wings of the afternoon I
should at this moment be with you & close to you – the
best & to me the dearest of all places in heaven or earth. I
love you more than life.

He hung the last of the glistening prints on the line to dry and
contemplated them. On the face of it, they were the usual bizarre
mixture of secret military intelligence and passionate declarations
of love. But it seemed to him the language was slightly heightened, the Prime Minister's ardour a degree or so more intense
than before. *The realest of realities* . . . He wondered if something
particularly significant might have happened over the weekend in
Penrhos.

There was no letter in the seven o'clock collection and he went
home for the evening. On Tuesday morning, he steamed open a
letter from Venetia to the Prime Minister.

Penrhos House,
Monday 28 Sept. 1914
My darling, the house seems so empty now that you have
gone, & writing seems such a terrible makeshift compared
to having you with me. Sometimes, I wish you had not
made me want more, because one always <u>wants</u> so much,
& of course it is unobtainable . . .

And at seven came the Prime Minister's reply.

Darling don't ever wish that I had 'not made you want
more'. Can we ever forget those divine hours on Saturday

& Sunday? They are part of us both, beyond the reach of
chance or change – an ineffaceable memory – the little
sheltered slope with the long grass, and the dogs in
attendance, and the delicious alternations of silence &
speech; and later on, the twilight on the wooden bench in
the garden, with the moon & the evening star and the
Great Bear, and – but it is too cruel to recreate what, until
the lapse of many weary days & nights, we cannot renew.
The price of absence & separation is heavy indeed, but not
too heavy if (as I firmly believe) there is even more for us
in the future than there has been in the past . . .

Now I will tell you a great <u>secret</u>. French intends – if he
can get Joffre's assent, and if Joffre can spare enough men
to fill the gap – to 'disengage' as they call it, i.e. to unlock
his troops from their present position, and to make with
his whole force a great outflanking march via Amiens,
Arras, Douai, Tournay, to the line across Belgium from
Brussels to Cologne . . .

Take a solitary walk tomorrow beloved to our dear little
hollow, and think of me & of our heavenly hour there.
How I try to recall all you said, and every turn of your
head, and every look of your face, and the touch of your
hand, and – I hardly dare: the contrast makes things look so
drab. I love you more than words can say – with every
fibre, & whatever I have that is worth having & giving.

Deemer could visualise exactly 'the little sheltered slope with
the long grass' and 'the wooden bench in the garden', and the two
lovers slipping away from the other guests. Sitting in the confined
space of his cell, waiting for the prints to dry, he felt a sudden nos-
talgia for the woods and the lawns, the curving beaches, the fresh

sea breezes and the wide-open skies of north Wales. And then he realised he felt something else, so unprofessional it shocked him even to admit it to himself: envy.

He gathered the photographs and locked them in the safe.

There is even more for us in the future than there has been in the past . . .

He thought about the phrase as he walked home that night. He wondered what exactly the Prime Minister might mean by it.

And so, the week went on.

Penrhos House
Tues. 29 Sept. 1914
Darling, please, <u>please</u> don't be alarmed & ask Winston to send a gunboat to fetch me to London or anything but I'm afraid I'm rather ill – aches & pains in every limb, a high temperature, & my eyes all out of focus – I don't know whether I caught a chill while you were here, or you've left me bereft like Mariana:

> She only said, 'My life is dreary,
> He cometh not,' she said;
> She said, 'I am aweary, aweary,
> I would that I were dead!'

I feel too 'aweary' even to visit our hollow . . .

10 Downing Street
Weds. 30 Sept. 14
My darling – I could hardly believe my eyes when I got your letter this morning and looked (as I always do first) at

the envelope – the writing was so evidently yours, & yet so
unlike. I needn't tell you how shocked I was when I read
the contents. Thank God I have now got your telegram –
but do <u>do</u> be careful. As you said on Monday in your letter
one <u>wants</u> so much . . .

Penrhos House
30 Sept.
Darling, Sorry for the awful scrawl – tho' my temperature
is down, my eyes are poor & I don't trust myself to use pen
& ink whilst lying in bed. I do hope the flanking attack
comes off – you are so sweet to keep me always in the
know. O Prime, I fear it's unlikely I can come & see you
speak in Cardiff on Friday, as tomorrow we leave Penrhos
for good, & go to Alderley, but if I can, I shall.

10 Downing Street
Thurs. 1 Oct 1914
My darling – Your little pencil note this morning shows
distinct signs of advance in the way of handwriting, but I
am distressed to learn about your eyes. I feel almost as sad
as you must be feeling, at the thought that this is the last
day of Penrhos for the year. What memories of association
it has, most dear, for you & me! And happily the latest are
the best. It is a lovely autumnal day with bright sunshine &
a keen edge in the air: and I wish I were at Penrhos, in our
hollow, or anywhere, & try to think that I am there: &
after a moment of vain reverie I realise that I am in the
Cabinet room.

The Germans are pounding away with their big guns at
Antwerp, and tho' the Belgians are in large numerical

superiority they seem to have lost morale & nerve, and are making the most piteous appeals for help. The French telegraph that they are willing to send a division (of 15,000 to 20,000) & to put it under a British general . . . Darling – I know all this doesn't bore you, but sometimes I am afraid that I may burden you too much with my preoccupations. After all, this is the biggest thing we are ever likely to see, and I shall & must take you with me every day until it is carried through, or I succumb . . . I feel honestly unworthy of all you have been, and are, & will be to me. My love!

On Friday evening, Deemer met Kell at his club. He travelled on the Underground, with the week's haul of photographs in a locked briefcase resting on his lap, and waited on the bench opposite the porters' glass-fronted lodge. Several dozen men in evening dress, braying loudly, strolled past him on their way to dinner. They reminded him of a colony of squalling pink-faced penguins. Presently, Kell appeared, also wearing black tie, and took him upstairs to the deserted library.

They sat in a corner. Kell said, 'Have you had a good week?'

'Quite fruitful, sir.'

He unlocked his briefcase and handed over the stack of prints. While Kell leafed through them, he glanced around at the shelves of leather-bound volumes, the shaded reading desks, the solid heaviness of the place.

'My God,' said Kell, 'I've never written to my wife like this. Have you ever written anything like this to yours?'

'I'm not married, sir.'

'But if you were?'

'He's certainly very eloquent.'

'Eloquent! That's one word for it! "Thinking and remembering and longing and hoping"? "I love you more than life"? And what about this: "the touch of your hand"? What does he mean by that?'

He seemed fixated on the declarations of passion. Deemer said, 'And then there's the secret intelligence.'

'Well, yes – quite! The entire Allied divisional strength on the Western and Eastern Fronts! Joffre's plan of attack! But you still say there's no evidence, either in her correspondence or the maid's, that they're leaking any of this?'

'No, sir.'

'But unfortunately, we know there are still enemy agents at large in the country, and German sympathisers at every level of society, so we can't afford to be complacent. Just because no secrets seem to have reached Berlin so far, it doesn't mean it couldn't happen.'

'Wouldn't the safest course be to simply stop it at source? To somehow let the Prime Minister know that *we* know?'

Kell sighed. 'It isn't as easy as that, I'm afraid. This operation is off the books, remember. How would we let him know? Who would tell him? He's in a very powerful position at the moment. The war isn't going well, but he's more popular than ever. We need to wait for the right moment. Besides – you've read the letters. He's in the grip of some kind of erotic obsession. I'm not sure he's even capable of stopping at this point. Perhaps it will all just die down. These things often do.'

'Perhaps.' Deemer was dubious about that. If anything, he thought, it was intensifying.

Kell looked at his watch. 'I must go. I was due at dinner ten minutes ago.'

'Would you like to take the photographs?'

'Heavens, no.' He thrust them back at him. 'I can't risk having all that in the office. Keep it under lock and key at Mount Pleasant. You're doing a first-rate job, Deemer. I won't forget it.'

They went down to the street together. On the club's steps in Pall Mall, they shook hands. The major turned left towards his dinner, and Deemer right – towards the Tube station and his cell-like office in Mount Pleasant where he would deposit the photographs for the night before his solitary walk back through Clerkenwell to his house.

CHAPTER TWENTY-ONE

THE PRIME MINISTER was in Cardiff that evening, to deliver the last of his capital city recruitment speeches. Accompanied by Margot, Violet, Elizabeth and Lloyd George, he was driven from the railway station in a procession of open carriages with a mounted escort, passing beneath the castle walls, through streets lined with thousands of cheering men and women, until he arrived at the American Roller Rink – whatever that might be – a vast modern edifice of corrugated iron, where an audience of ten thousand was waiting for him. The air shook with the ovation as he entered. The rafters were hung with flags.

He was a good platform orator. He had taught himself to overcome his natural diffidence in 1903 while pursuing old Joe Chamberlain from hall to hall at the time of the free trade campaign – and he'd beaten him. He knew how to put on a vulgar show. Remembering the tricks of the Nonconformist preachers of his youth, he always saved a final punch for his peroration.

'Men of Wales, of whom I see so many in this splendid gathering, let me say one last word to you. Remember your past. *(Cheers.)* Think of the villages and the mountains which in the old days were the recruiting ground of your fathers in the struggles which adorn and glorify your annals. Be worthy of those who went before you and leave to your children the richest of all inheritances – the memory of fathers who in a great cause put self-sacrifice before ease, and honour above life itself!' *(Loud cheers.)*

Afterwards, as the immense audience roared out 'Men of Harlech' –

> Rend the sluggish bonds asunder,
> Let the war cry's deafening thunder,
> Every foe appall!

– his glance kept returning to the one empty seat in the front row.

It had gone better than his speech in Dublin. He had hoped right up to the last minute that she might turn up. Her absence took the edge off his triumph. This was why he needed to involve her in everything, every day. If he didn't share the events of his life with her, none of them seemed to matter nearly as much – or, indeed, at all.

The recruiting offices had to stay open long after midnight to cope with the queues of men stirred by his words to enlist. Each signatory was presented with a tin token of a Welsh red dragon to remind him of the occasion.

By eleven the next morning, he was back in Downing Street.

Kitchener came round straight away from the War Office to see him in the Cabinet Room.

He began as usual without preliminaries, his curious blue eyes staring at everything and nothing. 'I need to bring you up to date, Prime Minister. We discovered late last night that the Belgian government was planning to abandon Antwerp and retreat to Ostend. There was a meeting at my house at midnight – Winston, myself and Grey. We agreed that to lose such a vital port would be a strategic disaster, therefore Winston left for Belgium at one o'clock this morning to take charge of the situation. He should be almost there by now. He proposes to send in his Royal Naval Division to help stabilise the front line. I hope you agree with our decision.'

Oc, thought the Prime Minister immediately. Oc was in the Royal Naval Division. He had received a letter from him that morning, from the divisional camp in Kent, describing his induction: sleeping under canvas, cross-country runs, tug-o'-war. He made it sound like an outdoor holiday.

'Are we sure they're fully prepared? My son only started his basic training three days ago.'

'Winston seems to think so.'

'Well, in that case – of course.'

What else could he say, without looking as though he was trying to keep his boy out of harm's way?

'I'll keep you informed of developments.' At the door, Kitchener turned, and added encouragingly, 'I'm sure they'll acquit themselves well.'

The Prime Minister tried to shut it out of his mind, but reminders were everywhere. On Sunday morning, he drove over to Oxford with Margot to visit Puffin at his preparatory school. The boy was young for his age, girlishly pretty, with blonde curls, like Millais' *Bubbles*: very much his mother's darling. He felt crowded out by the intensity of their mutual love – awkward, distant, grandfatherly. In the hall as they were leaving, a hundred pupils gathered round him with sheets of paper, cards and autograph books, and for a quarter of an hour he signed his name, with as much avuncular good humour as he could muster. Please God, he thought, after he had managed to escape back to his car, they don't grow up and have to fight, like their fathers and their older brothers.

That night, he received a three-word telegram from Oc at Dover pier: *Embarking tonight. Love.*

He went to bed holding it and fell asleep with it still clutched in his hand.

The next morning, he woke to a sheaf of telegrams, including one from Winston, sent via the War Office:

5 October 1914 Antwerp
8.00 a.m.
Prime Minister

If it is thought by HM Government that I can be of service here, I am willing to resign my office and undertake command of relieving and defensive forces assigned to Antwerp in conjunction with Belgian Army, provided that I am given necessary military rank and authority . . .

Kitchener had scrawled in the margin in pencil: 'I will make him a Lieut. General if you will give him the command.'

The Prime Minister had to read it again to make sure he wasn't hallucinating. General Churchill! A politician who as a young man had never risen above subaltern, the lowest commissioned rank in the Hussars! And his son – his beloved Oc – was trapped in Belgium somewhere with this delusional would-be Napoleon! He sent a stern reply, reminding him that his place was back at his desk in London. When he went in to meet the Cabinet that morning and was asked about the absence of the First Lord of the Admiralty, he felt he had no option but to read out the telegram.

The roar of laughter from the assembled ministers could have been heard halfway across Whitehall.

It was too good a story not to share. Naturally, as soon as the meeting was over, he sent the telegram to Venetia to add to her collection. *I know you won't show it to anybody . . .*

By half-past four, Churchill's telegram was in Deemer's hands, together with the accompanying letter.

> (Secret) French is on the move, & in the course of 10 days
> will have concentrated all his forces, including the Indians,
> at some point between Dunkirk & Lille. No one (including
> I hope the Germans) has the least idea of his
> manoeuvres . . .

'Secret' was ringed in red ink.

He had long since ceased to be surprised by the Prime Minister's indiscretions, or by his expressions of passionate longing – *Do you know how much I love you? No? Just try to multiply the stars by the sands* – but even so . . .

He finished his photography, resealed the envelope and took it along the corridor to make sure it caught the next mail train to north-west England.

Venetia received it the following morning – Tuesday 6 October – lying in her four-poster bed in Alderley Park, to which she had been confined from the moment she arrived the previous Friday. It was not like her to be ill. At first, she thought she must have caught a chill, either from lying in the hollow or sitting on the bench under the stars: the symptoms had started almost as soon as the Prime Minister left Penrhos. But they persisted and worsened, and her mother had become sufficiently worried to send for their London doctor, who had put her on a diet of raw meat – which she took in the form of steak tartare – and strychnine pills, to strengthen her heart.

He was an elderly man, with an excellent bedside manner, who over the years had become a kind of family counsellor. He had treated Venetia since childhood.

'I wonder,' he said, giving her a shrewd look, 'if the root cause of all these symptoms isn't nervous strain. Sometimes these illnesses are as much mental as physical. The war is creating an epidemic of anxiety, even among those not called upon to fight.'

He prescribed a complete rest.

'But Mama,' she objected, after he had gone back to Harley Street, 'all I do is rest. Day in, day out. Week in, week out. The truth is, I don't really *do* anything! And don't say that's why I need to get married.'

She propped herself up on her pillows and read the Prime Minister's letter. It was amusing gossip. Anything to do with Winston generally was amusing. And he *was* a darling, to keep her in the know all the time. But there was just so much of it! Each letter demanded a reply, and he became so anxious if she missed a day. She would have to write back at once, even though she neither felt like it nor had anything worth saying.

Wearily, she pulled back the covers, swung her feet to the floor and walked unsteadily across the Persian carpet to the dressing table, where she kept the key to her painted chest hidden in an old jewellery case. As at Penrhos, the box was tucked away behind her dresses at the back of her wardrobe. She pulled it out, knelt and opened it. She regarded her archive. So many decrypted telegrams, so much secret information, such a plethora of extravagant declarations of love! She had asked him what he wanted her to do with it and he had told her to keep it, so that one day they could read through it together. She placed that morning's delivery on top of the heap. Looking down at it all, she began to feel faint. She rested her forehead on the edge of the upraised lid. What if her illness became more serious, and someone else found the key when she was too weak to protest, or she became careless? She had already forgotten to lock it once, when she went to London at the beginning of September – at least she *hoped* she had forgotten; when she had returned, it was open, and the only other explanation was that someone had broken in during her absence.

It was a Pandora's box, she thought suddenly. One day it could release chaos and destruction into the world for them both.

On Wednesday morning, Winston reluctantly obeyed the Prime Minister's summons and returned to London. They met in the Cabinet Room.

The Prime Minister had intended to read him the riot act. But before he could launch his planned assault, a pre-emptive barrage of perfectly formed sentences and paragraphs started rolling across the table towards him, punctuated by vivid flashes of description – of the clatter of machine-gun fire and of German shells whistling overhead and exploding close to where he was standing, and of high-flying aircraft glittering like jewelled moths in the azure firmament. The monologue lasted at least a quarter of an hour.

The Prime Minister studied him as he spoke. Not yet forty, ugly really, pug-like, with his freckled bald head and his thin red hair, childlike almost, domineering certainly, and entirely self-absorbed; and yet sometimes when his blue eyes flashed it was possible briefly to glimpse that zigzag streak of lightning in his brain that someone had once defined as genius.

'I beg of you, Prime Minister, not to conceive of my future any longer in conventional terms, but to relieve me of my administrative burdens at the Admiralty and bestow upon me the honour of a military command. These great armies of Lord Kitchener's that are presently forming – are these glittering commands really to be entrusted to the dug-out trash of our present general staff, bred on the obsolete tactics of twenty-five years ago, mediocrities who have led a sheltered life mouldering in military routine? A political career means nothing to me in comparison to the glories of the battlefield. I have tasted blood, Prime Minister, and like the tiger I am hungry for more! I fear I shock you, but I make no apologies for it, because mine is the spirit that will win us the war.'

He stuck out his chin and lapsed back in his chair, seemingly – at least temporarily – out of ammunition.

'Well, perhaps at some point,' the Prime Minister found himself murmuring dubiously, 'it may be possible.' It was so much the opposite of what he had intended to say he couldn't help smiling. He tried to adopt a stern expression. 'But for now, your place is here. No more wild adventures. You're too valuable to lose.' Winston gave him a self-mocking, sad puppy-dog look of contrition. 'Anyway – you believe Antwerp can be held?'

'Most certainly. If the Belgians play their part and the French send the forces they have promised. But if the worst comes to the worst, we should be able to make a fighting retreat.'

The Prime Minister toyed with his pen. He said casually, 'Did you hear anything of Oc while you were over there?'

Winston shook his head. 'But I can make inquiries.'

'No, don't do that. He wouldn't want to be treated any differently to the rest.' As Winston rose to leave, he added, 'Why don't you and Clemmie join us for dinner tonight?'

'I should certainly like to, Prime Minister, thank you. Clemmie, unfortunately, I fear is indisposed.'

'I'm sorry to hear that. Nothing serious, I hope.'

'She had her newest baby last night, while I was in Antwerp. Another girl. We've named her Sarah.'

'Congratulations. Perhaps, under the circumstances, you had better spend the evening with her.'

'Oh no, she's all right. She'll understand.'

He saw a lot of Winston over the next few days – at dinner that night, when he was the modestly smiling war hero newly returned from the front, and then again the following morning, when he stormed over from the Admiralty in a rage. The Germans had bombarded Antwerp heavily throughout the night, the Belgians were in flight, the French had failed to move, and the commander of the Naval Division was proposing to abandon his position and escape to Ostend. Winston got through to him on the telephone from Bongie's office and shouted at him to stay in the trenches. But in the afternoon, Kitchener joined them in the Cabinet Room, studied the map, pointed out bluntly that the position was hopeless, and said they must evacuate that night under cover of darkness.

The Prime Minister escaped to his club. He sat in an armchair in the library of the Athenaeum with a whisky and soda on the table beside him and finished the letter to Venetia he had begun earlier in the day. *Poor Winston is very depressed, as he feels that his mission has been in vain.* He glanced up at the clock. It was ten to six.

. . . the sight of you, & the sound of your voice, & the
touch of your hand mean so much to me. I must stop now

as it is close to post time & I want you to get this letter before you get up. Mine alas! has not yet arrived, but I still hope for it. My own darling, I never cease to think of you – with all my love.

He dropped the letter in the club's post box and walked back towards Downing Street – down the steps to the Mall where the crowds had been singing on the eve of war but which was silent now, past the Admiralty and across Horse Guards Parade. The sun was just setting. It would be dark in Antwerp in less than an hour, and Oc, assuming he was still alive and unwounded, would be on the move. He wondered – and then checked himself again. Some things were best not thought about.

At the Mount Pleasant sorting office, seven o'clock passed with no sign of the Prime Minister's daily letter to Venetia. Deemer stayed on. He was sure it would come; the old man never missed. He must have posted it outside the Westminster district. It was Venetia's side of the correspondence that was causing him more trouble: forwarded from Cheshire, it generally reached him late.

When the PM's letter finally arrived, he opened it, photographed it and resealed it as quickly as he could and sprinted along the corridor to the collection room. But he had missed the deadline for the evening mail train to the north-west. And when he returned to develop the prints, he found they began with yet another of the Prime Minister's recent complaints about the late delivery of her letters: *My darling – there is certainly something rotten about your posts at Alderley . . . it is rather disquieting.* What would happen if his disquiet turned to suspicion, and he demanded an investigation? It seemed absurd that he would do such a thing in the midst of a general European war, but given his need to have a letter from her first thing every morning, it was not impossible.

For the second night in succession, Winston abandoned Clemmie and came to dinner, along with Sir Edward Grey, and Raymond, who tried to be amusing about his eccentric London Volunteer Defence Force but whose flippancy grated on his father's nerves. He poked at his food without an appetite. From time to time, Winston left the table to telephone the Admiralty to find out if there was any news. There was none.

The Prime Minister came downstairs the next morning to a telegram from General Rawlinson, reporting that two thousand men of the Naval Division had escaped overnight from Antwerp and were safely on their way to Ostend, where they would be evacuated. It was impossible amid the chaos to determine whether Oc was with them. Another two thousand were still in peril.

He went for the weekend to the Wharf and was told that the remains of the division had set sail for Dover on Saturday night: still no word of Oc.

It wasn't until Monday evening, late at night, when the rest of the household was asleep and he was working alone amid his collection of little glass figurines, that he heard heavily booted footsteps running up the stairs, and suddenly there in the doorway was Oc. He jumped up from his desk and, for the first time since his son was a boy, flung his arms around him. He was still in his uniform. His body felt thin and hard and strange, and he smelled of sweat and earth and cinders, like a visitor from the underworld.

Oc laughed and pulled away. 'Steady on, Prime! You'll break my ribs!'

They sat up drinking brandy until long past midnight, the Prime

Minister listening as Oc recounted his story – how the brigade had set off at five o'clock the previous Sunday afternoon and marched from Betteshanger camp to Dover behind a band playing music hall tunes – 'Hello! Hello! Who's Your Lady Friend?' – through cheering crowds to board a troopship, and how from that moment on, almost everything had started to go wrong. First, it had turned out there was no food on board for the officers, so he and Rupert Brooke – 'some kind of poet, apparently, a pretty odd chap for a soldier I thought at first, but he turned out to be a hell of a fellow' – had to disembark and buy provisions from a local hotel. Then, once they had crossed the Channel, they had been stuck anchored off Dunkirk, playing cards, waiting for the right tide. When they finally made the harbour, they had spent the afternoon unloading, and sat in a great empty shed a quarter of a mile long until after dark, at which point their senior officer, a lugubrious ex-subaltern in the Guards, had warned them they were probably going to be killed, either on the train taking them to Antwerp that night, or in the trenches when they arrived, so they had better write their farewell letters home.

The train was packed but they got through all right. More cheering crowds greeted them in Antwerp the next day, but they could hear the German howitzers pounding the outskirts of the city, saw enemy aeroplanes overhead, and as they marched towards the front, passed wagonloads of dead and wounded heading the other way. They arrived in darkness at a deserted chateau, statues of Cupid and Venus in the grounds ('very poor stuff, you would have hated them'), had a few hours' sleep on the stone floors, then, frozen and exhausted, just before dawn were marched off again to relieve the Belgians in the trenches around an antiquated fort. The trenches were collapsing but none of them knew how to use an entrenching tool; they had barely learned how to fire a rifle:

'Brooke had been in the division just a week, I'd had three days, and Dennis Brown – a pianist, another lovely chap – had only been a soldier for twenty-four hours.'

Thousands of shells screamed over their heads and smashed into the fort. By the end of the following day, it had been levelled to nothing. Finally, when it got dark, they were ordered to retreat – a twenty-five-mile march over cobbled streets that took them eight hours. The night was as bright and hot as a midsummer's day. Rivers of burning petrol ran in the gutters, spires of flames towered on every side, sending out billows of blinding acrid smoke. Dead horses and cattle sizzled in the heat. Half a million refugees were fleeing the city, pushing prams and handcarts piled with their belongings, the old men crying, the women tougher, the children trudging in a daze. The brigade reached a pontoon bridge over the Scheldt just as two German spies were discovered trying to blow it up. They were made to kneel by the roadside and a British major shot them both in the back of the neck. Oc and his comrades somehow managed to get across the river, 'but if the wind had blown the fire the other way, we would never have made it'. Fifteen hundred men had not been so lucky. They were doomed to spend the rest of the war in captivity.

When he had finished, the Prime Minister hardly knew what to say. Given his position, he didn't feel he could give vent to his true feelings, even to his son, especially as Oc seemed strangely unaffected by his experiences. On the contrary, he made his catalogue of horrors sound like a thrilling adventure and insisted he was eager to get back in the fight. But the next day the Prime Minister poured out his dismay to Venetia: *Strictly between ourselves, I can't tell you what I feel of the* _wicked_ *folly of it all . . . Nothing can excuse Winston . . . It was like sending sheep to the shambles.*

CHAPTER TWENTY-TWO

H E WAS INCREASINGLY preoccupied by death – by the lists of casualties published daily in the newspapers, the killing of his friends' sons, the letters of condolence he had to write. It had never occurred to him that he might be called upon to lead the country through such a war. He wondered what the world would make of him after he was gone. Often nowadays, before he went to sleep, he composed his own obituary in his head, or imagined himself standing in the dock before some heavenly tribunal, awaiting judgement.

Fifty years ago, when he was twelve, he had been walking up Ludgate Hill to school when he came upon the bodies of five convicted murderers, publicly executed half an hour earlier, trussed and dangling from the gallows outside Newgate Prison, their heads shrouded by white hoods. The image had stayed with him for years, then faded in the busy decades of middle age, but now it had started to come back to him in his dreams – those damned dreams!

How many years of active life did he have left? It was a matter of simple arithmetic. Ten? Fifteen?

He had to see Venetia. When he was with her, his melancholy lifted. Yet more than two weeks had elapsed since their blissful interlude in Penrhos. After his conversation with Oc, he made up his mind. If she was not coming to London, he would go to Cheshire.

Once he had settled on his objective, he set about to trying to achieve it, as if it were a piece of controversial legislation that needed to be pushed through Parliament. He informed Venetia that he thought he saw his way clear to coming up to Alderley on Friday (*I am counting the hours*). He wrote to Lady Sheffield and asked if he might stay next weekend. He instructed Bongie to clear a space in his diary, and ignored his raised eyebrows. And when he went to say good night to Margot that evening, he announced in a matter-of-fact way that he would be going away for a few days to Alderley to see the Stanleys.

'Surely we were with them only very recently?'

'I know, but they say we're always welcome, and we haven't had a holiday this year, not even to Scotland, and God knows when I'll next have a chance. I could do with a rest.'

'I can't join you, unfortunately. I've made other arrangements.'

'I realise that, but I do see a gap opening up this weekend, and I really think I must seize the opportunity.'

She stared over his shoulder, her lips compressed, and he braced himself for what he knew was coming.

'Venetia will be there, I presume?'

'I expect so. She's been rather ill. I get the impression she needs cheering up.'

'Well, I'm sure you'll do that.'

She leaned over and turned off the light.

He asked George to arrange to send his luggage on ahead and told him there was no need for him to come himself: he would use one of the Stanleys' valets. He wrote to Venetia, saying he could stay for four whole nights: *Are you glad beloved? Does it I wonder excite you at all as it does me? To see you again, not in a crowd – but near & close by & by ourselves, that is my idea of Heaven . . .*

He found her polite reply on Thursday slightly troubling, and reproved her gently – *You say 'we shall be glad to see you'. I shouldn't perhaps have put it quite that way* – but he set off after lunch on Friday undeterred. He took a taxi on his own to Euston station – no private secretary, no detective – and boarded the four o'clock train to Macclesfield. He felt gloriously free. His compartment was only half-full. None of the other passengers seemed to recognise him. He had brought with him a volume of Robert Browning – there was one poem in particular he wanted to show Venetia – and passed most of the journey with his head buried in that. Occasionally, he took a nip of brandy from his hip flask.

It was dark by the time he arrived at Macclesfield and changed trains to catch the local service to Alderley Edge. The Cheshire countryside was mostly invisible except for the odd pair of headlights on the winding lanes, the window a black mirror. He studied his reflection. In his youth he had been reasonably handsome, but time had done its work. His cheeks were purplish and covered in a filigree of tiny crimson blood vessels, his nose more bulbous, his mane of hair, once fine and thick, was white and wispy. *I have become an old man*, he thought. He had another sip of brandy. *Well then, all the more reason to live life while one could.*

The train pulled into the little village station just after half-past eight. The platform was deserted; he was the only passenger to alight. In the foggy autumnal evening, the gas lights were diffuse and yellow. It was eerily quiet, a muffled silence, colder than in London – he was glad of his overcoat with its astrakhan collar and his warm top hat. As he made his way towards the station entrance, the only sounds were his footsteps and the tap of his cane.

He had half-hoped she might be there to meet him, but of course that was unrealistic: it was already past dinner time. Waiting in the lane was Lord Sheffield's old Rolls-Royce, with a chauffeur standing by the rear door, smoking a cigarette. When he saw the Prime Minister, he dropped it onto the damp road and ground it under his toecap. Five minutes later, they were gliding down the familiar long drive from the gate lodge towards Alderley Park. The great house, with its sixty bedrooms, rose above the layers of mist drifting across the park from the lake, so that it seemed to float in its own landscape like a luxurious ocean liner, its windows ablaze with electric light along all of its immense facade.

To begin with, the weekend followed the same frustrating pattern as the one at Penrhos.

He was told the family were delaying dinner for him. He was shown up by the butler to his usual room, where his evening dress had been laid out for him, and a valet was waiting to help him change. Ten minutes later, he went down to the baronial drawing room to be confronted by the customary crowd of extraneous hangers-on who always made an intimate conversation with Venetia so difficult to achieve. There were her parents, obviously, and her sisters, Sylvia and Blanche, and a handful of others he knew well: the beautiful Gwendoline ('Goonie') Churchill, who was married to Winston's younger brother, and Roderick Meikeljohn ('Mikky'), a shy aesthete who had been his private secretary when he was Chancellor of the Exchequer. There was also, he was dismayed to see, standing with his back to the fire, the portly figure of Algernon Stanley, Lord Sheffield's septuagenarian brother, a worldly Catholic bishop who had spent much of his life in Rome.

And, of course, there was Venetia – paler and thinner than when he had last seen her – who came over at once to greet him, stopped at a discreet distance and leaned in to kiss him lightly on either cheek.

She said, 'This is an unexpected treat.'

'My dearest, how are you?'

'Much better, thank you, Prime.'

But she didn't seem entirely herself, and soon after they had gone into dinner and the first course was over, he saw her rise from the table, whisper something to her mother and leave the room.

Lady Sheffield said, 'I'm afraid Venetia is still feeling rather tired. I hope she'll be stronger in the morning.'

It was a grief to him, to have come so far and to have barely exchanged a word with her, but he was more concerned for her than himself. Unfortunately, the next day was scarcely an improvement. That little toad Meikeljohn attached himself to them from breakfast onwards, and when he wasn't engaging the Prime Minister in conversation about the war – a subject he was anxious to forget for a day or two – he was mooning around after Venetia. He was a confirmed bachelor of nearly forty, who still lived with his parents. It wasn't possible – was it? – that even he might be considering making a proposal of marriage? The Prime Minister had always rather liked him, but as that Saturday wore on, he conceived an intense irritation for the fellow which was not alleviated until Sunday afternoon, when he and Venetia finally found themselves alone together and she suggested they go up to her sitting room.

The weekend had not seemed to her a great success. She thought the Prime Minister looked exhausted and unwell. It was awkward for her parents that he had turned up so soon after his last visit, and without Margot or any of his usual entourage. And she couldn't help noticing how much he was drinking, and the glances that were exchanged behind his back whenever he accepted another glass. After they had gone upstairs, he went off to fetch something, and when he came to her room, they sat on the sofa and she put her arms around him. There was a fire in the hearth, two dogs lying asleep before it, a table with a chess set, shelves of books, framed etchings by Piranesi. Outside, the sky was already darkening. He sighed contentedly.

'Peace at last.'

He had returned with a volume of Browning, *Men and Women* – a first edition naturally, from 1855 – and suggested they should read one particular poem together, 'The Statue and the Bust', he taking the part of the Duke of Florence, and she the bride he glimpses for the first time on her wedding day as he is riding past her house. 'It reminds me of us.'

It was quite a long poem. It took them a quarter of an hour, passing the text back and forth.

> He looked at her, as a lover can;
> She looked at him, as one who awakes:
> The past was a sleep, and their life began.

But the bride was to be married that day and nothing could prevent it. The duke attended the wedding feast, and although each vowed to meet the other again, they never had the courage to act upon their desire, trusting instead to Fate to reunite them. *Weeks grew months, years; gleam by gleam / The glory dropped from their youth and love*, until all that remained of them at the end of their lives was his statue in the town square and her bust, set in the window of her house.

And the sin I impute to each frustrate ghost
Is – the unlit lamp and the ungirt loin,
Though the end in sight was a vice . . .

When they had finished reading, Venetia said, 'That's beautiful, but very sad. And quite a daring thing to have written in 1855, wouldn't you say – a poem advocating adultery?'

'It's not simply about adultery,' said the Prime Minister in a distant voice. 'That's an awful, legal term. It's about two souls who should have joined together in life and for eternity but failed to do it. Imagine it, darling – dying, and never having had the courage to grasp the thing one wants most in the world.'

She glanced at him. He was sitting with the book open on his lap, staring at the fire.

His mood was strange. She had never seen him like it. He took down her volume of Shakespeare's complete works and read her Hamlet's 'to be or not to be' soliloquy, as if he thought that suicide might be the best solution to his problems. And when on Monday morning they walked through the arboretum arm in arm, and sat on a wooden bench overlooking the lake, he returned to the same themes: duty versus love, convention versus passion, death as a welcome release from a life not worth living.

She started laughing, partly to conceal her alarm, partly because it all seemed so melodramatic and absurd. 'Oh, do chuck it, Prime! Your life's not as bad as all that!'

'I'm sorry, darling. But I do sense we've reached a crisis. Don't you feel it? The war, these constant separations? You do love me, don't you?'

'Yes, but what's the alternative? Anything more would be the end of your career.'

'Does that matter? I've been prime minister for six and a half years – more than enough for any man. No doubt my departure would be a sensation for a week or two, but I'd soon be forgotten.'

'Listen to me, sweetest. You will win the war. You will never die. And you will always have me. Now do let's get back to the house before anyone notices we're missing.'

He left straight after breakfast on Tuesday morning feeling better than when he had arrived. He had said what he wanted to say, and she had not ruled it out completely.

It proved impossible to say a proper goodbye. Goonie and Blanche had decided to travel down to London with him, and the family had all assembled in front of the house for their departure. The bishop made a sign of the cross and blessed their journey. The beautiful but air-headed Goonie actually curtsied.

Venetia kissed the Prime Minister on the cheek. 'Remember what I said. It's not as bad as all that. I'll see you in London soon.'

'Thank you for everything, my dearest. And *you* remember what *I* said. And *write!*' he added over his shoulder.

As the car pulled away down the drive, he twisted around in his seat to wave to her, but she had already gone inside.

On the train from Macclesfield, Goonie read *The Times* and Blanche knitted, while he took out a pencil and began a letter to Venetia. *My darling – as I move every minute under a gloomy sky to an ever-lengthening distance from you I wonder if you have anything of the same sensation – a sort of dull ache . . .*

By three, he was back in London and presiding over a Cabinet meeting. Afterwards, Winston stayed behind to speak to him about the First Sea Lord, Prince Louis of Battenberg: he was ill, declared Winston, he wasn't any longer up to the job, he had been born in Austria and he had a German name. The press was becoming more murderous by the day. It was time for him to go.

'Who do you want to replace him?'

'There's only one man. We must bring back Jackie Fisher.'

'Is that wise? It's four years since he retired. He's terribly old and egocentric.'

'His mind functions on a titanic scale, in harmony with the scale of events. I can handle him. And bringing him back will galvanise the Admiralty.'

'Well, if that is who you want. Now, if you'll excuse me . . .'

The Prime Minister was keen to get back to his letter to Venetia, which he wanted to finish in time to catch the post.

It arrived in the middle of the following morning. Yet again it was delivered slightly later than usual. She put on a fur coat and took it down to the lake to read.

I go back in thought, & often shall, to those delicious hours when we read together & were silent, & read again & talked. You remember what we said about short and long lives? Anything would be better than to <u>rust</u>. Better far to leave Ithaca & its rocks & 'twinkling lights' and to start on a new voyage:

> 'It may be that the deep will draw us down,
> It may be we shall reach the Happy Isles,
> And see the great Achilles who we knew.'

Modern conditions are not favourable to this kind of adventure; if so, the only attraction may be to shuffle off the coil, and, as I think Macbeth says, 'jump the life to come . . .' As I said yesterday – whatever is in store for us, you & me – we have not fallen into the feckless blunder of the 'frustrate ghosts' – the unlit lamp & the ungirt loin. Thank God for that.

She groaned and briefly bowed her head. First Browning, then Shakespeare, now Tennyson's 'Ulysses'. This fantasy of his was becoming tedious. Not that she believed for a moment he was serious. No prime minister ever gave up power willingly, however much strain they were under: if that was in their nature, they never would have acquired it in the first place. And if he was serious, what did he envisage? The two of them living in a little cottage somewhere? What about the scandal and social ruin it would entail for her? That didn't seem to have entered his calculations.

Her life was entirely on the wrong track. With the whole world being stood on its head, surely it must be possible for a single woman with some spirit and a decent brain to break free and follow a course of her own choosing? She must find something to *do*. And for the first time, as she turned to walk back through the woods to the house, she began to consider how she might try to extricate herself from her affair with the Prime Minister.

PART FIVE

HOSPITAL

3 December 1914–7 April 1915

CHAPTER TWENTY-THREE

S IX WEEKS LATER, on a cold, clear Thursday morning at the
beginning of December, Venetia stretched out one ele-
gantly shod foot and then the other, like an explorer arriving
on a distant shore, and stepped down carefully from her taxi onto
the crowded pavement of Whitechapel Road in the East End of
London.

Behind her as she paid the fare, she was conscious of a teeming,
noisy market selling clothes and pots and pans and all manner of
bric-a-brac. In front of her when the taxi pulled away loomed a
massive, soot-grimed eighteenth-century neoclassical building
with 'The London Hospital' engraved in stone above its entrance.

She stared up at it for half a minute. She had dressed for the
occasion in a demure dark hat with a stiff brim, a plain grey skirt,
and a three-quarter-length fur coat with matching stole. She
hoped that was appropriate.

She crossed the wide road, stopping in the middle to wait for
the traffic to pass, climbed the flight of steps and went through
the arched portico into the interior. At the porter's desk she gave
her name and was directed to a small waiting room off the main

lobby. The parquet floor was dark and highly polished. There was a pervasive smell of disinfectant. She was surprised to feel so nervous. This, she imagined, must be what it was like to go to school for the first time, or to have an interview for a job. But as she had only ever been taught by governesses and had never been interviewed for a position of any sort, that could only be conjecture.

After a few minutes, a nurse came to fetch her and took her up an echoing staircase and along a wide corridor with lime-green walls to the office of the head matron.

Miss Eva Luckes was seated at her desk – a small, plump, round-faced elderly woman, who bore a striking resemblance to Queen Victoria. Venetia had taken the precaution of looking her up beforehand: a friend of Florence Nightingale, a campaigner for health reform, chief matron at the London Hospital for a third of a century.

She was invited to sit.

'So, you are the Honourable Beatrice Venetia Stanley.' Miss Luckes enunciated each syllable slightly sceptically and scrutinised her application through a pair of half-moon spectacles. 'And what makes you believe you have the qualities necessary to become a nurse?'

'I don't know whether I have or not, Matron, but I want to try.'

'Why?'

'Because it seems to me the best contribution I can make to the war effort.'

'And why do you choose to make your contribution here rather than in Cheshire?'

'Actually, my first idea was to set up a hospital for wounded soldiers in my parents' house, but I was told I lacked experience.'

'Indeed. You do. Completely.' She looked up from the application. 'It is large, I take it, your parents' house?'

'It is, yes.'

'How many bedrooms?'

Venetia hesitated. 'Sixty.'

The matron laughed. 'Well, yes, that *is* rather large. Many of our patients live in slums where they have to sleep four or five to a room. This is a hospital for the poor, you know, as well as for wounded soldiers. We have five hundred of each.'

'I'm not afraid of poor people.'

'I'm sure you're not. But you do realise what being a nurse will entail? Ten-hour shifts, seven days a week, with three hours off per day and one day off per month. It means living in a hostel on the premises, at least to begin with, and sharing a bathroom with twenty others. Sweeping floors, emptying slops, dressing wounds, feeding and bathing male patients with running sores who may not have washed for weeks. A lot of young women like you from wealthy families give up very quickly.'

'I shan't.'

Miss Luckes folded her arms and studied her properly. 'No, perhaps you won't.' She picked up her pen and scrawled her signature on the bottom of the application. 'The normal training period for a nurse is three years, but for those who can afford a fee of thirteen guineas, that is reduced to three months. At the end of that time, if we believe you have passed your probation successfully, you will be qualified to work elsewhere – at one of the military hospitals in France if you really want to help the war effort. The fee must be paid in advance.'

Venetia opened her purse and counted out thirteen guineas. Miss Luckes swept the coins into her palm and put them in a cash box.

'The next induction day is Wednesday the sixth of January. You will be sent details of the uniform, which you must provide yourself. You should arrive the evening before, no later than six p.m., when you will be allotted a room.'

She locked the cash box and put it in a drawer. She handed Venetia a receipt.

'If you change your mind, the money is non-refundable. We shall see how you get on. Good day to you, Miss Stanley.'

Outside at the top of the steps, Venetia raised her face to the sky and closed her eyes. She savoured the moment. Never mind that she had had to pay for the privilege. For the first time in her life, she had a job.

They had arranged that the Prime Minister would pick her up from the corner of Mansfield Street the following afternoon for one of their Friday-afternoon drives, although she had told him it would need to be shorter than usual: she had to catch the four o'clock train back to Alderley.

He left Downing Street at half-past two to collect her.

It was an unsatisfactory arrangement from his point of view, and it fitted into a pattern of recent disappointments. A couple of weekends earlier, when they had both been staying at a house party in Kent, she had chosen to drive back to London with Clemmie Churchill rather than with him. Last week, she had stood him up for lunch. Her letters were as affectionate as ever, and when they were alone together, they were still as intimate. But he sensed a barely perceptible drawing-back. And now there was this foolish business with the hospital. He secretly – and, because she was so set on it, rather shamefully – hoped that her interview had gone badly, or that she had seen the conditions under which she would have to work and had come to her senses. But the moment she climbed into the car he could tell it was all settled. She had an air of purpose about her, a seriousness.

'Hello, Prime.' She quickly kissed his cheek.

'Darling. How was Matron?'

'Oh, you know – *matronly*. Fierce. Formidable. I liked her. She tried to put me off, but the more she listed the horrors, the more determined I became.'

'I could have warned her about that. So, you're in?'

'I'm in.'

He tapped on the window with the top of his cane. The car pulled away. He had instructed Horwood to drive them around Regent's Park.

She took his hand. 'Do at least *try* to be happy for me.'

'I am, of course, although as I've said from the start, I simply can't understand how a woman of your intelligence and refinement can bear to contemplate such demeaning work – it's beyond my comprehension. And when am I going to see you? I imagine the hours must be very long.'

'They are long.'

'How long?'

'Ten hours a day.'

He started to protest, but she cut him off. 'One *is* allowed three hours off a day for meals and exercise. And the course only lasts three months.'

'Three months of hardly seeing you – for me, that's an eternity!' He couldn't resist adding, 'I fear you seem less concerned about it.'

'Of course, I hate the prospect as much as you do, but I have to find a way of playing my part.'

'Surely there must be a better way? Charity work?'

She withdrew her hand.

'Let's not talk about it any more. I hate it when we disagree. Tell me what's been happening in your life.'

But he didn't much want to. Everything was black. Margot's nephew, Lachlan Duff, had been killed in action; Blanche's husband, Eric Serocold, seriously wounded. Raymond had finally been commissioned into a proper regiment, the Queen's Westminster Rifles, and Beb was in the Royal Artillery – so, along with Oc, that made three sons in uniform. He was proud of them, but what were the chances they would all survive unscathed? There had been terrible fighting around Ypres. The army had lost thirteen thousand men in two weeks. It was a war unlike any other. Industrialised slaughter.

He said, 'Now Winston's agitating for an attack on the Dardanelles to break the stalemate. But after his antics at Antwerp, I must say I have serious doubts about invading Turkey. That's just between us, of course.'

'Of course.'

They drove slowly around the Outer Circle of Regent's Park. He would have liked to draw the blinds, but she didn't seem in the mood, sitting slightly apart from him and leaning forwards. Suddenly, she said, 'Let's go to the Zoo.'

'If that's what you want.'

When the entrance came into view, he signalled Horwood to stop.

It was a cold, hard day, the temperature barely above freezing. But it had at least the advantage of deterring all but the hardiest visitors, and they had the place almost to themselves. As they strolled between the cages and the animal houses, she took his arm. He had always disliked the Zoo: the forlorn-looking animals, the heavy sour stench of dung, and rank fur, and scaly skin. They made their way from the aviary, past the monkey house – where she tried to cheer him up: 'It always reminds me of the House of Commons; look, there's Bonar Law' – and towards the bear pit.

'It smells of misery.' He pointed with his cane. 'That camel looks particularly depressed.'

'I doubt camels ever look cheerful, even in the wild.' She gave his arm a tug. 'Let's look at the penguins before we go.'

A thin crust of ice ringed the edge of the pool. The birds stood motionless on their rocks, waiting to be fed.

'At least,' she said eventually, 'my penguin had a taste of freedom. Every living creature deserves that, don't you think? It's cruel to deny them the chance of a full life.'

'I agree. I detest seeing anything in cages – birds, lions, elephants.'

'And people, Prime. People especially.'

Perhaps it was his imagination, but the remark seemed pointed – rehearsed, even. He wondered if that was why she had wanted to come.

They walked back to the car in silence.

At Euston station, he insisted on carrying her bag to the platform.

'Next week?'

She kissed his cheek. 'Next week.'

He lingered at the barrier until she boarded the train – third class, he noticed: her curious affectation – and then she was gone.

He wrote to her at midnight, sitting at his desk. A *cri de coeur*. He couldn't help it.

I sometimes think how much more you wd. think of me,
& how much higher you might possibly rate me, if I were
not so fond of you. It is rather sad that one shd. suffer in
the estimation & judgment that one most prizes, because
one loves so much.

He sighed and shifted around his little collection of figurines. If only neediness was attractive – how much happier the world would be! In the distance, Big Ben chimed twelve. He leaned over and unlocked the dispatch box in which he kept her letters and took out the only two photographs he had of her. Looking at them, he felt a twist of pain in his stomach as sharp as a pang of hunger.

I must now go to bed. If you were to fail me – I know you won't – I should go down – 'deeper than ever plummet sounded' . . . Good night beloved.

For Christmas, he sent her two more first editions: Alexander Pope's translation of *The Iliad* and Voltaire's *Candide*. But she outclassed him with her present, dispatched from Alderley: a large leather-bound 'Treasury of Love Sonnets', all beautifully copied out in her fine calligraphy, each capital letter coloured and larger than the surrounding text, with illustrations in the margins, like an illuminated medieval manuscript. He kept it by his bedside. It must have taken her days of laborious work. He wondered when she had done it. Not recently, he suspected. Probably in the summer, at Penrhos, when she had sent him the 44th Sonnet – *If the dull substance of my flesh were thought, / Injurious distance should not stop my way* – which he always now thought of as *their* sonnet. Things had been simpler then.

His New Year resolution for 1915 was to be more supportive, less demanding. If he couldn't talk her out of her decision to become a nurse, he could at least try to put on a show of being cheerful about it. He offered to give a dinner in her honour at Number 10 on Monday 4 January, the evening before she was due to move into the hospital – 'a farewell dinner', he half-jokingly called it – but she wrote to say that Montagu had beaten him to it, and that they were both invited to his house instead. *He bought me a dress for Christmas, and although I know you won't believe me, it's really rather fine. I suspect Violet must have chosen it.*

The dinner was, like all the Assyrian's entertainments, a lavish occasion – Lord and Lady Sheffield, Sylvia and Blanche, Winston and Clemmie, Margot and Violet, Raymond and Katharine, Oc and his new friend Rupert Brooke, Bongie and Diana Manners. Outside, it was snowing; inside, the house was warm and brilliantly lit. The 'silken tent' was an architectural conjuring trick. It looked narrow from the street but was five times as long as it was wide, running on and on towards the rear through several grand reception rooms that came to an end in a magnificent view over St James's Park.

Margot had taken charge of the *placement* and had put the Prime Minister at the far end of the table, well away from Venetia. The improbably handsome Rupert Brooke, who was becoming the Byron of the day, was seated next to Violet, and the Prime Minister thought they looked very intimate: that wouldn't be a bad match, he thought. He was between Clemmie and Sylvia and stared jealously through the candles and flowers as Venetia had a laughing conversation with Montagu, wearing the dress he had bought her, occasionally touching his arm. He had just made the Assyrian a Privy Councillor and planned to put him in the Cabinet at the end of the month. Looking at the two of them, he wondered for a moment if he might be making a rod for his own back but dismissed the idea: he really was too ugly and neurotic – the poor, loyal, clever fellow.

Sylvia, following the direction of his gaze, said, 'You exert too much influence over her, you know – both good and bad.'

'Me? I have no influence over her whatsoever! The influence is all the other way.'

The next afternoon, there was a meeting of the War Council, at which Winston's scheme to attack the Dardanelles was discussed for the first time. As soon as he could get away, he picked up Venetia from Mansfield Street to drive her to the hospital: on this at least he had insisted. She emerged carrying a large suitcase, which Horwood stowed in the boot.

He had never loved her more than during that journey through the heavy traffic to the East End. She was clearly nervous but determined not to show it, and he thought how brave she was, what spirit she was showing, to leave behind her comfortable life with her family and social circle and embark on God-knew-what. He was proud of her and ashamed of his selfishness and told her so. By way of an answer, she reached across him and drew the blinds on the dismal, dark winter afternoon.

But when she raised them half an hour later to reveal the depressing sight of Whitechapel Road in the early-evening darkness – the cars splashing through the filthy melted snow, the lights in the squalid shops and tenements, the pinched and ragged pedestrians hurrying home with their heads down – he felt all his old concerns returning. She straightened her skirt and asked him to tell Horwood to pull over.

'But we aren't at the hospital yet.'

'I don't want to be seen arriving in such a grand car.'

'Oh, I was hoping to carry your case to your room and see you settled in. I want to be able to visualise it.'

She laughed. 'It's a nurses' hostel, not a hotel. What if someone recognises you? That would be a good start, wouldn't it – arriving on my first evening with the Prime Minister! I'd like to be dropped off here, please.'

He signalled to Horwood to stop. She climbed out, leaned into the driver's window and asked him if he would be kind enough to fetch her case from the boot. The Prime Minister got out too and stood on the pavement. The wind was whistling down the street from the direction of the Mile End Road. When she had her case, she said, 'Well, this is it. Wish me luck.'

'All the luck in the world, my darling. And all the love. This is for you.'

He gave her the small parcel he had been nursing all week.

She smiled. 'Thank you.'

She wouldn't kiss him in public, even on the cheek. She hefted her case, waited on the kerb for a gap in the traffic, and crossed to the other side of the road. He felt their little intimate world vanish like a bubble.

He said to Horwood, 'Would you mind following her, at a discreet distance? I just want to make sure she's safe.'

They crawled along behind her for a hundred yards, a slender figure on the opposite side of the street. The weight of her case made her bend slightly to the right. Outside the entrance to the hospital, she set it down to rest her arm. Then she squared her shoulders, hoisted it again, and walked away swiftly up the steps. In his imagination, the Prime Minister heard the clang of a prison door.

He got back to Downing Street just before six to find the spartan figure of Major – now Colonel – Hankey, Secretary of the Committee of Imperial Defence, waiting to see him. The Germans had carried out the first ever air raids on British soil during the Christmas holidays, sending Zeppelins over to drop bombs on Dover and the Thames estuary. No one had been killed and not much damage had been done, but they would surely return, and Hankey said that Jackie Fisher, the new First Sea Lord, was proposing they should threaten to shoot all German prisoners as a reprisal.

'He cannot be serious! The Germans would shoot all our prisoners in return.'

'That's what Winston told him. Now Fisher has put in a letter of resignation.'

'I only wish we could accept it, but he's as popular in his way as Kitchener.'

'Winston is trying to dissuade him. Incidentally, Prime Minister, I think we should have a meeting of the War Council to thrash out this plan of Winston's for a naval attack on the Dardanelles.'

'Are you in favour?'

'I am, sir. And Lord Kitchener is coming round to it as well.'

'So, it's more than just another of Winston's hare-brained schemes? Very well. Schedule it for next week.'

After Hankey had gone, he went upstairs. The house was deserted. Margot had gone away for the week with Violet and Puffin to Walmer Castle on the Kent coast, lent to the family by Lord Beauchamp as a country retreat. Oc had returned to the Naval Division's camp at Blandford. He felt suddenly lonely. The thought of Venetia alone in her room in her hideous hospital haunted his mind. He put his overcoat back on, went out into the freezing night and walked down to the Athenaeum, where he ordered a brandy and soda, lit a cigar, and took a sheet of the club's notepaper.

My darling – tho' it is not 2 hours since we parted I must send you one little line for you to read in the morning . . .

CHAPTER TWENTY-FOUR

V ENETIA'S WORLD HAD shrunk in a matter of minutes
from two stately homes and a London mansion to a
locker and a pigeonhole on the ground floor of the
nurses' hostel, and a small room along a corridor at the top of
four flights of stairs. She had a narrow bed, a wooden table with
a wobbly wooden chair, a chest of drawers, a couple of wire metal
coat hangers that jangled on the back of the door whenever she
opened or closed it, a basin, a jug, and a chamber pot. It was so
grim it was almost amusing.

'Don't worry, Beatrice,' said the young probationary nurse who
showed her in, 'you'll soon be so tired you won't even notice.'

'Actually, I'm not called Beatrice. I'm Venetia.'

'Well, you're in the register as Beatrice. So I'm afraid Beatrice
you will be.'

After the nurse had gone and she had unpacked her things, she
unwrapped the Prime Minister's present: Shelley's 'Ode to the
West Wind'. It was kind, but it hardly matched her mood. She laid
the volume aside without even opening it and went downstairs to
explore the kitchen. A pan of stew was warming on the stove. A

couple of nurses were slumped at the table. She had hardly begun to introduce herself when she was spotted by a passing sister, who told her sharply she must always wear her uniform when she was on hospital premises. No one had spoken to her like that since she was a child. Meekly, she went back up to her room to change: a shapeless grey-blue shirt and skirt, an ankle-length white apron tightly belted at the waist, a stiff white detachable collar, a nun's white headdress. She felt she had become another person entirely. Nurse Beatrice Stanley. Why not? Grim. Amusing. She lay down on her bed.

Just after half-past eight, the hostel started coming to life – doors slamming, feet clumping along the corridor, women's voices calling to one another. She went down to the kitchen again. It was crowded now: the day shift was coming off duty, the night shift preparing to go on. Nobody took any notice of her. Eventually, she said to no one in particular, 'Hello, I'm Beatrice Stanley. I'm new.'

Heads turned.

'Pull up a chair, Beatrice.'

They were ordinary, middle-class girls, perfectly friendly. It wasn't long before they started calling her Bea – something else that had never happened to her before.

'Where do you come from, Bea?'

'Cheshire – a little village. Alderley. You'll never have heard of it.'

'Well, welcome to the madhouse.'

Someone made her a cup of tea. At nine o'clock, the door opened and in came three more nurses, just finished for the day, one of whom she recognised – her cousin Nellie Hozier, Clemmie's sister, the same age as Venetia, hoping to be engaged soon to a colonel in the Scots Guards. They fell into one another's arms. Nellie was another probationer trying to 'do her bit'. She took Venetia into the corner.

'When do you start, Vinny?'

'Seven o'clock tomorrow. You'd better call me Beatrice, everyone else does.'

'All right. Let's go on duty together. I'll show you the ropes.'

She set her alarm clock for 5.30, but was awake long before that, lying in her dressing gown under the blankets, trying to keep warm. She took her jug and chamber pot along the freezing corridor to the communal bathroom. Two women were already queuing. Their thin smiles were enough to signal that it was too early for a conversation. When her turn came, she found there was no hot water. She filled her jug from the sink. By the time she emerged, four more women were waiting. She washed in her room and dressed, then inspected herself in her hand mirror. No make-up. Red blotches on her cheeks from the cold water. Dark circles under her eyes from lack of sleep. She looked a fright already, in her sexless outfit, and she hadn't even started yet.

At half-past six, she met Nellie in the kitchen and tried to eat fried eggs and bacon, which slid around her plate on a film of fat. By ten to seven she was following her cousin and a group of others along the covered walkway to the hospital's east wing. Through the windows, the courtyard was in darkness. A few lights shone in the west wing and glittered on the frosty ground.

Nellie said, 'There are forty-one wards. Probationers usually start in Charrington – it's a men's ward, just to warn you.'

She pushed open a door to a large, dimly lit room with seven or eight beds on either side. There was another door at the far end and further interconnected wards beyond that which seemed to go on a long way before they vanished into the shadows. Some of the beds had screens around them. The ceiling was high. The hush, broken by coughs and groans, reminded Venetia of a church. Somewhere at the far end, a man was shouting in terror.

Nellie took her over to the ward sister. 'This is Miss Stanley, Sister. She's on a three-month probation. It's her first day.'

'One of the rich girls?' The sister had a Scottish accent. Her tone was not unfriendly. 'All right, let's get you started. The patient in bed four had a haemorrhage in the night. There's a lot of blood to be cleaned up. Fetch a mop, Nurse Stanley.' And when Venetia hesitated, not knowing where to find one, she added, 'You've seen a mop before, I take it? A pole with a wet cloth at one end and a maid at the other?'

'I know perfectly well what a mop is.'

Venetia cleaned up the blood as best she could. There was an awful lot of it to squeeze out into the bucket. When she thought she had finished, she was told by the sister to do it again – 'Properly this time' – and then to wash the linoleum with disinfectant. After that, there was a lot more sweeping-up with dustpan and brush. As the grey London daylight began to appear at the high windows, she had to go round the ward and collect all the chamber pots that had been filled overnight with urine and faeces, phlegm and vomit, and tip the slops into the lavatory. It made her retch each time, no matter how far she twisted her head away. Then she had to help serve breakfast and sit by the beds of a couple of elderly men who were unable to feed themselves and spoon soft-boiled eggs into their slack mouths as if they were babies, scraping up the residue from their stubbled chins and popping that in as well. Another old man started crying and whispered that he had soiled himself, so she fetched a bowl of water and a sponge to clean him up, and Nellie showed her how to turn a patient, the two of them standing on either side of the bed and sharing the weight between them,

Venetia pushing and Nellie pulling as they rolled him over and wedged him in place on his side with pillows, so that she could lift his nightshirt.

The day got busier. The ward was short-staffed. There was no chance to go off duty. She shared the patients' midday meal of bread and jam and strong Indian tea. She lost track of time until eventually she noticed that outside, the sky had turned dark again; the short winter day had gone. She went up and down the ward closing the curtains. By the end of the afternoon, she had at least discovered, to her surprise, that she wasn't at all squeamish. When one young soldier, newly arrived from France, was brought in with a bad leg wound and she was told to remove the dressing, she found the flesh was crawling with maggots. She held his hand and told him to lie still, and went to inform the sister, who in turn fetched a doctor, who removed the wriggling white grubs with a scalpel and tweezers and dropped them into the bowl she was holding.

At five o'clock, she walked back with Nellie along the covered walkway to the hostel for tea. They followed a group of other nurses. She was too exhausted to speak. In the entrance hall, the women clustered around the pigeonholes to check for mail. Nellie had been hoping for a letter from her colonel, but he hadn't written: 'the rotter'.

'I say, though, Bea' – she had started using her shortened name like all the others – 'look here – you've got *three* letters! I call that jolly unfair!' She had a loud, schoolgirlish voice which made everyone turn to look. She extracted the envelopes from their slot and glanced at them as she handed them over. 'Not only that – they're all from the same person! Come on then, darling – who is he?'

Venetia sighed. 'Oh, just the Prime Minister, I expect.'

She tucked the letters into her apron. They all laughed. They thought she was joking. Dear Bea! She was already turning into a bit of a card.

She left the others sitting in the kitchen eating their supper and slowly climbed the stairs to her room. She dropped the letters onto the table. Her back was stiff, her joints ached. She perched on the edge of her bed, pulled off her shoes, rubbed her feet. Dubiously, she eyed the letters. He had never sent her three in one day before.

She opened them in the order they had been written: the first in the Athenaeum the previous evening (*tho' it is not 2 hours since we parted I must send you one little line . . .*); the second in pencil at midnight (*you must tell me everything, but if you are hustled or tired, just write two or three lines; never less . . .*); the third that afternoon.

> We are going to have our War Council tomorrow morning
> when we shall begin to consider the merits and de-merits
> of various alternative 'objectives'. There, my sweetest that
> is enough for one bout, & I am sure you must be growing
> tired. But you will have to put up with a lot of letters
> now . . .

She knew he would be desperate for a reply before he went to sleep, which meant she would have to write to him now, to catch the evening post. She eased herself off the bed and onto her rickety wooden chair, pulled it up close to the table and reached for her writing case. She wrote rapidly, in a kind of trance.

Half an hour later, Nellie was knocking on her door, telling her it was time to go back on duty.

She dropped the envelope in the post box on their way to the ward.

*

The letter was in Deemer's hands by half-past seven that same evening – steamed open, photographed, resealed, and dispatched to the sorting room for onward delivery by eight p.m.

He developed the prints.

London Hospital
Whitechapel
Weds. 6 Jan. 15
Darling, thank you for your sweet letters, wh. were waiting for me when I came off shift for my break at 5. I can't write much as I'm already more tired than I've ever been in my life, & I still have a couple of hours to go before bedtime . . .

He read her account of her first day at the hospital with close attention. Intercepting her letters had become for him like following a character in a serialised novel. He had come to know her well during the past few months, and – unprofessional though it was – he couldn't help rather liking her. She was funny and clever; she had spirit. The Prime Minister, on the other hand, shocked him constantly: his appalling recklessness, his endless lunches and dinners and games of bridge, his possessiveness towards a woman half his age, his betrayal of his wife. And yet . . . the man wasn't vicious. There was something tragic about him: those reams of poetry, that hopeless yearning. The whole relationship, in Deemer's considered judgement – and he had little else to think about all day – was heading towards disaster. Occasionally of late he detected that the Prime Minister seemed to sense it too but was powerless to stop himself.

When the prints were dry, he locked them away in the safe with the others. It was nearly half-full. If this went on much longer, he would need to order a new one. He was becoming heartily sick of the whole operation, its tedium and loneliness. He was also beginning to doubt the point of it. There was no hint that Venetia had betrayed any official secrets, not even to her friends. But Kell was insistent it continue, until such time as either the affair was ended or there was a suitable opportunity for the Prime Minister's colleagues to discreetly intervene.

'Just because nothing has leaked so far doesn't mean it won't in the future. Let's maintain the surveillance at least until the spring. Then I'll find you a more congenial assignment, you have my word.'

Deemer put on his coat and hat and prepared to go home to his empty house. As he closed the door behind him and pocketed the key, he felt trapped more than ever by the dreary routine of his existence: locked into the affair as helplessly in his way as were Venetia and the Prime Minister – a secret, silent partner in a dangerous *ménage à trois*.

She had started her work at the hospital on the Wednesday. On the Friday afternoon, the Prime Minister picked her up from Whitechapel Road and took her for a drive. He found her more distant than before. The hospital seemed to have changed her. She showed him her swollen wrists and ankles. He found it baffling and horrifying that she should choose to do such work, and couldn't resist telling her so. Just before he dropped her back, she said, 'You know, you must remember, we are very different, you and I. Please don't try to turn me into someone I'm not.'

She thought no more about it, but he must have fretted over the remark all weekend, because on Sunday afternoon, when she was emptying bedpans, the matron who presided over the wards in the east wing came to find her, carrying a letter.

'Nurse Stanley, this has just been delivered by a special government messenger. I don't know how important it is, but it really is
very inconvenient for the hospital to have to cope with these kinds
of communications, especially when we're so busy. Letters should
only come through the post in the regular way. Please ensure there
is no recurrence.'

She felt her face colour, stammered her apologies, and promised it wouldn't happen again.

When she got to her room that evening, she found he had sent
her another secret dispatch from Sir John French, concerning what
he proposed to say at the forthcoming meeting of the War
Council.

Either burn it, or keep it, as you like: perhaps with your
present restricted space the former is the safest course. If I
am in chains, I cling tightly to them. The you that I see &
know & love is to me the real you, and I am pretty certain
that I am neither mad nor doting . . .

She glanced around her cramped quarters. She had no fire. How
on earth was she meant to burn it? In the end, she tore it into tiny
fragments and stuffed them in her pocket, and when she returned
to the ward, sprinkled them into a sack of surgical waste that was
being taken to the incinerator.

Darling, it was thoughtful of you to enclose the dispatch,
but really it isn't safe to send anything like that here; it
caused a certain amount of agitation & I got a rather stern
ticking-off about the special messenger. Please don't do
that again. I don't want to appear in any way 'special' . . .

★

The following Wednesday, 13 January, the War Council met at noon in the Cabinet Room to discuss strategy for the coming months. It was meant to be a national rather than a partisan body. The Prime Minister presided. Sir John French was on his left and Arthur Balfour, the former Unionist prime minister, on his right. Looking round the table clockwise, he could see Kitchener seated next to French – the two generals were being excessively polite to one another – then old Jackie Fisher, with his curiously Oriental face, Winston, Sir Arthur Wilson (the elderly Second Sea Lord, also brought out of retirement), Lord Crewe, Sir Edward Grey and Lloyd George. Hankey was taking the minutes, so at least he was spared that chore. You could not, he thought, have gathered a stranger collection of men around one table. French was all for taking an extra half-million new recruits and mounting a fresh offensive on the Western Front in the spring. Kitchener backed him, with reservations. Balfour and Lloyd George were opposed. Winston for once kept fairly quiet.

The Prime Minister said little. There had been no letter from Venetia for more than a day – nothing before breakfast, nothing waiting for him when they broke for lunch. Her silence tormented him. Just before the start of the afternoon session he left instructions with Bongie to bring him any private correspondence the moment it arrived, and at half-past three, his private secretary appeared in the Cabinet Room bearing an envelope addressed in her familiar darling handwriting. He opened it at once.

> Dearest, I'm sorry you are feeling the absence of letters so keenly, but I'm so rushed all day & every day it really is very hard for me to keep up with you . . .

He read through to the end, keeping one ear tuned to the discussion, and started his reply at once.

My darling – I have just received your most welcome letter, and quite understand why it couldn't have come sooner. I hope I didn't cause any further 'agitation' by sending my second letter by messenger this morning. I knew you were going out for the afternoon, & wanted you to get it before you started. I feel rather jealous of the Assyrian—

'Prime Minister?'

He looked up. Winston was staring at him. 'I wonder if I might now bring before the Council the matter of the Dardanelles?'

'Of course.' He quickly covered his letter with a few Foreign Office telegrams.

The air was stale with tobacco smoke after nearly four hours of discussions, the table littered with papers, the windows already growing dark. Hankey rose from his seat and went round the Cabinet Room drawing the curtains, as Winston set out his own documents and unrolled a naval chart of the Black Sea.

'Gentlemen, let us begin by acknowledging the truth: this war has reached a stalemate, with little prospect of one side defeating the other. A system of trenches now extends from the Channel coast to Switzerland. Are millions of men to chew barbed wire in France indefinitely, at an appalling cost in lives and treasure, or has the time come to seek more fruitful opportunities in more distant lands?

'The Royal Navy has so far in this war served mainly as a deterrent. The Admiralty's proposal is to bring this mighty weapon to bear at last, by employing it to force the straits of the Dardanelles, occupy the Black Sea, and open the possibility of a link-up with the Russian army and a back door into the German Reich.'

There was a stir of interest, even from Sir John French. Some members of the War Council half-lifted themselves out of their chairs for a closer view of the map.

'The commander of our squadron in the Aegean, Admiral Carden, has drawn up a plan for a bombardment of the forts that guard the narrow channel into the Black Sea, the clearance of the minefields, and an advance into north-western Turkey. For this, he estimates he will need a fleet of twelve battleships, three battle-cruisers, three light cruisers, sixteen destroyers, six submarines and twelve minesweepers . . .'

The Prime Minister surreptitiously took out his pocket diary, inspected his week's engagements, then pulled the letter he had just begun from beneath his pile of documents. He shielded it with his arm from Balfour's languid gaze as he wrote.

I have wired to you to say that if (as I suppose) you breakfast with Cynthia at Sussex Place, I will come and pick you up about 10.30 so that I could get you back to your place by 11.30, & myself keep a revised appointment with the King at Buckingham Palace by noon. Then you might come here to <u>dinner</u> in the evening. (This last I see is wrong: you say your free day is <u>Tuesday</u> i.e. next week. Of course I shall keep it free: tell me your hours.) & on Friday you will be here to lunch, & we shall have a <u>real</u> drive afterwards. <u>Friday</u> is all right. What do you say to this plan of campaign? We are now (4 p.m.) in the midst of our War Council, wh. began at 12, adjourned at 2, and is now sitting again. Sir J. French is here & sits next to me. A most interesting conversation, but so confidential and secret that

I won't put anything down on paper, but I will talk fully to you tomorrow (if we meet then) or if not in the course of our drive on Friday.

He folded his letter and returned his full attention to Winston's presentation. It was clear the First Lord of the Admiralty had made a tremendous impression. The torpor in the room was entirely dispelled by the vision he had conjured.

French said, 'And this will require no diversion of men from the Western Front?'

'No, this a purely maritime operation. Any men that may be required on land can be supplied by the Naval Division.'

'And when would this begin?'

'We can start the bombardment in a month.'

Nobody raised any objections.

The Prime Minister said, 'If we are all in agreement, then an operation to force the Dardanelles Straits is approved unanimously.'

Afterwards, as the others were leaving, Balfour said, 'Are you sure it was unanimous? Fisher didn't say a word.'

'Really? I didn't notice. Don't worry about Fisher. Winston says he can handle him.'

CHAPTER TWENTY-FIVE

V ENETIA FOUND IT hard to believe that despite her pleading, he had sent her a second letter by special messenger,
that had landed her in further trouble with the matron,
and all because he wanted to catch her before she met Edwin
Montagu for tea at the Savoy!

And the letter itself, describing a couple of near-misses he
had had in the car that morning motoring up from Kent, and
meditating on the reaction there would have been if he had
been killed – *lots of stuff in the Press – a 'nine days' wonder' in the
country – and after a week or 10 days at the outside, the world going
on as tho' nothing had happened* – it was simply too mawkish for
words:

And you – my most dearly beloved, to whom every day &
night I give my best thoughts, my most intimate
confidence, my unceasing devotion, my fears & hopes, my
strength & weakness, my past my present my future –
you! – what would it mean to you?

It would mean a relief, Prime, she thought savagely – a relief! –
and then immediately felt appalled at her own callousness. But
really, this could not go on, and her attitude towards him over the
next few weeks began to harden. By the middle of January, he was
still writing to her three times a day – in the morning, the afternoon and at midnight. She could not have kept pace with the
correspondence even if she had been living a life of leisure at
Penrhos or Alderley; working ten hours a day in the hospital, it
was impossible. She kept his letters, filled with military and political secrets, in her suitcase, locked and stowed beneath her bed,
and fretted in case someone tried to open it. And yet, by some
peculiar equipoise of rejection and attraction, the further she tried
to draw away from him, the closer he crowded into her life; the
less free time she had available, the more of it he demanded. She
tried to maintain the same affectionate, bantering tone in her letters, but she could not face him personally quite as often as she
once did and cancelled their next two Friday-afternoon drives.

On the twenty-seventh, in one of his midnight messages, he
told her that he had just a few minutes earlier offered 'the Assyrian'
a junior position in the Cabinet.

I am sure he has gone back to his tent – for once in his
life – a genuinely happy man. You, I know, will be glad too.
Sometimes – in my worst moods – I am jealous of everybody
who likes you & whom you like. But that does not last.

She *was* glad, and on impulse wrote Montagu an immediate
note of congratulation, to which he replied at once by telegram
asking if she might be free to come to lunch, just the two of them,
on Saturday to celebrate. He would send his car to fetch her. After

a brief hesitation, she wired him back: *WOULD BE DELIGHTED. FREE FROM ONE TILL FOUR.*

She was touched by all the trouble he went to – the Rolls-Royce to convey her to the silken tent, the best vintage champagne, flowers on the little table set up in the bay window of the first-floor library, an exquisite lunch overlooking St James's Park, sparkling with frost under a crystalline blue sky on the coldest day of the winter. Montagu, however, was typically gloomy, having convinced himself the main reason for his promotion was that Lloyd George wanted to get rid of him from the Treasury. And it was only a very minor Cabinet job – the most junior, in fact – Chancellor of the Duchy of Lancaster.

She laughed. 'Only you could find a reason not to be happy about such good news! I also happen to know that Lloyd George likes you.'

'And how do you know that?'

'Because the Prime Minister told me.'

'Is there anything he doesn't tell you?'

'No, not really. To be honest, he tells me far more than I want to know.'

'What do you mean?'

Perhaps it was the effects of the champagne, or the need at long last to share the burden with someone, but she found herself leaning in to him. 'Edwin, he writes to me *three times a day*. He sends me all manner of secrets – documents even. You wouldn't believe it. It frightens me to have such things in my possession, and yet I don't know how to stop it.'

'Can't you just say so?'

'I've tried. The thing is, he gets so upset at any hint that I might be pulling back from him. And I know it's absurd, but I feel it's almost my patriotic duty to keep him happy.'

'Do you want me to have a word with him?'

'God, no! He'd be appalled if he knew I'd mentioned any of this to anyone, especially you. I didn't even dare tell him I was seeing you – he'd be so jealous.'

'Oh, my dear Venetia!' He looked quite stricken. 'I knew how fond he was of you – everyone knows that – but I had no idea it had gone this far. He's putting you in the most awful comprom- ising position. There must be something I can do to help.'

'Oh, don't worry. I expect it will all sort itself out. You won't say anything, will you? Promise me.'

'Of course not.'

She changed the subject.

They had coffee in the adjoining drawing room. It really was a most beautiful house, she thought. Fit for the Cabinet's youngest rising star. He was only thirty-five, although he looked about fifty.

After a while, she glanced at the ormolu clock, ticking on the chimney piece above the blazing fire. It was already after three.

'I should be getting back.'

'Must you?'

He walked her down the curving marble staircase to the ground floor, through the main reception room to the hall. A maid handed him her coat, and after some clumsy fumbling he managed to help her on with it.

'That was lovely, Edwin, thank you. Better not mention it to the Prime.'

'I won't.' He added, earnestly, 'He's a good man, Venetia – the greatest statesman in Europe, as Winston says. I love him, you know.'

'And I love him, too. I just wish it hadn't become so difficult.'

As she was driven away from Westminster along the quiet winter streets, through the City of London and eastwards towards

Whitechapel, she watched the grand buildings and the wide streets gradually become shabbier and meaner, and she thought about Edwin and his fine empty house overlooking the snowy park. He was clever, amusing, kind, rich, rising in the world of politics, and he had loved her for years. But he was also neurotic, hypochondriac, melancholy, and not in the slightest degree physically attractive. He was also Jewish, and under the terms of his father's will, he would lose his inheritance if he married outside the faith.

The next day, she pulled her suitcase out from under her bed and sorted through the Prime Minister's letters until she found the quotation she wanted. She wrote a thank-you note to Edwin.

I know the P.M. has wanted to have you in for some time. He's <u>very</u> fond of you. He says in one letter 'It is one of the few real pleasures one has to feel one can open the door, without any misgiving as to capacity or merit, to a really great friend.' I am certain you won't stick in the Duchy for long, & as I am very ambitious for you (!) I welcome this step very greatly. Next time I have my day off I'm determined, if you can, to dine with you, get a 'late pass' & try to win or lose a little money. Will you arrange that? Yours ever, Venetia.

She hesitated before she dropped it in the post box. She knew the effect it would have.

His reply came the next day.

God bless you Venetia. You have been an angel friend to me, why not a wife? I cannot guess. Have you ever thought again of that? Yrs, Ed. Montagu

★

Ten days later, in the second week of February, the Charrington ward was suddenly cleared of local patients and turned over entirely to wounded soldiers. They brought with them, along with the mud on their boots and their khaki uniforms, the sights and smells of the field hospitals of northern France: trench foot and gangrene, amputated arms and legs, shattered jaws and skull fractures, and gaping shrapnel wounds that required cleaning and re-dressing daily.

Some of the young men flirted with Venetia. Some were silent and morose. A few talked to themselves, or shook uncontrollably, or shouted out visions only they could see. These she tried to spend more time with, sitting on the edges of their beds, holding their hands. For the first time she felt as though she was doing useful war work.

Early one afternoon, a porter came in with a stepladder and hung a Union Jack from the ceiling, imparting a patriotic touch. Not long after that, a dapper, well-dressed man in his late fifties appeared, followed by an assistant. Venetia, going through the ward pushing a trolley laden with bowls of clean water, bottles of antiseptic and fresh bandages, was too preoccupied to pay him any attention. She pulled on a pair of brown rubber gloves and began changing the dressing on the arm of a young man who had been badly cut up by a shell splinter. It must have been painful, but he tried not to show it. He was one of the flirtatious types. He kept glancing over her shoulder.

'Tell you what, miss, don't look now, but we're being painted.'

She turned to see. The visitor had donned a crumpled fawn linen jacket, of the kind a shopkeeper might wear, and had set up an easel. He was standing a few yards away with a palette of paints in one hand, a brush in the other, and was making rapid strokes across the canvas.

'Hello, Miss Stanley.' He gestured vaguely with his brush. 'I hope you don't mind.'

It took her a moment to recognise him. 'Mr Lavery?' She had met him at lunch in Downing Street.

'It's an official commission from the War Office,' he said, 'for the historical record. Please just carry on. Ignore me.'

'As you wish.' She returned to bandaging the arm and pulled a face at the young soldier. She said quietly, '*The historical record . . .* I say!'

'Is he famous?'

'He is rather. Hold still.'

'Well, fancy that – you and me in a painting together.'

'He specialises in society ladies. He charges a great deal of money.'

'You should be grateful to me, miss – you're getting yours done for nothing.'

'Very funny. There.'

She had finished. Tentatively, he tried to move his arm. 'Will it be all right when it's healed?'

'It will probably always be stiff. There's quite deep damage to the muscle. But you should have some use of it.'

'Pity it's my right. I've not been able to write a letter home since the day I got hit.'

'I can do that for you if you like.' She smiled at him. She liked his cheekiness. 'It's the least I can do – in return for the painting.'

Deemer heard the letter-box flap the following morning, just as he was shaving. It was an occurrence unusual enough for him to finish quickly, dry his face and go shirtless downstairs. When he bent to retrieve the letter, he suddenly stopped. Venetia Stanley wrote in a very distinctive style – high capitals and upward strokes, lowercase very small, almost print-like, the words widely spaced. The sight of his name and address in her handwriting was a shock. He carried the envelope into the kitchen and placed it on the table, and took a breath before he opened it.

Weds. 10 Feb. 15

Hello, old man, you'll never guess what, but I'm back in England. I took a bit of a hit from a Hun shell splinter, made a real mess of my arm, & I'm in the London Hospital being patched up – Charrington ward, if you fancy a visit. I'll be right as rain in a week or two, so not to worry, but thought you'd want to know. A lovely nurse is kindly writing this for me.

Your loving brother Fred

(As dictated; PS, <u>not</u> lovely)

His overwhelming reaction was relief – that Fred was alive and that Venetia hadn't written to him demanding to know why he was reading her letters. She was simply a nurse on his brother's ward – an outlandish coincidence, but not impossible. At any rate, he resolved to take it at face value.

On his way to Mount Pleasant, he stopped to send a telegram to Fred saying that he would call round that evening after work. There was a risk he might run into Venetia, but he calculated it was slim, and it certainly wouldn't deter him from going to see his brother.

The day seemed to drag even more slowly than usual. In the morning he opened a letter from the Prime Minister written the previous night:

A secret telegram came this morning, wh. has only been
seen by Winston, Grey, K & me, from the Admiral (Carden)
that the business out there, wh. was to have begun next
Monday, has had to be postponed for a few days, as the
requisite minesweepers could not be got together sooner.

He knew what the 'business out there' was: the attack on the
Dardanelles. Once again, Nurse Stanley knew more about military
operations than most Cabinet ministers.

In the afternoon there was a letter from Venetia, which seemed
to refer to Fred:

We have had an influx of wounded from France, some
quite bad (it is sobering to think that the worst cases are
too ill to evacuate & so these poor devils are the lucky
ones). They seem so <u>young</u>. I do what I can to cheer them
up, not just dressing their wounds but sitting with them,
lighting their cigarettes, helping them write letters to their
relatives . . .

The evening delivery produced a final letter from the Prime
Minister, posted at half-past five, with its usual inconsequential
gossip:

We have just had a huge & most heterogeneous lunch
party. Mrs Lavery sat next to me and told me that her
husband who is painting an interior in one of your wards
had seen you at the Hospital . . .

By eight, he was on his way to Whitechapel.

*

From the moment he entered the ward, he felt embarrassed. To be young and able-bodied and to walk in civilian dress past beds occupied by men of his own age who had been wounded fighting for King and Country – he found it shaming. It was late. The lights were dim. He was the only visitor. (He had managed to talk his way past the porter on the front desk by showing his police warrant card.) He felt as if he was intruding on some exclusive masculine society. There was a soldier in uniform, his left leg missing below the knee, obviously trying to get used to moving around on crutches, swinging his way along the aisle between the beds. Two men with bandaged heads were sitting in a corner smoking pipes and playing chess. Somewhere in the shadows, a patient started howling and was good-humouredly told to 'Pipe down, Jimmy, for God's sake,' by one of his neighbours.

He found Fred halfway down the ward on the right, propped up on his pillows, his arm in a sling, asleep. He looked small and thin and hollow-cheeked, yet smooth-skinned and oddly innocent, like a very young old man. He opened his eyes and smiled.

'Hello, Paulie.'

'Hello, Fred. How are you?'

'Bloody awful, what do you think? Still, better off than most.'

'I brought you a few things.' From his coat pockets he pulled a couple of cartons of cigarettes, a bar of chocolate and a half-bottle of whisky.

'Oh, lovely! Pull the screens round, will you, there's a good bloke? We're not supposed to have a drink.'

Deemer did as he was asked. Fred tried to hold the bottle in his right hand so he could unscrew the top, but he didn't have the strength, so Deemer did it for him. Fred took a couple of swigs then offered him the bottle. 'Your health.'

'And yours, more to the point.'

He swallowed a mouthful then lit a cigarette, inhaled, and handed it to Fred, who lay back happily on his pillows, smoking and sipping whisky. Deemer sat on the edge of the bed. As usual, there was a great sense of affection between them, and yet hardly any conversation. When he asked Fred what had happened, he said there had been a bloody great bang and that was all he could remember. He deflected every question about life in the trenches. He didn't want to talk about it. There had always been a gulf between them and now it seemed to Deemer that the war and their utterly different experiences had widened it still further.

Eventually, he said, 'You make me feel guilty.'

'Come off it, old man!'

'You know what I mean. I ought to be fighting.'

'Don't worry, you'll get your chance. I reckon every man in the country will be out there before it's finished. These buggers will take some beating.' He finished his cigarette and stretched over stiffly to the bedside locker to stub it out. 'You ought to be going.'

Deemer stood with relief. 'When you're discharged – come and stay with me. I have a spare room.'

'That's good of you. Let's see what the army says.'

'They won't send you back to France, surely?'

'Christ, I hope so.' For the first time, Fred looked distressed. 'What else can I do? I don't want to let the lads down.'

'Well, let's see. The important thing is to get that arm working again.' He pulled back the screens. 'I'll come again.'

'No need for that.'

'Of course I will. See you, Fred.'

'Night, Paulie.'

As he passed the sister's desk by the entrance to the ward, a nurse looked up from the chart she was filling out. The uniform threw him for a moment, then he registered the dark hair and eyes beneath the white headdress, the irredeemably aristocratic manner, and he realised he was face to face with Venetia Stanley.

She said, 'Can I help you?'

'No, thank you. I was just visiting my brother over there.'

'Ah, Private Deemer! He's a character. You received his letter then?'

'I did, thank you. It was good of you to write it for him.'

'How did you know *I* wrote it?' She looked genuinely puzzled.

Suddenly, he was flailing.

'I didn't. I'm sorry. I just assumed.'

'Deemer?' she said thoughtfully. 'Deemer. I thought I recognised the name. It's rather unusual.' She was studying him more closely now. 'We've met before, haven't we?'

'Have we?'

'You're the policeman who came to interview me after that awful river accident.'

He made a show of pretending to remember. 'Yes, I believe I did. It's Miss Stanley, isn't it?'

She nodded. 'That seems a whole lifetime ago. And yet here we are again.'

He shrugged. 'It's a small world.'

'Mine is a very small world indeed.'

It was an odd remark. He thought she was about to say something else, and for a crazy moment he felt a powerful impulse to warn her that her correspondence was being read by a government department, that she was under suspicion of breaking the Official Secrets Act, that she and the Prime Minister were on the brink of a scandal that could ruin them.

'Well, good night, Mr Deemer.'

'Good night, Miss Stanley.'

He touched the rim of his bowler. The door swung shut behind him. As he walked away along the corridor, he was sure she was watching him, but when he reached the end and looked back, the round window in the door was empty.

CHAPTER TWENTY-SIX

THE PRIME MINISTER had suffered a lapse in concentration. That brilliantly efficient mind of his – the precision instrument that had guided him like a sextant, through Oxford and the law courts, Parliament and government – had briefly slipped its focus on the afternoon when the War Council approved the Dardanelles operation. By the time he looked up from his letter to Venetia, its members had already been stunned by the force of Winston's rhetoric. Perhaps he would have been too – Haldane once complained that arguing with Winston was like trying to argue with a brass band – but the Prime Minister had the authority and the forensic skill to subject him to a more thorough cross-examination. He had missed his chance, and gradually, throughout the latter part of February and into March, he came to regret his error.

First, the naval bombardment of the outer forts protecting the entrance to the straits, which Winston had promised would begin on Monday 15 February, had to be postponed to the Friday because four minesweepers hadn't turned up. That caused him a slight unease. The navy had had a month to prepare. Surely the time needed to get them into position should have been foreseen?

On the day the warships began shelling the Turkish garrison, he went for a drive with Venetia, picking her up from the hospital and driving aimlessly into north London. In Islington, they passed the grim dark terraced house in Liverpool Road where he had lodged as a schoolboy for two joyless years with a Puritan chemist and his wife. The sight of it depressed him, and although Venetia could not have been sweeter, he sensed there was something dutiful about her solicitude, that a distance was opening between them he somehow couldn't bridge. They talked about the war.

'How are things going in the Dardanelles? Didn't you say it was starting today?'

'I haven't heard anything yet.'

He dropped her back in Whitechapel Road and Horwood drove him to Victoria station to catch the train to Walmer Castle.

On Saturday he sat on a bench in the castle grounds, his face turned to the winter sun, and thought about those two years in Liverpool Road, the way he used to creep out of the house as a sixteen-year-old to go to the theatre – strictly forbidden – and queue for an hour or more for the cheapest seats. That was where he first fell in love, with an actress named Madge Robertson, although he never spoke to her, merely gazed up at her with infatuated rapture from the pit. It was a relief from his present worries to retreat into the past. He was still waiting for news about the progress of the bombardment, but nothing came.

It was only on Sunday that Winston finally sent him a telegram saying that after an encouraging start the attack had had to be abandoned due to bad weather and that the fleet had retreated to its harbour in Lemnos.

When the news of the operation broke in the press the following morning, the tone of the reports in *The Times* struck the Prime Minister as somewhat hesitant. *The reasons in favour of this operation are overwhelming, provided that the risks and necessary preparations have been coolly calculated in advance.* According to the Turkish communiqué which *The Times* unhelpfully printed, the four hundred heavy-calibre shells that the British battleships had rained down on the forts had resulted merely in one man being injured by stone splinters. He dismissed it as another Northcliffe attempt to cause trouble.

On Tuesday, Oc came to lunch in his Naval Division uniform to say goodbye. He was due to take part in the landings once the forts had been subdued and had travelled up to town to buy the last of his kit, including a Baedeker guide to Constantinople, from which he read choice extracts at table. He was in his usual high spirits. It was all an adventure to him. The whole of London society seemed to know the Naval Division was heading to the Dardanelles, which made the Prime Minister wonder about the element of surprise. At the door, Oc's parting words were, 'Don't worry, Prime. I'll send you a postcard of the Blue Mosque.'

Margot went down to the West Country to see him off and returned looking anxious. On Friday, he wrote about it to Venetia.

At the eleventh hour it seems to have been discovered that they were without either doctor or drugs, & Clemmie showed a good deal of resource, with the result that they will pick up some necessary 'details' at Malta, but it doesn't look as if the organisation was well thought out. Rupert Brooke is quite convinced that he will not return alive.

He had never felt the need for her more, and he thanked God and more importantly the authorities of the London Hospital that she finally had been given a few days' leave the following week on the grounds that she had been overworking: her blood pressure was high. He told her that he would pick her up from Mansfield Street at 6.15 on Wednesday evening, 3 March, and that they would drive together to the Assyrian's for dinner.

From the moment she climbed into the car and gave him a peck on the cheek, he knew that their levels of anticipation about the week ahead were on entirely different planes, but he pressed on regardless, pulling out his pocket diary, trying to schedule as much time together as possible. She said she was going to Alderley at the weekend, and he waited for her to invite him, but she was silent.

'Listen,' she said eventually, 'please don't take this the wrong way, but I've hardly seen any of my friends in the past two months, and I simply can't make all these commitments to you. I don't think it's fair on them, and to be perfectly honest, I don't think it's fair on me either.'

He was so startled he didn't know how to reply. She had never spoken to him in such a way before.

'Of course. Forgive me.'

He put away his diary and tried to behave as if he understood, that it didn't matter, that she was tired, not quite herself. They talked as normal throughout the rest of the journey, but inside he felt quite wretched.

The dinner party was an exquisite hell for him. He didn't think she had ever looked more beautiful. The hard work and poor food of the hospital had caused her to lose weight. It was almost as if strain suited her. She had a kind of ethereal loveliness in his eyes – aloof, cool, untouchable, like one of the actresses he had fallen in love with as a shy young schoolboy, like Madge Robertson herself. He watched her laughing and gossiping with the Assyrian and the others, and although she spoke to him, and even touched his hand as he was leaving and whispered, 'I'm sorry about earlier, I didn't mean to speak so sharply,' he had a terrible sense of foreboding.

He lay awake after midnight, and finally, at one o'clock on Thursday morning, decided he had to tell her how he felt.

No greater blessing ever befell any man than has befallen me, in knowing & loving you: And whatever happens, nothing can ever take that away from me. Of course, it follows that you can (if you were so inclined) give me more pain than anyone else in the world. I have quite forgotten the little transient stab of last night, which you so quickly & so sweetly healed. I know well that you are far too kind by nature (even leaving out any special feeling you may have for me) ever voluntarily to inflict a wound.

He posted the letter first thing, and tried to concentrate on work, but it was hopeless, and he wrote again in the middle of the morning, just a couple of sentences, a cry of pain; he could not help himself.

My darling – I am so unhappy. It is no use saying anything – but I am. I think of Landor's lines – 'I warmed both hands before the fire of life; It sinks – & I am ready to depart'.

He waited all day for her reply. It didn't arrive until nine that evening, brought round by messenger to the house of the Home Secretary in Smith Square, where he was having dinner. He turned his back on the other guests to read it.

I'm so very sorry that you are feeling miserable, & that I am in any way the cause of it. Nothing has changed in my feelings towards you, it is only the circumstances wh. have changed, & we must try to make the best of what is possible. Please be happy, dearest, & try to understand. Ever yours.

He took it back to Downing Street after dinner and sat at his desk, reading it, and re-reading it, studying every word closely, trying to discern the deeper motivations behind it, as if it were one of the Kaiser's telegrams from last summer. There was no 'my darling', he noticed, only 'dearest'. He picked up his pen.

Midnight. My own darling – thank you with all my heart for your little note, which I got at dinner at the McKennas. It made me less unhappy. But I am. If you are free, I will call for you in the motor at 5 to 3 tomorrow (Friday) and we will have a drive. Your devoted – always –

For the first time that he could remember, he passed an entire night without sleep, a real *nuit blanche*, listening to every chime of Big Ben. I am losing my mind, he thought. It was not impossible. Men *had* gone mad in office. Castlereagh had slashed his throat out with a pair of scissors in 1822 when he was Foreign Secretary and had died in the arms of his doctor. It was a relief when morning came.

At 2.55 p.m. exactly, he drew up in the car outside the house in Mansfield Street. He could see her standing at the window, waiting for him. She came out at once, kissed him and took his hand, and as the Napier drew away said quietly, 'Now tell me exactly what is troubling you. I'm starting to become worried.'

They drove up to Hampstead Heath and he tried to explain to

her how he felt, the misery of loving her more than she loved him, her indispensability to his life and work, his terror of losing her, his thoughts of suicide.

'Really, there were times last night when I prayed for a heart attack. And the worst of it is, I know there's nothing to be done. I don't blame you at all, my darling. I don't want to monopolise your life. No one could have been kinder to me than you have been. I know I'm making unreasonable demands on you. But it's as if a fissure has opened up within me that simply can't be filled. Perhaps it's always been there.'

'Oh, poor dear Prime, you have everything entirely out of proportion.' She put her arms around him. 'You must see it's the strain of the war and worrying about Oc and Beb and Raymond, and everything else. I'm still here.'

'For now, yes – but for how much longer? You'll finish your training and go to some wretched hospital in France, and I'll hardly ever see you. Or you'll marry someone – I know it's bound to happen – I don't think I could stand that.'

'I haven't decided definitely to go to France, and if I do you can come and see me – make some official visit as an excuse. And as for marrying, I'm a long way off that, but if it happens, we can still meet.'

'It wouldn't be the same – it *couldn't* be the same. I can't bear the thought of sharing you.'

Still, he felt better for having poured it all out, and she couldn't have been kinder or more loving. When he dropped her back at Mansfield Street at half-past four, it was almost like old times. Even when he said, 'You know, I'm supposed to be going to Walmer for the weekend, but I could always change my plans and come with you to Alderley,' and she replied gently, 'I think that could be difficult,' he accepted the rebuff without demur.

He wrote to her from the train early that evening.

My own darling – I had a very healing hour & a half with you and feel far happier than 24 hours ago I thought wd. ever be possible. I didn't really exaggerate in what I said to you: the coup foudroyant (in the literal sense) would have been welcome all yest. aft. & night. It may not be wise to be so dependent: to have put everything that one has or hopes for into one investment: to stand or fall entirely by one person: but it is too late now to make these calculations . . .

And he wrote again at midnight.

My most beloved – I wrote you a little letter in the train wh. I hope you will get by teatime tomorrow (Sat.) I don't suppose it was at all adequate, but it will at any rate have conveyed to you that, after our divine drive today, I am no longer in a suicidal mood.

He wrote to her again the following morning, and in the afternoon, and at midnight. And he wrote on Sunday morning, and again at midnight.

And then it was back to London, and the Dardanelles.

On Wednesday, he chaired another meeting of the War Council, enlarged by the addition of Bonar Law and the Unionist leader in the House of Lords, Lord Lansdowne. What had begun as a purely naval operation had now, in the face of Turkish and German resistance, swollen to a plan for a full-scale land invasion. Kitchener proposed to send the best of his new armies training in England, the 29th Division, which together with French, Australian and New Zealand divisions would bring the task force's strength to almost seventy thousand men. They would land on the Gallipoli Peninsula. During the discussion, the Prime Minister kept his eye on Jackie Fisher, who seemed as usual detached, his faintly Oriental face with its yellowish complexion – a consequence of malaria and dysentery caught on active service in Egypt – staring out of the window, as if the whole thing had nothing to do with him.

The next day he sent Venetia a fragment of a sequence of sonnets he was writing about her.

> Love keeps no account of more or less,
> Gives without stint, exacts no recompense:
> Adds to its wealth by prodigal expense:
> Creates a Garden of a Wilderness.

My darling – would you, do you think, care rather more for me if I cared rather less for you?

London Hospital
Fri. 12 March 15
Dearest – I fear this will be a damnably boring letter, as I have done nothing all day except work. I have been thinking over what you have written & said, & how difficult everything now seems to be compared to how it was back in the summer. Do you remember Browning –

> We two stood there with never a third,
> But each by each, as each knew well:
> The sights we saw and the sounds we heard,
> The lights and the shades made up a spell

Till the trouble grew and stirred.
Oh, the little more, and how much it is!
And the little less, and what worlds away!

We need to find a balance, & I wonder if the best way
forward for us both wd. be if you tried the experiment of
loving me less . . .

Walmer Castle
Sat. 13 March 15
My darling – I didn't find your letter this morning
'damnably' or at all boring: on the contrary, it had one or
two passages of rather exceptional interest. The lines from
Browning (wh. I had forgotten for the moment) are most
true . . . No, I am not going to 'try the experiment of
loving you less'; the difficulty (if it is a difficulty) is all the
other way. But I have come quite definitely to the
conclusion that it is the best thing in my life.

Five days later, on Thursday morning, Kitchener asked to see him
in private, to discuss the general situation of the war. They sat
opposite one another at the Cabinet table. The Field Marshal,
normally so lofty and imperturbable, seemed for once agitated
and preoccupied. The new commander of the army task force,
General Hamilton, had arrived in the Aegean on Tuesday, and had
sent him a worrying telegram. He had brought it with him.

'He says we've been concentrating all our efforts on subduing
the outer forts of the Dardanelles, but according to him those
aren't the real problem. Apparently, the straits beyond the forts
are bristling on both sides with concealed field guns and howitzers, which are proving more or less impossible to destroy from

the sea. And it turns out there's an even greater danger from mines which have been sown in the channel.'

'I thought we had a flotilla of minesweepers to deal with that.'

'We do. But no sooner have we cleared the mines in the daylight than the Turks come back and lay new minefields at night. The fleet is in action even as we speak but it's a hazardous business, and up to now, it's not gone well. I'm very much afraid, Prime Minister, the Admiralty has over-promised what they could deliver by purely naval measures.

'And I must alert you to another serious problem developing on the Western Front. French has had to halt his offensive at Neuve Chapelle because he claims to have run out of shells.'

'Is he right?'

'Yes, but only because he's wasted so much ammunition. On the first day alone, it seems we fired seventeen days' worth of the country's entire shell production, and we've only succeeded in advancing just over a mile. That works out at two shells for every square yard of territory gained. We simply can't continue in such a profligate manner. We also suffered twelve thousand casualties, but that's of less concern. To put the matter brutally – men I can replace; artillery shells I cannot.'

The Prime Minister briefly closed his eyes. The worst crises in politics always occurred, in his experience, when two unrelated problems struck at once. The difficulties weren't doubled, or even squared, but cubed. 'I think you had better get over there and take a grip on the situation.'

'I shall. I fear French simply isn't up to the demands of modern scientific warfare, or commanding four hundred and fifty thousand men in the field. We shall have to make a change.'

The following day, before he could collect Venetia for their

Friday-afternoon drive, he had to deal with Winston and the War Council.

The First Lord of the Admiralty's gift for narrative was such that he could make a defeat sound as compelling as a victory – could make one believe, in fact, that a defeat *was* a victory. The Prime Minister and the other members of the Council – Kitchener, Lloyd George, Balfour, Bonar Law, Grey, Fisher and the rest – listened with rapt attention to his description of the previous day's naval action: eighteen battleships, including the *Queen Elizabeth*, the most powerful warship in the Royal Navy, protected by an armada of cruisers and destroyers, sweeping across the glittering waters of the Aegean early in the morning, beneath a blue sky flecked with white clouds, into the dragon's jaws of the Dardanelles straits, the *Elizabeth*, *Agamemnon*, *Lord Nelson* and *Inflexible* opening fire on the forts at a range of eight miles – a smashing assault. But then, unfortunately, the gods of war withdrew their favours. The French warship *Bouvet* either hit a mine or took a direct hit in her magazine from a Turkish shell – at any rate she disappeared in a cloud of smoke and steam, and sank at once, taking six hundred men with her. The Royal Navy minesweepers fled in the face of withering fire from the Turkish field guns and howitzers. *Inflexible* struck a mine, and began to list. *Irresistible* was torpedoed on her starboard side. The battleship *Ocean* exploded, her steering gear jammed, and she began to go round in circles. At the end of the afternoon the fleet commander gave the order to withdraw. Three battleships had been sunk, three crippled. One third of his force was gone. The forts were still intact.

Winston looked around the table. 'We shall more than make good the losses. *Queen* and *Implacable* are already on their way. *London* and the *Prince of Wales* will be sent today. A gale blew up last night, unfortunately, but as soon as it abates, we shall resume the attack.'

His voice was firm, but his hands, the Prime Minister noticed – surprisingly small and fine, almost feminine – were clasped tightly together, as if to stop them shaking.

Kitchener said, 'I shall order General Hamilton to ready himself to land on the peninsula as soon as practicable. It's obvious those guns will eventually have to be silenced by the army.'

The Prime Minister summed up. 'We must leave it to the commanders on the spot to decide, but I believe we are all in agreement that they should press on with the attack whenever they feel that conditions permit.'

The members of the Council, apart from Fisher, murmured their assent. What else could they do?

Venetia had been lunching with the McKennas. The Prime Minister picked her up from Smith Square to drive her back to the hospital and told her about the naval disaster in the Dardanelles. She said, 'It sounds to me as though the whole conception is flawed. Surely it would be wiser to abandon it now, before any more lives are lost?'

'I'm afraid that would be a disastrous blow to our prestige internationally, but especially in the Mediterranean. Just between ourselves, we have some hopes of bringing Italy into the war on our side in the next few weeks. Can you imagine the effect it would have on that? No, I fear there's no alternative except to double down.'

'Sometimes,' she said carefully, 'it's better to accept the inevitable and cut one's losses.'

In his heightened state of anxiety, he caught the implication at once. 'That's a rather double-edged remark. Are you talking about us? "Cut one's losses" – my God! You can't mean it?'

She turned away from him to look out of the window. After a while she said, 'There's never going to be a good time to tell you, so it might as well be now. My training at the hospital ends in three weeks, and I've applied to nurse in France.'

The fact that he had been expecting the blow didn't make it any easier to bear, and although he had sworn to himself he would accept it calmly and try to be supportive, he feared in retrospect he made something of a scene, demanding to know how she could desert him at such a critical moment in the war, when he needed her more than ever: what was dressing wounds in France – a job that could be done by any one of hundreds, thousands of women – compared to the unique contribution she could make by sharing the burdens of the nation's leader?

She absorbed it all, not with a stony face, or by arguing back – either of which he could have taken – but with a sad, sympathetic, almost *pitying* smile, and when they drew up at the hospital, she kissed him on the cheek and said she hoped she would see him next Friday.

He said plaintively, as she was getting out of the car, 'Not till then?'

'I'm afraid not.'

He felt so bereft that as soon as the car pulled away and they started on the long journey to Kent – he had decided to go to Walmer Castle by road – he began writing to her, jolting and swerving in the back of the Napier along the Mile End Road, a near-illegible scrawl. *My darling you have just left me & I feel very desolate . . .*

It was divine being with you & near you, watching you, hearing you; and looking back upon our heavenly hour I

am sorry that I dwelt so much on gloomy forecasts of a
selfish kind. My darling you know that I should never
quarrel with what on full reflection you thought right &
best for yourself – unless, indeed, it meant cutting me out
of your life. That I could not endure. But you won't ever
do that – will you? I can't say more. Write me a sweet little
letter. I am going to post this at the next office I find.

He stopped the car at Maidstone when he saw a post office on
the opposite side of the road, and after he had dodged through
the traffic and bought a stamp and handed over his letter to be
posted, he stood on the edge of the pavement and watched the
cars and lorries hurtling past, experiencing the noise and the wind
of them almost sucking him off his feet. It really would only take
a moment – *To die – to sleep, / No more; and by a sleep to say we end
/ The heartache and the thousand natural shocks / That flesh is heir
to* . . . He imagined his broken body flying through the air, perhaps
a moment or two of agony, and then nothing. He stayed poised
on the kerb for half a minute, an elderly gentleman in a frock coat
and top hat, unnoticed by the drivers, then made his way cautiously back to his car.

CHAPTER TWENTY-SEVEN

GOD BLESS YOU *Venetia. You have been an angel friend to me, why not a wife?*

She kept Montagu's letter in the same suitcase as the Prime Minister's. Not that she looked at it very often, or even at all. It wasn't necessary. She knew the relevant sentence by heart.

Why not a wife?

Sometimes the answer seemed so entirely obvious to her, it barely merited consideration.

Because she did not love him. What more needed to be said?

Still, she did not dismiss the possibility entirely, and throughout February and March made sure to see a lot of him. She agreed to let him drive her to and from the hospital. She went to tea with him at the Savoy. She attended his dinner parties. She even invited him to stay for the weekend at Alderley, where they read 'The Statue and the Bust' together in her library.

At no point during all of this did she make any reference to his tentative half-proposal, and nor did he. It hung in the air between them. But whenever she stole a look at him sitting next to her, or observed him across the room, and tried to imagine herself married to him, she found the notion simply impossible. It was not just that he left her cold physically. Rather, she felt a visceral . . . well, honestly, *repulsion* was not too harsh a word. Nowhere in that ungainly, heavy body of his, beneath its layers of thick old-fashioned suiting, could she discern a spark of sexuality. The idea of him kissing her – those teeth! that heavy black moustache! – made her recoil. As for the thought of going to bed with him, it was almost too horrible to contemplate.

But . . .

She *did* like him, more than almost anyone in her circle. Even though he could be fussy and nervous – 'Auntie' was another of his nicknames – he always managed to say something that was arresting or made her laugh. He never bored her, which was certainly no longer true of the Prime Minister. She had come to dread going to her pigeonhole at the end of her shift and finding it stuffed with letters. Their Friday-afternoon drives had become ordeals she tried to avoid – the most recent, when she had nerved herself to tell him of her plan to go to nurse in France and he had complained for half an hour, had left her not only bored, but angry. How could he expect her to sacrifice her life purely to be at his beck and call?

She had to find a way out.

It was in this unaccustomedly confused state of mind that on the Sunday after their last, fractious drive together she decided to seek spiritual guidance by taking Holy Communion for only the third time in her life. She didn't care in which church she did it, just as long as it was nearby.

St Philip's was barely twenty years old: a tall, red-brick Victorian structure, like a factory or a warehouse, standing within the precincts of the hospital, next to the isolation wing. The floor was parquet. Wheelchairs and crutches filled the nave. She sat at the back wearing her uniform with a group of other nurses and joined in the hymns, listened hard to the sermon, and tried to concentrate during the prayers. But although she mouthed the words along with the rest, she found herself unmoved. The boom of the organ and the chant of the vicar were mere noises in her ears. Her father was an atheist, one uncle was a Muslim, another a Roman Catholic bishop. She decided she was definitely of her father's persuasion.

She joined the queue to go up for communion. When her turn came to kneel at the altar and receive the wafer and the wine, the utter absence of any feeling was itself a kind of revelation. Whatever other obstacles might stand in the way of her marrying Montagu, his religion was not among them. She realised she could convert to Judaism as easily as crossing a road. In fact, it would rather amuse her to outrage conventional society by doing so. She left the Anglican church that morning never to return, head high, solitary, and defiant.

The following Tuesday, Edwin Montagu proposed again.

By now, she was allowed to sleep outside the hostel a couple of nights a week, and he came to Mansfield Street just after two, straight from a Cabinet meeting. She was due back at the hospital at three and he had asked if he could drive her. She met him in the hall. Her parents were still at the lunch table. She could tell at once he was agitated. He asked if he might have a private word with her before they left. She took him into the morning room and gestured for him to sit in an armchair, while she sat on the sofa.

'Would you like a drink?'

'No, thank you.'

He seemed unable to sit still, crossing and uncrossing his legs.

'Are you all right, Edwin? What on earth's the matter?'

'I'm sorry to ask this, but did the Prime Minister send you a letter yesterday – rather a long one, written in the morning during a Cabinet committee?'

She frowned at him, puzzled, and reached for her handbag. The letter, which had reached her at the hospital the previous afternoon, was yet another extravagant effusion of his feelings. It included a quotation from Milton's *Comus* and ended rather abruptly:

My own darling – I am writing in the stress & tumult of a windy & wordy controversy about munitions &c between Ll. G., Winston & A.J.B. – and I daren't abstract myself more. I will write you a real letter tonight. But this I felt I must say – at once & now.

'Yes,' she said, glancing through it. 'He mentions he's in a meeting. He writes to me throughout the day from all over the place. What of it?'

'I thought it must be to you. I was sitting next to him. The point is the others noticed it as well. Not Winston, who was gassing away as usual, but Lloyd George certainly did, and so did Balfour. I saw the pair of them watching him. They kept exchanging glances.'

'Oh God! But they didn't know it was me?'

'Probably not. But you know how you've always argued that the reason you need to make yourself available to him, and meet him so often, is because it helps him cope with the strain? I suddenly saw the other side of it. What if the opposite is true, and you're such a distraction he's no longer functioning properly? It isn't the first time he's done it in the middle of a meeting.'

She stared at him. It was such an inversion of how she had

perceived her role in the Prime Minister's life, and how she had always justified it to herself, that for a few seconds she couldn't respond. And Edwin didn't know the half of it – all the recent wild talk of elopement and suicide.

She said quietly, 'I can't believe it's as bad as that.'

'I think you know it is, and unfortunately colleagues are becoming aware of it too. In normal times it might not matter, but the war isn't going well. There's a shortage of artillery shells – you must have seen the press is on to it – and there's a battle royal in progress behind the scenes between Kitchener, who wants to keep control of the munitions factories, and Lloyd George, who says he isn't up to it. And meanwhile the Dardanelles is going from bad to worse. It's a great secret, but I might as well tell you, because I know the Prime Minister will: Winston had to inform the Cabinet this morning that the operation is to be postponed for yet another three weeks because the army isn't ready to go ashore, and the navy is in a funk. God knows, it's turning into a fiasco!'

He uncrossed his legs again and leaned forwards, his hat clasped between his hands, urgent, imploring. 'The fact is, Venetia, people are starting to plot – Lloyd George especially. I'm picking up rumours on all sides, and I'm not sure the Prime's position is as secure as he thinks it is. Forgive me for speaking frankly, but I thought you ought to know. Any breath of a scandal could be disastrous – for you, as well as for him.'

'No, no. You're right to tell me. I'm grateful.' She was anxious to bring the conversation to an end. 'I ought to go. You've given me a lot to think about. The last thing I want to do is damage his career.' She stood. 'Are you sure you want to drive me? You must be very busy.'

'Of course I want to drive you! I cherish every minute with you.'

In the car, they sat well apart. The sliding glass window

separating them from the driver was closed, but there was a rear-view mirror, and she was conscious of the chauffeur's eyes occasionally glancing at her.

Montagu said, 'I'm sorry you've been placed in such an invidious position.'

'I've rather placed myself in it, don't you think?'

They were silent for a few minutes.

He said, 'There is a way out for you, of course.'

'And what is that?'

'You could always change your mind and marry me.'

She had guessed this was coming. She shook her head. 'You are kind to renew the offer. But can you imagine what that would do to him, given the state he's in?'

'Kindness has nothing to do with it! As for the Prime – I love him, as you know. I owe him everything. He's practically made me a member of his family. But on this, his position is indefensible, and in the end it will prove self-destructive. You'd be rescuing yourself from an impossible situation and saving him from himself – as well as making me very happy.' His hand crept crab-wise across the seat and touched hers. 'I'm sorry, this isn't very romantic. But knowing the way your mind works, I thought it might be a more productive approach. There are so many practical arguments in favour of us being together.'

'And only one against.'

'Which is?'

She turned to face him. 'Love, Edwin. I like you enormously – more than I like almost anyone. I just don't think I love you as a wife should love her husband, and I'm not sure I ever will.'

But she let his hand rest in hers – cool, limp, entirely without pressure: not unpleasant, just nothing – and there it remained until they pulled up outside the hospital.

He said, 'You will think it over, won't you? Promise me. Don't say no just yet.'

'I'll think it over.' She squeezed his hand. 'Thank you.'

She needed time alone, to think, and for the next two weeks she withdrew into herself, taking refuge in the hard, mind-dulling work of the hospital. She even volunteered for extra shifts. It was difficult to feel sorry for oneself when one was surrounded by wounded soldiers. She didn't contact Montagu, ignored his letters, and as far as possible, she avoided seeing the Prime Minister as well, although there was no escape from his correspondence. When she cancelled a drive with him the following Monday, he wrote to her in the middle of the afternoon in anguished terms.

> I cannot tell you in any words what a blow it is to me not
> to see you this afternoon. I have built so many hopes &
> desires upon it. I feel like someone who has had his day
> turned suddenly from possible sunshine into assured &
> unrelieved darkness. It is especially sad to me today,
> because I longed above everything to talk to you frankly &
> fully about the strange & new situation wh. is now being
> evolved. There is, as you see in the Tory press, a dead set
> being made against me personally. Witness the articles in
> The Times & the Morning Post . . .

In the early evening, he wrote again. His letter arrived just as she was coming off duty.

> I had an extraordinary & really very interesting talk with
> Ll. George. He declared that he owed everything to me;
> that I had stuck to him & protected him & defended him

when every man's hand was against him; and that he wd. rather (1) break stones (2) dig potatoes (3) be hanged & quartered (these were metaphors used at different stages of his broken but impassioned harangue) than do an act, or say a word, or harbour a thought, that was disloyal to me. And he said that every one of our colleagues felt the same. His eyes were wet with tears, and I am sure that, with all his Celtic capacity for impulsive & momentary fervour, he was quite sincere. Of course, I assured him that I had never for a moment doubted him – wh. is quite true: & he warmly wrung my hand & abruptly left the room. Darling, does that interest you?

Interest her? It did far more than that. It alarmed her. If he really did regard his Chancellor of the Exchequer – dynamic, charming, cynical, ambitious to the point of mania – as 'quite sincere', he most definitely was losing his touch. Despite her tiredness and her resolution to keep her distance, she could not turn her back on him – especially if, as Edwin said, she was responsible for his lack of grip. She replied at once.

London Hospital
10 p.m. Mon. 29 Mar.
Dearest Prime, I am so sorry this afternoon proved to be impossible, esp. as you seem to be more than usually in need of love & care.

Here is what I think:
The Tory papers, esp. Northcliffe's, are your natural enemies – as far as possible, ignore them.
There are always tricky times in politics, especially in war – this is one of them, you will get through it.

Your position in the Party & the Country is strong. Your colleagues are devoted to you. I know that Winston is absolutely loyal to you. (About Lloyd George I am not so confident – he is the most ambitious man in the government & his loyalty is always & only to himself; I shd. <u>strongly</u> advise treating his tearful protestations with a certain degree of caution.) Remember that the only person who can bring you down is <u>yourself</u>. Stop all this morbid thinking that has been so disturbing lately. Cease hankering after what can never be. Remember <u>I am with you</u>. I finish at the hospital next week. Then I shall be able to see you more.

All love.

10 Downing Street
Tu. 30 March 1915
Your letter today has made a new man of me. I shall always remember it, because it came just at a moment when I was beginning to be a little doubtful about myself.

Not for the first time, or the tenth time, you have readjusted my point of view, recreated my fading resolves, and given me new confidence & life.

I bless & adore you: and all my life is yours. Dearest & best, good night. <u>Your own.</u>

The following Wednesday was her last day at the hospital. She was called upstairs in the morning to see the head matron.

Miss Luckes sat behind her desk, ancient, spherical, arthritic. A spider had spun a thread between her chair and the desk. The line of gossamer caught the sunlight. Venetia wondered if perhaps she hadn't moved in the last four months.

'Well, I must congratulate you. Your weekly reports from the ward sisters have been excellent.' She consulted one of the papers in front of her. '"Probationer Beatrice Stanley is very nice, she is anxious to learn, willing and intelligent . . ." That was near the start, and they have gone on getting better ever since. The patients respond to you. You have the makings of a fine nurse, Miss Stanley – or rather, *Nurse* Stanley, as you may call yourself from now on.'

'Thank you, Matron.'

'It cannot always have been easy, given the attentions of a certain eminent gentleman.' Venetia started to protest, but Miss Luckes cut her off with a wave of her plump hand. 'Nothing goes unnoticed in a place like this. He's been seen parked outside, waiting for you. Messages delivered by courier from Downing Street. You will be aware, no doubt, that the Prime Minister has written to the chairman of our board of governors, Viscount Knutsford, suggesting you transfer to the hospital at Millbank rather than go abroad?'

'I told him I didn't want to do that. I intend to go to France.'

'Good for you, Nurse. I gather he's paying us a visit next Tuesday. You'll be accompanying him, I assume?'

It was the first Venetia had heard of it. She managed to cover her surprise. 'I expect so, yes.'

'So it isn't quite goodbye.' She rose with difficulty. 'This is your certificate of qualification. Thank you for your hard work. You leave with our best wishes.'

When Venetia packed up her belongings that afternoon, she pulled her suitcase out from beneath her bed and counted the number of letters the Prime Minister had written to her during her time at the hospital. The total was one hundred and forty-seven.

PART SIX

CRISIS

7 April–17 May 1915

CHAPTER TWENTY-EIGHT

I N DOWNING STREET, as Venetia packed, the Prime Minister was chairing an informal meeting of the War Council. He was in a great good humour. Sir Edward Grey was absent – away on sick leave, lying in a darkened room in a cottage somewhere in Hampshire, trying to recover his eyesight – and he had taken temporary charge of the Foreign Office. He relished these opportunities to show his mastery of government, especially as he had hopes of accomplishing one of the great diplomatic coups of the war – bringing in Italy on the Allied side. The rumours of a plot against him had seemingly come to nothing. Lloyd George was friendly to the point of obsequiousness. And Venetia was finishing her sentence in that hellish hospital prison and had finally promised to come to Walmer for the weekend; he would drive her down to Kent on Friday.

Only the Dardanelles was giving him cause for grief. It was like a stone in his shoe. He didn't seem to be able to get rid of it. Now Hankey, whose judgement he trusted, was making an impassioned plea for further postponement, quoting the opinion of General Robertson, Sir John French's Chief of Staff, that an opposed landing on the exposed barren cliffs of Gallipoli, some four thousand miles distant from England by sea, was 'the stiffest operation any army could undertake'.

Winston glowered at Hankey across the table. 'That is pure defeatism.'

Kitchener said, 'We should bear in mind that every hour we delay gives the Turks more time to strengthen their defences. Intelligence suggests they may have close to a hundred thousand men in place.'

'All the more reason to put it off,' replied Hankey. He was only a colonel, but he was not afraid to take on a field marshal. 'We need to outnumber them, not the other way round.'

'If we *do* suffer a setback,' said Balfour, in his usual slightly arch and feline manner, 'it would surely be *better* if it were to happen *after* Italy has declared war on Germany rather than *before*, otherwise they might change their minds. I favour delay.'

The Prime Minister, whose instinct was always to procrastinate, agreed. The landings were put off again.

The next day, Thursday 8 April, was the seventh anniversary of his appointment to the premiership. The Assyrian gave a dinner in his honour in the silken tent. Half the Cabinet was present, and Margot, Violet, Raymond, Bongie – but no Venetia, he was disappointed to see. After the dessert, he made an off-the-cuff speech, reminiscing about the day in 1908 when he kissed hands. King Edward had been on holiday in Biarritz, avoiding the English climate, and had refused to return to London to appoint him, so he had been forced to go to him, catching the boat train from Charing Cross station, entirely alone, wearing a thick overcoat with a travelling cap pulled well down over his eyes – 'Like one of Mr Conrad's secret agents' – and had stayed the night at the Ritz in Paris before continuing south.

'I found the old King at the Hotel du Palais, a most luxurious belle époque establishment, and he consented to see me after breakfast – mealtimes, you may recall, being always a sacrosanct ritual for His late Majesty *(laughter)* – and within half an hour, after a reviving glass of champagne, I was back on the train to Paris, the business done, leaving behind me, with more than a little regret, the sea sparkling in the sunshine. I . . . I . . .'

He was dismayed to discover his voice choking, his eyes filling with tears. It was a few moments before he could continue. 'What a vanished golden world that is to look back upon. My dear friends and colleagues, I hope in the seven years since, I haven't disappointed your trust. I have striven to do my best. Of one thing I am certain: no leader could have been better or more loyally served. These are difficult, deadly times we must all endure, but together I am certain we shall come through them to victory.'

It seemed a good moment to stop, before he broke down completely. He raised his glass.

'To victory!'

Everyone rose.

'To victory!'

The applause was loud and prolonged. The table was pounded until the cutlery clattered.

Afterwards, he said to Montagu, 'No Venetia?'

'She wasn't free.'

'Thank you for organising this.' He added on impulse, 'Come to Walmer this weekend. I've persuaded Venetia to stay at last. No, no – I insist. Don't think of refusing. It will do us all good to get some sea air.'

He collected her from Mansfield Street the following afternoon. As soon as she had settled into the back of the Napier, he said reproachfully, 'I missed you at the Assyrian's last night.'

'I was sorry not to be there. Did it go well?'

'Yes, pretty well. He's always a very generous host. But it would have meant much more to me if you'd been there. I've invited him down to join us for the weekend.' He noticed her eyes widen slightly. 'Was it a bad idea? I thought you'd be pleased.'

'I really don't mind one way or the other.' She sounded as though she did. 'And I gather from the head matron you're going to visit the hospital next week?'

Again, a slight edge to her voice.

'*We* are going – together, I hope. I'm longing to see the place where you've been hiding yourself all this time. I assumed you would find it less of an embarrassment, now you're no longer working there.'

'I just wish you'd told me.'

'I wanted to surprise you.'

They were not yet across Westminster Bridge but already he sensed that clouds were gathering over his perfect weekend. His response, as always when faced with potential unpleasantness, personal or political, was to ignore it, in the hope it would go away, which it mostly did. And the same seemed true today, for not long after they left the endless suburbs of south London and pushed out into open country, her mood began to improve. They talked about mutual friends. He brought her up to date on the Dardanelles. He showed her the latest telegrams from the embassy in Rome about Italy's entry into the war, but when he started to lower the window to dispose of them, she stopped him.

'Don't do that. You don't want another police inquiry.'

'Yes, quite right.' He put them back in his dispatch box. 'What would I do without you?'

He wanted to close the blinds and hold her, but the brittleness of her mood deterred him.

Just before six, they turned off the Dover Road onto a narrow country lane. It was an idyllic spring late afternoon, the hedge-rows rising on either side like green waves capped by a froth of white blossom, the immense Kent sky alive with singing skylarks.

'"Oh, to be in England",' he murmured, '"now that April's there . . ."'

'Browning!' She smiled and shook her head. 'Always Browning!'

He felt obscurely put out, as if she was mocking him.

They reached Walmer, passed through a little seaside town of whitewashed terraced houses, not unlike Holyhead, and climbed the sloping drive to the castle. He could have had it for himself if he'd wanted – it was the official residence of the Lord Warden of the Cinque Ports, a ceremonial office of the Crown, and the King had offered him the position – but he couldn't afford the upkeep, so instead he had arranged for it to be awarded to the wealthy William Lygon, Earl of Beauchamp, a member of the Cabinet, on the informal understanding he would be able to use it at week-ends. He was immensely proud of it, almost as if it were his own. It was not a faux-castle, like Penrhos, but the real thing – four centuries old, composed of great round towers with walls that were fifteen feet thick, a circular keep, topped by a flagpole from which the warden's standard flapped nosily in the breeze, its ram-parts looking across a stony beach to the sea. Not bad for a middle-class lad from Yorkshire! He studied Venetia's expression as she viewed it for the first time.

'Oh, Prime,' she said, 'I see now what you mean – it is rather wonderful.'

The others had already arrived. They were having tea on one of the crenellated terraces. He relished this spot in particular – the four antique cannons poking out through the battlements towards the English Channel, the little pyramids of cannonballs heaped beside them, the encompassing blue of the sea and sky, the weathered grey wooden benches that caught the morning sun. He conducted Venetia out into the warm early evening towards most of the people he knew and loved best – Margot and Violet, Raymond and Katharine, Montagu and Bongie – and for a moment at least, with her at his side, he was the king of his castle, and his world was complete.

Venetia regretted accepting the invitation from the moment she arrived.

There was the presence of Margot, for a start, who greeted her with glacial politeness, offering two hard cheekbones, right then left, like a pair of knives, for a lightly grazing contact; and Montagu, who looked at her reproachfully, and whispered that they had to talk; and Raymond, who seemed to find the whole arrangement intensely amusing; and Violet, who had once been her best friend, the repository of every secret, but now was not, so that their past intimacy lay like a shadow between them.

And then there was the castle itself, designed in Tudor times to be a fortress, not a residence. The rooms were small, the corridors narrow and draughty. Suits of armour lurked menacingly in odd corners. On the walls were pikes and swords and regimental banners, dusty tapestries and grimy oil paintings. Her room had a stone floor, no bathroom, and a hard four-poster bed so high it had to be mounted by a step. As she dressed for dinner – Violet lent her the services of her maid – the sky beyond the arrow-slit window darkened, and a wind got up and howled around the battlements. She thought how carefully Margot must have chosen this room for her. Therefore it was a pleasure, when she went down to dinner, to tell her how much she loved it.

'Really?' Margot looked taken aback. 'I worried it might be rather spartan.'

'Not at all, it's charming. I *adore* it.'

The Prime Minister was on good form over dinner, telling stories of recent guests – how Lady Tree, driving back from a round of golf at Deal, had said, 'Tell me, Mr Asquith, do you take an interest in the war at all?' ('Rather sharp, I thought!'), and how he had mischievously invited Henry James over from Rye to stay for a weekend and have dinner with Winston. 'It wasn't exactly a meeting of minds! You can guess who did all the talking. I asked James afterwards what he had made of him. His reply was a Jamesian masterpiece: "I confess I am often struck at the – er, er – *limitations* with which men of power pay the price for their domination over mankind."'

Everyone laughed, apart from Venetia, who couldn't help bursting out, 'Well, personally I prefer Winston any day, with all his absurdities, to that dried-up old maid!'

The table fell quiet. The Prime Minister changed the subject.

When she went to bed, she locked her door, and not long after midnight heard a gentle tapping on the thick oak. She pretended to be asleep, and lay wondering which it might be, the Prime Minister or Edwin. Whoever it was, they soon gave up, and neither made any mention of it the next morning.

Over lunch on Saturday, the Prime Minister announced he had to go to Dover that afternoon and inspect some troops preparing to embark for France. 'Venetia, my dear, I wondered if you'd care to come with me.'

She glanced across the table at Margot, who immediately turned her head away. She felt embarrassed. 'I'm afraid I've rather a bad headache. Would you mind very much if I didn't?'

'That's a pity. I'd prefer not to go alone.' He looked around, his gaze travelling past Margot. 'Montagu, would you mind?'

'Of course not, sir.' He stared helplessly at Venetia.

After they had driven away, she went for a long, solitary walk along the stony beach. She experienced a spasm of irritation with Edwin, always so feeble in the presence of the Prime Minister. It was as if he, rather than Margot, was the third member of this wretched love triangle. When she returned to the castle, she went straight up to her room and stayed there, lying on her bed, reading, until dinner. In the evening she spoke mostly to Bongie and Violet and watched Edwin becoming more and more lugubrious and withdrawn. What a curious, moody creature he was. Could she really contemplate a lifetime with him?

That night, she was woken by the rustle of a note being pushed under her door. It was from Edwin. *Dearest*, it began.

Glowing with happiness at staying with you, it has resulted in my being like a caged beast raging up and down at a delectable being separated by the bars of a cage. Time – the biggest part of my stay here – has gone by with hardly a word to satisfy my appetite and I've been all the time consumed with hunger and jealousy. I could not let him go to town alone – could I, even though I should have loved to get that golden opportunity. If only you felt as sorry about it as I do – (always the same 'if'!) Shall I ever have any rights? I shall be ready tomorrow for the walk that must not be tampered with and I want to arrange something for Monday.

Yrs. separated, yearning, anxious E. S. Montagu

What did he mean, would he ever have any *rights*? The word chilled her. Was that his conception of marriage? She couldn't bear the thought of any man having *rights* over her.

Nevertheless, the next morning, after breakfast, she went out onto the terrace where he was smoking a cigarette and asked him if he would like to go for a walk through the castle grounds.

He looked at her – rather coldly, she thought. 'Yes, as it happens, I would.'

He threw away his cigarette.

They descended in silence to the gravel path, and she realised he was still sulking, waiting for her to open the conversation. She had just begun it, without knowing where it would lead – 'We seem to have been rather distant from one another of late' – when a woman's voice called out behind them, and they turned to see Margot hurrying down the steps. They waited to let her catch up.

'Do you mind if I join you?' She moved in between them without waiting for an answer and slipped her thin arms through theirs. 'This part of the castle is so lovely at this time of day. I always try to walk here in the mornings.' They went on a few more paces and then she stopped. 'Oh, Edwin dear, I've forgotten my gloves. Would you be a darling and fetch them for me? They're on the table in the drawing room.'

Venetia gave him a beseeching look, but he said, 'Of course, Margot. I shan't be a moment.'

As soon as he had gone, Margot gestured to a bench and said, 'Let's wait here, shall we?'

They sat awkwardly together, facing the lawn. Venetia's throat was dry, her defences on alert. She couldn't remember the last time they had been alone together.

'Do you hate me, Venetia?'

'No, Margot. Not in the slightest.'

'Then why are you pursuing this relationship with my husband?'

She felt as if she had been struck in the face.

'I'm not *pursuing* him.'

'Very well, then – why are you encouraging him to pursue *you*?'

'I'm not doing that, either.'

'Really?' Margot snorted and poked the gravel with the sharp toe of her fashionable shoe. 'I noticed you weren't at his anniversary dinner the other night. He told a wonderful tale of the day he went to Biarritz to see the King to be sworn in. What he didn't mention was the telegram he sent me straight after he kissed hands. I remember it exactly: "BACK FRIDAY ASK GREY DINNER AND ONE OR TWO NICE WOMEN." Actually, I didn't invite any women on that occasion, nice or otherwise, much to his irritation. But you see, this is how he's always been. I can't pretend I've ever liked it much, this need of his for the company of pretty young women to cheer him up and flatter him – Pamela, Viola, Dorothy and the rest – it was simply something I put up with for his sake. They were decent, well-bred girls. I knew them, and I knew they wouldn't let things go too far. But then you came along.'

She turned to look at her then – a terrible, searching stare, full of anger and pain, and worst of all, because it was so out of character, vulnerability.

'You *have* encouraged him in a way they never did. You are cleverer than they were, for a start – more political – and you are careless of other people's feelings in a way they weren't. I blame a lot of it on this selfish "Coterie" you belong to, which you all think so terribly modern and daring. And tell me: where are all your cynical young men now? Hanging on barbed wire! This war is the punishment for your generation's hubris.'

Venetia managed to find her voice at that. 'I don't think you can blame us for the war!'

'No, but it's a just reward, nonetheless. It's your *deception* I can't abide, Venetia. I have invited you to lunches and dinners and parties. I have had you to stay under my roof. And you have not been honest with me. Not *honest*. I shan't ask you to give Henry up – I know that's useless. I shall *never* beg. But I want you to understand that what you are doing is immoral, and wrong, and that I know *everything*. And really that's all I have to say to you.' She glanced over Venetia's shoulder. 'Now here is Edwin with my gloves. I shall leave you two to continue your walk.'

But a walk with Montagu was the last thing Venetia could face at that moment. She rose and rushed back the way they had come, past the astonished Edwin, up the steps into the castle, and rapidly mounted the winding staircase to her room.

The remainder of that Sunday, she kept herself apart, pleading a headache. It was not a mere diplomatic excuse. This time it was genuine. She closed the shutters and lay on the bed, almost blinded by the pain behind her eyes, Margot's words chasing endlessly round in her mind. She didn't feel angry or ashamed, so much as bruised and exhausted, as if she had been physically assaulted. She missed lunch and dinner and declined an offer from Violet to have something brought up to her on a tray. Shortly after nine, she packed her own suitcase and carried it downstairs to the dining room, where the others had just finished dinner.

Her reappearance provoked a ripple of anxious inquiries about her health.

'Thank you. I think it's passing off. I'm sorry to have been such a bore. It's been a memorable weekend, but what I'd really like now is to get back to London.'

The Prime Minister said, 'You must come with us. We've plenty of room.'

Margot said, 'Yes, come with us, Venetia.'

'I can drive you,' said Montagu. 'I'm on my own.'

She looked from one to the other. It was Raymond who came to her rescue.

'Why don't you come with Katharine and me? But we need to leave right away.'

'That suits me if you're sure it's all right. I'm packed and ready.'

She made the round of goodbye kisses. Margot embraced her as if nothing had happened. The Prime Minister said, 'I'll see you on Tuesday.'

'Tuesday?' inquired Margot sharply.

'Venetia is showing me round the London Hospital.'

'But we're staying with the King and Queen at Windsor on Monday and Tuesday nights.'

'I'm afraid I shall have to go back to London during the day on Tuesday, to work.'

'To work,' repeated Margot. 'Well! How very nice for you both.'

Montagu hissed in Venetia's ear, 'I *must* see you.'

'I'll send you a line when I get back to town.'

Raymond was driving his own car. She asked if she might sit in the front next to him. 'I think it might be better for my head.'

'Of course. You don't mind sitting on your own in the back, do you, Katharine?'

Katharine said she did not. 'I'm tired. I'd like to sleep.'

Five minutes later, they were driving down the slope towards Walmer.

Venetia glanced over her shoulder at the receding lights of the castle and groaned with relief. 'God, what a draining weekend! I feel like a character in an Ibsen play.'

Raymond said, 'Strindberg, darling, surely? There was so much going on below the surface, I really found it hard to keep up. Wasn't Margot at her magnificent best!'

'She ambushed me this morning. She seems to think the war is all the fault of the Coterie.'

'You know, she may have a point. Nothing's gone right with the world since poor old Denis jumped in the river. Wouldn't he just have *loved* the war? It was invented for chaps like him. Such a shame he missed it. Mind you, he'd probably be dead by now.'

Katharine interrupted, from the back seat, 'Don't say things like that, Raymond. I still have dreams about that horrible night.'

Raymond turned to Venetia and gave her a wink. They stopped talking. By the time they reached the main road, Katharine's genteel snoring signalled she was asleep. Raymond glanced at her in the mirror and said quietly, 'I haven't told her yet, but my commission's come through. I'm going to France with the Guards at the end of the month.'

'I thought you didn't believe in the war?'

'I don't. I think it's absurd. Winston and Lord Kitchener of Chaos haven't the first clue what they're doing.'

'So why go?'

'Because I don't want to spend the rest of my life – assuming I survive – having to explain to people why I didn't. Can you imagine how boring that would be?'

'You'll survive, Raymond. You're indestructible.'

'Will I? The way things are going, I sometimes think we'll all end up under the sod.'

He lapsed back into silence.

Venetia said suddenly. 'Do you think I ought to marry Edwin?'

'Why not? He's rich. He's nice. It would annoy all the right people. And you'd make a lovely Jewish wife.'

'I'm just not sure I can face going to bed with him.'

'You probably wouldn't have to.'

'What do you mean?'

'Oh, Vinny!' He laughed. 'Don't say you've never realised? I don't think his inclinations lie in that direction.'

CHAPTER TWENTY-NINE

T HE PRIME MINISTER left Downing Street with Margot late the following afternoon to drive to Windsor Castle. George, his valet, sat in the front next to Horwood, and alongside Margot's maid.

He was not in a good mood. He sensed that the Walmer weekend, to which he had so long looked forward, had for some reason been a failure. Venetia had not written to thank him. Margot was being difficult. He had a mountain of papers to read and decisions to make. And now he had to interrupt his work for this tedious expedition. The days when he might have derived any frisson of pleasure from staying with the King and Queen of England had long since passed.

The company at dinner was even duller than he had feared – Lord and Lady Minto; Lord and Lady Mieux; the former Portuguese ambassador, the Marquis de Soveral, whom the Kaiser had nicknamed 'the Blue Monkey'; the elderly Lady Coke, who told him she had twice stayed at Walmer Castle with the Duke of Wellington; the Prince of Wales, who at least provided a touch of glamour and who spent the evening flirting with Portia Cadogan, the only halfway decent-looking young woman. But the worst aspect of all was that the King had joined in the temperance campaign dreamed up by Lloyd George to stamp out drunkenness among munitions workers and had signed a pledge not to drink or serve alcohol for the duration of the war. The Prime Minister had to choose between mineral water and elderflower cordial. It was a relief when His Majesty announced that he and the Queen were turning in for the night and they were all free to go to bed.

He stalked back irritably with Margot along the wide curving corridor that led to their separate rooms.

She said, 'You were very quiet this evening. Were you tired? Were you cold?'

'No, I was simply bored out of my mind. I'm leaving early in the morning. I'll see you back here tomorrow night.'

He left her standing in the passageway and went into his room.

He regretted almost at once the harshness of his tone, but when he opened the door to apologise and kiss her good night, she had gone.

The next morning, as he was getting into his car, George handed him a letter. 'Mrs Asquith asked me to give you this, sir.'

Windsor Castle
5 a.m.
My dearest Henry,
How <u>can</u> you treat me so cruelly? I have lain awake all night, alone & in the depths of misery. I know you think me cocky, snobby, loud & <u>plain</u>, but is it really necessary to bewilder & humiliate me? I have <u>never</u> tried to interfere in your relationship with Venetia, even though I have been chaffed about it often. But of late I fear she has entirely ousted me in your affections. She has many fine

points – unselfish & kind &c – but from the start she has conspired with Violet behind my back. She leads the sort of life I <u>hate</u> & lacks intellectual & moral sensibility or any sort of direction. I know I am no longer young, & men as they get older like different kinds of women, but to have our precious intimacy destroyed in this way destroys <u>me</u>. I am sorry to write in these terms, because I know how beset you are with problems, but I had to tell you, dearest Henry –

Your (still) ever loving –

Margot

As they drove back to London, he stared out of the window, the letter grasped in his hand, his mind playing back and forth over the past twenty years. No one had called him Henry before her. She had decreed Herbert 'too common' and insisted on using his middle name. He hadn't minded: 'You may call me whatever you like.' But he knew old friends like Haldane thought he had been corrupted by all that came with her – the enormous house in Cavendish Square, the endless entertaining, her relentless ambition. It was possible he might not have become prime minister without her money to free him from his legal work. He hated the thought of her feeling bewildered and humiliated. It was so *not Margot*.

When he got back to Number 10, he went straight to the Cabinet Room and wrote a reply. What he wanted to say was that the human heart had many chambers and that it was possible to love more than one person. But the politician in him made him construct a careful answer that skirted the edge of deception without ever quite tipping into it.

My own darling – Your letter made me sad, and I hasten to tell you that you have no cause for the doubts & fears wh.

it expresses, or suggests . . . My fondness for Venetia has never interfered & never could with our relationship . . . I <u>never consciously</u> keep things from you & tell them to others.

(He liked that phrase, *never consciously*.)

These last 3 years I have lived under a perpetual strain, the like of which I suppose has been experienced by very few men living or dead . . . I am reputed to be of serene 'imperturbable' temperament, & I do my best in the way of self-control. But I admit that I am often irritated & impatient, and that then I become curt & perhaps taciturn. I fear you have suffered from this more than anyone, and I am deeply sorry, but believe me darling it has not been due to any want of confidence & love. These remain, and always will, unchanged.

Ever your own <u>husband</u>

He dispatched it to Windsor Castle by special messenger and then turned his attention to all the other problems that had accumulated in his absence. On top of the pile of papers was a copy of that morning's edition of *The Times*, with a note from Bongie clipped to the front page directing his attention to the main leader article. It laid all the problems of the war at his door, blaming him for his failure to get a grip on the ammunition shortage.

If he had undertaken it from the outset he would, no doubt, have done it well, for when he stirs himself to take hold of a crisis, he generally succeeds in finding a way out of the difficulty. The

*unfortunate thing is that he seldom does so until the imperative
need is forced upon him by the hopeless mess into which matters
have drifted, when irreparable harm has already been done. Irreparable harm has already been done in the matter of ammunition.*

He rang for Bongie.

'This is vicious,' he said, 'even by Northcliffe's standards. We
shall have to answer it. Where is Kitchener?'

'He's in France, sir.'

'Send him a telegram saying I want him to raise the issue immediately with Sir John French and find out the truth of it. That
speech you've been suggesting I should make to munitions workers in Newcastle – schedule it for next week.'

At noon, he chaired a Cabinet meeting. He looked around the
table at his colleagues, and wondered which of them was leaking
information to the newspapers, who was loyal and who was not.
His gaze kept returning to Lloyd George.

At one o'clock, Venetia arrived.

Her mind was still teeming with the events of the weekend, especially Raymond's oracular comment about Edwin: *I don't think his
inclinations lie in that direction . . .*

She had asked him what he meant.

'Oh, nothing, probably. Just some gossip I heard about his time
at Cambridge and a fellow named Keynes. It's so cold and flat out
there, people go mad and get up to all sorts of strange practices.'
He had changed the subject.

Her first instinct had been to dismiss it. But the more she had
considered it since, the more plausible an explanation it seemed
for his various neuroses. It would account for the fact he had never
seemed much interested in women in the romantic sense, and for

her failure to detect any spark of sexual attraction, either towards him or emanating from him. It was all such a mess. The last thing she wanted to do was accompany the Prime Minister to the hospital, but he was insistent, and after a brief lunch in the smaller dining room, just the two of them, they set off.

From the moment they arrived, she knew it was a mistake. The senior staff, including Miss Luckes, leaning on a pair of sticks, and the chairman of the board of governors, Viscount Knutsford, were already lined up in the entrance hall, waiting to greet their eminent visitor. She tried to linger in the background, but he called her forward to introduce her. 'You must know my dear friend, Miss Stanley. You've rather been keeping her from me these past three months.'

They toured the west wing and the out-patients' department. They crossed the garden field where some of the wounded soldiers were sitting out in the sunshine, and he stopped to talk to them. He was shown the medical college and the operating theatres and then he asked if he could see the Charrington ward, because that was where she had worked. He promenaded down the aisle past the amazed patients and their relatives, nodding right and left as if he were at a garden party. He is showing off his power to me again, she thought – that peacock strut. When he announced he wished finally to see the nurses' hostel, she wanted to run away and hide.

Lord Knutsford looked at him in surprise. 'It's not really part of the medical facilities.'

'Nevertheless, I'd like to visit the place where Miss Stanley has lived all this time.'

'There's nothing much to see, but if you really want to' – Knutsford glanced at Miss Luckes, who shrugged – 'then, of course.'

As they set off along the covered walkway, Venetia slipped in next to the Prime Minister. 'Honestly,' she whispered, 'this is *mortifying*.'

He glanced at her, puzzled. 'Why?'

'Can't you see the way they're all looking at me?'

'No, I haven't noticed anything. What's wrong with us visiting the hostel?'

She prayed the kitchen would be empty, but by now it was nearly four o'clock, the time when many of the day shift took their tea break. The table was crowded with exhausted nurses. As the senior management entered with the Prime Minister, they scrambled to their feet. He insisted on being introduced to them one by one and shaking their hands. To her horror, some of them – young women who had been her colleagues until less than a week ago – curtsied. She felt them staring at her, and suddenly her carefully constructed alternative existence, in which she was simply dear old Bea – 'Busy Bea' – a cheerful hard worker, 'no side to her at all, posh, but one of the good ones', was exposed as a sham.

After refusing a cup of tea, the Prime Minister smiled at her. 'There's only one more thing I'd like to see, my dear – your room.'

'No!' She was surprised at her own vehemence. 'That's absolutely out of the question, isn't it, Matron?'

Miss Luckes planted herself and her sticks between the Prime Minister and the door. 'I'm afraid we do have a rule, sir – no male visitors – and I fear we can't make an exception, even in your case.'

The firmness with which she spoke pulled him up short. 'Well, if I've learned nothing else in politics, it's not to argue with a head matron!' He beamed around the kitchen. 'Thank you, ladies, for all that you're doing. The nation appreciates it.'

And with that, mercifully, it was over. Once they had said goodbye to Lord Knutsford in the lobby of the Front Block and descended the steps, he said, 'That was such a pleasure, darling, to see it all. I hope it wasn't too embarrassing for you.'

'Embarrassing?' She gave a sharp gasp of laughter. 'I must say I found that last part excruciating. I think I ought to go back in and explain.'

'Explain what?'

'That I wasn't a fraud all the time I was working there, pretending to be just like them when I wasn't at all.'

'But you're not like them.'

She had no answer to that. 'Even so – I think I should.'

'Don't you want me to drive you back to Mansfield Street?'

'No, thank you. I can make my own way.'

'When will I see you again?'

'I'm not sure. I'm going to Alderley tomorrow.'

'Will you be there for the weekend?'

'Yes.' She knew he was waiting for an invitation. He looked so forlorn she took his hand. 'Goodbye, Prime. I do hope you enjoy Windsor a little better tonight.'

'You'll write?'

'As soon as I know my plans.'

She watched him drive away. Everything seemed suddenly much clearer to her now. As soon as his car was out of sight, she turned her back on the hospital and walked along Whitechapel Road, through the East End crowds. She found a post office and sent a telegram to Montagu in his office at the Treasury Chambers: *PLEASE COME AND STAY AT ALDERLEY THIS WEEKEND. WE MUST TALK. DON'T FAIL ME. LOVE VENETIA.*

The Prime Minister returned to Downing Street and did another two hours' work, then in the early evening he drove back along the Great West Road to Windsor. Stepping out of the car in the shadow of the great round tower, he braced himself, as if in preparation for a tricky Cabinet meeting or a Commons debate, and went straight to Margot's room.

He knocked lightly and called her name. There was no reply. He opened the door.

She was lying in darkness.

'May I come in?'

No reply.

He climbed up onto the bed and lay beside her.

Finally, she said, 'Thank you for your darling letter, Henry. It was sweet of you to answer so quickly.'

'I hope it's reassured you. We've been through so much together. Nothing can ever really come between us.'

She turned onto her side and kissed him. 'That's all I wanted to hear.'

They lay together for a few more minutes without speaking.

He sighed. 'Well, I suppose I had better go and change for this ghastly dinner. Imagine it – to be the King-Emperor of nearly five hundred million subjects and to be able to locate the twelve dullest, then gather them together around one table. It takes a kind of genius. Still, at least this time I've brought a secret weapon.'

'And what is that?'

He reached into his inside pocket and produced a flask of brandy.

'Henry, you are incorrigible!'

In his room, he stood at the window and looked out across the Great Park, at the deer grazing upon the immense sweep of grass beneath the ancient trees, and thought of Venetia.

The next day, soon after he had returned to London, Bongie came into the Cabinet Room with a letter from Kitchener.

I have had a talk with French. He told me I could let you
know with the present supply of ammunition he will have
as much as his troops will be able to use on the next
forward movement.

That afternoon, he wrote to Venetia in Alderley.

My most dear – I had a faint hope that before you left
today you might have sent me a line . . . But I have no
doubt you were too busy . . .

    I send you – to keep secret or destroy, as you think
best – a letter I got about noon from K, recording the result
of his private interview this morning with Sir J. French. It
shows how wicked was the lie invented by The Times
yesterday that our lack of ammunition at the front was
holding back not only our own Army but the French. Of
course, you won't breathe a word of it.

    It is now arranged that I shall go to Newcastle next
week – Tues, Wed, or Thurs – and address a big town's
meeting on the whole subject. I think it might be a good
occasion, if only I can make the most of it. I am sure,
sweetest & most wise, that you agree. If only you
could be there! Could you? I should speak 1000 times
better . . .

    I shall go on telling you everything – inside & outside:
until you tell me to stop. And if ever that shd come, I shd
say with Hamlet 'The rest is silence'. And the curtain
would fall. But that is not going to be – is it? My own love
& hope.

    Your own.

★

Early on Friday evening, Venetia drove over from Alderley House to meet Edwin at the station. She stood at the end of the platform as the little branch-line locomotive pulled in and halted beside her in a gush of steam. She watched him climb down from his compartment. He was wearing a top hat and an ankle-length overcoat far too thick for the warm weather, with a cane in one hand and a large suitcase in the other. He paused, apparently bewildered, peered around, set off in the wrong direction, realised his mistake, turned back, saw her, took off his hat, waved it, and hastened towards her. She advanced to meet him and kissed him on either cheek. His skin was flushed, hot, damp, and smelled of eau de Cologne.

'It's very good of you to come.'

'My dear Venetia, I'm delighted. I can hardly believe my luck – two weekends in a row!'

'Let's hope this one is more successful than the last.'

'It could hardly be otherwise.'

The house was full of elderly single relations – Uncle Algernon, now permanently exiled from his home in the Vatican; Aunt Rosalind, the Dowager Countess of Crewe; and Aunt Maude, a spinster of eighty-one, whose life had been spent in charity work in the London slums, and who had now retired to Alderley suffering from a bad heart. On the stroke of the dinner gong, they all descended for dinner from their various rooms, and she observed how artfully Edwin dealt with them, attentive to the deaf old ladies, respectful towards the elderly men, even when Algernon, wearing a heavily jewelled pectoral cross that rested against the swelling front of his purple silk shirt, asked him loudly if he intended to observe the Jewish sabbath.

'No, Bishop, I do not observe any of the rituals of Orthodox Judaism.'

'Might I ask why not?'

'Because I do not believe in them intellectually, and culturally I am entirely assimilated into English society. If I have any free time, I usually spend my Saturdays birdwatching.'

'Well, you can do what you like in this house,' said Lord Sheffield. 'The Stanleys have God covered from every angle – and from none.'

She accompanied him the next morning when he set out in his tweed suit and flat cap, his binoculars slung around his neck, to scrutinise Alderley's birdlife. It seemed to her an incongruous hobby for a man so urban, but he was utterly absorbed, leading her through the woods and around the lake, pointing out birds she had never noticed before – mistle thrushes, chiffchaffs, goldcrests – handing her the binoculars, unselfconsciously standing behind her and putting his arms around her to help her steady the glasses. It moved her to see him so happy. Perhaps I do love him, she thought; or perhaps at least I *could* love him.

On Sunday morning, they went out together again, trudging for an hour through the woods and coming upon a perfectly charming little bird which he said was a coal tit. He entered it in his notebook. As they turned for home, he said, 'Have you heard from the Prime at all?'

'Yes, of course – constantly.'

'Anything interesting? You don't have to tell me if you'd prefer not.'

'His letters are always interesting. On Thursday, he sent me a note from Kitchener about the shell crisis.'

'The actual note itself?' He sounded surprised.

'Yes. Do you want to see it?'

'I don't want to put you in an awkward spot.'

'No, I'm sure I can show it you – as long as you keep it to yourself.'

She took him up to her sitting room, knelt on the rug and

unlocked the painted box, now filled almost to the brim with letters.

'Voilà.'

'They're *all* from him?'

'All. I'd guess there must be five hundred or more.'

'I had no idea of the scale of it.' He looked at her with concern. 'This is quite mad, you know.'

'I know. Here's the Kitchener letter.'

She handed it up to him. He read it, standing over her, shaking his head slowly in disbelief. 'This is classified information. This ought to be on file in Number Ten. Does he often send you this kind of thing?'

'All the time. Some of them are marked secret. It worries me, just having them in the house. He also shows me telegrams when we're driving around together.'

'What kind of telegrams?'

'Decoded Foreign Office telegrams, from ambassadors. He got into a stupid habit last summer, after I'd read them, of screwing them up and throwing them out of the window. They started turning up all over the place. Members of the public handed them in to the local police.'

'The *police* have been involved?' He sat down on the sofa. 'What happened with the police?'

'They gave the fragments to the Foreign Office. Apparently, only five men receive those particular telegrams – Grey, the Prime, Winston, Kitchener and Harcourt. Grey sent the pieces round in a box and demanded to know which of them was responsible for littering the country.'

'And did the Prime own up?'

'No, he denied it.'

'What happened after that?'

'Nothing, as far as I know. I assumed it had all gone away. Why? Do you think it hasn't?'

'I've no idea. But presumably it must have been Scotland Yard who brought them to the Foreign Office, which probably means the security service were involved as well.' He chewed his lip, thinking it over, musing aloud. 'Would they have just dropped it, I wonder? Perhaps they would, given the nature of the suspects involved. You haven't noticed anything suspicious lately, have you?'

'Such as?'

'I don't know.' He gave a nervous laugh. 'Men in overcoats hanging around the gates. Things going missing. Letters that look as though they might have been tampered with.'

'The posts *have* been rather slower than usual – half a day late, sometimes a day. I put it down to the war. And once, at Penrhos, after I'd been in London for a week, I came back and found the box was open, whereas I'm pretty sure I'd locked it before I left.' She had forgotten about that. She felt a twinge of alarm. 'Do you think I'm being investigated?'

'I shouldn't think so, but then again, they're absolutely obsessed with finding German spies.' He handed her the Kitchener letter. 'You might want to consider either giving all this back to him or transferring it to a bank vault – something a bit more secure than a toy chest.'

She returned the letter to the box and locked it. She had her back to him. 'It's all a bit of a mess, isn't it?'

'It certainly is.'

This was the moment, half-longed for, half-dreaded. It had to be done.

'Edwin, darling.' She turned to face him. 'Do you still want to marry me?'

'You know I do.'

'Can we talk about it?'

'Yes, please! I've been wanting to talk seriously the entire weekend.'

'And can I be honest?'

'Always.'

She sat next to him on the sofa. 'Do you remember the first time you proposed to me, at Penrhos?'

'Of course.'

'And do you remember, when I asked you why you loved me, you said it was because I had a man's mind in a woman's body?'

'Did I really say that? How crass of me. I'm sorry.'

'Don't apologise. I wasn't offended. I thought it rather shrewd. And do you recall that I retaliated by saying that perhaps you had a woman's mind in a man's body?'

'Yes, I do remember. Also shrewd.'

'Well – do you think *that* could be the basis for a marriage?'

He cocked his head and squinted at her. 'I'm not sure I follow.'

'I'm not especially feminine – never have been, mentally or physically.'

'I disagree! You're beautiful. I—'

'No, listen.' She patted his knee to silence him. 'I'm not fishing for compliments. I'm quite happy with the way I look. I'm simply saying that I'm the sort of woman who's generally described as handsome rather than pretty, and I suspect that's probably what makes me attractive to you.'

'What are you driving at?' He had started to look uncomfortable.

'Oh, for heaven's sake, do I really have to spell it out? You're attracted to me because I'm quite – *masculine*.'

There was a moment's silence.

'Good God!'

'Please don't be offended, Edwin. I don't mind where your desires may have led you in the past, or where they might lead you in the future, for that matter. To be honest, I'm relieved, because I can see now how a marriage might work for us both. You'd rescue me from an awful situation and offer me a life and a purpose. And in return I'd happily give you almost everything I have – my loyalty, my companionship and, insofar as I possess any capacity for it, my love.'

'And what is it you *wouldn't* give me?'

'My freedom. And I wouldn't expect you to give me yours.'

He was quiet for a minute.

'It's not exactly what I'd hoped for.'

'I understand. But it's the best I can offer.'

Another silence.

'I'd like to try it – you know, the physical side.'

'Yes, let's. But if it doesn't work, we'd both be free.'

'Not to separate?'

'No, to see other people. Discreetly.'

He nodded slowly. 'All right,' he said. He took her hand. 'I can't say I like it. But all right.'

Because they had agreed not to tell anyone until they had devised a strategy for informing the Prime Minister, their secret engagement felt quite unreal to her. There was no fuss, no excitement. She sat at lunch watching Edwin talk to her father, and thought: in a few months he will be my husband – can it really be true? Everything had changed, yet nothing had. And afterwards, when she drove him to the station to catch the train back to London, and they walked up and down the platform together, she had a sense of being disconnected from the whole situation. He was saying he would have to talk to his elder brother in general terms about what her conversion to Judaism might entail, what would be expected of her, how long it might take, the details of the financial settlement, and so forth.

This couldn't be happening, could it?

When the train arrived, she closed her eyes and kissed him on the mouth. It was not nearly as unpleasant as she had feared it might be.

'You have made me so happy,' he said.

Back at the house, she started to write to the Prime Minister.

My dearest, it is only fair to warn you that soon I may have to talk to you about my future. When I do, it will be a real test of your love for me. But if that love is as great as you say it is – & as I firmly believe that it is – then I hope you will find it in your heart to be happy for me & give me your counsel. I know I have the potential to make you feel wretched, but I promise you it is the last thing I shd. ever seek to do. And although my situation in life may change, nothing will ever change my feelings towards you . . .

Normally, words came to her without much effort. But this was a tortuous composition, designed to hint rather than reveal – a letter to prepare the ground – and she laboured like a diplomat over several drafts before she was satisfied with the result.

CHAPTER THIRTY

T HE PRIME MINISTER found her letter waiting for him on
his desk the following evening just before midnight, when
he returned to Downing Street from dinner. He had to
deliver his great speech to five thousand munitions workers in
Newcastle the next day, and only half of it was written; he was
planning to work on it into the small hours. Nevertheless, he
immediately pushed it to one side to discover what she had to say.

It took a while for the blow to register.

My situation in life may change . . .

He thought – hoped – at first that she might simply be referring
to her decision to nurse in France. But a second and then a third
reading left him in little doubt that she was referring to . . . marriage.
He sat numbly in the pool of lamplight, surrounded by his figurines,
trying to guess who her potential fiancé might be. He couldn't
imagine. It was several minutes before he was able to pick up his pen.

My own darling – when I got home just now I received &
read your letter of Sunday. I understand every word of it,
and (what is more important) I can read between the lines.

If you were to tell me tomorrow that you were going to be married, I hope I should have the strength not to utter a word of protest or dissuasion. I should honestly try to the best of my judgment to forecast your chances of happiness; and, from that point of view, I should mind quite enormously, who & what was the man. But whoever it was, life wd have lost for me its fountain, its inspiration, its outlook . . .

He poured himself a glass of brandy and glanced at the opening of his speech – *I have come here tonight to speak not only to the men of Newcastle and Tyneside, but through you to the workers of the whole of the north-east coast* – and then back again at his letter to her – *all that I am or can be are yours, now and for ever* – and for a moment he had a crazy impulse to shuffle the two: to call on Venetia to redouble her patriotic efforts to manufacture more artillery shells, and to tell the workers of the north-east how much he loved them. What would Northcliffe make of that!

Reluctantly, he finished his letter to Venetia – *I must try & think of something to say at Newcastle! Good night, most dear* – and forced himself back to work.

He left King's Cross station at ten o'clock the following morning. The Chief Whip had arranged for a small delegation of junior ministers and backbench MPs to see him off – a thoughtful gesture. As the guard blew his whistle and the train pulled away, he leaned out of the window and waved his hat in elegant circles towards them before flopping down into his seat opposite Margot. She had Elizabeth next to her. To his right sat Bongie with two red dispatch boxes. Violet was to his left. Poor Bongie. Things had rather cooled between him and Violet since she had taken such a shine to Rupert Brooke. George Wicks and Margot's maid were in third class with the luggage.

He felt tired before the day had even properly started. A combination of Venetia's letter and the need to stay up late to write his speech had ensured he had not slept well – and the wretched speech still wasn't finished, and now he had a stack of urgent papers and telegrams to work through. He ploughed on steadily as the train headed north, taking documents from Bongie, reading them, initialling them, adding instructions, handing them back, dispatching government business with his usual relentless concentration. It was a relief to lose himself in work. Only when they were past York did he at last find time to write to Venetia.

I will try to make my love for you more <u>unselfish</u>, and more worthy of you, my darling.

He looked across at Margot, who was sucking a peppermint and watching him beadily.

I must stop now & get back to my speech. I will write tomorrow to Alderley, where I assume you are likely to remain. I know you are thinking of me & wishing me good luck.

At 3.30 p.m. they pulled into Newcastle station, gliding to a halt next to a civic reception – the mayor and council, a brass band playing, flags strung from the ironwork, a large crowd. He went along the line of dignitaries, shaking hands, and at the end whispered to Bongie, 'I need to get to the hotel and finish my speech.'

'They've laid on a launch to take us along the river and look at the shipyards.'

'How long will that take?'

'A couple of hours.'

'I can't do that!' He beckoned to Margot. 'Darling, you and the girls will have to represent me on the tour of inspection. I need to work.'

There was a groan of disappointment from the crowd as he was led away along the platform. Like any politician, he hated to turn his back on a group of voters, but it couldn't be helped – the speech was the purpose of his journey. He was conducted by the manager of the Central Station Hotel across the grand reception area and up the staircase to the first-floor suite where the prime ministerial party were staying for the night. Bongie laid out his papers on the desk and left him alone.

The moment the door closed he resumed his letter to Venetia.

I have a blessed 1½ hours of peace & solitude, wh. I shall employ partly in my conventional task, & partly (I expect) in reading over again some letters I carry in my pocket: which is not at all conventional. Do you think I would have been a happier man if (in some ways) I had been more conventional?

He only wished she was with him, but writing to her constantly was the next best thing.

According to the figures Bongie had prepared for his speech, the munitions workers of north-east England were working an average of sixty-eight hours per week. Armstrong, the vast armaments company building battleships and field guns and making artillery shells and bullets, had arranged for five thousand men to be brought straight from the yards and factories to the Empire Palace Theatre in the centre of Newcastle to listen to the Prime Minister. Many were still in their overalls and were carrying their evening meals, wrapped up in red cotton handkerchiefs.

The Prime Minister entered to a tremendous roar of welcome. As he surveyed them from his seat on the stage, half-listening to the introductory speaker, he experienced the best kind of pre-performance nerves – keyed up, surging with adrenaline, anxious but confident. A lot was riding on this speech. Weeks of hostile press coverage, whispers that he was losing his grip – it demanded a firm response, and he was going to give it. An all-male audience was the perfect forum. He proposed to come out swinging like a fighter. The introduction over – 'Gentlemen, I give you the Prime Minister' – he strode to the lectern.

'I have come here tonight to speak not only to the men of Newcastle and Tyneside, but through you to the workers of the whole of the north-east coast! I have *not* come here, let me say at the outset, as the mouthpiece of either apology or panic! *(Cheers.)*

'This war was not of our seeking. Our honour, our security, our most glorious traditions, our best hopes, our most cherished ideals – all these were put in issue, and history will record that without an instant's hesitation, the challenge was taken up, and with a unanimity and an enthusiasm which can hardly be paralleled in the annals of the world! *(Cheers.)*

'I do not believe that any army or navy has ever entered upon a campaign or been maintained during a campaign with better or more adequate equipment. *(Cheers.)* I saw a statement the other day that the operations not only of our army but of our Allies were being crippled, or at any rate hampered, by our failure to provide the necessary ammunition. There is not a word of truth

in that statement! *(Loud cheers.)* I say there is not a word of truth
in that statement, which is the more mischievous because, if it
were believed, it is calculated to dishearten our troops, to discourage our Allies, and to stimulate the hopes and the activities of our
enemies!'

The words Northcliffe and *The Times* never left his mouth. He
would not sully himself to utter them. He did not need to. Everyone knew who he meant. He spoke for forty minutes, ended with
a paean of praise to the country's workers – 'To supply in these
times of stress our country's needs may show a heroism as real, a
patriotism as deep as theirs who are every day hazarding their lives
in the fighting line' – and sat down to a standing ovation.

Backstage afterwards, he was embraced by Margot and his
daughters. 'Henry, that was magnificent!' 'I'm so proud of you,
Papa!' 'Brilliant, Prime.' Only Bongie seemed somewhat muted.

'Well, what did you think?'

'That was very strong stuff, sir. Very strong indeed.'

'Too strong?'

'When you said there was "not a word of truth" that the army
has ever been hampered by a shortage of ammunition – may I ask,
what was the basis for that?'

'Sir John French said as much to Kitchener last week – don't you
remember? Kitchener sent me a note of their conversation.'

'I'm not sure he *did* say exactly that, sir. I thought he merely
said that he had enough ammunition for his *next attack*. We ought
to check to make sure. Do you have Lord Kitchener's letter?'

'Not with me, no.' He felt a sudden irritation with his private
secretary, not least because, now he came to think of it, he realised
he might be right. It was a mistake to have sent the letter to Venetia the moment he received it. He should have kept it by him while
he was writing his speech. 'Well, it's too late now. There's no point

in worrying about it. Northcliffe's always going to hate us, whatever we do.'

The next day's press was hostile. Not just *The Times*, which expressed its 'deep disappointment' at his 'petty attempts to prove that he and his colleagues have made no false calculations and no mistakes': such sanctimony he had expected, as he had the predictable sneers of Northcliffe's other penny rags, the *Daily Mail* and the *Daily Mirror*. But papers normally supportive were also critical. He had travelled to Newcastle to prove he was neither complacent nor out of touch, yet somehow he had managed to appear as both. He surveyed the newsprint, spread out like a stain across the white linen of the breakfast table, and felt a sense of foreboding. It would not end here, he thought. From now on, every time there was a shortage of munitions, his words would be thrown back at him. Even Margot, normally ferocious in her denunciations of his critics, was quiet.

They left the hotel after breakfast for a tour of the Armstrong works, a vast smoke-shrouded enterprise strung along the banks of the Tyne. According to Mr Marjoribanks, the manager who showed them round, it now employed thirteen thousand workers – ten times the number at the start of the war – and was the largest centre of armaments manufacturing in the world. They inspected the blast furnaces and the foundry where some of the navy's immense fifteen-inch guns were slung in their steel cradles, and the shipyards and the railyards and the aircraft factories. In the plants dedicated to filling shells and bullets with explosives, the machines were operated mostly by women. It was a revolution, he thought, women no longer working as maids and secretaries and nurses but doing men's jobs. With so many millions in the army, the war could not be won without them. He saw in that instant that his old opposition to female suffrage belonged to a different era. How could they be denied the vote after this?

In the train back to London, he was unusually quiet, staring out of the window, churning everything over in his mind – the Stygian foundries of death along the Tyne working round the clock to feed the mincing machine in France; Beb due to go to the front on Friday and Raymond the following week; Oc about to land at Gallipoli; the press against him; his colleagues conspiring; Venetia on the brink of marriage; his world sliding away beneath him.

The following day, Thursday, he woke to find a letter from her.

Alderley Park
Weds. 21 April 15
My dearest Prime,
I read the text of your Newcastle speech in <u>The Times</u> with pride & delight. How inspiring it was, & how beastly was their treatment of it! I hope you weren't discouraged by their sneers. Papa (who as you know has a temperament as detached & equable as yr. own) says that Northcliffe's treachery and megalomania is such that he should be horsewhipped the next time he appears in public!

I'm afraid you won't be pleased to hear that your uplifting words have only made me more determined to play my part in the struggle, & I shall be coming to London next week to receive my inoculations before I leave for France. I have been accepted to nurse at Lady Norman's war hospital at Wimereux, nr. Boulogne . . .

He read it with see-sawing emotions. She liked his speech – good. She was going to France – bad. She was coming to London – good. She made no further mention of marriage – good.

Or was it? As the day went on, his doubts grew. No mention of an engagement did not necessarily mean it wasn't happening; it might mean the opposite.

And so, at midnight:

My own darling – you will tell me, won't you? the real truth at once. However hard it may be to me. I would rather know the worst – without disguise or delay. You once said a thing that wounded me – only once – about 'cutting the loss'. Do tell me – yes or no! Then I can settle my account. The only thing I mind is suspense & uncertainty. Deliver me from that.

Your own lover.

She did not reply.

On Friday evening, Margot flung open the door of the Cabinet Room, where he was sitting working. He looked up and saw that she had tears in her eyes. She was holding a telegram.

He said at once, without thinking, 'Is it Oc?'

'No, it's *from* him. Rupert Brooke died this afternoon of blood poisoning. Oc's just returned from his burial on Skyros.'

'Blood poisoning?'

'From an insect bite.'

The news shook him. Apollo killed by an insect! It seemed to sum up the futility of it all.

'We'd better warn Violet.'

'She's gone to Dublin. I'll telephone her.'

Forty-eight hours later, in the darkness just before dawn on the morning of Sunday 25 April, an armada of two hundred ships closed in on the coast of the Gallipoli Peninsula. Winston showed him on a chart where the various divisions were going ashore – the Australian and New Zealand Army Corps at Gaba Tepe, the French at Besika Bay and Kum Kale, the 29th Division at Cape Helles, the Naval Division more than sixty miles to the north, along the Gulf of Saros to Bulair.

There was no mention of the invasion in the newspapers the following day. A press blackout had been imposed.

After that, there was nothing much he, or Winston, or Kitchener, or anyone else could do, except wait.

CHAPTER THIRTY-ONE

THAT MONDAY EVENING, Deemer met Kell at his club. This had been the pattern of his life for months now – reporting to the chief once a fortnight after office hours, usually on a Monday, unless he had something urgent to convey, in which case he would send him a telegram requesting a meeting. The loneliness of his existence had been alleviated briefly at the end of March, when his brother had come to stay. But Fred had returned to his regiment in France, to some unspecified clerical duties behind the lines, and Deemer was once again living and working entirely by himself. Kell had promised him in January that come the spring, he would find him a 'more congenial assignment'. Spring had arrived, and he was still stuck in Mount Pleasant. He braced himself to raise the matter again.

He was nodded through by the porter – his face had become familiar – and he found Kell as usual upstairs in the library, in a corner of the huge, deserted room.

'Good evening, Deemer. How are you?'

'Well enough, sir, thank you.'

'Take a seat.' He pointed to an overstuffed leather armchair. 'So, what do you have for me tonight?'

'A couple of things worth mentioning, sir.' He opened his brief-case and took out half a dozen photographs. 'Ten days ago, the Prime Minister sent Miss Stanley an account of a Cabinet meeting, which seems to have been extremely fractious. Lord Kitchener accused Mr Lloyd George of revealing secret information about the number of troops in France. According to the Prime Minister, I quote: "He declared that he could be no longer responsible for the War Office under such conditions, tendered his resignation, rose from his chair, & was about to leave the room."' Deemer handed over photographs of the letter. 'He claims he then man-aged to smooth things over, but he says he hasn't dared tell anyone else about it and asks her to keep it entirely to herself.'

'I'd heard things were becoming pretty strained between Kitch-ener and Lloyd George, but I'd no idea they were as bad as that. And has Miss Stanley kept it entirely to herself?'

'As far as we know, sir. At no time since the autumn has she shared any confidential information, to the best of our knowledge.'

'We must be thankful for that. Any suggestion that Kitchener was threatening resignation would be a gift to the enemy. You said there were a couple of things. What's the other one?'

'He wrote to her about the shell shortage and enclosed a letter he'd just received from Lord Kitchener, reporting a conversation with Sir John French. This is obviously a clear breach of the Offi-cial Secrets Act.'

'Let me see.'

Kell reached out and took the photograph. He spent a while frowning over it, as if he couldn't quite believe it. 'How long after he received this did he make his speech in Newcastle?'

'Six days, sir.'

'But this letter doesn't in any way support what he claimed. If anything, it implies the opposite.' He looked at Deemer. His face was clenched with anger. 'He deliberately lied to the country.'

'He exaggerated, certainly.' For some reason, he found himself wanting to defend the old man. 'Perhaps if he hadn't sent the letter to Miss Stanley – if he'd kept it by him when he was preparing his speech – he wouldn't have gone so far.'

'That's a very charitable explanation. And even if it's true, it means at the very least he's losing his judgement.' Kell glanced at the photograph again. 'I'd like to hold on to this, for now. You can make another copy, can't you?'

'Of course.'

Kell slipped it into his inside pocket. Deemer wondered why he wanted it. He'd never taken anything away with him in the past. He put the rest of the intercepted mail back in his briefcase.

Kell said, 'Is there anything else?'

'Nothing of much interest. On a general note, relations between the PM and Miss Stanley have become rather strained of late. I sense the affair may be coming to an end. She seems to be planning to marry Edwin Montagu.'

'That would be a pity,' said Kell, 'from an intelligence point of view.'

Deemer glanced at him in surprise. 'But surely we want the Prime Minister to stop sending her classified information?'

Kell said quickly, 'We do – of course we do! Although you must agree it has given us an extraordinary insight into what's happening at the very top of the government. You and I and Miss Stanley must be three of the best-informed people in the country. Won't you miss it if it stops?'

'No, sir.' He hesitated. 'To be honest, I've come to feel rather uncomfortable with the entire operation, especially as it's obvious none of the secrets are reaching the enemy. It's rather a disreputable business, and I'm not sure it's worth the risk of continuing. I think we should consider closing the case.'

'Do you indeed! Well, I'm afraid that's not a decision for you. But I hear what you're saying. I know how repetitive and isolating the work must be. Perhaps I could draft someone in to replace you. Let me know if anything important comes up in the meantime, otherwise I'll see you here in two weeks.'

And so Deemer returned to Mount Pleasant to continue his dutiful surveillance of the correspondence between the Prime Minister and Venetia, and also now – increasingly – between Venetia and Edwin Montagu. Over the next fortnight, he maintained his regular log of the dates and the main events. It was more than ever like following a romantic novel published in instalments, its story propelled towards its inevitable climax by forces the reader could see more clearly than its characters. Deemer found himself hurrying in to work each day, not so much to monitor secret information any more as to discover what would happen next.

On Tuesday 27 April, Venetia returned to London from Alderley and went for an afternoon drive with the Prime Minister. It left the PM, he confessed in a letter written to her that night, 'puzzled & bewildered':

It was strange – what you said today – of your detachment
from yourself & your own future. It fills me with surprise
& forebodings . . . I am far from happy about other
things – foreign & domestic. I have to make a fresh draft

every day upon my already overdrawn account of
optimism . . .

On Wednesday, it was Montagu's turn to complain to Venetia:

To tell you the honest truth, nothing worries me now but
you. I can't expect to be loved much or nearly as much as I
love you, but dearest you are a perplexing person. You
decide to spend your life with me if it can be done, then
without a word to me fix up 3 months at least in France.
You come to London and use most of your time here being
inoculated . . .

On the Thursday Venetia and Montagu met to discuss the
details of her conversion to Judaism, and clearly reached an agreement, because afterwards he wrote to her:

Most desperately beloved of all women,
    Yesterday was the greatest day of my life. Its net result
was that the most wonderful woman in the world
delivered herself into my safe keeping, into my hands for
better or worse, in the hope that with me she could lead a
happier life than was possible without me, or with any
other man.

On Friday, she left London to spend the weekend in Alderley
with the Prime Minister and his usual entourage. She wrote to
Montagu from the train:

Darling, I wish I felt the faintest inspiration, but this
infernal train shakes so that I find it impossible to

concentrate either my mind or my pen. Opposite me sits the P.M. in a more cheerful frame of mind I think, but I've a feeling in my bones that this party isn't going to be a success. I feel I shall quarrel with Bongie, be odious to the P.M., & have to avoid Violet's questions if she bothers to ask any . . . I am always impressing on you the fact that I'm completely & cold-bloodedly detached from all interest in my life. It doesn't sound good on paper. And yet I'm simply longing for you to be here & miss you horribly. It's again such a lovely day & we should have been so happy . . .

On Sunday, she wrote him a second letter, from Alderley House:

Boulogne, darling, is cinched. I go on Monday week. Don't be angry with me for settling this, I know it must seem to you to show lamentable lukewarmness, but it isn't that I want to postpone things, but I do want to have a slight first-hand experience of what the conditions are like not 60 miles away from a vast war.

To which Montagu replied:

I'm miserable about Boulogne. Well so be it, only swear to me you will be back by a certain date, and let's try to fix all things before you go. Will you?

On Monday 3 May, the Prime Minister wrote her a thank-you letter from Downing Street:

I had a heavenly time in Alderley to look back upon during these coming weeks of separation & absence. True there were some depressing moments, for which I hold myself accountable. I only hope I did not infect you with any of my bad spirits.

On Tuesday, he visited her in Mansfield Street, and afterwards wrote to her again:

Midnight. My darling – I don't think you were really <u>very</u> glad to see me this evening. I walked almost the whole way back to Downing St (nearly run over) ruminating over these things. I sometimes think that Northcliffe & his obscene crew may perhaps be right – that, whatever the rest of the world may say, I am, if not an imposter, at any rate a failure, & <u>au fond</u>, a fool.

On Wednesday, from 5.30 p.m. to 6.30 p.m., they went to Selfridges in Oxford Street, where he bought her a present of a bag for her journey to France.

On Friday afternoon, they had a final two-hour drive.

We had one of the most heavenly of our drives – hadn't we? When shall we have such another? I despair when I think of the Fridays that lie before me. I wonder if you feel the same. Whatever the future has in store for you in the way of companionship and intimacy (with some undisclosed person, whom in advance I loathe more than words can say) I shall be ready at the day of judgement to mention that I had the best of it!

After that, there was silence.

★

Deemer arrived at Mount Pleasant on the morning of Monday 10 May ready to begin yet another week's work. He was due to meet Kell that evening.

But although he lingered in his office all day, there was no delivery in the morning, and none that afternoon – the first time there had been a complete blank. He wondered if Venetia had already left for France. Impatient for information, he sat at his table and read *The Times*. He couldn't remember a grimmer day's news. A passenger liner, the *Lusitania*, had been torpedoed off the coast of Ireland by a German submarine; twelve hundred lives had been lost, more than a hundred of them American; there were pages of eyewitness reports and commentary. The Germans had started using poison gas on the Western Front. Column after column listed the names of dead, wounded and missing – almost three hundred on Sunday at Gallipoli alone. He felt guilty, sitting safely in his cell in north London, while the conflict raged with such increasing savagery across Europe.

At six, he locked up for the day, took the tube to Charing Cross and walked the rest of the way to Pall Mall. He had nothing of any significance to report to Kell. His briefcase was almost empty. He savoured the spring evening.

He arrived at the club earlier than usual. A Rolls-Royce was parked outside, its chauffeur resting his bottom against the bonnet, reading a copy of the *Daily Mail*. He nodded to the porter and passed unchallenged, up the staircase to the library. In the doorway, he heard voices, and paused just beyond the threshold. Kell was sitting in the corner with his back to him. Opposite him was a burly figure with a fleshy, powerful, almost brutal face. They were talking very quietly. Deemer thought he recognised him – but it couldn't be, could it? The man's gaze flicked in his direction and rested on him for a moment. He took a hasty step backwards, turned, and hurried downstairs.

'The man with Major Kell,' he said to the porter. 'Who is he?'

'I'm afraid I'm not at liberty to disclose that, sir.'

'Isn't it Lord Northcliffe?'

The porter smiled and winked. 'You said it, sir, not me.'

He sat on the leather bench and waited.

After ten minutes or so, Northcliffe walked past him, climbed into the back of the Rolls-Royce and was driven away.

He went back upstairs to the library.

'Deemer!' said Kell cheerfully. 'What do you have for me this evening?'

'Very little, sir. Nothing, in fact. Their letters were entirely personal. No political information, no official secrets. The relationship seems to be coming to an end.'

Kell frowned. 'Really – nothing?'

'No, sir.' He gestured to his briefcase. 'I can show you it all if you like.'

'No, there's no need. Anyway, I have some good news for you. I'm taking you off the case. I'll send one of my officers round to Mount Pleasant tomorrow morning. You can show him the ropes and leave him to take charge of everything.' He paused, smiled. 'Aren't you pleased? You look rather disappointed.'

'No, sir. I shall be glad to get out of there.'

'Good man. Take some leave for the rest of the week – you've earned a break – and report to Captain Holt-Wilson next Monday. We'll try to find something interesting for you.'

'Thank you, sir.'

He stood. He yearned to ask about Northcliffe, but he wasn't sure how to broach it.

Kell said, 'I think that's everything. I wish you a good evening.'

'Thank you, sir. The same to you.'

Venetia should have been on her way to France. Instead, she was lying in bed in Mansfield Street with a fever – a reaction, according to her doctor, to her typhoid inoculation. What made it so frustrating was that she didn't even feel particularly ill. But her mother was insisting on treating her as an invalid, putting her to bed, cancelling her Channel crossing, and telegraphing the hospital to say she would not be arriving until she had fully recovered.

Edwin had come to visit her, bringing flowers and sufficient fruit to feed a family for a week. He sat beside the bed and held her hand, while Edith went off to find a vase.

'Poor darling,' he said. 'I think this is a sign from God. Forget about France. Stay in London. Let's announce our engagement.'

'Don't be silly, Edwin. Mother's already making enough of a fuss as it is, without adding an engagement on top of it.'

'You're always finding an excuse to put it off. I honestly wonder whether it will ever happen.'

She wondered herself. Secretly, she wasn't sure whether she wanted the marriage to go ahead or not. Either option seemed to offer nothing but difficulties. Were other women like this, or was it just her?

Edith returned with a vase. 'The Prime Minister is downstairs, asking to see you.'

Venetia groaned and lay back on her pillows. Ibsen and Strindberg, and now Feydeau!

'Tell him I'm too ill.'

'No,' said Edwin. He turned to Edith. 'Tell him to come up.' And then to Venetia, 'This is the perfect opportunity for us to share our news. Come on, darling – let's get it over with once and for all.'

'Edwin – I can't.' Edith was standing patiently, vase in hand, waiting for confirmation of her instructions. She sighed and surrendered. 'All right, Edith, but warn him he can't stay longer than ten minutes. And Edwin, you're not to say a word.' She pulled her hand away. 'Go and stand by the window.'

The Prime Minister hurried in a minute later, his expression full of concern, his eyes only for her. 'Darling!' He was carrying two books, which he held out to her. 'Tolstoy and Bulwer-Lytton – the sublime and the ridiculous.' Then he noticed the figure at the window. 'Montagu,' he said in surprise.

'Prime Minister.'

Venetia said, 'It was lovely of you to come, Prime – for both of you to come.'

There followed an excruciating ten minutes of elaborate politeness – the Prime Minister trying not to show his resentment of Montagu; Montagu shooting her occasional pleading looks; she determinedly restricting the conversation to banalities – her symptoms, the risks of inoculations, her mother's over-reaction, the beauty of the flowers, her plans for the week, the chances of her being well enough for lunches and dinners.

Eventually, she felt she had done enough. 'Would you think it awfully rude of me if I said I'd like to rest now? I'm feeling very tired.'

They competed with one another in the sincerity of their apologies for tiring her and the fervour of their hopes that she would soon feel better. She rang the bell for Edith to show them out, and after a final round of goodbyes, and the door had closed, she rolled onto her side and pulled the blankets over her head.

*

They left the house together and walked down the street towards Cavendish Square in the direction of Westminster. Deemer watched them go. He recognised them both. If nothing else, their presence told him that Venetia must be at home. He crossed the road and rang the bell.

A house maid opened the door.

'Good evening. I'm Detective Sergeant Paul Deemer of the Metropolitan Police.' He showed his warrant card. 'I wish to see Miss Venetia Stanley.'

'I'm afraid Miss Stanley is ill, and not receiving visitors.'

'It's a matter of great urgency.'

'I'm sorry, sir. Those are my instructions.'

'In that case, could I have a word with her personal maid, Miss Winter?'

'Very well. I'll see if I can find her. Would you mind waiting in the hall?'

She disappeared upstairs. He stood on the black and white tiled floor, his bowler in his hand, and studied his reflection in the mirror. He straightened his tie and ran a finger through his hair. He felt oddly calm. In the time it had taken him to travel across London, he had considered the position from every angle and each time had arrived at the same conclusion. There had never been any evidence that Venetia Stanley had passed on secrets to the enemy. It might have been a possibility at the outset, and therefore worth investigating to make sure, but after seven months of constant monitoring, it was inconceivable. In other words, Kell had kept him embroiled in an illegal operation for purely political reasons, and now he was determined to damage the Prime Minister, perhaps even to bring down the government. What other reason might he have for meeting Northcliffe, except to pass on information? He felt used. He felt ashamed. He felt angry.

He heard a tread on the staircase and turned to see Edith Winter descending. 'Sergeant Deemer?' She stopped and stared at him. 'And also Mr Merryweather – isn't it?'

'One and the same, I'm afraid. I need to see Miss Stanley, immediately.'

'What a nerve you have, whoever you are! She is not seeing anyone. She most certainly will not be seeing *you*.'

'Miss Winter, she must. It concerns her relationship with the Prime Minister.'

A door opened and Lord Sheffield appeared, holding an evening paper. 'Is everything all right?'

Edith said, 'Yes, your lordship. I am dealing with the matter.'

He grunted and went back into the room.

Deemer said quietly, 'I have to see her. Please. She knows who I am. And I am truly sorry to have deceived you. It was only because of my work.'

'And what work is that?'

'I shall explain it to Miss Stanley.'

She studied him – he remembered that cool look – then sighed and turned away.

He followed her up the stairs. On the landing, she told him to wait, opened a door and slipped inside, closing it behind her. A minute later, she was back.

'She will see you.'

She stood aside to let him enter.

There was still some daylight from the windows. The lamps were on. Venetia was sitting up in bed with a quilted jacket over her nightdress.

She said, 'The mysterious Sergeant Deemer. You seem to be haunting me.'

'I'm afraid I have been somewhat. I apologise.' It was strange to see her lying there – to know so much about her, and yet really not to know her at all. She looked quite different with her hair let down and lying across her shoulders. He stood at the end of the bed. 'Perhaps I might explain?'

'Please do.' She seemed more amused than anything.

'We met in July, as you remember. After the investigation into the accident on the river, I was assigned to a department of Scotland Yard that deals with national security. Later in the summer, I was ordered to look into the discovery of a number of Foreign Office telegrams that had turned up at various places. You know what I'm referring to?'

She hesitated then nodded cautiously. 'I do.'

'In the course of that inquiry, it came to our attention that the Prime Minister was writing to you regularly. There was some concern about the possibility of espionage. To put the matter briefly, ever since September, the correspondence between the two of you has been monitored.'

'Monitored?' She was no longer looking amused. 'By whom? What do you mean?'

'Your letters have been intercepted and read by the government agency for which I work. I've come to warn you that I've reason to believe some of the details of that investigation may have been revealed – or possibly may be *about* to be revealed – to the press, and that you need to take action urgently.'

'How do I know you're telling the truth?'

'Well, for example, he wrote to you on Friday. He said you'd had a most heavenly drive.'

'This is outrageous.' Her face had turned pale. She was silent for a while. 'What sort of action do you suggest I take?'

'It's not really my place to say, but my advice would be to end your relationship with the Prime Minister as soon as possible, remove the letters to a secure location – and leave the country; go to France.'

'You're right about one thing – it's not your place to say!'

He bowed his head. 'I am profoundly sorry.'

'Why are you telling me all this? I don't understand. Won't you get into trouble?'

'Perhaps. It depends whether anyone discovers I've been to see you. I can't say I mind much either way.' He shrugged. 'It's wrong – that's all there is to it. I ought to go.'

'I think you better had.'

Edith was waiting for him on the landing.

At the front door, he said, 'Thank you for letting me in to see her. And again, I'm sorry for misleading you in Penrhos. I really would have liked that walk.'

He went straight to Oxford Circus Tube station and caught an eastbound train, then changed lines and travelled north to King's Cross.

The lights were on all around the Mount Pleasant sorting office. It was as busy at night as in the day. Nobody paid him any attention as he walked down the corridor to his little room. He locked the door behind him, took off his coat, and lit a fire in the stove. Once he had a decent blaze, he started emptying the safe, feeding the photographs and the negatives into the flames. He didn't bother to read the letters, just glimpsed the occasional phrase – 'My darling' 'Do you know how much I love you' 'My dearest Prime' – as they browned and curled and burst alight. It took him several hours. When he had finished, he left the keys to the empty safe on the table, took a final look around, and went home.

Early the next day, he presented himself at the army recruiting office in Clerkenwell. He was waiting on the doorstep when it opened. A sergeant looked him up and down.

'You're keen,' he said.

Venetia lay half-awake for much of the night, drifting in and out of a tempestuous sleep. In the morning, her fever had lifted, and her mind felt sharper. She didn't doubt that the policeman had been telling the truth. He seemed an honest man. She knew what she had to do. After taking her breakfast in bed, she put on a robe, sat at her dressing table, and wrote to the Prime Minister.

She sealed the envelope and addressed it. When Sylvia, who had temporarily moved back in with her parents while Anthony was at the front, looked in to see how she was, she asked her to post it. 'But not till this evening. I don't want him to get it until the morning.'

Sylvia held the letter close to her ear, as if it might whisper to her. 'What are you telling him now? Who to put in the Cabinet?'

'No, I'm letting him know I'm marrying Edwin.'

Sylvia's mouth dropped open.

'Good God – you're not?'

'Marrying Edwin or telling the Prime?'

'Both!'

'I *am* marrying Edwin. And obviously I must tell the Prime before he hears about it from anyone else.' She held Sylvia's hand. 'Will you do me a favour, darling? He's bound to come round at some point today. Tell him I'm too ill to see anyone.'

She stayed in her room all day. At six, she heard the doorbell ring. She opened her door and stood on the landing, listening. She could hear his voice, and Sylvia's, but not what they were saying. She returned to her room and stood at the window. About twenty minutes later, he emerged onto the pavement, settled his top hat on his head, and set off. As he neared the corner, he stopped and looked back at the house. For a moment, she thought he might have seen her, but if he had, he gave no sign. He stood there for at least a minute, as motionless as a statue in the May evening sunshine, until eventually he turned on his heel and walked away.

CHAPTER THIRTY-TWO

ER LETTER WAS brought to him with his tea and the rest of his correspondence early the following morning, while he was still lying in bed. The envelope felt disappointingly thin. He slit it open with his paper knife and pulled out the single sheet.

18 Mansfield St.
Tues. 11 May 1915
Dearest,
There is no easy way of saying this, so I shall come straight out with it. Edwin Montagu has asked me to marry him & after much thought I have accepted.

I know how fond you are of him, & that this will come as a shock to you, maybe even as a betrayal. No doubt I should have warned you of the possibility sooner, but my mind was not made up, & besides there never seemed a good moment to tell you when you weren't beset by one crisis or another. The last thing I have ever wanted – or want now – is to add to your burdens. Still, I can't help feeling, after all the joy you've given me, that mine is a very treacherous return.

Will you come and see me, & we can talk?

Ever yours.

Please forgive me & try to be happy for me.

Disbelief was his first reaction.

He had to go back to the beginning and read it again before his brain could absorb the information.

Montagu?

The prospect of her marrying any man had always been an agony for him. First, he had pleaded with her not to desert him. Then he had spent weeks trying to guess whom she might choose. Finally, he had sought to armour himself against the blow.

But *Montagu*!

His most loyal friend, or so he had always thought. Intelligent, good company, but not really a *man* at all – a neutered, self-absorbed bundle of moods and nerves and symptoms . . .

He thought of Monday. He remembered the three of them in her bedroom. Afterwards, he had walked back with the Assyrian the entire way to Whitehall, talking of Venetia and of politics – and not a word, never a hint of what was coming. And that last unsatisfactory weekend in Alderley when she had been so distant – she had known then, surely. They must have been plotting behind his back for weeks. It was the most grotesque, humiliating betrayal. And it would be a disaster. He knew them both too well to imagine they could ever sustain a proper marriage.

With shaking hands, he shaved and dressed and went directly to Margot's bedroom.

'Henry, what's the matter? You look as if you're about to faint.'

'A terrible thing has happened.'

Her hand flew to her mouth. 'Has Beb been killed?'

'No, not that, thank God. No – Venetia's agreed to marry Montagu!'

He knew she must be secretly delighted, but she managed to conceal it. 'Oh, Henry!' She held out her arms. 'Come here.'

He sat on the bed and leaned into her. She patted his back. For an awful moment, with his forehead pressed against her bony shoulder, he thought he might start to cry. He pulled away and cleared his throat.

'Well, there it is.'

She said, 'Is it really as bad as all that?'

'For her it will be. She doesn't love him. I know she doesn't. It will be a most miserable liaison.'

'I'm not sure Venetia's capable of loving anyone. But she knows what she's doing. And if she decides it won't work, even now, she'll end the engagement. She's entirely ruthless.'

For a moment he felt a spark of hope. It was true. Her family would be appalled: their daughter marrying a Jew – dear God! Give her a day or two, and she might well change her mind, or have it changed for her. But when he went downstairs and sat at the Cabinet table, he remembered her streak of recklessness, her vast capacity for indifference – both to what might become of her, and to what anyone might think of her – and in his heart he recognised it was hopeless. He reached for a sheet of notepaper.

Most Loved –
As you know well, <u>this</u> breaks my heart.
I couldn't bear to come and see you.
I can only pray God to bless you – and help me.
Yours.

★

But God – or Fate, or History, or whatever one wanted to call it – did not help him. On the contrary.

All across the country that day – it had started the night before in reaction to the sinking of the *Lusitania*, the use of poison gas in France, the Zeppelin raids, and an official report into the atrocities committed in Belgium during the first weeks of the war – a wave of anti-German rioting swept the major cities. In London, in Camden and Kentish Town alone, a hundred and fifty shops owned by naturalised Germans or Austrians were attacked – stocks looted, living quarters wrecked, staircases hacked to pieces, walls and ceilings torn down. Mobs carted away pianos, dressers, chests of drawers, tables, armchairs from the homes of neighbours they had known for years. It was the same in the East End. In Liverpool, two hundred shops were gutted. In Southend, the army had to be called out to restore order.

The reports penetrated the Prime Minister's misery, gave him something else to fix his mind upon.

He summoned a meeting of the Cabinet and urged the Home Secretary to take measures to protect the innocent – he suggested drafting in more police and troops – but McKenna said the simplest solution would be to intern every enemy national still at liberty, some twenty-four thousand men and sixteen thousand women.

The Prime Minister's Victorian Liberal instincts recoiled. 'But surely we must discriminate between those few who may pose a potential threat and those law-abiding citizens who have lived here most of their lives?'

'Impossible. We haven't the time or the resources.'

The argument went back and forth between the libertarians and the hard-liners. Kitchener was worried about German reprisals. Lloyd George wanted to set up special tribunals to decide on individual cases. In the end, the Prime Minister drafted a short holding statement he could make in the Commons that afternoon, expressing dismay at the rioting, understanding of the causes, and promising action in the near future. That seemed to satisfy both sides.

For a blessed hour, he had been able to forget about Venetia, but the moment the meeting ended, the anguish welled up again. Somehow, he managed to get through an official lunch with Prince Paul of Serbia, despite not being able to eat more than a mouthful, and then it was off to the Commons to answer questions – a lot of hostile barracking from the Tory benches about Winston's frequent trips to France – before he made his statement about internment. 'No one can be surprised that the progressive violation by the enemy of the usages of civilised warfare and the rules of humanity, culminating for the moment in the sinking of the *Lusitania*, should arouse a feeling of righteous indignation *(cheers)* among all classes in this country . . .'

Afterwards, he retreated to his room and sat staring into space. Normally at this time he would have written to Venetia. Instead, he poured out his heart to Sylvia.

I don't suppose there is in the kingdom at this moment a much more unhappy man. I never had any illusions, as I often told Venetia, and she also was always most frank about it – as to her some day getting married. But this! I don't believe there are two living people who, each in their separate ways, are more devoted to me than she and Montagu: and it is the irony of fortune that they two shd. combine to deal a death blow to me . . .

He hoped there might be a further letter from Venetia, but there was nothing. There was only one from Montagu:

Dear Prime Minister,
    You will by now have heard that Venetia has made me more than happy by consenting to marry me . . .

To which he managed to dredge up the grace to make a one-sentence reply:

My dear Montagu,
    You are more than fortunate, and I pray that Heaven will bring you both all happiness.
    Yrs always,
    H.H.A.

First thing the next morning, Hankey came to see him and asked if he would meet Jackie Fisher: the First Sea Lord was once again threatening to resign.

'Really? Must I?' He had no energy for such a task.

'He and Winston are at one another's throats over the Darda-nelles. I think if he felt he had your confidence, it might make him easier to manage.'

The old admiral came to the Cabinet Room that afternoon. He was a short man, not much taller than Winston, but stocky, like a wrestler. Outside, it was dark and cold, more January than May. The rain beat against the windows.

'*Bad* news, PM.'

He had an oddly emphatic way of speaking, putting the stress on certain words as if they were in capital letters.

'What now?'

'*Goliath* was torpedoed last night off the Dardanelles, and she went down *fast*.'

'How many casualties?'

'Six hundred. According to a report from *Majestic*, half an acre of sea was nothing but a mass of struggling, drowning men, being carried away by the current. There was nothing they could do.'

'God, how appalling.'

'We can't go on losing ships at this rate, sir. To add to the dangers, we have intelligence that two German *submarines* have just arrived in the area. One well-aimed torpedo, and there goes the *Queen Elizabeth*! We must withdraw her.'

'What does Winston say?'

'Winston is a man *obsessed*! He's *hell-bent* on forcing the Dardanelles and *nothing* will turn him from it – *nothing*! The whole thing is *madness*. He has the entire Admiralty running around thinking *only* about the Dardanelles, and meanwhile we're ignoring the increasing submarine menace in our own home waters.'

He said wearily, 'Winston sets policy. You're in charge of operations. Withdraw the *Queen Elizabeth* if that's your judgement and tell him I said so. Rely on me. I'll back you up.'

After he had gone, the Prime Minister sat alone looking at the rain lashing against the window. He ought to talk to Winston and tell him to make peace with the First Sea Lord, but he couldn't face it. His mind no longer seemed to be functioning properly, circling round and round the void that had been left by Venetia. His letters to her had always helped him focus his thoughts. Without them, he felt adrift. He went next door to Bongie's office, to see if a message had come from her. To his astonishment, he found Margot and Fisher dancing a waltz together around the table, the admiral humming a creditable rendition of 'The Blue Danube'.

She called over his shoulder, 'Darling, Lord Fisher is a wonderful dancer!'

She had been in an excellent mood ever since Venetia's letter. Her high spirits added to his gloom. As for Fisher – dancing after bringing him news of the deaths of six hundred sailors: the man was mentally unstable. He closed the door and returned to his reverie.

Friday was the worst day.

He barely slept all night and woke to yet another morning without a word from Venetia. When he went downstairs, he found Bongie hovering like an anxious waiter beside the Cabinet table, where a copy of *The Times* lay open at the headlines:

NEED FOR SHELLS

BRITISH ATTACK CHECKED

LIMITED SUPPLIES THE CAUSE

A LESSON FROM FRANCE

Northcliffe – again!

He sat and read the article, an account of the latest failed attacks at Fromelles and Richebourg: *The want of an unlimited supply of high explosives was a fatal bar to our success.*

'At least this time it doesn't blame me personally.'

'There's also a leader.' Bongie leaned over the Prime Minister's shoulder, turned the page, and placed his finger on the relevant paragraph: *The Government, who have so seriously failed to organise adequately our national resources, must bear their share of the grave responsibility.*

'Where are they getting their information?'

'Presumably, from the Commander-in-Chief. It really would be useful, sir, to have that letter from Lord Kitchener.'

'As I told you, I'm afraid I no longer have it to hand.'

'Might it be possible to . . . *find* it?'

The Prime Minister gave him a sharp look. He didn't care for the implication. He momentarily contemplated the prospect of asking Venetia for its return – unthinkable after everything that had happened. In any case, for all he knew, she had destroyed it. 'No, I'm afraid it's not.'

'Well, that's unfortunate. The Opposition are likely to make a lot of trouble over this.'

'Yes, yes, yes – I'm aware of that!'

He didn't have much time to brood over it. At ten o'clock he had to chair a meeting of the War Council. He could tell it would be rancorous, from the moment Kitchener strode in without a word to anyone and sat glowering around the table. The War Secretary opened the session by summarising the situation at Gallipoli, which was deteriorating fast.

'The British, Australian and New Zealand divisions have so far lost fifteen thousand men. The French have lost thirteen thousand. We have barely penetrated beyond our original landing sites and are trapped – as in France – by a combination of barbed wire and machine guns. Our latest estimate is that the Turks have deployed an army of one hundred and fifty thousand in the zone of battle, well dug in, led by good German officers, and outnumbering us by two to one.

'I must remind the Council that we were assured by the Admiralty in January that forcing the Dardanelles would be a relatively quick maritime operation. We were told that the *Queen Elizabeth*, as the most powerful of our battleships, would practically destroy the forts single-handed. Last night, I was informed that she is to be withdrawn, leaving the army to do the job on its own. This is quite intolerable.'

Fisher, who was sitting next to Winston, raised his hand. He had never spoken at a meeting of the Council before.

The Prime Minister said, reluctantly, 'The First Sea Lord?'

'As the Secretary of State for War knows full well, I was *against* the Dardanelles operation *from the start*. I believe the Prime Minister is also aware of that fact.'

There was a startled silence. Winston stuck out a petulant lower lip, and half-turned his back on him. Bonar Law glanced at the pair in astonishment.

Kitchener resumed his grim survey of the war – stalemate and huge losses in France; Russian defeats on the Eastern Front; the danger, if the French collapsed in a similar fashion, of a German invasion of the British Isles; the need to keep some of the new armies back for home defence. 'It is impossible, in present circumstances, to send more men to Gallipoli.'

Winston could control himself no longer. 'The Germans are not going to invade this country! They would be insane even to contemplate such a stupendous folly. Let our armies in France remain on the defensive for now. The entrenched positions are too strong on either side for a breakthrough. That is why our whole military effort, including our new armies, should be directed at Gallipoli, where victory is within our grasp.'

There were groans around the table, and after that, it was a free-for-all, an awful, sulphurous meeting – the worst two hours the Prime Minister could remember in the entire course of the war – with Winston, like some stricken warship, battling away against the combined forces of Kitchener, Lloyd George and Haldane, while Fisher sat beside him, staring at the table, saying nothing. Lloyd George, Winston's great ally before the war, was especially bitter towards him: 'How can we possibly send enough men to dislodge one hundred and fifty thousand Turks, fighting to defend their native soil? You have consistently underestimated their ability, as if they are some kind of inferior race. We can't go on drifting from day to day, losing men in their thousands, simply to save your pride!'

For the first time, the Prime Minister had a sense of impending disaster. He sat listening, silent, judge-like as usual, waiting for the storm to blow itself out, before intervening at the end to sum up the argument with the only practical solution: that the army commanders on the ground should be requested to provide, in explicit terms, the exact size of the force they estimated they would need to reach Constantinople. Then a final decision could be taken.

As he gathered his papers, he cursed himself for not asking the question back in January.

That afternoon, he went for his regular Friday drive, alone. He directed Horwood to take him to Mansfield Street. They parked on the opposite side of the road, and he studied the impressive house, so familiar after so many years. The facade was blank. There was no sign of life. He sat there for at least ten minutes, trying to decide whether to ring the bell, but in the end his nerve failed him, and he signalled Horwood to return home.

At midnight, he broke the vow he had made to himself to wait for her to end the silence, and wrote her a note.

This is too terrible. No Hell can be so bad. Cannot you send me one word? It is so unnatural. Only one word?

The following morning – Saturday – he was due to attend the wedding of Geoffrey Howard, a Liberal MP, formerly his parliamentary private secretary, now a government whip. Howard was a relative of Venetia. Montagu was to be his best man. It would be a big political occasion. He knew they would both be there.

He dressed more carefully than usual in his formal morning suit and inspected himself in the mirror. He had scarcely eaten in the past three days. He definitely looked thinner, but whether it made him appear handsome or merely haggard he couldn't decide.

He went down to the Cabinet Room to see what telegrams had come in overnight and had barely made a start when Winston appeared in the doorway.

'Fisher has disappeared.'

'What?'

'He's left me a note.' He flourished it.

'What does it say?'

'"First Lord, After further anxious reflection I have come to the regretted conclusion I am unable to remain any longer as your colleague . . . I am off to Scotland at once so as to avoid all questionings. Yours truly, Fisher."'

The Prime Minister sat back in his chair, appalled. The resignation of the most popular sailor since Nelson at the exact moment when Gallipoli was on the knife-edge of disaster, and just as the munitions shortage was back in the papers, would make a deadly combination.

'But he can't just run away! He's a serving admiral in wartime! That's tantamount to desertion.'

'I agree entirely. It's intolerable'

The Prime Minister rang for Bongie. He came at once. Like Winston, he too was dressed for the wedding.

'Fisher is missing without leave.' He scribbled a note.

Lord Fisher,

In the King's name, I order you at once to return to your post.

H. H. Asquith

'Find him, give him this, tell him I want to see him immediately.'

'Where might he be?'

'I've no idea. He says he's planning to go to Scotland. If necessary, you should call in the police to help you track him down. And make sure nobody else hears about it.' After he'd gone, he said to Winston, 'Are you coming to this wedding?'

'I think I should return to the Admiralty. Why? Are you still going?' He looked surprised.

'I don't see why not. There's nothing I can do until Fisher gets here.'

The ceremony was in King Henry VII's Chapel at Westminster Abbey. He drove to it with Margot and Violet, both dressed as if for a fashion show, his wife in a black net coat and tiny hat, his daughter in a striped yellow tunic. Margot gabbled away cheerfully about everything and nothing. Violet mostly ignored her and looked out of the window. He didn't mention Fisher's resignation. He knew that if he did, Margot wouldn't be able to resist telling half the congregation.

The ringing of church bells was forbidden in wartime. At the North Porch of the Abbey, a crowd had gathered in the silence. When he stepped out of the car, they gave him a faint cheer. Inside, the small chapel was already packed, the organ playing. He was conducted to the front, Margot clinging to his arm, Violet walking behind them. As he drew closer to the altar, in the third row he saw Venetia – his heart jumped when he glanced at her; he put his head down quickly. Montagu was in the first pew next to the bridegroom. They nodded to one another. No sooner had he taken his place than the organ struck up the 'Wedding March'.

He passed through most of the service in a trance – the prayers, the hymns, the sermon – but the solemnisation was an agony for him, as if he had never really heard the familiar words before. *May they ever remain in perfect love and peace together* . . . Margot nudged him and gave him her handkerchief. He blew his nose noisily. What was this awful sentimental old man's habit he had got into lately, of blubbing in public?

Afterwards, in the interlude when the bride and groom had gone off with the Dean of Westminster to sign the register, he felt a presence arrive beside him and turned to find Bongie crouching in the aisle. His private secretary whispered, 'The police located Admiral Fisher in the Charing Cross Hotel. He's in Number Ten waiting to see you.'

He said to Margot, 'I have to go,' and before she could ask him why, he rose and followed Bongie back down the aisle. He was conscious of the whole congregation swivelling to look at him, and this time, as he passed Venetia, their eyes met, and she gave him a faint smile. She couldn't have been more than five feet from him, and that was the awfulness of it, he reflected in the car back to Downing Street – she might as well have been on the other side of a chasm.

He found Fisher in the Cabinet Room with Lloyd George. As he opened the door, the Chancellor – who was sitting in *his* chair, he noticed – jumped up. 'I'll leave you two to talk.' On his way out, Lloyd George touched the Prime Minister's elbow and beckoned him into the lobby. He said quietly, 'I just happened to come round to see you on another matter and found him waiting. He told me what he's done. I've tried to persuade him to stay but he's having none of it. I hope you have better luck.'

'If even you, with your silver tongue, couldn't talk him round, I very much doubt I shall manage it.'

'Well, I hope to God you can, because if he resigns, it will put the whole government in jeopardy.'

'You think it's as bad as that?'

'I do.'

The Prime Minister watched him walk away along the corridor towards the connecting door to Number 11. He remembered Venetia's warning – *he is the most ambitious man in the government & his loyalty is always & only to himself.* It seemed an odd coincidence, that he should have 'just happened' to call round on a Saturday morning, when he might have guessed they would all be at the Howards' wedding. He sensed something was going on, but if so, there was nothing he could do about it.

'Now then, Admiral,' he said, stepping into the Cabinet Room and closing the door behind him, 'what's all this talk about resignation?'

For the next half-hour, he deployed every weapon in his lawyer's armoury. He reasoned. He flattered. He bullied. He cajoled. He reminded him of his patriotic duty. To no avail. Fisher declared that fond of Winston though he was – 'And I *love* that man: he is a *genius*' – he could not work with him for another hour. He would not return to the Admiralty even to clear his desk – 'If I do, he'll only *out-argue* me and *browbeat* me into staying; I know what he's *like.*' He would not support a policy he did not believe in. He could not defend the Dardanelles operation. He was *out.* The only concessions the Prime Minister could extract from him were that he would not go to Scotland but would stay in London; that he would talk to McKenna – Winston's predecessor, to whom he remained close; and that he would keep his resignation secret until Monday.

After that, he drove down with Margot and Violet to the Wharf, although he was careful not to mention anything about Fisher's resignation until Margot came over the bridge from her bedroom to say good night.

'Your dancing partner may be about to waltz us all over the cliff!'

Reggie McKenna arrived at five-thirty on Sunday afternoon and came straight up to the Prime Minister's study, while Pamela sat in the garden with Margot.

'I've spoken to Fisher.'

'And?'

'He's quite immovable, I'm afraid.'

The Home Secretary was in his early fifties, bald of head, mournful of face, one of those senior politicians commonly described as 'a safe pair of hands', who could be relied upon to run whatever department they were given with machine-like efficiency. He had modernised and expanded the navy with Fisher and still deeply resented the Prime Minister's decision in 1911 to make him swap jobs with Winston at the Home Office. Now was his moment of revenge.

'You realise Winston will have to go?'

'Keep Fisher, you mean, and lose Winston?'

'That would never work. You can't take him back after this. He'd be intolerable. He's far too old and unstable. But Winston can't survive his resignation. The Tories will tear him to pieces in the Commons tomorrow.'

There was truth in what he said, but the Prime Minister couldn't quite bring himself to accept the situation was so cataclysmic. 'Winston has more fighting spirit than the rest of us put together. He would be a terrible loss.'

'Maybe so, but look where he's got us.'

'I'll think about it. Will you stay for dinner?'

'No, thank you. We should get back to London.'

The Prime Minister went downstairs to see them off. Their car had only just rounded the corner when the telephone rang. Margot went inside to answer it. When she came back, she said, 'That was Winston's private office. He and Clemmie are on their way down to dine with us – if that's all right?'

'I suppose it had better be, if they're already on their way.' He knew she was waiting for him to tell her what had happened with McKenna, but he didn't want to be hectored. 'I'm going for a walk.'

It was a glorious summer's evening. The garden was a mass of tulips. He went down to the river's edge and sat on a wooden bench. Beyond his feet the Thames flowed wide and slow. He had never felt more lonely. He composed a letter to Venetia in his head: *My dearest darling, I am so besieged by problems, I don't know which way to turn. There is no one I can speak to, whose judgement I can trust, who isn't self-interested in some way. If I sack Winston, I'm not sure how long the government can survive. If I try to keep him, I foresee nothing but problems. Ever since you left me, the whole world seems to have turned against me. Can I meet you tomorrow, if only for an hour, to seek your reassurance and your counsel? I love you and I always shall. Ever your beloved . . .*

If he sent it by special messenger, she would have it that night, and he could see her in the morning. But what if she refused to come to him? That he couldn't bear. So he stayed where he was, as the river flowed and the shadows lengthened, trying to find a way out of his problems, until he heard Winston's car arriving, when he rose and walked back to the house.

As he often was when things were going badly, Winston was in splendid form. Before they went into dinner – Bongie and Raymond were there, as well as Clemmie, Margot and Violet – they had a talk in the Prime Minister's study. He had spoken, he said, to the other Sea Lords. None of them would resign in support of Fisher, and Sir Arthur Wilson had agreed to step up and take his place. As for Fisher, he had agreed in writing to every executive telegram on which the Dardanelles expedition had been mounted. Winston had assembled the documents to prove it.

'If he tries to cause us trouble, I shall get up in the House of Commons, and I fear I shall destroy him. It will afford me no pleasure, I can assure you, but he will have brought it on himself.'

The Prime Minister listened, nodded, and said nothing.

He motored up to London the following morning. As soon as he got to his desk, he checked the newspapers. There was not a word in any of them about Fisher. *The Times* had printed a list of the latest casualties from the Dardanelles. The columns of names, set in small type, took up the whole of page three, and spilled over onto page four. He was sitting studying them, running his finger down the list of officers to see if there was anyone he knew, when there was a knock at the door and Lloyd George came in.

'Good morning, Prime Minister. How was your weekend?'

'Fraught. Yours?'

'The same. I need to have a talk. Do you have a minute?'

'Of course.'

Lloyd George closed the door and sat down opposite him. The Prime Minister could see at once he was nervous, shifting in his seat, clasping his hands on the arms of the chair and then unclasping them.

'Bonar Law came to see me last night when I was sitting in Number Eleven, smoking a cigar with McKenna.'

'Bonar Law? Well, well, the company you keep!'

'He'd heard about Fisher's resignation. He's also worried about how some on his side might try to exploit the munitions crisis. In fact, he's concerned about the whole state of the war. To cut a long story short, he's offering to form a coalition.'

'What did you tell him?'

'I said I'd need to speak to you, obviously.'

'But you're in favour?'

'I am.' He leaned forwards, elbows on his knees, entreating, determined. 'We can't go on as we are. This war is clearly going to last for several more years at least. To win it will require a supreme national effort, and that demands a united, all-party government.'

'You may be right. I shall need to think about it.'

'I'm afraid there's no time for that. Once news of Fisher's resignation breaks, there will be a political bloodbath. We need to come to an agreement in principle immediately. Bonar Law is waiting in my office for an answer. I suggest I go and fetch him now.'

The Prime Minister stared at him. He had never before encountered such a brutal démarche. 'And if I refuse?'

'I strongly advise against that. McKenna feels the same.'

'That sounds like a threat.'

Lloyd George didn't answer.

'And what would be the terms of this agreement in principle?'

'Bonar Law has only two fundamental conditions. Winston would have to leave the Admiralty, and Haldane would have to leave the government altogether.'

'Haldane? Why? For the crime of once studying in Germany? He's my oldest friend! And I thought Winston was one of yours.'

Lloyd George's voice was ice. 'We have moved beyond considerations of friendship, Prime Minister. As far as Winston goes, he wanted this war from the start, he saw in it a chance for personal glory, and he embarked on a risky campaign without caring a straw for the misery and hardship it would bring to thousands.

Yes, he is a friend, but I have to say, in this instance, my sympathies are minimal. Now, shall I fetch Bonar Law or not?'

The Prime Minister weighed it up. Winston was a brilliant debater – he might well be able to refute Fisher's charges. And as for himself, he could face down the shell crisis – he had got through worse. He still had a majority in the Commons. The party would rally behind him. He could call Lloyd George's bluff: he doubted he would resign, and McKenna certainly wouldn't. But he felt a great exhaustion overcoming him at the prospect of such a lonely, bitter fight.

He bowed his head.

'Go and get him.'

That morning, after Bonar Law had been and gone, after they had agreed on an equal division of seats in the Cabinet, on the dismissal of Winston and Haldane, and they had shaken hands over the corpse of the Liberal government, a letter finally arrived from Venetia.

My darling (do you mind if I use the possessive one last time?),

My heart was broken to see you at the wedding on
Saturday & not to be able to speak to you. It felt so cruel &
unnatural, & you looked so sad and careworn. I tried to
find the best time to tell you about my plans, & I seem to
have picked the worst.

I can't undo what's been done, nor would I if I could –
not just agreeing to marry Edwin, but most of all, I would
not undo what went before it: two years of constant
intimacy of thought & feeling with <u>you</u>, my dearest Prime.
When I am old & grey, I know that ours is the time I shall
remember best of all others in my life.

We shall meet again, & it will be painful for us both I'm sure, but the time after that it will be less so, & then again, & then again, until we recover our old easy joy in one another's company.

All love

He carried the letter over to his desk, cleared a space among his little figures. He thought for a while. He was so tired. But eventually he wrote his reply.

Darling, your most revealing and heart-rending letter has just come. What am I to say? What can I say? I was able to keep silence for the two most miserable days of my life, and then it became unbearable; and like you I felt that it was cruel and unnatural, and that anything was better. So I scrawled my 2 or 3 agonised sentences, and thank God you once more speak to me and I to you . . .

Never since the war began had I such an accumulation (no longer shared!) of anxieties. One of the most hellish bits of these most hellish days was that you alone of all the world – to whom I have always gone in every moment of trial & trouble, & from whom I have always come back solaced and healed & inspired – were the one person who could do nothing, & from whom I could ask nothing. To my dying day, that will be the most bitter memory of my life.

I am on the eve of the most astounding & world-shaking decisions – such as I wd never have taken without your counsel & consent. It seems so strange & empty & unnatural: yet there is nowhere else that I can go, nor would I, if I could.

HISTORICAL NOTE

Thus ended the affair between the Prime Minister and Venetia Stanley, and with it the last Liberal government ever to hold office in the United Kingdom.

Venetia sailed for France the following Monday, 24 May, to take up her work as a nurse. *The Times* that morning carried preliminary details of the new Cabinet: six Liberals – the Prime Minister, Grey, Lloyd George, Crewe, McKenna and Simon; six Unionists – Bonar Law, Balfour, Lansdowne, Lord Curzon, Carson and Austen Chamberlain; one Labour – Arthur Henderson; and one non-party – Kitchener.

As part of the coalition agreement, Edwin Montagu was dropped from the Cabinet and his junior position was given to Churchill, newly dismissed from the Admiralty. But Churchill soon thought better of it and left to join his regiment in France.

By the time the Dardanelles campaign was abandoned as a failure in January 1916, the total dead amounted to more than 110,000 – 34,000 British, 10,000 French, 10,000 Australian and New Zealand, and 56,000 Turkish; in addition, roughly a quarter of a million men were wounded or missing.

Lord Kitchener was drowned in June 1916 when the warship taking him on a mission to Russia struck a mine a few miles off the coast of Scotland in a gale force wind; his body was never recovered.

Raymond Asquith was killed in action on the Somme in

September 1916. He smoked a cigarette as he was carried away on a stretcher so as not to demoralise his men; his last words were to ask for his cigarette case to be given to his father.

Oc rose to the rank of brigadier general, and was badly wounded in December 1917, when a leg had to be amputated.

Beb served in France with the Royal Artillery, suffered from shell shock, but remained in the army until the end of the war.

Violet married Maurice ('Bongie') Bonham Carter in 1915, was active in Liberal politics, standing unsuccessfully for Parliament, and became a life peer in 1964.

After almost nine years in office, Asquith was finally ousted as prime minister by Lloyd George in December 1916. On his final day in Downing Street, he burned most of his private correspondence, including all his letters from Venetia. He continued to lead the Liberal Party until 1926, but never returned to power. He died in February 1928 at the age of seventy-five. The last person he visited before his final illness confined him to the Wharf was Venetia.

Margot Asquith died in 1945, aged eighty-one.

Venetia married Edwin Montagu in July 1915. The Prime Minister did not attend the ceremony but sent two silver boxes as a wedding present. Montagu eventually returned to the Cabinet and served as a reforming Secretary of State for India, helping to create the legislation that led ultimately to Indian independence. A passionate anti-Zionist, he opposed the Balfour Declaration of 1917 establishing a Jewish homeland in Palestine. He died in 1924 at the age of forty-five.

Venetia had by then given birth to a daughter, Judith, born in in 1923. Decades later, DNA tests established that her father was not Montagu but the Earl of Dudley, one of several affairs Venetia had during her married life and widowhood; another, which began around 1918, was with the press proprietor Lord Beaverbrook. Venetia died in 1948, at the age of sixty. By then, the Stanley family's fortunes were in steep decline. Today, Alderley Park no longer exists; all that remains of Penrhos House are parts of the walls and corner towers, mostly overgrown with ivy, hidden in the woods.

All this, of course, was in the unforeseeable future. I prefer to think of Venetia on that day in May 1915, on the deck of the Channel ferry, her face turned to the wind, free and independent, following her chosen course at last, one of the most consequential women in British political history.

ACKNOWLEDGEMENTS

My greatest debt is to the estate of the late Lord Bonham Carter for permission to quote from Asquith's letters to Venetia, and in particular to Jane Bonham Carter for her generosity and encouragement over several years. I would also like to thank her fellow trustees, Virginia and Liza Bonham Carter, and Dr Mark Pottle, who allowed me access to the edition of Margot Asquith's pre-war journals which he is preparing.

The 560 letters to Venetia, amounting to some 300,000 words, are held in eight boxes at the Bodleian Library in Oxford, and I am grateful to Jeremy McIlwaine, Senior Archivist, and Dr Christopher Fletcher, Keeper of Special Collections.

The letters – which are for the most part in pristine condition and were obviously well looked after – first surfaced about fifteen years after Venetia's death. The physical ownership belonged to the Montagu estate; the literary rights were controlled by the Bonham Carters. Mark Bonham Carter made them available to his friend Roy Jenkins, who was writing a biography of Asquith, published in 1964. His mother, Asquith's daughter Violet – who had no idea of their existence and was shocked by their contents – strongly opposed allowing him access, but was eventually prevailed upon to permit their use, albeit with certain omissions, designed to protect her father's reputation.

In 1982, a scholarly edition of 'something over half' of the letters was published by Oxford University Press, superbly edited by

Michael and Eleanor Brock. This edition, which I read when it first appeared, has been utterly invaluable to me – inspired this book, in fact – so it seems churlish to point out that I have since discovered there are certain passages and letters that were rather surprisingly left out, most notably perhaps the last two paragraphs of this novel. It seems incredible, in the literal sense of that word, to suggest, as some historians have done, that Venetia's ending of their affair had little impact on Asquith's decision to agree to a coalition government on 17 May 1915. Of course, she might have advised him he had no choice, and probably in the long run he did not, but that is a different matter. I also think it strains credulity to breaking point, given the characters of Asquith and of Venetia, to suggest, as the Brocks do, that the affair was not, at least in some sense, physical. But this is where a novelist has a freedom a historian does not.

One writer who has spent longer studying the letters than perhaps any other is Dr Stefan Buczacki, who wrote and self-published an excellent and informative biography of Venetia Stanley, *My darling Mr Asquith*. He has read all the letters and made available to me his transcripts of many passages which are not in the Brocks' edition; I salute his scholarship and generosity.

I wish also to record my special thanks to Anna Mathias, Venetia's granddaughter, both for her insights and encouragement, and for giving me permission to quote from the Venetia–Edwin Montagu correspondence.

I am grateful to the staff of the National Archives at Kew, to the London Library, and to my friends at the Cornerstone division of Penguin Random House, especially Helen Conford, Venetia Butterfield and Gail Rebuck. I thank, yet again, for reading the manuscript and making suggestions, Jocasta Hamilton. My wife, Gill Hornby, was, as ever, the most invaluable adviser and support.

Our first grandchild was born shortly before I started writing *Precipice*: this one is for him.

The work of a great many historians made this novel possible, and it is a pleasure to cite below a list of those books which were especially useful.

Robert Harris
11 June 2024

Christopher Andrew, *The Defence of the Realm: The Authorized History of MI5*

H. H. Asquith, *Letters to Venetia Stanley* (edited by Michael and Eleanor Brock)

Herbert Asquith, *Moments of Glory*

Margot Asquith, *Great War Diary 1914–1916* (edited by Michael and Eleanor Brock)

Violet Bonham Carter, *Champion Redoubtable: The Diaries and Letters of Violet Bonham Carter 1915–45* (edited by Mark Pottle)

Rupert Brooke, *Letters* (edited by Sir Geoffrey Keynes)

Stefan Buczacki, *My darling Mr Asquith: The Extraordinary Life and Times of Venetia Stanley*

John Campbell, *Haldane*

Winston Churchill, *The World Crisis 1911–1918*

Christopher Clark, *The Sleepwalkers: How Europe Went to War in 1914*

Colin Clifford, *The Asquiths*

Diana Cooper, *The Rainbow Comes and Goes*

Martin Gilbert, *Winston S. Churchill, Vol. 3 1914–1916* and *Companion Volume 3*

Lord Hankey, *The Supreme Command, 1914–1918, Vol. 1*

Christopher Hassall, *Rupert Brooke*

Max Hastings, *Catastrophe: Europe Goes to War 1914*

Simon Heffer, *Staring at God: Britain in the Great War*

Charles Hobhouse, *Inside Asquith's Cabinet* (edited by Edward David)

Roy Jenkins, *Asquith*

John Jolliffe, *Raymond Asquith: Life and Letters*

David Lindsay, *The Crawford Papers: The Journal of David Lindsay, Twenty-Seventh Earl of Crawford, 1892–1940* (edited by John Vincent)

David Lloyd George, *War Memoirs*

Lyn Macdonald, *1914*

Margaret Macmillan, *The War that Ended Peace*

T. G. Otte, *Statesman of Europe: A Life of Sir Edward Grey*

J. A. Pease, *A Liberal Chronicle in Peace and War* (edited by Cameron Hazlehurst and Christine Woodland)

Sir Oliver Popplewell, *The Prime Minister and his Mistress*

Robert Rhodes James, *Gallipoli*

Keith Robbins, *Sir Edward Grey*

Stephen Roskill, *Hankey: Man of Secrets, Vol. 1 1877–1918*

Frances Stevenson, *Lloyd George: A Diary* (edited by A. J. P. Taylor)

Barbara W. Tuchman, *August 1914*

Nigel West, *MI5 in the Great War*

Philip Ziegler, *Diana Cooper*

ABOUT THE AUTHOR

ROBERT HARRIS is the author of *Act of Oblivion*, *Pompeii*, *Enigma*, and *Fatherland*. He has been a television correspondent with the BBC and a newspaper columnist for London's *Sunday Times* and the *Daily Telegraph*. His novels have sold more than ten million copies and been translated into thirty languages. He lives in Berkshire, England, with his wife and four children.